SECRETS
OF THE
LORE

True Nature Series: Book Two

Karen Lynn Bennett

I0563622

WHAT IF PRESS

What If Press

San Jose, California

Dedicated to you, Mom.
Your faith in me kept me going.

*"The liar gives birth to another liar,
until they become a generation of liars."*

–ANCIENT GREEK PROVERB

Prologue

Zander Hughes
Ten Months Ago

THERE SHE WAS AGAIN. The crying girl. I could see her in the distance, curled up among the ferns of a redwood forest whose giant trunks surrounded me like old friends. I breathed in the odd spicy scent that reminded me of ...something. I couldn't remember, but déjà vu clung to me like cobwebs. The girl's sobs grew louder, her anguish digging deeper into my heart, demanding my attention. I followed the sounds, but she remained out of my grasp, like an elusive phantom. The thought pulled me up short. Was she a ghost?

A jagged bolt of pain cut through me and I bent over, pressing a hand to my chest and sucking in air. Despite the agony, my eyes remained fixed on my prey. Unable to look away, I watched as the girl clutched her t-shirt with both hands, hunching over in the same manner as I did. Was it possible that we shared the same pain? Something inside me screamed, "Hell, yes," and I believed that if I could reach her, touch her, wrap myself around her, then and only then would our shared suffering go away.

My stomach twisted like a wind-up clock and I inhaled and exhaled slowly trying to calm myself. In the silence of my controlled breathing my heartbeat grew louder, ticking ominously like Poe's "Tell Tale Heart," signifying imminent danger.

More motivated than ever, I re-evaluated my options. The trees were as wide as cars and so tall that I couldn't see where they ended. They spread out like prehistoric birds above me blocking most of the light. If only I could leap from tree to tree like a squirrel. Caw! Caw! From above a raven startled me, flapping and rattling out a deep, throaty warning. Flying would be nice, too. No such luck. Back to running, then.

Prickly branches left bloody scratches across my bare arms and sticks dug into my shins whenever I tripped over a bare root or broken log. I gritted my teeth against the pain and mentally cursed the waning evening light that hid the details of the forest. But I pushed harder, some seed of faith making me believe I could reach her. I stopped to regain my sense of direction and to listen for the sound of her distress. Combined with her foggy image, it served as both lure and guide.

As I approached the base of a wide tree, my confidence was rewarded. The girl huddled there, hugging her knees. My eyes squinted curiously. She was no phantom. Long hair curled over her shoulders, beckoning me forward. I almost called out to her, but fearing I would scare her away, I kept quiet and inched forward, around a massive fallen log. Crack! The girl let out a short squeal, jumping up and spinning toward me, her face inscrutable in the shadows.

Fearing she would run again, I rushed her, but the moment it seemed I would touch her, she disappeared like smoke. I scoured the entire area, circling the tree and looking for a trail. But I found no sign of her. Had I really almost touched her or was my mind finally breaking? I bellowed in frustration, jamming a fist into a tree trunk and relishing the pain it brought, because I understood that kind of agony.

Failure tore through my gut like barbwire. *That was it then*, I thought as I found a trail leading me out of the forest. It was finally over.

When the lights of civilization came into sight, a sound pulled my head to the left. I sighed heavily. It was the girl again, her sadness wrapping around me like vines, pulling me back into the forest.

Part of me recognized the futility of my actions. I could even hear my best friend's mocking voice in my head. "Dude, pull your head out. You're never going to catch her." Nevertheless, I started after her again, sucked into the hellish loop that repeated over and over.

1

BREAKING UP IS HARD TO DO

Tru Parker

Today

ISAAC PRESSED ME UP against the school lockers, one hand behind the nape of my neck, the other flattened out next to my shoulder. His handspan was so wide it covered the breadth of the locker next to mine. I chewed on my lip with worry, knowing that Alton Lee, my locker neighbor, would be here any minute to exchange his books for his lunch. He was a small and jumpy sort of boy, easily intimidated by tall guys like Isaac, who was half Tongan. Sure enough, from the corner of my eye I saw Alton all but skip toward us before stopping short in astonishment, his eyeballs popping out with alarm. Several other students knocked into each other as they moved to avoid him. A stocky, unibrow boy shoved him out of the way with a foul curse. Alton quickly dropped his gaze and skittered back the way he had come.

Angry and irritated on behalf of my locker mate, I pushed against Isaac, but he didn't seem to notice. He hummed a tune close to my ear and his woodsy scent tingled my nose pleasantly. I closed my eyes, thinking Isaac wasn't all that bad. Then two sapphire eyes flashed through my mind like lightning. I mentally berated myself for letting this get out of hand. Ashamed, I tried to melt into the painted gray metal at my back, my conscience prickling as I imagined how Zander would feel about this. Good thing he wasn't here. Not that he hadn't wanted to be, but I'd convinced him I had a plan.

But today's breakup plan sucked big time. The original plan had been to break up with Isaac Monday, but when the moment had presented itself, I'd pulled a G-roy—that's what my best friend and I called an uber coward who didn't deserve to live. We'd coined the name after the character Gilderoy Lockhart in one of the Harry Potter movies. I swallowed loudly, self-disgust like heavy slime in my throat.

But were we really "together" if I'd never kissed him? Unless you counted the chase around the quad at lunch when he'd caught me and embarrassed me by smooching me with his milk mustache mouth in front of everyone. Because if that counted, then my first kiss had been with Hottie Efoti—Ruthie's nickname for Isaac Efoti. He was Scotts Valley High School's beach babe—times ten. I used to think that, too, until last week. And that felt like forever ago.

Isaac gently nudged me closer and I pushed a hand against his stomach to keep from colliding with him. I stared up at his face in open-mouthed shock. He seemed to take it as an invitation, bending down, his mouth on a direct course with mine. I quickly tilted to the side, dodging him by inches. His lips grazed my cheek. He recovered faster than I did, though, and my heart raced as I continued to lose ground. His mouth pressed against my ear, moving like a soft feather down my neck, while a nameless tune wove its way into my senses. My brain fogged over with pleasure, but my heart seized with guilt. I shook my head and squirmed away. No matter how pleasant the sensation of Isaac's lips pressing along the juncture of my neck and shoulder, they weren't the right lips for me.

"Isaac," I begged, desperate to put an end to this. "Let's get to lunch before someone takes our table."

"How about we have our own lunch today," he suggested with a hungry grin. "We could eat right here." He herded me backward up against the lockers again, gazing down at me with liquid brown eyes. What I saw in them raised my panic level, motivating my hands to move with renewed strength up to his chest before he came too close.

"Isaac!" My voice raised in alarm as he crooned a tune again. I increased the distance between us, pushing against him and locking my arms straight out. I blinked at my hands, which looked small against the width of his chest. His tight t-shirt outlined his large muscles.

"Dang, Isaac," I gushed.

He leaned in.

"Wait!" I squeaked, realizing he'd misinterpreted my expression as permission to suck face. Seriously, couldn't a girl ogle for free these days? My desperation must have finally penetrated his thick skull, because his roving hands stopped. I peeked up through my eyelashes to see him scowling. I saw that he'd finally received my message and relief coursed through me.

Just being here like this with Isaac felt wrong, like Judas Iscariot kind of wrong. Yet, at the same time, one could argue that it wasn't that bad—because technically I was still *with* Isaac. On the other hand, my heart wasn't into it ... it never had been ... Geez. I never knew I had such hussy tendencies.

He finally moved away. "What's wrong?"

Recognizing the opportunity to escape, I hurried to put some distance between us. Fully aware I had yet to officially break up with him, I clenched my hands with determination. He folded his arms and leaned one powerful shoulder against the lockers, wrinkling up his face in confusion.

Did this have to be so awkward? Why couldn't I be direct and confident like Ruthie? I imagined my best friend's pep talk in this scenario and found my voice.

"Isaac. I don't know how to say this." My tone carried its own weight and Isaac's usual air of confidence slipped, pulling his shoulders down. He blinked rapidly as if knowing the direction of this conversation. I couldn't take the vulnerability that I saw in his face. It seemed too private, so I took a sudden interest in the trash littering the walkway.

The silence dragged for a moment before I steeled my nerves again.

"Isaac—" I finally said, dragging it out.

"Are you kidding me?" He bellowed, interrupting me. His expression altered between disbelief, pain, and anger, each emotion all too clear on his face. "I thought ... I mean don't you feel anything for me?"

"No," I blurted, the truth spilling from my lips despite the hurt spelled out in his brown gaze. "At least not like ..."

He slammed a hand against the locker, the loud bang making me jump. Alton's locker now had a dent. I peeked over my shoulder toward my escape route before looking back at Isaac. His shoulders curled inwardly, telling me that genuine pain fueled his outburst. I hadn't realized he liked me so much and I suddenly felt awful.

I reached out a hand. "Isaac—"

"No! This is not happening," he muttered between clenched teeth. "It's not supposed to happen," he mumbled.

I thought, *Wow. Someone's a little full of himself.* At least he had figured it out and I wouldn't have to actually speak the words.

I couldn't leave without apologizing, though. "I'm really sorry—"

He turned and walked away, ignoring me. I watched him stride down the now empty corridor toward the quad where all of his friends would be sitting, make that *our* friends. Oh well. I didn't want to hang out with them now anyway.

I blew out a puff of air as a sudden throbbing in my skull threatened to split my head wide open. Consequently, the idea of food curdled my stomach. I dialed the combination on my locker and wondered if Ruthie had something for this awful pain. As the door swung open, I paused with one hand stretched toward a pile of books. This might be the first headache I'd ever had. *Geez, it hurt!* No wonder Ruthie refused to get out of bed when she had a migraine.

But it was nothing compared to being shot, and I'd healed from that. I rubbed my temples with both hands, wishing Zander could hold me and take the agony away like he did two days ago. Even as I thought it, the splintering pain mellowed into a tiny ache before fading away. Would I ever understand this strange healing gift of mine?

Grabbing my lunch sack, I debated how to spend the next forty-five minutes. Zander was probably already waiting for me on the quad, and I should reassure him that my Isaac problem had been resolved. But he would ask questions, and I didn't want to rehash what had just happened. Whatever I'd seen in Isaac's face had taken up residence in my stomach like some alien parasite. I rubbed it absently, wondering what was wrong with me. *Probably karma*, I thought with a guilty twist of my lips. Because I'd hurt a nice guy.

Why did Isaac have to take it so hard? It wasn't like there had ever been anything between us.

The strange nausea disappeared and my stomach growled. My rumbling, bipolar body reminded me that I hadn't eaten much breakfast this morning because Dad had served it with a lecture on better communication. He'd nailed me for lying about going home with Ruthie on Monday. Apparently, her mom had called Dad this morning to check on me I'd stayed home yesterday, too traumatized to deal with school after everything that had happened the day before. Now I had a feeling he suspected that I'd also lied about being sick yesterday. But I had been sick—emotionally, anyway.

I imagined telling him the truth.

"Sorry, Dad. I didn't mean to worry you, but I was kidnapped and held hostage by a raving lunatic with supernatural powers. But no worries, because Zander rescued me and everything's cool now."

No, I'd never tell Dad what really happened. I'd felt so hopeless lying there in Dante's cellar. When Zander had found me, I'd never felt such relief.

My shoulders drooped as I munched on some carrots and stared into my locker mirror. It revealed some of my internal turmoil but none of the peril from the night before. Not even a bruise. I squinted into the glass surface. Did my eyes look more golden today? Perhaps. My wavy blond hair bulged on one side, giving me a lopsided appearance. I tried to smooth it down, but it bounced back. Sighing, I dug out an elastic band and pulled it into a messy bun at the nape of my head, the ends of my hair sticking up. I shifted my gaze to the wreck in my locker, acknowledging that it resembled the current state of my life.

At least I could do something about this mess. Halfway through reorganizing I stopped. What was I doing? Delaying the inevitable, that's what. I stared at my reflection, trying to look past my bright eyes and messy hair. Where was that reinvented girl from the other night? I had been pumped up on adrenaline and I-heart-U feelings for Zander. Now, among slamming lockers, backpacks, and "normalville," my insecurities had returned. I blushed, thinking of Zander's words of confidence and admiration.

...You saved me. You saved both of us ...

You were amazing ...

I can't think when you're touching me ...

I leaned the back of my head against the lockers, and as I closed my eyes, Monday's events replayed in my mind. To say that Zander and I kicked the bad guy's butt didn't do it justice. But that's what we did. Dante was gone, permanently. I had misgivings about how it went down, sure. I mean, did I have to kill him? Zander said it wasn't my fault, that it was self-defense, and that Dante was a crazy, lost cause.

But if I was this great "healer" that Dante seemed so sure that I was, then why couldn't I have found a way to save him from his own madness? I recalled the way he had transitioned from nice to mean to plain old creepy. Talk about multiple personalities. I still had whiplash from his rapid switchbacks. No, I wasn't some magical healer—I was the opposite.

Murderer. Didn't murderers go to hell? I hadn't read much of the Bible that Ruthie gave me to help me fall asleep, but I didn't have to read it to know murder was one of the unforgivable sins. *Unforgivable.*

I slid to the ground thinking about my dreams since that day. They fed into my guilty feelings. I'd dreamed about a younger Dante, with parents and a sister, and they were happy. I'd also seen an older Dante, who'd found and kidnapped people for the Collector with the zeal of a fanatic. But, despite Dante's disciple-like behavior, by the end of my dreams I'd realized that he had been simply surviving.

His ability to see auras allowed him to identify hybrids, half human and half something else. *Something else* turned out to be horror story creatures, only not so fictional. I wouldn't have believed him if I hadn't seen them with my own eyes—werewolves in my own backyard. Their eyes had been too human, their reactions otherworldly, like they had understood what I'd said. The thought of them changing forms, becoming human-like, having children with humans ... The thought that I could be one of those children ... That one of my parents could be something like that ... I shook my head.

Even as I refused to believe it, I recognized that sensation, that "bull's-eye" feeling I got after considering the answers on a test and knowing which was right. Comprehension stole the air from my lungs and I sucked in a deep breath. It was happening now. Like the click of a lock when it opened, or the "ta-da" moment when you placed the final piece in a puzzle. This had to be more than mere intuition. Did that make me less human? A hybrid human? A monster? Whatever the case, I was definitely a freak show. But the crazy stories Dante told me, that Zander told me? They seemed more than a little farfetched. I mean, deep down I knew they held some truth, but how much?

The truth.

My name was Tru Parker and I could sense the truth. What kind of freaking coincidence was that? Add super healing and night sight, and I guess that put me in the inhuman, hybrid, or freak of nature category.

According to Dante, my specific kind of freakishness had a name: *idimmu.*

And that's what had landed me in my current disastrous state. Apparently, idimmu had unique gifts that the Collector wanted, that he could use, such as Dante's ability to locate other idimmu. Yeah, that ability would be valuable to a despot looking to build up his power and influence. And since they could be anywhere in this world, he needed a "finder" like Dante who had some kind of inner "idimmu GPS," because without that, it would be like looking for a needle in a haystack.

Although Dante had been able see the true nature of a person, or their *aura*, he'd only been able to identify these hybrids when they used their abilities, because that's when their auras changed.

I had saved a bunch of future victims by eliminating Dante. That was the good news. The bad news? The Collector was not going to be happy when Dante didn't return. He'd come looking for him. I stuffed my carrots into their bag, my appetite deserting me again.

Dante. I couldn't seem to stop dwelling on him. Zander said that although Dante had been an innocent child once, he'd become a predator. Dante had fooled us all. He'd wormed his way into Bobby's group at school. And then, when I'd foolishly stepped into his car, he'd attacked, zapping both Bobby and me with his other superpower. His soporific touch. The brush of his hand had shut out our lights, leaving us unconscious and defenseless.

Zander was right. Dante had been dangerous, even evil. But I wasn't convinced he'd deserved death. People could change, and I couldn't help but wonder if Dante had been redeemable.

My dreams the previous night made me think that he could have changed. These dreams were another talent of mine, if that's what you'd call it. My jaw tightened. I was embracing a lot of new ideas, particularly regarding myself. I'd dreamed about actual events happening to real people, some that I'd never met before. It had been a peculiar kind of misery. But I didn't know how to control it. If I did, I'd turn it off, because I rarely dreamed a happy dream these days and I usually awoke exhausted and distressed. Most of the time the dreams were about people or events that had some kind of reference to my life. Sometimes not. I used to shrug them off as nightmares. Only recently had I begun to think that some of these dreams were real.

With this new perspective, I saw Dante in a different light. He had been threatened and manipulated. One could even argue that he'd been physically abused. Medical treatment had been denied him until he fulfilled the wishes of his tormentor, a man known as the Collector.

Dante had grown to love the Collector like a father. In my dreams, I'd seen the Collector berate him with cruel and belittling words. Then later he'd praise him and Dante would practically glow with gratitude and admiration. This struck me as bizarre until I thought about the way victims of Stockholm syndrome developed affection for their captors. They'd had a disturbing relationship for sure.

His medical treatments turned out to be a temporary cure from insanity, which was something that afflicted all idimmu. In last night's visions, I'd watched Dante's sanity slip away. And he'd been aware of it, truly fearing that dark path. He'd been willing to do anything for a treatment from the "fixer." *Therapist* seemed like a better term, but that's how Dante had referred to the woman who had repeatedly healed him from his schizophrenia.

Me? I would have called her Aunt Caroline.

Yes, it seemed that I was having all sorts of revelations now. Dante's fixer was actually my mom's sister.

Could it get any weirder?

During this morning's classes I'd been mulling over all of my dreams and matching them up to events in my life. One particular dream had been the catalyst that changed everything. While lying helpless in Dante's cellar, I'd fallen asleep and dreamed about Zander searching for me with such amazing clarity, I'd felt like I'd been there with him. At that moment, I hadn't had the time or energy to ponder the dream, but I had since then, and it had changed everything.

Last night I'd seen Zander do something that really happened in his past—mere minutes had gone by, but it was still his past. My dreams about Zander and my dreams about Dante had felt real. I compared both experiences, and with the knowledge that what I'd seen Zander do had really happened, a light went on in my head. My dreams about Dante must have been visions of earlier events, too. I had actually seen Dante's past.

Then I began to wonder if my other dreams worked the same way. They couldn't all be visions of the past, though. I had to have some normal dreams. But which were real and which were not? That would take longer to figure out.

The worst part had been about my aunt. Recognizing her had been a twisted sense of reality. I'd never met her in person, but she'd looked exactly like her picture in our family photo album. My dreams were like pieces to a giant puzzle, one piece leading to the next—only the puzzle never seemed to end. An exhausting task lay before me because I wouldn't be satisfied until I saw the entire picture.

2

PARANOIA

"TRU!"

I looked up at the boy running down the corridor. It was Bobby. He kicked away an empty chip bag and slid to the ground next to me. He had suffered from years of depression after his parents were killed. And according to Dante I had unintentionally "healed" him.

Bobby hugged me, which was awkward since I didn't think we were the hugging type of friends. "You're okay! I tried to call you, but you didn't answer. Ruthie said you were sick."

"I'm fine now, Bobby." I pulled free from him as kindly as possible.

"Sorry." He moved away, clearing his throat. "I was just worried. Shrina thinks I'm nuts, but I swear I woke up in the skate park Monday night and I can't remember what happened. The last thing I remember was driving home with you and Dante. When you both didn't show up yesterday, I got really worried."

Shrina was his crush, and soon to be girlfriend. Or so I hoped. She'd been in the car with us last Monday, but Dante had dropped her off before the drive had taken a dark turn. I'd believed Dante when he said he'd left Bobby unharmed at a park and filed his involvement in my kidnapping under "Deal With Later." But in retrospect, I'd been a bad friend.

"Sorry, Bobby. I should have called you. I really was just sick yesterday."

"Okay," he said, looking me over, but the doubt in his eyes didn't go away. "Do you know what happened Monday?" he asked, shoving his hands into his pockets and staring across the walkway.

My thoughts swirled and I looked down, scrambling for an answer that wouldn't reveal the supernatural world I'd accidentally stepped into because one, Zander said to tell no one, and two, no one would believe me.

"Dante is a total loser." I chuckled dryly, trying to lighten the conversation. "He, uh, did some weird Vulcan move." I made a pinching motion with one hand. "On your, uh, shoulder, or something like that, and you collapsed. I started freaking out, but he laughed and said it was such a cool trick I wouldn't believe it until he showed me." Had I thrown in a Star Trek reference? Geek-tastic. I had to sell this better.

"Huh?" Bobby looked stunned.

"Yeah. He stopped the car and did the same thing to me when I tried to get out. I woke up in my backyard in one of our patio chairs."

I tried to be convincing, but the lies made my tongue

feel twice its size. I probably sounded like a total dope-face.

His eyes bulged. "No way! Are you okay?"

"Don't worry. I don't think he did anything else. But even so, we should stay away from him. He's a whack job." There. That sounded better.

"What a douche!" Bobby pulled up his knees and leaned his elbows on them, running his hands over his eyes. "I'm sorry I ever introduced him to you. I thought he was, you know, *cool.*" He clenched his hands together causing his knuckles to whiten.

"Are you sure that's all that happened?" he asked, peering at me with doubt.

Great. Now he thought I had been molested or something.

"Yes, really. Nothing else happened, Bobby. Like I said, he went on and on about being some kind of Vulcan alien. He's mental, like straightjacket crazy." At least I wasn't lying about the crazy part. I racked my brain for something more to say, something that would make Bobby drop this for good.

An idea formed in my mind. "He also said that he was moving when he got home," I told him. "He said it wouldn't matter if I told anyone what he did because he'd be gone—or, something to the effect that we wouldn't see him anymore. Maybe that's why he thought it was safe to try his new trick." I blew air out my lips, wishing for better acting skills. "Or, I don't know. Maybe he just wanted to shut me up and give himself enough time to get out of town."

Red splotches had popped up on Bobby's face during my long-winded explanation. His eyes glinted with anger.

"If I ever see him again, I'm going to kill him!" He slammed a white-knuckled fist into the lockers behind him. They were getting quite a beating today.

"Whoa! Chill out," I said, worried that a teacher would hear him.

"Don't worry," he spat. "If that asshole shows up at school, he's the one who's going to get hurt." He stared at me, his eyes practically reaching out and grabbing me. "We should tell someone. What if he's a potential serial killer and we don't do anything about it?"

Don't worry, Bobby, I thought, blinking rapidly in the face of his intensity. *I already took care of him. He's never going to hurt anyone again.* But, of course, I couldn't tell him that.

"Well," I swallowed, pushing away the remorse I felt for lying to him and hoping he'd forget all about this. "I doubt he's a serial killer—"

"But he could become one," he insisted, warming up to the idea. "What if we could stop him from hurting someone later?"

Man! Why didn't Bobby let this drop? This was becoming paranoia. Wait. Could his anger involve something more, like his parents' deaths? They'd been in the wrong place at the wrong time, a highway drive-by shooting, their murderer never brought to justice. He and his brother had been split between family members. Bobby lived with his grandmother and I got the impression he hated it.

"He's long gone now," I said softly. "Let's leave it alone. We need to be choosier about our friends, that's all. I did have a weird feeling about getting in the car with you guys," I admitted. "But I didn't understand it, so I ignored it. Lesson learned. I won't make that mistake again."

"Don't act like it's your fault because you didn't figure him out, Tru. You clearly have a better sense of people than me because I totally thought he was legit."

I shrugged and started to get up. Bobby jumped to his feet, pulling me with him. "Tru, if you see him, call me." He shook his head. "No, call the police." His face twisted. "I really should talk to them." His eyes pleaded for permission.

I was so done with this conversation. "Seriously, Bobby. I'm fine," I said sharply.

He wilted. "Okay. But if you ever decide to talk to the cops or ..." He hesitated, looking at the dirty floor. "Uh, I spoke to the school counselor. After that day in the quad when you first talked to me." He looked hopeful. "She's surprisingly cool."

He'd talked to a shrink about his parents' tragic deaths? I tried not to grimace. No way was I talking to a therapist, counselor, or whatever watered-down title she went by. I shook my head. "Not happening," I said.

Bobby's shoulders dipped lower, making me feel wretched for not agreeing with him. "Okay," he mumbled. "But if you need to talk to anyone about this, I'll be there."

"Thanks, Bobby. But I'm okay. I don't need to talk to anyone. Really."

He stared at me for a moment, and then shrugged. "All right. See you later." With a nod, he headed toward the quad. "Wait!" he yelled before pivoting back my way. His forlorn face had perked up with excitement. "I forgot to tell you something." He jogged back to me. "Notice anything different?" He struck a pose with one fist under his chin.

I looked him over. Same average brown hair, brown eyes, and dark eyebrows.

"Nope," I responded.

His eyes rotated in their sockets as he let out an exasperated puff of air. "No contacts."

I hadn't even realized he'd worn contacts. "So?"

He heaved another sigh. "Don't you see? I don't need glasses or contacts anymore. It was the strangest thing. When I put my contacts in this morning, it made my vision worse. My grandma is taking me to the eye doctor today, but I swear I can see just fine. Weird! Right?"

Suspicion wound up my neck. Was it a coincidence that I had healed Bobby's depression and he suddenly didn't need contacts anymore? Shoving that thought away, I forced a smile.

"Yeah," I agreed. "But a good weird."

"I know!" He grinned. "Later." As he took off, I reconsidered Ruthie's campaign to turn me into a normal high school student. The more friends I made, the more I realized that they had baggage, too. Perhaps weird was the new normal.

3

MOXIE IS FOXY

I WANTED TO AVOID Isaac until he cooled off, which meant I couldn't go outside to my friends. Zander would be waiting for me out there, but suddenly I had no idea how I should act around him. I dug my phone out of my backpack to see how much time I had to kill before class.

Twenty-five minutes.

That seemed like forever. Maybe I should hang out in the library until my next class, because if I went out to the quad Ruthie was going to pester me about my dreams. As my self-appointed dream analyst, she'd been anxious to begin as soon as possible. But I'd stayed home yesterday and ignored as many of her texts as I could. Then, I'd bailed on her again this morning to be with Zander. I'd lied to her, telling her that I was still feeling sick and that I was running late. She knew I was holding out on her though. I could see it in first period. She'd had her "you're-full-of-it" detector running at full strength. I'd tried to make excuses, but it had been like room spray that couldn't quite hide the stink.

After everything Ruthie was trying to do for me this year—well, it was a BFF all-time low. When she had returned from a long summer away with relatives, she'd been all about "project Tru" and how she was going to turn my life around. Last year, when my mom died in the hit-and-run accident, I'd been so depressed that I'd become a zombie, numb to my friends who had tried to help but had eventually given up. When I emerged from my personal black hole, I had one friend left. Ruthie Robles. My best friend. And when school began this year, she became a BFF on a rescue mission—Mission Restore Tru's Social Life. I wasn't totally on board with the plan, but I was thankful for her support all the same.

And how was I repaying Ruthie for sticking with me through thick and thin? Avoiding her. Lying to her.

I glanced toward the quad, wondering if she was going to question me about my dreams or make a big deal about being ill. Maybe she'd have a Ruthie bubble going on. That's what I called it when her already deficient attention span produced an extra gear for obsessive-compulsiveness. Whatever or whoever wasn't involved in the object of her current obsession could disappear under the radar, like I wanted to this morning. Yes, right now I would love a Ruthie bubble.

But lunch was half over and I doubted there was enough time for her to get worked up about me. Isaac might be ticked, but at least he understood we weren't together anymore. That's all that mattered right now. In fact, the "breakup thing" went a lot better than I thought it would, minus the "almost kiss." And Zander would just have to wait for the details.

I sighed. I couldn't avoid the quad forever and I couldn't hang out in the library every day.

As I reached for my discarded lunch, a folded piece of paper floated down to the ground. I picked it up and opened it.

Although his power builds faster and faster,

Your true nature still eludes the master.

But all too soon the blood shall reveal

What you are and break the seal.

A shiver slid up my spine. It had to be a dumb joke. I could see Zena conning someone into writing this to make me feel like the social pariah she considered me to be. But I wasn't such an easy mark anymore. I had bigger fish to fry than my arch-nemesis since middle school. Crunching up the paper, I stuffed it into the dark recesses of my locker, promptly forgetting it, and headed down the walkway toward the sound of a thousand conversations in the outdoor eating area we called the quad. I peeked around the corner to observe my usual table. Isaac and his twin sister, Phoebe, were sitting with Ruthie and her boyfriend, Val. But where was Zander? He was supposed to wait for me on the quad. I'd assumed he'd be saving me a seat next to him. Insecurity wiggled its way into my mind. We were together now, weren't we?

Yeah, last week, when I thought Zander was messing with my mind, I had avoided him. And yeah, I'd even told him it was better that we didn't hang out. He had moved to a different lunch table only to be bombarded by a dozen drooling girls. Zena had pushed her way to the front of the line quicker than the Math Club could calculate the square root of negative sixteen. But I'd assumed things were different now. As my eyes zeroed in on Zander, I saw that Zena was doing a lot more than calculating this time. She sat squished up to him, with one arm around his back and her substantial boobs pressing into his shoulder. As she whispered something into his ear, he smiled.

I fumed. Zander and I so needed to talk. Years and years of Zena's malicious behavior toward me had evolved into a living, breathing animosity. But it was nothing compared to the black tar that threatened to pull me under and light me ablaze at the sight of Zander smiling at her. So what if I'd told him to pretend we weren't together yet. He was taking my suggestion too far. At least I hoped this was an act. I blinked away angry tears. He was pouring salt in an old and nasty wound.

I was upturning my whole life for him, wasn't I? I'd ditched my best friend this morning to ride to school with him so we could talk, but he'd shown up at my house with his doofus brother, Peter. Zander's apologetic look had not lessened the awkwardness of the quiet drive. Arriving a few minutes before the bell, we hadn't had a chance to talk about the important stuff, like what the heck we were going to do moving forward.

And now I'd broken up with Isaac, only to find Zander and Zena mauling each other at lunch. Man! This hurt worse than when Zena stole my training bra in middle school and taped it over my locker. I gripped my shirt with a clenched fist, tightening my lips when they began to tremble. Was Zander messing with my mind like his brother, Peter?

Peter had tried to wipe my memory, which had been extremely painful—like a baseball bat to the head kind of painful. Zander had led him to believe he'd been successful, that I didn't remember the afternoon in my backyard with the wolves. But I did. Since then, I could barely contain my dislike for him, hence the awkward drive to school.

Even though Peter had taken care of Dante's body for us, I didn't trust him. Zander said I didn't need to worry about it anymore, but I did. He didn't know that his father was the Collector, the real villain behind my kidnapping yesterday. If Peter knew, that meant he was playing Zander for some reason. To complicate things, I couldn't tell Zander my suspicions about Peter if I wasn't ready to tell him about his father.

This morning I'd only had enough time to tell Zander we needed to act like we were just friends for now, until I broke up with Isaac. Zander hadn't been happy about it, insisting that he also be there when I talked with Isaac. Seriously. That would have been a total disaster. When the warning bell had rung, I'd dashed away to first period, giving Zander no choice but to comply.

I smoothed out the wrinkles in my shirt as I debated my next move. My chest caved in a little more as I watched Zena continue to slither over Zander. The hot ball of anger in my chest grew larger. He was such a hypocrite. The tables had turned and he was—what the heck? Now he was letting her sit on his lap?

Another surge of betrayal swept over me, but I refused

to show any sign of weakness. I walked as gracefully as I could, trying to channel Phoebe, who moved like a majestic elk, never missing a step. Feeling like hitting back at Zander, I sat down between Isaac and Ruthie, keeping my face expressionless despite the dreadful hammering of my heart. *Take that, Zander*, I thought.

My skin prickled suddenly and I knew he was looking at me. But I resisted the urge to peek at him. Seconds later I gave in, hoping that the daggers in my glare were stabbing him and that he felt some of the torture and humiliation that I did. He was attempting to untangle himself from Zena, but she slid around his efforts like an octopus refusing to give up its prize. Zander's face burned bright red, like Rojo Roger's face did whenever Ruthie walked by. I smirked as I compared Zander to the geeky kid who'd been crushing on Ruthie since the eighth grade.

I looked away from Zander. *You feel nothing,* I told myself. A small voice in my head whispered, *liar*. No mantra could close up the meteor-sized cavern forming in my heart. It took everything in me to paste on a smile and blink away the moisture in my eyes.

Ruthie turned away from Val. "Tru!" She clapped her hands together before hugging me. Three hugs in less than thirty minutes. Ruthie would say it was a sign, that three was a magical number, that there was a message in it for me, like the world was sending me love, blah, blah, blah. Instead, I felt like someone had stuck an ice pick through my back.

"How are you feeling?" she said sarcastically. I grimaced. Yep. She hadn't believed my sick lie.

But on closer inspection, she changed her mind.

"Wow," she gasped. "You really are pale!" With a look of chagrin, she made "tsk tsk" sounds as she buzzed around me with fresh concern.

"I'm fine," I whined, brushing her hands away. "Just one of those overnight bugs, I guess." The lie sent an arrow through my chest, but when it seemed to appease her, I eased out the breath I didn't realize I'd been holding.

"I *was* worried about you," she added, settling down with a hurtful frown. "Were you avoiding me in Algebra class? Because I saved a seat for you—until Big Joe took it." She pulled out a tube of lipstick and began applying it, somehow speaking without getting any color outside the lines of her lips.

"I didn't have the heart to shoo him away because dork one and dork two were harassing him before he sat down. But then you left before I could catch up and ..." She covered her mouth with a hand and whispered, "We seriously need to talk, you know. About the other night!" But her whisper was so loud everyone heard.

I glanced over at Phoebe. She was in the process of rolling her eyes, which made the corners of my mouth lift despite the cloud of depression hovering over me.

"And you didn't want a ride again this morning. I knew something was wrong!" Ruthie complained in an even louder whisper. Her eyes somehow conveyed sympathy while her voice chastised.

"You were sick?" said Isaac, clasping one of my hands on the table. I tried to pull away and only succeeded with great effort. I looked away, doing my best to ignore him.

Casually, I squeezed Ruthie's arm under the table and caught her eye when she turned. "Nobody wants to hear about it at lunch," I said lightly. "I'll tell you later." Her BFF radar finally clicked on, and she shut up.

"*No problemo.*" She winked at me. "Guess what? Val was just trying to convince me *Living Large* is more awesome than *Glass Shadows*. Can you believe it?"

I glanced over at Val, who was in the process of shoving half of a hamburger into his mouth. *Glass Shadows* was Ruthie's favorite band. She thought the lead singer was her future husband and that they would make beautiful babies together.

"Come on! *Glass Shadows* sucks! What a stupid name," mumbled Val, as he added a couple of French fries to the disappearing burger.

Ruthie whipped out her iPod. "Uh uh!" She gestured to the rest of us. "Who do you think is best?"

"*Glass Shadows.*" The twins and I replied in unison. Ruthie yelled triumphantly.

"No contest." Isaac's deep voice startled me. He'd scooted closer, our thighs almost touching. I wrenched my body away from him, belatedly realizing what a mistake it had been to sit next to Isaac after our earlier conversation.

"What do you think, Zander?" asked Phoebe, her voice a tad higher than normal.

I whipped my head around. Behind me stood Zander, looking like I'd just slapped his mother. I snuck a peek at Zena's table. She chattered with her fan club while sending hate laser glares my way. I pursed my lips, the hurt still too fresh to speak to him. I didn't get it. He had wanted to "help" me break up with Isaac because he couldn't stand the thought of Isaac and me talking. But it was okay for Zander to let Zena sit in his lap? If I were a mature person, I suppose I'd lead him away somewhere to talk this out. But I remained glued to my seat by his duplicity.

"Never heard of them," Zander muttered, his jaw clenching. I wasn't surprised he'd never heard of the band. He had been raised by a secret cult-like group called sethians who ruled over the rest of the non-human folks, even the ones who didn't fit into any of their categories. Zander's parents were not exactly mainstream people. So, it was no wonder that edgy music band names weren't part of his vocabulary.

"Which one?" asked Val.

"Either." Zander rounded the table and sat next to Phoebe, across from me. Phoebe looked from me to him, one eyebrow up. But as he settled in by her side with a smile, she grinned, her eyes sparkling with appreciation. I gritted my teeth.

"Seriously?" said Ruthie. "Okay, listen." She yanked the earphones out of the iPod, but we could barely hear the music.

A foot nudged me under the table. I jumped and looked at Zander. When he raised an eyebrow at me, I realized it hadn't been him. I glanced at Isaac. He winked at me, bumping my foot again and nudging me with his knee. I dropped my eyes down to my lunch, but not before I caught a jolting glare from Zander, his eyes electric blue. What the heck? Isaac was getting friendly? How thick could one person be? He leaned down to whisper in my ear.

"Sorry I lost my temper." His warm breath tickled the hair curling down my neck and I pulled away. But he followed. "I'm okay if you need me to move a little slower." He dropped an elbow on the table, rotating his shoulder into me to get closer. "I get it. You aren't feeling well today and I was rushing things. I'll back off, I promise. Maybe by Homecoming I'll earn that kiss, but I won't push."

My jaw dropped. Isaac chuckled and reached out a long tan finger to lift my chin up.

"Ruthie, I can play that song for you if you want," offered Isaac. He had that dental commercial grin going on and a suspicious gleam in his eyes, which were still fixed on my reddening face.

"No way," said Phoebe, her voice lowering with firmness. "Isaac ..."

"Chill out, Feebs," said Isaac, chuckling. Phoebe bristled.

"Really?" Ruthie smiled gleefully. "Yes, that would be awesome! But, where's your guitar?"

"I'll just grab Roger's over there." He loped over the pavement to a table filled with band kids. They always seemed to have instruments with them, even instruments they didn't use in class. A guitar case was propped up next to their table.

After a brief conversation, Isaac returned with the guitar. A good portion of the band team followed, carrying their instruments. They smiled with excitement as they tried to recall the tune, humming pieces of it to each other. Roger smoothed down his bright red hair and grinned at Ruthie like a besotted fool, his pale freckled skin lighting up like Christmas. Ruthie pointedly ignored him.

"What a stupid idiot!" muttered Phoebe, her eyes following her brother with an incinerating scowl.

"Is he going to sing in front of everyone?" I asked with shock. Singing on the spot in front of the whole school was definitely on my list of scariest things to do. But I shouldn't have been surprised, knowing from Drama class that Isaac loved the spotlight.

"That boy has some serious brass ba—" started Ruthie. But Phoebe cut her off with a loud sputter of disgust. "Moxie," Ruthie amended. Then she lifted her chin in defense. "And moxie is foxy!"

4

EX-BOYFRIEND

ISAAC APPEARED IMMUNE TO Phoebe's fiery scowl as he settled down on the retaining wall across from our table, giving us the best seat to the show. The rest of the band kids took up spots around him. They plucked a few chords and then Isaac led out with the intro, his deep voice sending a tingle up my spine and his words going down like warm chocolate. Ruthie giggled next to me.

The familiar music seemed to dance in the air, and although I knew the song, it felt completely different when Isaac sang it. A boy and a girl. Forbidden romance. Nothing that original, but it mesmerized me. Isaac's voice started out rich and velvety, then changed, becoming gravelly like a rock star, which elicited several squeals and sighs around us. He lingered over words like "love" and "heart," layering them with his own brand of charm as he stared at me.

They said we weren't supposed to love each other

That you and I were like oil and water

But if that's the case, why can't I erase

You from my mind, from my heart, from my sight

Even when my eyes close. Oh, oh, oh.

Goose bumps shot up the side of my neck, causing me to tilt my head. Part of me wondered if everyone else felt it, but I didn't bother to look around—or I couldn't. Because the music was speaking to me. It was like Isaac and I were alone on a desert island where he built me my own tree house and cracked open coconuts for me, and I let him because I liked to watch the way his muscles clenched and released as he worked. I blinked away the tropical fantasy and stared at the god in front of me. I couldn't take my gaze off his languid eyes, his strong neck. Why had I broken up with him? How could I think of canceling our Homecoming plans? I couldn't believe he was into me, and I couldn't wait to get him up against the lockers again.

I've been looking, looking everywhere

But you've slipped away like a beautiful sunset

Then morning comes and suddenly you're here

The sun shines with our love and I feel we'll never split

But when the night comes again, I get nervous

That we're drifting apart, that soon you'll vanish

One kiss from you provides the cure,

Shows me that our love's so pure—

Isaac abruptly stopped singing, and I looked down at something squeezing my arm. It was Zander's hand. Annoyed, I started to pull away, but a wave of warmth flowed across my skin, jolting me out of my trance. I blinked slowly and stumbled, but Zander steadied me. We stood several feet away from our table. I'd been mid-stride on a direct course to Isaac. I shook my head, dazed.

"What just happened?" I whispered. I didn't even remember standing up.

"I'm not positive, but I have a damn good guess," he grumbled.

Huh? I stared around the quad with confusion.

Val was scowling at Ruthie, who was urging Isaac to keep singing. Her voice was so breathy and star-struck, I felt embarrassed for Val. Isaac was holding his head in his hands. Phoebe crouched next to him, looking concerned. The band kids complained about the interruption. Isaac apologized, telling them he was feeling sick. He wiped at his nose and his hand came away with blood. A few people gasped with concern.

"Sorry, guys," he said once more, ducking his head and moving away with a wave goodbye. Phoebe gripped his arm before grabbing both their backpacks and taking off, tugging Isaac out of the quad.

The band kids decided to keep playing. It was only a shadow of the song that Isaac had been singing. Its spark had disappeared with him and my connection to the music was gone. How had Isaac done that? I recalled the first day of school, when Isaac sang to Ruthie and me. This experience carried an eerily similar feeling.

"Hey. How do you feel?" said Zander, carefully spinning me toward him. I pressed a hand to my temple, still confused. Why had I been thinking about Isaac like he was my favorite flavor of ice cream? How embarrassing. I must have looked as stupid as Ruthie had. My face reddened under Zander's pointed gaze. He clasped my arm and led us to the big oak tree, away from our lunch table, away from the music, and away from Ruthie's prying eyes. She watched us with raised eyebrows, giving me the signal for "do you need rescuing?" I waved her off.

"I'm, uh, okay. But I don't remember getting up. That's weird, isn't it?" So many strange things had been happening to me that I was beginning to wonder what normal was. I rubbed my head, trying to piece it together.

"Yeah. I could have lived a long and happy life without hearing you gush over Isaac," he muttered, his face dark. "I'd like to kick that siren's a—" Zander cut himself off at my bewildered look.

I wrinkled up my nose, not remembering what I'd said out loud, but embarrassed by Zander's words. I squinted at him. "You think he's a siren?" He'd mentioned sirens Monday night, saying they were some type of idimmu that created fake feelings in others.

"I don't know. It doesn't make sense ..." Zander squeezed his eyes shut and drew in a deep breath. He expelled it with frustration. "But it would explain a few things." He stared at me with a truly perplexed expression. Then he shook his head. "Never mind. Maybe I'm just reaching for a reason to …"

I blinked, waiting for him to finish while trying to understand his odd rambling.

Then something shifted in his eyes and they narrowed. "What's going on with you and Isaac? I thought you were going to break up with him."

"I did." I yelped defensively. "I swear!"

Why was I feeling guilty? Then I remembered that I'd been staring at Isaac's lips, that my neck had tingled in response to his singing. I groaned, pressing my palms into my eyes. But I didn't like Isaac that way. Yuck! I peeked at Zander from under my eyelashes. I thought of Zander's kiss last night and my whole body heated up. Did just the memory of our kiss light him on fire like it did me? I closed my eyes again.

The image of Zena sitting in Zander's lap flashed at me from the insides of my eyelids like a lewd peep show, producing a Godzilla-sized knot in my stomach. The resulting wave of nausea reminded me why I was mad at Zander. He'd been the jerk, not me.

I glared. "But you are starting to make me wonder why I even bothered. I think Zena almost had her tongue down your throat."

"What?" His strangled cry warped his voice. He sounded genuinely surprised, which made me doubt what I'd seen. "I was waiting for you and she came over to my table," he explained. "It's not like I sat down by her. Besides, she's … she's like a boa constrictor."

Still hurt, I snorted in disbelief. "Really? You didn't look like you were trying very hard to get away." I hated that I sounded jealous.

He swung his hand through the air as if that could erase my feelings. "Forget Zena. She's nothing. I want to know about Isaac and you. He didn't act like you broke up with him. What's really going on between you two?" Zander's shoulders puffed up, like he was preparing to deflect a blow.

Isaac's song drifted through my mind. *One kiss from you provides the cure* ... I felt light-headed all of the sudden. What the heck? "Uh, I don't know." I lifted out my hands to balance myself and then the feeling was gone. "I mean ... nothing," I clarified.

My reaction to Isaac had not been real, but it had felt powerful. Something was not normal with Isaac. Suspicion began to worm its way into my mind. Could a guy be a siren? Impossible. I almost laughed out loud. Sirens were gorgeous and dangerous women of the sea, luring sailors to their death with their beautiful voices. Isaac was a hot Tongan with a temper, but dangerous? Murderous? I shook my head.

I was starting to suspect everyone around me. What were the odds that there was another non-human long-term resident here in Scotts Valley? No, he was just being ... Isaac. He even drove his twin sister nuts. Plus, if he didn't realize I'd broken up with him, then he was too stupid to be a siren.

"I think maybe he didn't understand what I was trying to tell him," I finally admitted.

Despite being obtuse and arrogant, he was remarkably talented. People like him became superstars. They called that charisma, right? I'd been wrapped up in it momentarily, but once I had come back down to earth, the temporary magnetism had vanished. That was the power that music bands like The Beatles had. I recalled a clip from a documentary. Girls were crying and fighting each other to get to them. I'd thought the fans were so over the top, but I'd acted just like them.

"Obviously." Zander's caustic voice cut into my thoughts and my head jerked up. His nostrils flared and he kept clenching and unclenching his jaw. "You couldn't have tried very hard," he mocked.

"It's not easy to do!" An ugly darkness unfurled itself in my gut.

"What was he whispering to you at lunch?"

I twisted the hem of my shirt. "Something about Homecoming," I confessed, regretting it immediately. This was one of those situations where a small lie would have been better than the truth.

Zander's lips thinned.

I tucked a wayward lock of hair behind one ear and shifted my weight. "I'm not with him, Zander. He asked me to go to Homecoming before all this stuff started happening, that's all." I looked at the ground, trying to rein in my anger because I knew I'd behaved questionably. Still, I felt that Zander had no room to criticize. He'd been worse than me.

"I tried to tell him it was over. I mean, I thought he understood. He got all mad and everything ... I mean, it seemed like he got the message. He even stormed off down the hall. But then at the lunch table he apologized and said he was going to take things more slowly, so now I don't think he interpreted me the right way—"

"Hey Zander!" Tori, one of Zena's groupies, ran up to us. "Zena's *waiting* for you outside of Algebra. She has your backpack." She winked at him like she'd just spoken in code. Then she swung her eyes my way, tweaking her lips in a way that told me I was yesterday's news.

"I'm sure Tru wants to go check on Isaac, anyway. Bet you want to get some more of that Hottie Efoti action I saw happening at your locker before lunch, don't ya!" She pretended to fan herself and winked suggestively.

For the love of—she was not helping here.

Zander's eyes burned as he glared at Tori. He looked like he wanted to choke her, but I knew it was me he wanted to throttle. Tori quailed under the weight of his anger before scuttling off and leaving me to face Zander's wrath alone.

"You are not going to go check on Isaac." His voice was low but it triggered a tsunami of fury inside of me. "You are not going to talk to him!" he growled.

The dark sensation I was feeling billowed out and I clenched my teeth to try and stem the flow, afraid of what it could do. But a little voice whispered that I couldn't let him treat me this way.

I gritted my teeth together. This was a side of Zander I definitely disliked. My heart pounded like the beat of a funeral dirge. He had misunderstood, assuming the worst and believing Tori without question. She was a Zena groupie. She'd sell her own mother for Zena's approval.

Who the hell did Zander think he was, anyway? "Since when do you get to tell me what to do?" I said.

His shoulders jerked up and down, his mouth a thin line. "Look, I just don't think he's safe."

"What?" Surprise stopped the pounding of my heart for a moment. I hadn't expected him to say that. It reminded me of Isaac's ferociousness the other day at my house when he'd caught Zander leaving. Then Zander shot me another disgusted look, like I was dog crap under his foot and my defenses shot sky high.

Oh no. I couldn't put up with this. "Well, you don't get to decide who I talk to, so you're wasting your breath!"

"You're seriously going after him?" he asked, a vulnerable expression flitting across his face.

When I didn't respond, his jaw tightened. "You may not know him as well as you think you do," he ground out, pulling himself up to his full height and looking down at me. The fact that I had wondered the same thing about Isaac didn't lessen the irritation I felt at the moment. Nobody told me what to do.

"So what if I don't know everything about Isaac?" I said furiously. "I know him better than I know you."

My brain said, *No, you don't. Shut up. Shut up.* But my mouth was on autopilot, and the words flew out faster than I could reel them in.

"Do I need to stay away from you, too, Zander?" The pitch of my voice peaked, like a screech, and I winced.

"Are you kidding me?" scoffed Zander. "After every-thing— Wait. What have you been doing with him?"

"What?" I'd created a trap for myself and could only hang my mouth open in shock, knowing exactly where this was heading but too dumbstruck to do anything about it. It was like watching a train wreck in slow mo-tion and I blinked away tears of frustration, embarrass-ment, and dawning despair.

"You and I have been through a lot in a short time, *idimmu.*" The way he drawled out the word felt like the basest insult. "A lot," he emphasized, his face like pale marble, his voice a razor. "And if you know him better than me …" Zander snickered rudely, letting his words hang. "Maybe I don't know you at all." His eyes glittered, regret flashing in them.

I felt my face heating up at the insinuation. Maybe a tiny part of me hoped he'd save us, that he'd have the strength that I didn't have to stop the disaster of our short-lived relationship. My nails dug into my palms and I knew I'd have crescent dents in them for the rest of the day.

Zander sighed, opening his mouth to say something, but I cut him off.

"Whatever," I snapped, filling the word with layers of disgust and disappointment. I pushed past him, knocking into his shoulder. And for the first time since we'd met, there was no hum when we touched.

"Tru! Wait!" he called out hoarsely.

I heard the misery in his voice, but all I felt was the gulf between us clawing at my chest.

Drama dragged. Isaac never came to class, and I suspected that he and Phoebe had ditched school. Sure enough, Phoebe didn't show for PE, either. Eventually, English class arrived and I walked in, stoic as a Greek statue, pointedly ignoring Zander, my ex-study partner, ex-frenemy, ex-crush, ex-everything. My eyes stung and I blinked, praying for some control over my tear ducts. He was talking to Zena, who caught my eye as she leaned in close to Zander, laughing. *Stupid boy,* I thought.

I told myself I didn't need him. Ruthie and I would figure out this supernatural insanity without him. He and his brother could take a flying leap off a cliff. I stared toward the front of the room, feeling forsaken and betrayed. Pushing those thoughts down deep, I stubbornly refused to even acknowledge the widening crack somewhere in my bleeding heart or the little whisper that said I'd just broken up with the wrong person.

5

HEY, HEY, WE'RE HERE TO STAY

RUTHIE DROVE ME HOME in silence. It was her way of
acknowledging that I was miserable and needed space.
After the epic argument at lunch, she had to know my
mood had something to do with Zander. But it was also
everything I couldn't tell her.

She didn't know what Dante had done to Zander and
me, or how close the experience had made us—at least I
thought we'd been close. I choked down a sob. Only Zander understood what I'd been through that night, the
confusion I struggled with, the danger I was still in. And
right now, he hated me. He thought I was some kind of
tramp or something. He'd practically said it today. That
hurt. It brought back the feelings of self-hatred and
worthlessness that I'd felt after Mom's accident.

I wanted to tell Ruthie what happened, the whole
Dante nightmare. I wanted to tell her about Zander, how

he'd rescued me, everything he'd admitted to me, and that we'd shared the most perfect kiss ever. And then how he'd shattered everything by flirting with Zena and then assuming the worst about Isaac and me. How I'd wanted to hurt him.

Monday night had been the best feeling ever, but only two days later we'd eclipsed our good memories with the suckiest ones ever.

As much as I wanted to, how could I confide in Ruthie when it was potentially dangerous for her? Things were getting more complicated and perilous. For the first time I wondered if my mother's death had anything to do with what I was. Was it just a coincidence that the strange dreams had started around the time of her accident? Pieces of that night were still blank. I already blamed myself for putting her in the wrong place at the wrong time, but was there more to it? An invisible hand squeezed my already wounded heart. What if I inadvertently caused something to happen to Ruthie or my dad? I shuddered. I couldn't take it if anything happened to them, too.

I looked out at the passenger-side mirror just as a black Tesla peeled away from our bumper and revealed Zander's truck. Was he watching out for me or just watching me to see what I'd do next? I felt completely alone without him.

When we arrived at my place, Ruthie followed me inside and dropped onto the sofa with a dramatic sigh. "Come on, Tru. What's going on?" Her head tilted, one eyebrow lifted, and her lips settled into a sympathetic line. It was her "you can tell me anything" face. But I forced myself to picture her at the bottom of Dante's cellar, her body broken.

"Sorry, Ruthie. I don't think I should involve you. It's just not a good idea." I stared through the window. The light outside was already beginning to dim with the incoming fog.

Fuchsia tipped fingers gripped my arm, yanking me around and bringing me face to face with a seething Ruthie in pre-banshee mode. "Oh no you don't. That's a bunch of cow poop! You don't get to shut me out like this." The compassion was gone, replaced by a mixture of anger and hurt. I tried to back away, tried to keep my resolve to protect her, but she wasn't letting go.

"I don't want anything to happen to you," I whimpered. "It's getting real shady—like we could die kind of shady! And I still don't know what's really going on." She would never understand I was doing what was best for her.

Ruthie let loose an indelicate snort. "It's too late. I already know too much." She giggled. "Good gravy! I can't believe I said that out loud." She giggled again, contagiously, hiding her grin behind her hands like she was five years old.

Against my better judgment, I cracked a smile. But a crack was all Ruthie needed to squeeze her way in.

"There's my girl!" She reached out again and pulled me down beside her on the sofa. "It might not be as bad as you think. We all feel like the world is going to end sometimes, but it never does." She gave me a sheepish smile. "I can't believe I'm repeating my mom." She rolled her eyes. "She says we create mountains out of molehills. But who freaking cares? We're teenagers. That's what we do!"

This was not a molehill. This was peril the size of Mt. Everest. Maybe if I left town, no one else would get hurt. I could empty out my college fund. But how long would that last? I would have to keep moving, because Dad was sure to come after me. Images ran through my mind— me homeless, me looking like a pile of dirty rags, and me hiding on street corners watching Dad and my friends get older. Not very appealing. And I couldn't do that to my dad. I had to stay. I needed to make sure everyone I cared about remained safe.

"Hey," Ruthie pestered, poking me with a finger.

She was going to keep bugging me until I spilled. I could feel myself caving. It wasn't hard to rationalize away my concerns as overactive imaginations. And I'd always felt better knowing the why, how, and when of everything. Now everything I didn't understand, all the secrets I kept from Ruthie, all the suspicions that I couldn't stop wondering about—they were interfering with the normal life I wanted. Today had been a total bust. In fact, I would have been better off not going to school at all. If I didn't tell Ruthie what was going on, she might stop talking to me, too. I didn't think I could stand that.

Maybe I was making up excuses to justify telling her, but I didn't care anymore. What was that saying about being armed with knowledge? Whatever. Bottom line, I decided that Ruthie was better off knowing the entire story so she could avoid future trouble. Right? I hoped so, because Zander was history and I needed to talk to *someone.* Besides, she was a force to be reckoned with when she wanted something. I let out a long sigh and folded my legs on the couch. Ruthie mimicked my actions and crisscrossed her legs too, facing me with a beseeching look, waiting for me to divulge my secrets.

"Okay," I finally said. "But if you never want to talk about this stuff again, I will understand." I rested a hand on one of her knees. "You will always be my best friend."

"Yeah, yeah." Ruthie bobbed her head up and down with impatience. "Spill it already."

"Okay, okay." I paused, not sure how to start. "Um. Something really bad happened to me after school Monday." I blinked away sudden tears. Weird that saying it out loud could bring back all the terror.

"Oh my gosh! I knew it! Zander is such a pig!"

"What?" I blinked at her. "It wasn't Zander. Why do you assume he did something?"

She shrugged. "I don't know. Some guys are super pushy, that's all. But something is going on with Zander. I can tell." She squinted her eyes. I marveled that she could see through some of Zander's disguise. She was right that he wasn't your average student. He wasn't really a student at all. But that wasn't as important as Ruthie's comment about pushy guys.

"Hey. Is someone bothering you? Is it Val?"

"Oh seriously," she heaved a sigh and rolled her eyes. "Can't a girl get into the drama of the moment without you assuming the worst?"

Her hypocrisy wasn't lost on me, but her theatrics were part of her charm, so I let it pass.

"Look," I continued. "This is going to sound completely nutters—"

"Tru, everything going on with you lately has been off the charts, so just say it!"

"Okay. You know Bobby?"

"Yeah. You were talking to him the other day. Uh-uh, he didn't—"

"No! Listen first. He had this friend named Dante ..."

IT TOOK FOREVER TO rehash everything with Ruthie, especially since she rarely let me finish a thought without interrupting. I tried to gloss over the supernatural creatures, but Ruthie peppered me with questions. She wouldn't let me skimp on any details. I told her how Dante could put you to sleep with a touch. How he could see colors in peoples' auras, and how my aura was more colorful than any Dante had ever seen before, and that Zander's aura was similar to mine, too. I told her how Dante pushed me into the cellar, how messed up in the head he had been. And I explained my strange vision of Zander trying to find me.

Ruthie sidetracked me for a while, making me describe exactly how I saw her with Phoebe after school when she was looking for me, as if I had to prove that I saw her. Surprisingly, that seemed to interest her the most—the idea that a dream had revealed what she'd been doing. I had to provide evidence by telling her bits of her conversation with Phoebe. Once I did that, she finally believed me. Her eyes glowed with awe as she tilted her head, her mouth curling up on one side. She made me slow down and explain certain details of my rescue, savoring them like the Godiva chocolate.

By the time I got to the part about healing Zander and escaping out of the cellar, only to be shot, I noticed the time. It was getting close to her family's dinner hour and her parents were strict about it. But Ruthie completely ignored my reminder.

"Good gravy!" gasped Ruthie. "You were shot? Show me your stomach. Now!" She demanded.

I lifted my shirt to expose the smooth flesh where the bullet had entered.

Ruthie ran a hand over my skin. "It looks totally normal to me. Are you sure that's what happened?"

"Oh, I was shot, all right." I shuddered, remembering how close to death I'd been. "At first, all I could think about was that I'd killed Dante. I didn't even realize I was hurt." A tear rolled down my cheek. Ruthie wiped it away and clasped my hand. "But then I felt the worst pain I've ever felt in my life," I whispered. "I was sure I was ..."

"You thought you were going to die," filled in Ruthie. "And be with your mother?"

I looked up sharply. Had I? No. My only thought had been that I was dying, that I couldn't heal myself, that I was leaving Zander before I got a chance to know him like I wanted. Why had I not thought of Mom? My shoulders slumped.

"No," I confessed. "I wasn't thinking of her."

"Oh," said Ruthie, before waving the thought away. "Still, you're so lucky you don't have a nasty scar. That would be the end of bikinis for you."

I smiled, knowing she wasn't that shallow. She was simply trying to lighten the mood.

I pressed on, telling her about how I got home and even all the mushy stuff with Zander. It wouldn't hurt to get her opinion about that, especially after today's breakup. Once again, I didn't trust what I felt. I didn't understand why he went all caveman on me today.

"Tru, I'm never going to believe your texts again."

"I know. I'm really sorry. But it wouldn't have helped for you to come over that night, and you *would* have come over if I had told you what was happening, for reals. We couldn't take the chance. It would have mucked things up, or you could have been hurt if someone had come after me. Zander was afraid there was an accomplice, but I don't think there was."

"Still," whined Ruthie. "We need some kind of code. Something that means 'I'm okay, but I can't go into it right now' or 'Get help because I'm being held hostage,' or whatever." A corner of Ruthie's mouth winged up.

I clasped one of her hands and squeezed. "We can work on that, I promise."

"Plus," she continued, "for Freakin' Fried Chicken! You can heal people! Man, girl! That is so awesome!" She bounced up and down on the sofa.

"Really?" I still couldn't get over the fact that she believed me. Her acceptance bolstered my soul, strengthening areas that had been weakened by doubt and loneliness. And fear. She made ideas that were almost impossible to believe seem normal. Her positivity was like a shot of confidence and despite my current heartbreak, my heart rallied in a way that only best friends could understand. My eyes grew misty with gratitude.

"Yeah!" gushed Ruthie. "I always thought seeing in the dark was pretty awesome, but magic healing is way better." She held out a hand and said, "Bring it in."

Knowing what she expected, I laughed and brought my own hand down on top of hers. We bounced our joined hands and chanted in a loud whisper:

Hey, hey, go, fight, win.

Hey, hey 'til the end.

Hey, hey, get out of the way.

Hey, hey, we're here to stay.

Team cheers were the only aspect of school sports that Ruthie excelled at. She brought up her other hand to trap mine in hers.

"We'll always be a team, Tru," she said, locking eyes with me. This time absolute seriousness reflected there. "No matter how crappy life may get," she added.

Ruthie had kept my oldest secret since we were kids, namely my ability to see in the dark. It was one reason I trusted her. Now that I knew there were others out there called idimmu with strange talents like mine, I didn't feel so weird anymore. And there were sethians like Zander and Peter who could do amazing things, too. It made me feel less alone in a way that my relationship with Ruthie could never do. But I loved her for her enduring and un-swerving friendship, nonetheless.

"Thanks," I whispered, moved by her loyalty.

"Okey-dokey," she trilled, releasing my hands and shaking off her uncustomary seriousness. "That other 'psycho Dante' and Collector stuff is super scary. It's so scary I don't want to think about it yet." She faked a shiver. "And, I'm not letting you out of my sight for a long time. I'm going to be your personal chauffeur."

"Sounds good to me," I admitted. "Part of me can't believe all of that happened. I mean, just telling you makes it sound—" I shook my head, at a loss for the right word.

"Zander was right, Tru. It was self-defense. You're not a killer. You're a survivor."

"I know. Still … I can't help wondering if there was something I could have done differently."

"Sweetie, you're thinking too much about it. Leave it alone. Seriously, you went through a lot. You should have stayed home another day so you could let it process."

"Maybe. But, besides being tired, I felt fine. I didn't think Dad would fall for it two days in a row. Plus, I thought I'd go stir crazy here all alone today." I'd been on cloud nine thinking about Zander this morning. What a difference a few hours could make. "I wish I'd stayed home now, though."

"If wishes were dimes—" Ruthie started.

"I'd be a millionaire," I finished. She grinned.

"Oh man! What time is it?" She pulled out her phone. "Bleeping halibut! I wish I could stay longer." She stood up jingling her car keys in her fingers.

"It's okay," I said. "Call me later."

"Will do. I want to talk more about your dreams, anyway. I think they're trying to tell you something, but I need to write some of this stuff down first. It will help me figure it out."

"Oh!" I pressed a hand against the side of my head. "I forgot about my dream last night!" As long as she was tracking my dreams, I should keep her up to date.

Ruthie settled back down on the sofa with a sigh. "Now I have to stay longer. I'm so in trouble. But lay it on me anyway."

I told her about Dante being fixed by "the healer." And I told her about how the Collector manipulated him, how he'd become brainwashed.

"I feel sorry for him," I admitted.

"I guess I do, too," she agreed, tucking her dark hair behind her ear and fingering one long dangly earring. "Maybe God will cut him some slack because he was abused, though. You can't be blamed for protecting yourself against a crazy person, even if he wasn't in control of himself."

She was right and I knew it. But it didn't erase the guilt. I had taken a *life* from someone.

"I want to show you something." I pulled her off the sofa and dragged her up to my bedroom. They said a picture was worth a thousand words, and I could use some help with the last thing I wanted to tell her.

6

AUNT CAROLINE

RUTHIE THREW HERSELF ACROSS my bed as I grabbed a photo album and wiped off the dust that blanketed the tops of the pages.

"I know it's in here somewhere," I said, sinking down next to her and turning the pages. "I used to look through this album all the time as a kid. Oh, here it is."

I pointed to a group of people. A bright blue banner stretched across a backyard patio, indicating that it was Dad's thirtieth birthday party. While I didn't recognize the place, I did recognize the people. And one person in particular grabbed my interest and confirmed my suspicions. Dang it. Sometimes it sucked to be right. I sighed. *Time to introduce Ruthie to the whole family*, I thought. *But I'll leave that woman for last.*

"This is Mom." I pointed to the people as I said their names. "And Dad." They looked so different, younger and happier. And they had better hair back then—something Ruthie couldn't resist pointing out.

"Wow," she gushed. "Hair really does change their look." Mom's blonde hair hung past her shoulders and Dad's light brown hair sported some serious waves. His thick sideburns looked so funny they made my lips twitch.

I tapped on another man with layered blonde hair and a beard. "This is Uncle Ira. He owns the rec center where I worked, remember?" He looked much the same now, although now he styled his hair short and shaved his beard. Every line on his chiseled face looked the same now, despite the twenty years plus that had passed since then. But his eyes had a carefree glint in them that I hadn't seen before. Uncle Ira was always kind, but sober and intense. And now that I thought about it, sad. I'd seen him lost in thought more than once, but he always made an effort to smile and tease me.

"And my mom's sister, Caroline." I rested a finger next to the woman with straight blond hair and pretty cerulean blue eyes. She grinned into the camera. Taking a deep breath, I voiced the idea I'd been thinking about all day, the idea that became a fact as soon as I looked at this picture.

"She's the woman that healed Dante."

Ruthie's mouth formed an 'O' shape and she blinked several times as she digested my announcement. "Are you sure?" She peered at the picture.

"She's the same woman," I insisted.

"I guess you get your healing gift from her."

"Hmmm," I shrugged. "I don't know why I didn't remember these pictures before. I haven't opened up this album in a long time." I scowled. "I never thought my dreams were real before, so it didn't matter."

"You saw her in your dreams before you met Dante?"

"Yeah." I hesitated. "Remember that dream I had with the girl and the vampire. The one where the wolf bit her?" I paused as Ruthie gasped, both of her hands covering her mouth.

"And ..." I continued, cringing as I told her my worst discovery. "I saw her in another dream, as the driver of the car that killed my mom." I chewed a nail.

Ruthie's face drooped. "Oh Tru! That totally sucks! Are you absolutely sure? I mean, do you think it was really her?"

"Yeah, it was her," I repeated, nodding. "I kind of suspected it during school today, but was hoping I was wrong. This photo removes any doubt now." I sagged into the bed somewhat relieved to get it off my chest.

"Wow," said Ruthie, her face uncharacteristically serious. "This is getting super twisted. Are you going to tell your dad?"

"I can't until I find out more. And even then, I don't know. I doubt he would believe me. And what good will it do?"

Dad would haul me off to a shrink if I told him my aunt might be a murderer. Besides, I still couldn't remember what happened the night Mom was killed. I could remember portions of it, like her being hit by a car and me holding her. But then there was nothing. Dad said I had passed out from the shock and I was blocking the memories because they were too painful. But I'd always thought there was more to it, because I felt so guilty all the time. Maybe I couldn't handle the truth. For the thousandth time, I wished I'd been less selfish and shown more understanding toward my mom. She hadn't had time to drive me that night, but she had done it anyway. If I had thought of her before myself for once, then she would still be alive.

I blinked away my depressing thoughts and continued. "There's more," I said, lowering my voice. "During school today I remembered the name that Zander and his brother called the wolf, you know, when Peter tried to wipe my memory and believed I was unconscious, but I wasn't." I flipped the pages, searching for the one I wanted. "Here. My aunt's wedding announcement." I pointed to a card stuck in the photo album.

"That's a wedding invitation?" asked Ruthie with a grimace, as if the plain postcard offended her. When she got married, we'd have to rewrite the definition of bridezilla.

"Not an invitation. My parents were never invited."

If I remembered correctly, Mom said she met Caroline's husband only a couple times before they both died. But now I knew Aunt Caroline was alive. Was her husband alive, too? Uncle. The mysterious husband was my uncle.

"Well. Lamest announcement ever," stated Ruthie, grabbing the card from me and reading aloud its faded cursive scroll.

Dear Lydia and James,

Surprise! I'm a married woman now. Uriel and I tied the knot two weeks ago in a private ceremony in the forest! It was beautiful and lovely

and spontaneous. Like a fairy tale! I wish you could have been here. Just know that I'm absolutely happy and we'll visit you as soon as we can.

Lots of love,

The new Mrs. Dubois

"Dubois! I knew it," I blurted, leaping up and running a hand across my forehead.

"What does it mean?" asked Ruthie with big round eyes.

"When Zander and his brother referred to the wolf in my backyard, they used that name, Dubois."

She set aside the announcement and photo album and perched herself on the edge of the bed. "So, you think that the wolf you saw in your backyard was, in fact, your Aunt Caroline?"

"Yeah. It makes crazy sense." Another thought popped into my head. "Oh, and I almost forgot. Dante said 'the fixer' was different, that she was usemi, you know, a wolf shape-shifter. But she used to be idimmu. Idimmu are hybrids—a mix of human and something else." I air quoted "something else."

"And that makes her way more unusual than just being usemi." If my aunt was Dante's "fixer" then I had as much reason to pity her as I had to hate her.

"No way! Your aunt is a werewolf?" Even Ruthie's extensive limits of believability were being stretched thin, but her voice said she had already accepted it. "Your dream about the fight between the wolf and vampire, where the girl was bitten by the wolf. You think it's her, don't you?" she said.

I shrugged.

"What about the vampire guy?" Ruthie asked. "Do you think he's the husband? This Dubois guy?"

"Usemi. They call themselves *usemi*, not werewolves. And I don't know. He could be the husband." Even as I said it, my gut told me I was correct.

"So, you might have a werewolf and a vampire in the family. Awesome." Ruthie shook her head with envy.

I rolled my eyes, ignoring her comment. "I don't get why she would have killed Mom, though. Mom never said anything bad about her. Maybe Caroline is a psycho or something. It's just so weird. I'm mad, but not mad, you know?"

Ruthie's head bobbed up and down in understanding.

"And it's weird that I wasn't afraid of her as a wolf," I continued. "If she were a psycho, wouldn't she have ripped me to shreds? But she didn't hurt me. That must mean something, right? I mean she licked me, remember?"

"Hmmm. Licking," mused Ruthie. "A bit tame for a villain."

"Right."

Then I remembered Dante, how he'd been nice sometimes. But he'd definitely been the bad guy. "Maybe she's crazy like Dante," I wondered aloud. "If she's part idimmu, then she could have that weakness, right? Dante said that eventually *all* idimmu go insane."

"But why wouldn't she heal herself?" Ruthie asked.

"I can't heal myself," I whispered.

"What?" Ruthie yelped, her pitch high with disbelief.

"I can't heal myself," I repeated, louder.

"But you do it all the time. Remember, you're never

sick." Ruthie pointed out what I had conveniently forgotten.

I thought about my headache earlier today. It had
disappeared fast. I thought about other times, childhood
injuries—scraped knees, twisted ankles, minor stuff. My
wounds didn't heal instantly, but I did heal faster than
anyone I'd ever known. Mom had always been surprised
about that. Now that I thought about it, she sometimes
said I recovered faster than Aunt Caroline.

I recalled one injury in particular. "Remember when
we crashed our bikes on your street trying to go off that
jump stand your neighbor set up?"

"Oh yeah! I still have a scar from that," she said with
a frown, flipping over one arm to display a curved white
line.

"I was hurt worse than you," I said.

"I remember." Her nose crinkled. "But your scrapes
mended fast and you don't have any scars."

"Huh. Maybe you're right." I pulled up one leg of my
jeans to display a smooth, scar-free shin.

"See!" Ruthie pointed vigorously in the air, tilting to
her head as if to say "I told you so." "Hey," she continued. "What about that knife cut you got when the
whatchacallit, was in your backyard?"

"Oh yeah." I rotated my arm, once again amazed to
see smooth, unmarked skin. "But I think *she* made me
better that time. Caroline. Remember? She licked my
arm with her wolf tongue."

"Right. Now I get it. I mean I believed you, but, well,
it was weird that there wasn't any sign of the wound.
Except for the dried blood."

I plopped down on my bed, Ruthie following me. We

scooted backward to lean against the headboard.

"So, I can heal myself sometimes," I said, letting that marinate for a moment. "But there's some kind of threshold. Some point of no return. Maybe I can heal the small stuff, but at a slower rate. Like when Zena's minions made me fall and scrape my hands before English. They healed before class was even halfway over. But when I was shot, I wasn't healing at all. I felt like I was *dying*. Maybe I couldn't heal faster than I was dying." I crinkled my face in confusion. "Then Zander helped me somehow."

"Sweet. You two really do hum!" Ruthie started making kissing noises and I swung out with my arm, catching her in the shoulder.

"Umph," gasped Ruthie. "Sorry. I forgot you two are fighting."

"Ruthie! It's over!" My voice cracked.

Deep down I felt it was impossible. An invisible and binding force connected Zander and me. And no matter how we argued, we were stuck with each other. Unfortunately, it didn't make me feel better. In fact, it sounded miserable. If we didn't want to be together but were forced to be together, well that sounded like hell.

"Whatever," I mumbled.

"Tru, you have serious boy drama going on." She smiled proudly.

"Like that's a good thing!" I waved it off. "Back to the current problem. Maybe *Aunt* Caroline can't heal herself either, and she's gone bonkers."

I remembered something else Dante said.

"Oh, oh!" I leaped off the bed and paced. "That dream I had of the girl, the Euro guy and the wolf? Right?" My hands were starting to sweat. I rubbed them on my jeans.

"Yeah!" she said, picking up my line of thought. "Like we said," she continued, leaning forward with a jerk that caused her hair to fall into her face. "He might be your long-lost uncle."

She dug around one of her pockets and pulled out a hair band. With quick, skilled fingers, she wove her hair into one long braid as she babbled, not missing a beat.

"That was the dream about the vampire and the girl making out in the woods," she said, her face animated. "And then a wolf sneaks up on them and fights with the vampire and kills it—or so you thought. And after taking down the vampire, it—what did you call it?"

"Usemi," I said.

"Yeah. The *usemi*," she corrected, over-enunciating the word, "bites the girl. And that's when the vampire made a surprise recovery and woke up. Then it jumped up and killed the wolf."

I chuckled at her dramatic summary. "You did write it down, didn't you?"

"Of course!" She grinned with pride.

"Anyway," I said. "I think there's a connection between this dream and Aunt Caroline. Dante said 'the fixer' (aka Aunt Caroline) had a child with an akharu (aka vampire)."

"Which would be her husband and your uncle." Ruthie gasped. "Uncle Uriel!"

"Yes!" I yelped, grateful she was making the connections without me explaining.

"Good Gravy! You mean—"

"Yes. I could have a cousin out there," I burst out. We stared at each other in astonishment.

I plopped down on my bed, letting its softness comfort me. It was my safe place and the site of many conversations with Ruthie. We told each other everything here. And now we could add supernatural secrets to the list. Rubbing a hand along the yarn tied into the quilt, I thought of my mother making it. I realized she was wrapped up in the sense of security I felt here, making my bed like sacred ground to me. And as our lives had taken such an ominous turn, I drew strength from both the blanket and my best friend.

We batted around the implications of this mysterious cousin and where he or she could be. Perhaps the child had been adopted. Maybe the kid was dead. I hoped not. The upside was that I might not be the last hope for my family's gene pool. Maybe it wasn't all up to me.

Ruthie's phone cackled suddenly, startling both of us. It was the laugh of the wicked witch from *The Wizard of Oz.* I smiled and shook my head at Ruthie. Her mom was a lot cooler than she gave her credit for.

"Oh, crap on a stick! It's my mom," she said, reading the text aloud.

Tell Val to leave you alone and get your butt home ... with the groceries!

She pursed her lips into a pout. "I totally forgot!"

"Oops." I sympathized, knowing she was going to be in trouble when she got home.

"But I'm not with Val!" she whined. Her thumbs flew across the keys. "How does she even know about him anyway?"

"Hey, I forgot to ask what happened the other day! Did Val ask you to Homecoming?"

Ruthie frowned, finishing her text message. "No. I was supposed to meet him at Froyo Dream after his practice, but I couldn't find you and well ..."

"Oh my gosh! Sorry for messing up your plans."

"Yeah, like it's your fault you got kidnapped." She cracked a half smile. "Besides, I think he stood me up. On my way home I saw him with Jim and Dalton at the 7-Eleven with a whore horde. I'm losing faith in him." Her eyes drooped at the corners for second. "But then he seemed okay at school, and—ugh! He's so messing with my mind. Do you think he's just using me?"

I squeezed her hand, an apology spilling out. "Honestly, I have no idea. I haven't been paying attention like I should have been. Sorry." I felt like such a lame friend.

"Not like you don't have enough going on." She rolled her eyes.

"I'll do better," I promised. "Wait. He did seem angry when you went all sappy fan girl while listening to Isaac singing today."

"Really? Jealousy is a good sign." A hopeful note entered her voice. "You know, later I felt stupid about how I acted with Isaac."

"Me, too. I don't get what happened." Something had felt wrong with that whole situation. And, now that I thought about it, Zander hadn't seemed all that surprised by my reaction to the singing. He'd been angrier about my bumbled breakup with Isaac.

"Well, we are hormonal teenagers," Ruthie mused, excusing our behavior. "And Isaac is pretty dang hot. Seriously. His muscles make me want to go all-damsel-in-distress sometimes. Who could blame us?"

Her face was stone cold serious. My lips twitched with

amusement. But then I recalled the disaster that followed Isaac's impromptu concert and frowned.

"Zander and Val, that's who," I answered flatly.

"Y-e-a-h ... Alright-y, then." She scrambled off the bed. "We could make them cookies. Works every time. I'd stay and get all Betty Crocker with you, but I'm in enough trouble as it is. Are you going to be okay if I take off? I was supposed to stop by the grocery store for milk and stuff. Crap. I need to find Mom's list." She checked her pockets and came up empty. "Why doesn't the woman just text me her list like a normal person?" she muttered.

"Don't worry about me. I'll be fine. Dad will be home soon anyway." I followed her downstairs to the front door.

"Oh man, Tru. Now my head is full of all this crazy crap." She stared my way for a second before nodding her head, as if she'd made a decision. "I'm picking you up in the morning, okay?"

I smiled in agreement.

"And maybe it will make more sense after we sleep on it, or in your case, dream on it."

"Definitely." I gave her a hug, then looked through the peephole. When I didn't see anything but an empty porch, I cracked open the front door, cautiously letting the outside air drift in, bringing with it a sense of autumn. A bird cawed loudly.

An early fog drifted around the trees along our street. The moist air accentuated the smell of redwoods and eucalyptus. I loved and hated the fog. On one hand, it kept our small niche in the world alive and green, the redwoods tall and mossy, the ground covered in ferns, the wildlife vast and varied. It literally vibrated with life. On the other hand, the fog created the only darkness I couldn't see through—a sinister and wet wall that deadened my super sight.

Remembering another creepy day involving giant wolves, I grabbed the bottle of bear spray from the drawer in the entry hall before we headed out to the front porch. Although we didn't get bears in our area, Dad said it worked as a protection against mountain lions and burglars. Hopefully, against usemi as well.

Misty clouds hovered low to the ground, making me feel like I lived in a fishbowl. The Collector, the usemi, a crazy aunt—anything or anyone could be right there, hidden in the fog. Dante had told me that people were coming to relocate me to some unknown cell, in which I might never see the light of day again. For all I knew, they could already be here. Then there were the wolves in my backyard. I reminded myself that Zander and his brother had wounded the grey wolf. It probably wouldn't be returning anytime soon ... unless it healed magically like the ones in the movies or was healed by Aunt Caroline. Dang! Why did I have to think of that?

We stood on the threshold of my home, our hearts speeding up at the thought of traversing the distance from the porch to the car. Ruthie clutched my arm as I chewed my lower lip. After a moment, she released my arm, squared her shoulders, and seemed to say, "Do your worst," to the fog.

A long wail echoed in the distance followed by several dog-like yips. But they were deeper and more menacing.

"Please tell me that was just a dog," said Ruthie, pulling us back against the front door.

"I don't know. Doesn't sound like it, does it?"

"Damn it," she swore. "No, it doesn't."

Grabbing her hand and giving it a squeeze, I said, "Nothing would even think of coming at you, girl, because you look like Jana Jegger, and she totally kicks butt."

She choked out a laugh. Jana was one of the tv stars on *Court of Palms* who had wicked tai chi moves. Ruthie knew some tai chi herself. I had witnessed her take down a cocky tourist visiting from the east coast when he'd literally rubbed her the wrong way. Now Jana Jegger was one of my favorite nicknames for her.

"Okay. This fog is messing with my mind. I'm running for it!" Ruthie's hushed voice echoed across the front porch.

"I'll watch your back," I promised, holding up the bear spray.

"Thanks," she whispered. "Lock yourself in the house as soon as I get in the car."

"You, too!"

Ruthie took off, dashing to her car and wrenching open her door. As she pulled away from my street, I laughed at our paranoid behavior. But then Dante's crazy eyes popped into my head and I shivered.

Across the street, the shadowy form of a familiar truck surprised me. It had to be Zander. I couldn't believe he was still watching out for me. Despite our current disagreement, the fact that he would still do that melted away some of my earlier ire. Not sure what to do about that problem, I went inside and locked the door.

As the lock slid into place with a resounding click, my phone buzzed, its vibration startling me so much I yelped. I took a deep breath, one hand over my heart. I needed to calm down.

It was Bobby. "Hey there. What's up?"

"Are you all right?" he gushed.

"Yeah," I replied. "Why?"

"Oh. Sorry. I just had a weird feeling about you. Strange, I know. Maybe it's residual stuff from Monday."

"No worries. I'm fine."

"Okay. Are you at home?"

"Yeah."

"Lock the door for me, would you?"

"Sure," I said, as I bolted the top latch.

Why was he worried? A howl ripped through the night air again, this time closer. A second later I heard something scratching across our porch and I jerked away from the door as the handle rattled. I held my phone with one hand and reached for the bear spray with the other, pointing it toward the door. Something growled and the rattling stopped. I heard another growl followed by a guttural whine. A second later tires squealed as a vehicle pealed out of our street.

"Tru? Tru? Are you still there?" Bobby's urgent voice broke through my fear. I set the bear spray down with shaky fingers and assured Bobby I was fine before hanging up. One last peek out the window told me Zander's truck was gone.

Despite my assurances to Bobby, I didn't feel safe at all. Keeping the bear spray with me, I ran up to my room and climbed under my bedcovers, counting the minutes until Dad came home.

7

VEXED

IN THE MORNING I was surprised to hear the doorbell ring instead of Ruthie's car horn. I zipped up my backpack and headed downstairs, following the voices to the kitchen. Dad and Ruthie huddled around the counter.

"What are you two up to?" I called out, already guessing.

Ruthie whipped around, a toothy grin on her face. "It's hot cocoa day!" she quipped, holding out her paper cup. I looked out the window to see a bright sunny day awaiting us. Last night's cold fog had disappeared and been replaced with brightness and warmth. It didn't seem cold enough to warrant hot cocoa, but this was Ruthie Robles we were talking about.

"Every day is hot cocoa day for you," I countered, with a knowing smile. Dad stocked up on disposable mugs just for Ruthie's requests.

"It's the least I can do for Ruthie since she won't take any gas money," inserted Dad, topping her cup with a large helping of whipping cream.

Ruthie's head vibrated with excitement. "Thanks Mr. Parker! You've got the best recipe. Plus, I love the whip cream!"

Dad nodded his head and puffed out his chest. I rolled my eyes.

"Come on. It's just a half-day of school and we're going to be late," I said, leading out the front door and waving goodbye to Dad.

"So," Ruthie said, as soon as we piled into her red Mini. "Any dreams?"

I shook my head. "No, just crappy sleep."

She raised one perfectly manicured eyebrow.

While I admired her perky attitude this morning, I couldn't wipe away my fatigue or gloominess. "If my REM cycle isn't going to be interrupted by psycho dreams, you'd think I'd get some decent sleep," I complained. "My brain wouldn't shut down and I kept thinking about Caroline. Maybe that's why I didn't dream."

"Well, I suppose you can't always be weaving your dream magic."

A bitter laugh escaped me. "Yeah, right. More like dream curse."

"Call it what you want, it's magic to me," she declared, reaching for her cocoa.

When she closed her eyes in bliss, I yelped. "Hey! Watch the road!"

"I got it," she murmured, her voice full of confidence. "Did you decide what to do about Zander? Did he call you?"

"No and no." I stared out the window.

"He's a loser." Ruthie shrugged as if to say it was his loss, but I couldn't let go so easily.

"I know. I think we did break up," I mumbled. Until now I'd believed Zander would call, that he would apologize, that he wouldn't let us break up.

"Which is pretty amazing since you are officially with Isaac," chuckled Ruthie. Her eyelids were at half-mast as she continued to glory in her chocolate nectar.

"No, we aren't!" I whined. "At least I tried to break up with Isaac. I mean, I *did* break up with him. He's just confused."

"Oh, Isaac." Ruthie made a "tsk tsk" sound. "Maybe I should dump Val and go for Hottie Efoti. A girl would always know where she stood with him." One side of her mouth pulled up dreamily.

"Be my guest."

She threw me a look of disbelief. "You really don't like him?"

"Nope. I mean, he's super good-looking and everything. We just don't ... you know."

"Yeah, I get it. Too bad, though. 'Cause Zander's trouble, if you ask me. He's hot and all, but your life has been seriously crappy ever since he showed up."

She was right. But I didn't blame Zander. I wouldn't even be here if he hadn't been around to save me.

"Hey, you know what we need today?" Suddenly Ruthie looked giddy.

"What?" I asked with some trepidation. She had a mischievous twinkle in her eye. She giggled at my wary look.

"Don't be so scared! Geez." She squeezed the steering

wheel tighter as she leaned forward to look up at the sky. "I was just thinking ... Well, this day is way too nice to waste on homework. Let's go to the beach after school."

I grinned, nodding with enthusiasm. No need to sit at home stewing. "Excellent idea!" I agreed, giving Ruthie a quick high-five. There was something therapeutic about going to the beach. When I dove into the cold sea, I forgot all my troubles. I could sure use some of that today.

DESPITE THE SHORTENED CLASS schedule, I was itching for school to be over even before I made it to first break. Knowing that I'd be sunning on the beach this afternoon made every minute feel ten times longer. Isaac and Phoebe hadn't shown up, and Zander was keeping out of sight, mostly. I caught a glimpse of him now and then, and quickly came to the conclusion that he was avoiding me. That worked for me because my motto today was "no worries."

Of course, the last person I wanted to see was everywhere I turned. Zena Taylor. She and her entourage smirked at me as I passed them coming out of the bathroom. I gritted my teeth when I caught the words "crazy bitch." But it didn't affect me like it normally did. Now that I had enemies more dangerous than her it didn't seem to matter as much. The way she tended to hang all over Zander, however, would be harder to ignore. Not for the first time, I wondered why Zena was such a narcissistic pain in the butt. I considered skipping English later. I knew I could convince Ruthie, but I didn't want to risk getting detention when I had such awesome plans for my afternoon. I sighed as I decided to tough it out.

Students bumped into me as they hurried to class, turning the walkways into punishing gauntlets. I made it to Drama and grabbed a front row seat near the door. As I settled in, I noticed an unfamiliar woman wearing a tracksuit at the front of the room, her feet propped up on the desk. *Great,* I thought. Another substitute teacher. Isaac sure knew when to miss class. If this teacher understood a lick of drama, I would eat my gym shorts. Sure enough, as soon as the bell rang, she announced that we had free time to work on homework. Yeah, right. Like anyone was going to do that. Well, besides me anyway. Maybe I could finish the English project without Zander.

I cracked open my project notes and attempted to pick up where we left off. But my mind kept wandering to Zena and to all the hurtful things she'd done to me over the years. In fourth grade she told everyone I had three nipples, knowing full well I wasn't going to strip down to prove her wrong. In middle school, she sabotaged the science experiment Ruthie and I were presenting by replacing the sugar in our yeast-growing demonstration with salt, which gave us an epic fail. We never proved it, but the secretive smile on Zena's face was enough evidence for us. There were other embarrassing jokes, all designed to humiliate. I didn't understand her and probably never would. What made a person so cruel?

For the first time I realized that my feelings of hate toward her had become toxic. I tried not to think about them, but knowing I'd be facing both her and Zander next period wound the dark emotions tighter and tighter around my heart, and I couldn't ignore them. She was like VX, the most lethal nerve gas in the world and cat-egorized as a weapon of mass destruction—or so Mr. Neff said in freshman Biology. If one drop of its gas made contact with your skin, you were toast. Yeah, that was Zena. Or should I start calling her VeX? I chuckled to myself, drawing a few curious gazes. Ruthie would get a kick out of the new nickname. Until then I needed to concentrate on this stupid project.

I closed my eyes, trying to think of something that would erase Zena's nastiness from my mind. For some reason, I thought about a time when Ruthie and I were eight years old. We'd gone into the woods by her house to look for fairies because Ruthie believed they were real. Just like now, I'd been willing to follow her pretty much anywhere. Instead of fairies, though, we found the cutest kittens ever. They were curled up in a black and white pile. We gushed over them, creeping closer to pet them. They woke up before we reached them, sniffing the air curiously and allowing us to pick them up and feed them some of the food we'd brought with us to give to the fairies. We marveled at their beautiful markings. They were unlike any kittens we'd ever seen and we decided to show our parents. By dropping food along the path, we led them away from their bed. When we reached Ruthie's backyard, her dad saw us and called out in a desperate voice, commanding us to drop everything and run to the house as fast as we could. We didn't understand why he was yelling. It scared us and we froze. When I looked at our line of kittens, I saw a bigger one not far away. It had larger white markings, long white stripes up its back, and I realized our kittens were not cats, but skunks. Ruthie figured it out about the same time. We looked at each other and screamed so high and loudly we could have broken glass, and that scared the momma skunk. Suffice it to say, we had a vinegar bath that night and several more over the next few days. We'd learned a great lesson about the difference between kittens and skunks—and skunk mommies, too.

I smiled to myself as I rested my head on my arms. My sleepless and dreamless night suddenly caught up with me, and before I knew it, I was snoozing.

I was in an unfamiliar house, furnished with denim and suede fabrics, heavy draperies, and shiny crystal chandeliers. Clearly this was another vision. My eyes followed the patterns along the hallway rug until I noticed Zena pressing herself against the wall beneath an ornately framed Monet-like painting. She bent her ear toward the sound of voices arguing in the next room.

"How much longer do we need to prove ourselves to the Kasadu? I'm sick to death of this nowhere town. We're stuck here while our friends back home are getting blessed. Millisande must laugh every time she thinks of us."

"Your sister would never do that," said a man.

"I can't believe it! You still have a thing for her," accused the woman in an acrid voice. I recognized the voices now. They belonged to Mr. and Mrs. Tayler. Zena's parents.

"We have a good life here," Mr Taylor said. "Why can't you be happy?"

"Because we deserve more! We've been monitoring this area for years! There's nothing here! No usemi, akharu, or half-breeds. And definitely no child like the one he's looking for. They're just horrible, boring humans. It's no place to raise our daughter. What kind of connections can w-she make here?"

The Taylors knew about supernaturals! Could they be from the same place as Zander and his brother, Peter? Did Zander know them?

"Eleria, we don't have a choice, thanks to your neverending snooping. Remember? You had to know everything. And, now that you know the truth about our people, are you any better off?" Then his frustrated tone softened. *"I realize you want to return, but this is our home now. Complaining to Kasadu won't help. We're fortunate he's allowed us such a comfortable life here."*

Mr. Taylor sounded worn out, which wasn't surprising. Being stuck with Zena's mom must be hell on earth. Store clerks cringed when she walked into their shops. And our school principal, Mr. Millard, lost his suntan every time her high heels clicked across school property. She was a master manipulator and the coldest person I'd ever met. I couldn't imagine anyone making her do something she didn't want to do.

"We've been punished enough for my ... indiscretions." She let out a frustrated sigh. *"If only Millisande had been on my side ..."* There a pause before she

spoke again, but more softly and with obvious restraint. "I just wanted to help our people. I always have. But I can't here. So, we're going to do something about it." Then her voice took on that condescending tone I was used to hearing. "Have you learned nothing after all this time?"

I heard a long forfeiting sigh. "What would you have me do?" asked Zena's dad. "Do you want me to request a transfer? I bet the Kasadu would move us in a heartbeat—to the lower levels, that is."

Zena's face whitened.

What did she know? Who the heck was she? I'd known Zena most of my life, and it was hard to think of her as anything other than a pain-in-the-butt school bully. Could her parents know about the Collector? I imagined Ruthie rolling her eyes and saying, "That figures."

Mrs. Taylor's oily laugh chased goose bumps up my arm. "Oh Gary. We can't have that. No, we need to find something important enough to draw his attention here, to us. In a good way, of course."

"But you agree that there's nothing here."

"Well, there could be ... we just have to make it appear that way ..."

"I'm not making up—"

"Gary." Her voice slammed down like a cleaver, causing my heart to thud. "Sweetheart," she whispered in a softer voice. "We have to do something. How can you *just sit here while the children of our peers get what is rightfully Zena's?"*

"You mean your sister's kid. And it isn't even about them. You can't stand the idea that Milli has been blessed while you haven't. This is really about you. Zena's fine," *he insisted.*

A long silent moment followed and Zena tensed in expectation. When Mrs. Taylor finally spoke, Zena breathed out a long, pent up sigh.

"No, she's not. You've never recognized Zena's potential. You've lowered your standards. You might as well throw your hat in with these humans."

Something banged. "You push her too hard." Mr. Taylor sounded angry.

"I'm molding her. A child is like a piece of clay, and with help from us she can become a masterpiece. I'm only trying to help her become more, be what she's truly capable of becoming. I'm trying to resurrect her true nature. How can you deny that for her? If we went home, she could be trained, as she should be. We would receive the blessing and evolve as we were meant to evolve. You must see that!"

Zena moved away from the voices and the floor creaked beneath her feet. Her head shot up, her eyes bulging with panic.

"Zena? Is that you, darling?" Mrs. Taylor asked. Her voice was polite but I still heard the threat in it.

Zena appeared torn between running away and facing her mother.

"I know you're there." This time the voice crackled like lightning. "You know what they say about eavesdropping. Come here now." To my surprise, Zena started shaking. I'd never seen her scared before, at least not like that, and I suddenly felt like the intruder that I was.

Zena had always been the bully, the tormentor, and the one manipulating the situation. At school she never had to deal with the consequences of her actions. But she looked terrified now, which begged the question.

What would her mother do to her?

Someone shook my shoulder and I snapped up my head, disoriented to see that I was still in drama class. A bobbing brown ball with blue glasses flashed in and out of my vision.

"Wow! You were in a deep sleep." Kelsey Perkins smiled at me, her mouth full of multi-colored rubber bands that were attached to the brackets on her braces. "Sorry. I just wanted to warn you that the bell is about to ri—"

The loud peal over the sound system indicated that the period had ended and I jumped again, gripping the edges of the desk.

Kelsey chuckled. "Like I was saying, class is over."

Students hustled down the aisle between us with swinging backpacks. The substitute still had her feet up on the desk reading, not in the least ruffled by the sudden clang of the bell or the students bumping their way out of the room as fast as possible. Without looking up from her magazine, she lifted her hand to wave goodbye as they passed her.

"Are you all right?" asked Kelsey with concern.

"Yeah, I'm fine. Thanks," I mumbled. She smiled kindly before taking off. As I gathered up my things, I leaned against the desk, feeling my world teetering on its axis as my life-long nemesis and her family started changing shape before my very eyes. They had to be sethians, an ancient race of people like the usemi and akharu. Questions and assumptions piled up in my mind. They were looking for non-humans?

I walked in a daze to my last class: English. I wanted to tell Zander about my dream, but I couldn't if we weren't talking to each other. And we definitely weren't. When I arrived, Zena had already parked herself next to him. She was trying to catch his attention, but he appeared to be ignoring her. I stared at Zena with new eyes, wondering about her home life. I'd always thought her mom was scary—*Sleeping Beauty's* Maleficent kind of scary—but now I wondered if she might be more like the mother in *Flowers in the Attic* kind of scary. I began to feel something new for her. Pity. I felt ... *sorry* for her. Zena looked up, meeting my eyes. Something undefined passed between us. Then it was gone and she looked at me like she always did. If anything, her gaze held more disdain than usual. I sighed and moved to an open seat.

Toward the end of class, Mr. Mac dumped extra reading on us, eliciting a class wide grumble.

"And don't forget that your projects are due next week," he added. A few kids were dumb enough to admit they hadn't even started it. Guess things could be worse.

At least my project was mostly done.

Later, as the final bell rang, students scattered, anxious to begin their stint of freedom. Mr. Mac shouted over their glee. "Extra credit to you if your parents come to Back to School Night!"

I groaned inwardly. The last thing I wanted was Dad coming to a school meeting. That was Mom's job. I hoped that Dad would have to work late.

ON MY WAY HOME, I weighed the pros and cons of telling Ruthie about the Taylors, because it led to another secret I'd been sitting on. Should I tell her that Zander's father was the Collector, too? How much could I divulge if I didn't? I wondered again if I was risking her life in some way.

Before I stepped out of her car, I casually dropped the first bomb, as if it was simply another item on our list of things to bring to the beach. She gasped dramatically. The car lurched forward before she remembered to slam on the brakes and put the car in Park.

"You think the Taylors are freaking spies for the Collector?" she screamed at me.

I nodded, shut the car door, and walked off toward my front door. The hum of the car window rolling down had me spinning back to see her raising a shaking fist. She didn't leave without extracting a promise of details once she returned from grabbing all her beach gear.

She showed up twenty minutes later with the top down on her convertible and her bodyboard sticking up out of it. Record time for her.

"Now will you tell me what happened?" demanded

Ruthie as I picked up my bodyboard from the garage.

She seized my board with impatient hands, marched to her car, and threw it into the back alongside hers.

"Yes," I stated. I tossed in my beach bag and dropped into the passenger seat. "One second." I sent a short text to Dad letting him know we were leaving—his final request when granting permission to let me hang at the beach today. I looked to the parking spot that Zander had staked out days ago. Our neighbor's car sat in it and I couldn't see the truck anywhere. I wondered what he was up to.

As Ruthie pulled away from the curb, the wind zipped over my sunglasses and through my hair in a you're-about-to-have-an-adventure kind of way. I tipped up my chin, smiling.

"Seriously, will you finally tell me why you think the Taylors are evil scouts?" Her knuckles whitened as she squeezed the steering wheel.

"I had another dream, in drama class, of all places."

"Oooh. Fell asleep in class, did we? Any drool?" She pulled one corner of her mouth down with a finger.

"Shut up." I smacked her shoulder playfully.

She pretended to be in pain. "Ow!"

I explained almost everything, deciding at the last second to withhold what I knew about Zander's father. I also didn't tell her my theory that the "home" Mrs. Taylor referred to was also Zander's home, and that this Kasadu character was most likely Zander's father. I didn't mention how much I pitied Zena, either. It felt too much like I'd be betraying the friendship between Ruthie and me, which was built, in part, on our mutual hatred of Zena.

"Don't they have relatives in Southern Cal?" asked Ruthie. "Zena's always bragging about the movie stars she's related to. Do you think they're from the same place? Oh my gosh! Hollywood could be full of them!"

"Ruthie," I tried to get her back on track. "All I know is that the Taylors are dangerous."

"And different? Like you and Zander? And Dante?"

"Different is right," I hedged.

"Whatever," dismissed Ruthie, waving a hand in the air. "I always knew something was wrong with that girl. But I never would have guessed she wasn't human."

Neither am I, I thought. *At least not completely human.*

I suddenly remembered my new nickname for Zena. "Hey!" I told Ruthie, who of course needed more graphic details on what VX would do to a body.

"Good one," she said with a grimace. "Still. VD isn't bad either."

I sputtered out laughing. "As in Venereal Disease?"

"Yep," smiled Ruthie. "Seriously, she was all over the football team today in the halls. And yes, I meant the entire team. She's such a slut."

"I still think we should go with VeX."

"Fine, but don't be surprised if I slip up and say VD once in a while." She nodded with satisfaction. "But back to your spy theory. Who do you think her family is spying on?"

"I don't know. She said they've been monitoring this place for a long time and they haven't found anything. I'm not sure what that means. Could go all the way to San Francisco or down to LA, for all I know."

"Maybe the Collector has spies like the Taylors all

over the country," suggested Ruthie. "So many interest-ing characters." She drummed her fingers on the steering wheel, taking the next exit toward the beach. "Dante. The 'fixer.' Your aunt. A mysterious uncle, and possibly a cousin out there ... What if—"

"The Collector is sending out spies to search for this mysterious child? And maybe the father, too?" I finished for her. "Dante said the fixer had a child, half usemi and half akharu. Yes, that could explain the spies every-where. Plus, they did mention they'd been looking for some kid."

"That child would sure be something for his freaky zoo," she observed. Then her mouth formed a circle. "Sh-oot! Maybe they think you're this mysterious kid." She rubbed her arms. "Oh my gosh! I just got goosebumps."

I groaned. The same worry had been etching a crease in my forehead since school ended. "But I'm not that mysterious kid. We don't know if Aunt Caroline had a baby, anyway," I countered. "Plus, if they thought it was me, I'd already be toast."

"Well, never say never," she declared. "Something or someone brought them here to Scotts Valley. And the fact that Dante said they suspect there's a child ... that means the Collector thinks so."

"How would the Collector ever find out I was the per-son Dante kidnapped?" I asked, knowing that there was a way. Peter knew. Dante's chant ran through my mind. *The Collector's silly sons* ... Zander said his brother wouldn't tell anyone, but Zander didn't know what I knew.

"Don't know," Ruthie answered. "I'm just saying, with things getting weirder around here, and with the

Taylors *watching*," she air quoted, her hands lifting from the steering wheel for a moment. "Well, you need to avoid that family at all costs."

"Kind of hard to do when Zena and I go to school together." I massaged my temples, hoping a brilliant solution would pop into my brain.

"Yeah. Also, difficult to do when Zena wants to jump your boyfriend's bones." She raised an eyebrow and smirked.

"Actually, I don't think Zander is into her anymore," I admitted.

"But you said ..."

"Yeah, I was jealous. But he's ignoring her now." I'd watched them throughout English class. It seemed like he was going out of his way to avoid her.

"So, you guys are back together?"

"I didn't say that!" I didn't mean to snap at Ruthie, but I couldn't explain to her what I didn't understand myself.

"Geez! Only asking." She pretended to be offended, but an understanding smile played along her lips. "Just so you realize, hanging out with Zander is going to put you in Zena's line of fire and maybe in her parents', too. Not a very good idea if they are who you think they are."

"I know, I know," I said between pressed lips.

Then Ruthie pointed out the obvious. "You need to tell Zander about the Taylors."

At the moment, though, I preferred singing karaoke in front of the whole school rather than talking to Zander. Well, almost. Besides, even though he had ignored Zena today, it didn't make up for what he'd said to me. I rubbed my neck, massaging the tension bunching up my muscles.

"Yeah, I know I do," I acknowledged. "And it isn't the only thing I should tell him."

I had to unload the truth about Zander's dad on someone or my head was going to blow. So, I told her. Looking back, I should have made Ruthie pull over first because she let loose a long string of vegetarian swear words, completely over-reacting and swerving too close to the car next to us. Zander's face flashed before me as I screamed for her to watch the road. Ruthie quickly pulled into the nearest parking lot, ignoring the driver she'd cut off and his obscene hand gesture. She put her car in Park and swung around to me, her eyebrows sky high in outrage.

"Zander's dad is the evil Collector? Are you freaking kidding me? Do you have any sense of self-preservation? It's a good thing you broke up with that jerk."

My heart rate slowly leveled out. "It's not Zander's fault his father is secretly evil. It must be his alter ego, because Zander would never go along with what he's doing. Ruthie, he helped me escape from Dante, remember? And Dante was super surprised to see Zander. No, I don't think Zander knows. Possibly Peter, but not Zander."

Ruthie just shook her head from side to side, looking somber. "Doesn't matter. You need to stay away from him."

"What about telling him the Taylors are spies?"

Ruthie sighed. "That was before I realized they might be on the same side."

"They aren't. I mean, I'm mad at Zander. He was a jerk. But he's trying to protect me from the Collector. He has no idea he's protecting me from his own father. Man! This is so messed up."

"Why didn't you tell him before?" asked Ruthie, her eyes squinting at me as if I were a bug under a microscope.

I dropped my gaze. "I was afraid to. I knew it would be devastating. And I didn't know if he'd believe me. Remember Cora's brother?"

Ruthie cocked her head to the side. "Yeah. Glad she moved. I was getting sick of her dirty looks."

We knew from experience that people don't like to hear bad truths about those close to them. Once, Ruthie and I told a friend that we saw her brother shoplifting and she stopped talking to us. When her brother was caught stealing later, she hated us even more, acting as if it was our fault he was sent to Juvenile Hall.

"Exactly," I said. "I don't know how Zander will react."

"*Chica*, he's got to be told sometime." When I remained silent, Ruthie let out a sigh. She shrugged her shoulders and pulled back into traffic, darting a mischievous look my way. "So, you aren't going to tell him that his dad is the bad guy or that the Taylors are ... whatchacallits ... Moles? Narks? Dicks?"

"Dicks?"

She chuckled. "Yeah. Didn't you know that's slang for spies?"

I shook my head. "You mean private investigators."

"No kidding?" She seemed surprised, but shrugged. "Oh well. Then that's for Zander and Peter. I think you had it right earlier. VeX."

I snorted out a dark chuckle. "I'm certainly feeling vexed lately."

"Oooh," breathed out Ruthie in appreciation. "Good

one."

"Whatever they all are, everything's getting more and more complicated. I'll tell Zander soon. Just not yet."

But the idea of talking to Zander was on par with Zena's brand of torture, so I decided to put the whole idea aside and enjoy our beach day.

8

MIRACLE

"IT'S COLD!" WHINED RUTHIE.

We were piled high with our towels, bodyboards, food and sunscreen. Ruthie was disappointed to see new clouds forming in the sky, obscuring the sun. And without the naked blast of sunlight, the cold air caused goose bumps to spread along our uncovered legs. I was glad I brought a sweatshirt.

"I thought it was going to be a nice day." Ruthie scrunched up her shoulders and made a face.

"It will heat up soon. Positive thoughts."

"I hope so," she whined.

"It usually does. I bet the water is warm, though. Well, warm-*er*."

Movies like *Blue Crush* or *Point Break* built up expectations of bikini babes, hot sun, and bath temperature water. That was southern California, not up north in the

Monterey Bay. More often than not the fog didn't dissipate until late morning and then it crept back in by mid-afternoon, providing a short window of warmth.

"It better be warmer than last time," grumbled Ruthie, referring to our last foray to the sea when we hadn't thawed out until we hit the shower at home. "Maybe we should stay on the beach today. Last time it took forever to get all the sand out of my hair, not to mention everywhere else."

I chuckled. The sand had a way of getting into every nook and cranny, but we didn't care when we were out riding the waves. "Let's just play it by ear."

We finally made it to the sand and plopped down our bodyboards so we could load the rest of our things on top and drag them like sleds to the perfect spot on this lesser-known corner of Santa Cruz. We were hoping to avoid as many tourists as possible.

"I haven't been to this beach in ages," I said, comforted by the normalcy of our activity. "Why did you pick it?"

"Because Isaac and Phoebe always come here. They said most tourists don't know about it."

"I thought it was just going to be you and me," I pouted. I wanted a drama-free day. A day to mull over my new discoveries and have some one-on-one time with Ruthie. Now Isaac and Phoebe were coming? My stomach twisted.

"Oh shish-kebab, I didn't think about the weirdness between you and Isaac. Sorry," she said, her face begging forgiveness.

I shrugged. "It's all right," I said, not wanting it to ruin our day. Besides, I still wanted to be friends with the twins.

"Don't worry," said Ruthie. "They aren't getting here for at least an hour. Family stuff, as usual." She took in my droopy face and rolled her eyes. "I know you don't want to talk to Isaac, but you've got to rip off that Band-Aid eventually. Might as well be today." Then she marched ahead, determined to find the warmest spot, while I followed pensively.

We settled on a patch of sand where bushes blocked the cold breeze, shook out our blanket, and peeled down to our swimsuits, shuddering at the cold. Seagulls eyed our bags and crept closer. Ruthie threw a handful of sand at them with a scream. They ran away, cawing and setting off a stream of seagull screams.

"Damn, birds," she muttered.

I chuckled. "Remember your sunscreen," I reminded her.

"Yeah, yeah," she said. "Don't know how I can burn in this temperature." She tried rubbing away the goose bumps along her legs.

"Do I need to bring up eighth grade?" It had been a similarly overcast day for the end of year field trip and Ruthie had received the worst burn of her life.

Her face twisted in annoyance. "Fine, *mother,*" she mocked. We lubed up before spreading out on our blanket, which was angled toward the best light.

Much later, after the sun made up for lost time, we roasted on our blanket, listening to the crashing waves, grateful for the occasional cool breeze. My phone suddenly dinged. Then dinged again. Someone was sending me a text. Zander? I wanted it to be him. I wanted him to come crawling back to me. I sat up and dug through my bag. Ruthie looked like she was passed out. And she was turning pink. I toyed with the idea of waking her to lube up again, but thought better of it as I fished out my phone.

Bobby: Are you all right?

Bobby: Can you call me?

I frowned with disappointment. Why was Bobby worried about me again? I texted him that I was fine and asked why he thought I wasn't.

Bobby: Just a feeling. Sorry.

Bobby: Are you sure? Where are you?

"Geez!" I muttered. I repeated that I was okay and he shouldn't worry about me.

Bobby: Don't know what's wrong with me, Tru.

Bobby: I keep having these feelings like you're in trouble.

I told him he didn't need to feel guilty about the Dante episode. I was one hundred percent fine. A lie.

Bobby: Okay. I won't bug you. Just needed to know.

I threw my phone into my bag with an exasperated sigh.

"Who was that?" asked Ruthie, through stiff lips.

"Bobby. He was worried about me. It's starting to freak me out. There's something different about him."

"Like what?" Ruthie pulled up on her elbows,

squinting at me sleepily.

"Well, for starters, all of the sudden his poor eyesight is twenty-twenty."

"You mean his eyesight healed? That's kind of odd, right?"

"Yes." I chewed my lip. "And then he was pestering me about talking to the school counselor, about what happened with Dante. I got the feeling Bobby didn't believe me when I said that nothing happened."

"He can't prove anything did." Ruthie pulled out her sunscreen and reapplied. I sent her a proud smile. She stuck her tongue out at me.

"No, he can't prove anything. But he can still make trouble. And he's called me twice to check on me."

Ruthie stopped what she was doing. "Oh no! What if Zander's dad, aka the Collector, tracks Dante to you because Bobby says something or because you and Bobby hung out with Dante?"

"Exactly."

"Does anyone else know? Besides us and Bobby?" asked Ruthie. I knew what she meant by it. We had to contain the knowledge that Dante drove me home from school that day.

"Zander does, of course. I don't think Bobby told anyone other than Shrina, at least so far. I'll remind him to keep his gob shut when we get back to school. And to tell Shrina the same thing."

Ruthie nodded. "Well, his eyesight getting better is kind of odd."

I clenched the blanket tighter.

"Do you think Dante changed him when he knocked him out?" asked Ruthie.

"He didn't change me." I met her gaze as she raised an eyebrow. "You know what I mean. Anyway, what if *I* did something to Bobby, that day at lunch when Dante first noticed me? Dante said I fixed him. He could tell I was doing something, through my aura. Man, I wish I could jump back in time and do things differently."

I flopped down and I tried to move back into the body mold I'd burrowed into before, but I couldn't quite find it, and now ridges of sand pushed my legs and arms out in weird angles. I felt like a dead body outlined in chalk.

"You mean when you cured him of his depression?" Ruthie's voice softened. "That was a good thing, Tru. He looked gross before—two seconds from stepping in front of a train, if you ask me."

"Do you think I turned him into an idimmu? Is that even possible?"

"Wow. So you think maybe you gave him superpowers? Not bad, *chica*."

"Well, I don't think I should try healing anyone until I know for sure I'm not going to change them permanently, in a supernatural kind of way at least."

"Hmmm ... I think it's a small price to pay for being happy." Ruthie wore her mocking smile. I ignored the taunting angle of her eyebrow.

"And why is he always worried about me? Does that mean something bad is going to happen?"

"Not necessarily. A lot of bad stuff has already happened to you. Maybe he picked up on that." She made a good point.

My mind wandered to Zena again, to the irony that her mother wished there were supernaturals in Scotts Valley. If they found out about the usemi and idimmu roaming around here it would point back to me. The same thing would happen if Zena found out about Dante and me. I'd be doomed.

"I guess I should talk to Zander about the Taylors," I admitted grudgingly, wondering if Bobby sensed any impending danger involving them.

"Probably," she said with a frown. "Even if you don't tell him about his dad."

"But then again, he hasn't even tried to contact me," I countered. "And I'm still mad at him."

"So, be mad. Doesn't mean you can't talk to him. For your own sake, suck it up."

"Ugh!" I lifted up on my elbows, seeking an errant breeze. "I'm sweating and tired of lying here."

"Time to take the boards out." Ruthie started tucking things away in her bag.

"No wetsuits," I said, opting for vanity over comfort. She agreed. Neither of us wanted bad tan lines.

We grabbed our bodyboards and strapped them to our wrists before jogging out to the water. Some guys down the beach whistled.

"You are so Bay Watch right now," I said, giggling.

"We both are!" she yelled, laughing.

As we reached the water and walked into the waves, Ruthie screamed, destroying our confident demeanor. "It's f-freezing!" She stopped dead in her tracks as the frigid water splashed up her body.

"It's always cold!" I yelled over the crashing water, blocking some of the splashes with my board.

"But it was supposed to be warmer!" she wailed.

"Oh, come on!"

"Fine, let's do this," she conceded. We walked out into

the sea, squealing as the numbing water surged higher and higher over our skin. When we reached a depth where we could tread water, we plunged under, coming up with a scream.

"There!" I pointed to a promising swell rising before us in the distance. We paddled over as quickly as we could, but we were too late to catch it and dove under as it began to crest. Better swells started forming north of us, and we swam fast to catch them.

"Ouch!" yipped Ruthie.

"What happened?" I asked, stopping to tread water.

"Oh, nothing. I must have kicked against a rock." She waved me on. "Keep going. I think a good one is coming in."

We pulled harder against the water, trying to get into position in case this was the one. Suddenly, a dark head popped up ahead of us. I caught my breath.

"Seal." I pointed it out to Ruthie.

"Dangit!" she spat. Hanging out with seals was never a good idea in these waters.

"Yeah," I huffed. "Shark bait." Dad regularly reminded us, "*When seals pop, time to stop.*"

"Hey look!" Ruthie pointed out toward the endless line of water. A big swell started forming.

"This is it!" I yelled. We kicked along the latent wave, letting it raise us up. "Now!"

We positioned our bellies on our boards, turned them toward the beach, and paddled with the wave until suddenly we *were* the wave. I held tightly to my board as it carried me in, screaming with delight.

Just as I was about to hit the shallows I looked over at Ruthie with a big grin, but she wasn't there. Maybe she missed the wave. I fought the shallow surf as it tried to pull me back out to deeper waters and hauled myself up. The strap around my wrist yanked my arm as my bodyboard was sucked away by a receding wave. I jerked it back to me, scouring the water for Ruthie, but she was nowhere to be seen. Looking around the beach, I wondered if she had come in before me. But she wasn't here either. As I dithered around with worry, I heard my name and turned to see two faces jogging toward me with bright smiles.

I raised my hand as they drew near, and then shaded my eyes as I peered out into the waves, panic beginning to bubble up inside me.

"Nice ride in, Tru," smiled Isaac, his eyes glinting with appreciation.

"Where's Ruthie?" asked Phoebe.

"I don't know," I said, breathing fast. "She was right next to me."

"Is that her board out there?" asked Isaac, pointing to a red spot far from shore.

A bodyboard bobbed, like it was being pulled down, its end tipping all the way up.

"Holy crap!" I screamed. "That's her!" It looked like something was pulling her under.

We ran into the water.

"Maybe she's stuck in a riptide!" I cried, fear for my friend choking me.

Isaac and Phoebe swam so fast that they outdistanced me in no time. Then they dove under just as Ruthie's head bobbed up. She sucked in a gulp of air before shrieking in terror, her arms crawling toward us. A dark fin poked out of the choppy water near her. My heart stopped. *That is no riptide,* I thought before she went under again. "Sh-shark!" I gasped.

Frozen in place, I started to sink, only remembering to tread water when I got a mouthful of seawater. Coughing and panicking, I swam toward the shore until I could feel sand beneath me again. I scanned the beach, hoping for a lifeguard. No such luck. Isaac and Phoebe were still out there with whatever was attacking Ruthie. I needed to get help but I vacillated between looking for a lifeguard and swimming out to Ruthie.

I waded into the sea waist deep, my eyes pinned to Ruthie's board, which was just a small spot of red against the choppy water at least twenty-five meters out. A dark fin appeared again, but it looked different. It wasn't as pointy, but more curved on the backside. I squinted my eyes as I pushed through the waves with my legs. A head popped up again, then another. Isaac was towing someone in.

With Isaac's strength, it only took a few minutes for him to make it to shore. I tried to take Ruthie from him, which proved how flustered I was.

"I've got her," he insisted, his voiced clipped. She clung like seaweed to him, her head tucked into his chest. Blood dripped from her arm where the skin hung open.

"Get your phone," ordered Isaac. "Call an ambulance."

"It's way over there on the other side of those rocks." I pointed south. "What about Phoebe?" I bit my lip so hard I tasted blood. If he were worried, wouldn't he leave Ruthie with me and go after her?

"Um." He gave me a blank look before shaking his head. "Oh, she swam south to the next beach to find a lifeguard."

"In the water? With the shark?"

"Don't worry." Isaac reassured me. "It's gone. She'll be all right."

I nodded and focused on my friend clinging with terror to Isaac. "Is Ruthie going to be okay?"

Isaac's lips thinned. "I can't tell until I lay her down and check. Her face is bleeding, too."

I finally noticed the blood dripping down his chest, and sucked in a gasp of air.

"Can you run with her?" I asked. He raised an eyebrow, perhaps offended by my question. I nodded and took off toward our towels, Isaac right behind me. He tried to lay her down, but she grasped at his neck, not letting go, not saying a word.

My lifeguard training kicked in and I scooted closer, placing one hand on the side of her face and tilting it toward me. Her eyes were glossy and almost black. "It's okay, Ruthie. You're safe now." She stared at me without recognition, unblinking. She was in shock. I needed to check her injuries and warm her up fast.

Carefully, I pried her hands from Isaac's neck. She latched onto me as if I were a lifeboat.

"It's okay," I repeated, pulling away so that I could see her better. I gulped, about to go into shock myself. Long, jagged lacerations slashed across the side of her face, the skin splitting open, gaping and weeping multiple shades of red blood. Although they weren't lethal, they would be disfiguring. And that was if no infection set in. If that happened …

Finally, she looked up at me, eyes still dilated. I smoothed out my expression.

"Grab my towel," I ordered Isaac. Grimly he obeyed. As I took it from him, he looked out to sea and his face darkened.

"Do you think she made it to a lifeguard?" I asked, almost too afraid to hear the answer.

"Of course, she did," he insisted, his tone gruff. "She'll be back any minute." But because he kept looking toward the horizon, I didn't believe him.

I wrapped Ruthie in my sun-warmed towel, running my hand up and down her uninjured arm. After inspecting her legs for bites and cuts and finding none, I tucked the extra lengths of cloth around them. As far as I could tell, she'd only sustained injuries to her face, her arm, and her shoulder. Most importantly, all appendages were solidly intact. She'd been lucky in that regard. With trembling fingers, I dabbed at the rough edges of her torn skin, knowing she needed medical help, asap. Thankfully, the cold ocean water and Ruthie's lowered body temperature slowed down some of the blood flow. But she was definitely in shock. To some extent, so was I.

I could barely believe that a shark had attacked Ruthie. We'd been swimming along these shores our entire lives without a glimpse of one. Dolphins were common, not sharks. I paused. That's what the second fin looked like, I realized. The first had been large and triangular, the second smaller and curved in the back. Had a dolphin scared off the shark?

It was so bizarre. The fact that Phoebe wasn't freaking out next to me was almost as strange. Isaac ducked his head, avoiding my questioning look.

"Are you sure Phoebe's okay? Did you see her get out of the water?"

Isaac's eyes leaped to mine. "Maybe I should check," he decided. "What about Ruthie? We need to call 911 in case Phoebe can't find help."

"I will if we have to. She's, uh, not too bad," I lied. I had a better plan than calling for an ambulance. However, I wasn't sure I could do it if Isaac stayed here with us.

"Remember, I've had lifeguard training," I reminded him. Like that would help right now. But I hoped I could bluff until he left. "Go ahead and check on Phoebe."

He looked torn, but nodded, standing up. "Are you sure?"

"Yes. Go."

"I'll be back as fast as I can." Isaac sprinted down the beach.

I turned my attention to Ruthie. Dark eyes blinked at me. "I hope he didn't get her," she whispered between chattering teeth.

"He?" I asked, relieved to see her responding. She was going to be okay.

"Ja-jaws."

I cracked a smile. "You're all right."

She coughed, a hiccup-like explosion that I recognized as a poor attempt at laughter. "I look like Edward Scissorhands, don't I?" Her mouth turned down, trembling.

I hugged her, grateful to hear her talking, no matter how self-deprecating she sounded. She lifted a shaky hand to touch her face.

"Don't!" I blocked her hand. "You'll make it worse."

"Worse?" she croaked. "Why doesn't it hurt?"

"You're still in shock, sweetie, but at least you're talking now. I'm glad you can't feel them yet." Before peeling off the towel to look at her injuries again, I lowered her down to the sand and grabbed our backpacks. I stuffed them under her feet.

I found another scratch down her back and a cut on her foot. None of her injuries would kill her—unless she got an infection—but they were going to be nasty scars. I was worried most about her face.

"You can fix me, Tru, right?" Her eyes were round, imploring me to heal her.

I bit my lip, unsure. What history did I have? With Zander's help I'd healed from a gunshot wound, which was way worse than Ruthie's injuries. But he wasn't here. There was Bobby. I'd cured his depression. Maybe improved his eyesight. But now he was acting strange and paranoid.

"Ruthie. What if I caused Bobby's new weirdness when I fixed him? Maybe he's starting to go insane. What if I do something bad to you?"

"S-superpowers are-are not bad," she stuttered. "B-besides, you can't do anything w-worse than this." She touched the side of her face, despite my warning, letting out a yelp when her hand came away bloody and shaky. Her face was beginning to swell, the cuts oozing more blood. One gash started mere millimeters from her eye, pulling it down slightly. I needed to put pressure on the wounds right away or try to heal her myself.

"Please, Tru!" she whispered, beginning to pant. "I can feel how seriously bad it is, and-and it's starting to hurt."

"I'm freaking serious, Ruthie! What if I turn you into an idimmu and you start to lose your mind? What if you end up in a mental hospital like your uncle?"

Her eyes widened further. The odd people Ruthie saw when her family visited her uncle at the asylum bothered her for weeks afterward. But she clenched her jaw and I could see the possibility of going crazy wasn't going to dissuade her.

"Plus, they may heal fine on their own," I added. "Or, you can have plastic surgery."

"My parents can't afford plastic surgery," cried Ruthie. She sat up and rummaged through her bag, groaning at the strain, which caused more blood to seep from the wounds. Regardless of the obvious pain, she continued to dig away until she pulled out a makeup compact and flipped it open. I tried to stop her, but she pushed me away.

"Shiiiit!" Tears dripped down her face, turning pink as they ran with blood. "Damn shark shit, Tru! I know this makes me super shallow, but I'd rather chance it. Make me crazy, but fix me, please!"

I bit my lip, wondering again if I could. Was it really me who had done it before? Or did I need Zander? Doubt crept in as I considered what I should do. How did I do it? The truth was that I didn't have a method. It just happened. But for Ruthie, I'd try.

"Are you sure?" I whispered, hoping she would say no even though I wanted to help her.

She nodded with a wince.

Please God, let me do this right, I thought.

"Okay, then I need to try before Isaac and Phoebe get here. Lie still, okay?"

I placed a hand over Ruthie's swollen skin, hovering a second before touching it lightly. She squeaked anyway. I ripped my hand away.

"No," she protested, grasping my wrist. "Do it, Tru. I-I can handle it."

Her eyes glinted with determination and I couldn't say no, so I returned my hand, pressing ever so gently. Ruthie swallowed hard, shuddering at the effort not to strain away from me. Tears continued to slip down her face and I had to blink like mad to prevent myself from crying. Placing another hand on her wounded shoulder, I worried that I wouldn't be able to heal every wound because they were too widespread for me to reach all of them. Ruthie must have sensed my thoughts.

"It will work, Tru. It's not like you could touch Bobby's brain and you still fixed it."

I nodded and concentrated, squeezing my eyes shut. I thought about how my hands had healed when Zander held them, the warmth that had radiated across my palms. I'd mistaken that for the delicious hum I felt whenever Zander and I touched. *Aha.* Heat was involved in this process. Although my skin still felt cold from the ocean, the hot sun and sand were beginning to warm me. I imagined the sun shooting bolts of hot energy our way, then me grabbing the warm, golden rays and directing them into Ruthie. *Like plucking dandelions,* I thought, *gathering them together and blowing their tops off to float away like mini parachutes.* Opening my eyes, I saw the sun's rays dropping and scattering all over Ruthie. They migrated to her injuries like magnets to metal. Ruthie moaned, but pressed her lips together, her eyes begging me to keep going despite her apparent pain.

A moment later, I stared in amazement as Ruthie's face glowed, more so on the injured side.

She wrinkled her nose. "Oh my gosh! It itches so bad!"

"Don't touch it," I ordered, startling myself because my voice sounded deep and powerful. It echoed in my ears. "And hold still," I added, just to hear my voice again. Strange. This was different than before. I felt strong and full of energy.

Her eyes bulged as she stared at me. She shook with the effort to hold still and beads of sweat broke out along her lips. She opened her mouth to say something, but a scowl from me shut her up.

I imagined the cuts on her face closing up, the seams smoothing, their lines fading. Then I moved to her shoulder, each tear in her flesh disappearing as the good skin spread over the deep red slashes. I slowly turned her onto her back and watched as the raw, bloody gash closed, fading to pink, then brown. Gradually, it disappeared, along with the tear in her arm and the other more minor injuries.

When everything seemed normal again, I whispered, "Thank you," over and over, talking to each ray of light as it stretched out in a thin line across Ruthie's skin before blinking away altogether. As the last ray of healing light disappeared, so did that euphoric feeling I'd been riding. I swayed before falling over on the sand.

"Tru!"

I heard Ruthie's wail, the concern in her voice, and opened my eyes to see her perfect face peering into mine.

"Are you all right?" she asked. "You passed out!"

"Sorry. I'm fine, really. Just mega tired." I sat up feeling sluggish, but I shook off the fatigue and hugged her. "You look perfect! Better than perfect." I pulled away to smile tiredly at her. "I even think your zit is gone."

She didn't laugh like I wanted her to, but pulled away.

She picked up her compact, pausing before flipping it open to stare at her flawless face, now only marred by dried patches of blood. She soaked one edge of her towel with her water bottle and scrubbed the blood away. As she stared at her healed skin, her face began to crumple and she broke down into sobs. I reached out to hug her.

"I believed you, Tru," she said, a catch in her voice. "I really did. But hearing you say it is so different than seeing it for myself." She stared at me, her face the picture of humility, a rare look for her. "You're like a ... a goddess, Tru!"

I scoffed, embarrassed. "Yeah, right. Me and my adoring fans." I stretched, feeling stronger by the second.

"If you showed people what you could do, you'd have plenty of fans."

My heart raced at the thought. "Sure. They wouldn't be able to get enough of me. Until, oh, I dunno, the government takes me to Area 51 and dissects me. Or, the Collector puts me in a cage and does science experiments on me."

I realized anew that no one could know what I did and grabbed Ruthie's arm. "You can't tell anyone about this, Ruthie, nobody, you understand?" It was imperative that she kept this secret.

"I promise, Tru," said Ruthie, her voice low and grave. "Really. I'd never let anyone experiment on you." It was one of the sincerest looks I'd seen on her face since my mother died.

I smiled, realizing I was overreacting.

Ruthie sighed. "But man, what a waste of talent. Can't even flaunt it."

Even though I trusted Ruthie, I couldn't quite shake

my anxiety. "Speaking of flaunting it," I said. "What are we telling Isaac and Phoebe?"

"Is Phoebe here? Wait, Isaac went to find her, didn't he? Where has she been?" Ruthie was babbling, probably a post-trauma reaction. "Thank goodness Isaac saved me. And that dolphin!"

My eyes widened. "What the heck are you talking about, Ruthie? Isaac *and* Phoebe swam out to save you. I was on my way, but they swim mega fast! I didn't know if I should run for a lifeguard or not.

"But you are a lifeguard," Ruthie reached out to squeeze my hand.

"I'm not a beach lifeguard. I definitely never learned how to handle shark attacks."

She rolled her eyes as if to say I did now.

"Anyway, I wondered if there was a dolphin out there with you guys."

Ruthie hugged herself, nodding. "Isaac and the dolphin saved me. I think Isaac hit the shark on the nose and then the dolphin attacked the shark."

"You're kidding me!" How bizarre was that? It would make a great news story. Too bad we couldn't tell anyone without explaining how Ruthie looked pretty as a peach now. They'd never believe us.

"You were probably too freaked out to notice Phoebe."

Ruthie let out a long sigh. "I guess so." She grabbed her bag and extracted her beach dress, pulling it over her head before wrapping my towel around her again, covering most of her face, too. Then she curled herself into a ball. I could see a different kind of shock setting in—the post-trauma shock that lasted an indeterminate length of time. Like what happened to me when my mom died. But Ruthie was stronger than me. She'd snap out of it fast. I knew she would.

"You don't need to talk about it yet, Ruthie, but we have to decide what to tell the twins before they get here."

"Too late," she said, her eyes looking past me. I swung around just as Phoebe and Isaac skidded to a stop next to us.

Their arrival kicked up a shower of sand. I scrambled up, shaking off the briny particles and drops of water that flew from their hair. "What the heck? Geez, guys!"

"Double Geez-burger with fries!" added Ruthie, her voice muffled behind the towel that she'd quickly pinched shut over her face.

"Sorry!" said Phoebe. "We were so worried. We need to get you to a hospital, Ruthie. I couldn't find a lifeguard."

Ruthie poked her head out, smiling sheepishly and shaking off the towel. "Naw. I'm going to be okay."

Isaac sputtered. "What the hell happened to your face?"

"Seriously? Do I have to respond to that?" Ruthie replied, outraged.

"Yes," demanded Isaac. "When I left, you were all Bloody Margarita!"

I bit my lip as I realized Ruthie's towel was covered in blood. Hopefully they wouldn't notice it against the bright, busy pattern of the pink towel.

Ruthie laughed. "Good one."

Phoebe smiled, but it didn't reach her eyes. "Yeah, I would have definitely gone with Virgin Daiquiri."

Ruthie sputtered "Hey! Virgin and proud of it, you tramp!"

Phoebe smiled for real this time. "There's my girl," she whispered.

Isaac narrowed his eyes. "Seriously, guys," he said, his voice deepening. "What the hell happened?"

Ruthie and I looked at each other guiltily, but we didn't say anything.

Isaac clenched his jaw, and for a second I was afraid he might rip off Ruthie's towel and examine her himself. Phoebe reached up and pressed her hand to his arm. I could see him wrestling with doubt.

Finally, he turned to Phoebe with a burst of irritation and muttered, "I know what I saw." Then he stomped down the beach, heading toward an outcrop of rocks.

"Where's he going?" I asked.

"Don't worry about him," sighed Phoebe. "He was just scared. Boys get mad when they get scared. Actually, we were both scared. Are you sure you're okay, Ruthie?" She paused, peering at her. Softly, she added, "Maybe I can take a look at your shoulder?"

"I'm fine!" insisted Ruthie, pulling the towel tightly to her.

"She's okay," I murmured, not quite meeting her eyes. "I checked."

Phoebe let it go, but her eyes squinted in disbelief. Before she could start asking questions that I couldn't answer truthfully, I started toward Isaac, who had stopped near the shoreline to stare out into the waves. With his arms wrapped around themselves and the tide sweeping in on him, he looked like one of the hunks of rock down by the water. It crashed against his legs, unable to nudge him in or out as it pulled back out to sea. I felt horrible for lying to him, but fortunately he hadn't pressed for answers to the unexplainable phenomenon.

A hand on my arm stopped me from going any further. "I'll check on him," said Phoebe kindly. "Stay with Ruthie."

Ruthie and I silently cleaned up our mess, casting surreptitious looks at the twins. They, in turn, seemed to be arguing. Isaac glared at us enough that I started worrying that he hadn't been fooled after all, that my secret was out. They returned just as we filled our arms with the beach boards and bags.

Isaac stopped in front of us and rested his hands on his hips. "What really happened?"

I looked nervously at Ruthie, who rolled her eyes and said, "Okay, okay. I'll tell you. But you won't believe me."

My throat went dry. Isaac and Phoebe smiled doubtfully.

Ruthie threw up her hands. "All right. You guys know how religious my family is, right?"

They nodded.

"Well, I asked Tru to pray for a miracle with me." She then waved a hand around her face. "And I got a miracle."

Phoebe made a sound somewhere between a laugh and a cough, but shut up when she connected with Ruthie's deadly glare. The corners of Isaac's mouth pulled down in disbelief.

"See," Ruthie said. "I knew you wouldn't believe me. And I don't want you getting all loud-mouthy about it.

This is private stuff."

"Tru." Isaac gave up on Ruthie and stared at me. "What really happened?"

I bit down too hard on my lip and winced. Ruthie wrapped an arm around my shoulders. "It's okay, Tru. A miracle's a miracle. Don't you agree?"

It had been a miracle. And I'm pretty sure I'd invoked God's help with it.

"She's telling the truth," I said.

Isaac gave us an exasperated look.

"We won't tell anyone," said Phoebe. "But I'd love to hear the complete story sometime."

"Yeah," sighed Ruthie. "Sometime. I'm kind of wiped now."

"Well," I said, taking Ruthie's cue to skedaddle. "I guess we've all had enough beach for one day."

"Make that a lifetime!" threw out Ruthie. "The beach sucks. Well, except for dolphins. Wish I could adopt one."

We forced a laugh, not ready to completely let go of the terror we'd felt minutes before. It could have been so much worse.

This healing gift of mine was indeed a miracle, but a mystery, too. I was sure there was a limit to what I could heal, assuming I could control it. I knew Ruthie was thinking about it, too, perhaps thinking that she could be missing an arm or leg, or worse. This experience would haunt her for some time. And the "cure" I'd given her might haunt us both. I bit my lips as I continued packing up our stuff, concerned for my friend. One more favorite place ruined for the unforeseeable future. Werewolves in my backyard, psycho hybrids at my school, and sharks in the water. Nowhere was safe anymore.

9

SPECIAL EFFECTS

RUTHIE ENDED UP SPENDING the rest of the day at my place. Dad worked on his car for hours while we hid away in my room. We pulled up re-runs of *Court of Palms* on my computer and covered our faces in green goo, Ruthie's homemade face mask. It was nasty, but it took her mind off the shark attack. Once in a while I'd watch her eyes dilate as she stared off at nothing. I could almost see her sucking in the fear. Sometimes I put an arm around her and she leaned on me, saying something snarky like, "Good thing you have big shoulders." When I dropped her head and she giggled, I knew she was going to be okay.

I was still trying to derail Ruthie's dark thoughts after dinner. Ruthie was supposed to head home, but she was dragging her feet. We'd gone through most of the emergency junk food, painted our nails, and watched a lot of YouTube videos. I drooped in my desk chair, exhausted from trying to keep up with her.

She, on the other hand, was high on soda and Oreos and currently going through my clothes to find me a hot outfit for school. She said I needed to show Zander what he'd passed up on and rub it in his face. As if. I felt the most intense sense of hopelessness for my future with Zander, rivaling the dark feelings of my mother's death. I knew I should snap out of it for Ruthie's sake, but negative thoughts crept into my mind anyway.

"Please don't pull all that junk out," I pleaded. Irritation threatened my best intentions to be supportive. I frowned at the various piles of clothing and shoes that covered the floor of my closet. "I know where everything is and you're going to ruin my organization."

"Do you mind explaining why you have a computer hidden in your closet?" She extricated a laptop from a pile of t-shirts, mismatched socks, and one of my new lacy bras. Even as I recognized the laptop, I made a mental note to wear that bra to school tomorrow. Sometimes, the way my mind compartmentalized things surprised me.

"That's Dante's computer! What's it doing here?"

"You don't know?" asked Ruthie.

"No."

"Maybe Zander stashed it here."

"He must have. Let me see it." The sight of the laptop cleared my cobwebby brain. "Dante showed me a bunch of stuff on here ..."

"Wait! What if we trigger something and it explodes?

Or, maybe there's a tracker on it?" The way my mouth fell open in astonishment put her on the defensive. "Don't be so shocked. Thing One and Thing Two like watching movies with big explosions."

Thing One and Thing Two were one of many nick-names for her rambunctious younger brothers. "You never know," she said.

I gave her an impressive nod. "Well, I doubt this computer has a self-destruct booby trap. At least I hope not. And a tracker would have led them straight to me already." I powered it on, drumming my fingers as it booted up, hoping it was still charged.

Elbow to elbow, we sat on my bed anxiously watching the screen.

The login window appeared. "Do you know the password?" asked Ruthie.

I wracked my brain. What was that word he'd used? "I saw him type in his website information. But the password was encrypted."

"Could you guess it?"

I tried to remember my conversation with Dante. My stomach clenched as I thought about how scared I'd been. I hadn't believed anyone would ever find me. But Zander did. I shook away those memories and tried to recall Dante's words about his secret website.

"He had this lame-looking website with all sorts of supernatural secrets. I mean it didn't look like much until you got past the Hello Kitty login page. There were tons of pictures and videos of usemi and akharu and their locations."

"The creatures that act like vamps and werewolves?" Ruthie crinkled up her nose in disgust.

"Yeah. He showed me a video of a guy with fangs fighting a wolf. They moved fast! And it was creepy to see the wolf flip around like a ninja."

"Wow! How do you know it was real stuff? Not special effects, I mean."

"The wolf's eyes weren't animal eyes. It sort of looked like the one in my backyard." I shook my head. "I don't know why I think it was real. It just was."

"I believe you." She nodded. "So, can you remember the login stuff?"

"I just saw the login name, not the password."

"Should we try guessing it?"

"It may lock up on me if I get it wrong. I think we need some help with it."

"Like who?"

"Maybe Maverick from the rec center. He's good with computers."

"Oooh. What a contradiction. A jock with a cowboy name who is also a computer geek." Ruthie's dimples beamed. "And he's cute."

I rolled my eyes. "I wonder why Zander put it in my closet," I said. The night that Dante shot me I'd passed out after being healed and awakened in my bedroom with Zander by my side. How long had he sat here waiting for me to wake up?

"Guess you'll have to ask him." Ruthie's know-it-all voice pulled me out of my own thoughts. She was poking the beast in me on purpose, hoping it would force me to talk to Zander.

"I don't wanna think about it." I shut down Dante's computer and returned it to my closet. My bra sprawled at the top of the pile of clothes. I cringed wondering if

Zander had seen my underwear when he'd stashed the laptop. So embarrassing. I snagged the bra and shoved it in a drawer.

Ruthie's phone beeped again. "Phoebe and Isaac are sure worried about me," she sighed as she read a text. "They've got to be super confused by what happened. I mean, I was all ripped up and freaking out, and the next time they see me I'm good as new, no scratches." She paused to run a hand over her perfect cheek. "It's hard to believe it happened at all."

I rubbed my neck, stretching it as tension set in. "I know. I can't believe they fell for your miracle story. And I don't know what to do about them other than to keep lying. I hate that."

"It's okay, Tru. I'll keep your secret. Maybe I should fake some bruises on my shoulder or something." She ran a hand over her shoulder almost reverently.

"You can do that?"

"You doubt my makeup skills?" She lifted one eyebrow, daring me to suggest otherwise.

The earlier tension evaporated and I fist bumped her with a smile, feeling a second wind. "Let's see your magic. You've got to make it look good, though. Plus, we'll need a story for your mom."

Thirty minutes later, I asked, "When did you learn how to do all this?" I could have watched her makeup magic forever. I'd known that she loved this stuff, but I'd had no idea how good she was.

"Huh?" She was putting on the finishing touches—a little powder to blend everything together. "Oh, YouTube. Like the stuff we looked up today. There. All done. What do you think?"

Ruthie pulled her hair out of the quick bun she'd worn as she applied the makeup. Her skin puckered near the hairline, where a jagged, two-inch cut seemed to be healing. A line of black-red blood peeked around the edges of the partially healed wound and faint red lines that looked like scratches ran down the side of her face.

"Well," I smiled. "It looks real. But I think you may have gone overboard. You were miraculously healed, remember? Besides, your mom is going to freak out."

She pursed her lips and stared at her reflection in the mirror. "Dang it!" She muttered. "I totally got carried away. Guess I'll have to wash it all off."

"You don't have time," I said, helping her gather up her things. "You are mega late already."

She shrugged and threw up her hands. "Well, I'll just tell Mom I was practicing my special effects, that's all."

I nodded. "She'll figure out that it's fake no matter what you tell her."

She rolled her eyes. "Yep. She's going to poke and prod." She made a face.

I smiled sadly, thinking my mom would have done the same thing.

"Thanks for hanging out with me after ..." Ruthie bared her teeth and raised her hands like claws.

"No problem." I gave her quick hug. "One more thing, though." There was still something on my mind. Something I was afraid she wouldn't tell me because she wouldn't want to worry me. "How are you feeling? Really. And you know what I mean," I said, squeezing her hand.

Her eyes widened. "Oh! You mean that whole business about giving me superpowers?" She smirked. "Nope.

Nothing. Figures I wouldn't be that lucky."

Relief flooded through me and I pulled her in for another hug. "Tell me if it changes," I insisted.

"Sure, sure," she said, patting my back. Then she left through the front door. I headed to the kitchen for a soda. The bubbles tickled my nose as I stared out the kitchen window into the backyard. Reality was a funny thing. I shook my head thinking about the strange wolves I'd seen out there. Then I pictured the shark fin in the water and Ruthie getting pulled under. Her face had been a wreck. That had been real, too, and I was glad I'd healed her. The truth was, I would have tried it even if Isaac and Phoebe had seen me.

I almost had a heart attack when the doorbell rang. I tiptoed to the peephole. Sapphire blue eyes, wavy auburn hair, perfect mouth. Now *those* were special effects.

I eased open the door to see Zander, one hand stuffed in his jeans. His face looked pale and strained.

"What happened to Ruthie?" he asked.

I sighed, understanding his stress now. "She's fine. Just makeup."

He looked confused.

"Stage makeup," I explained. "She was just practicing for, uh ..." I scrambled for a reason, looking past his shoulder to our neighbor's house across the street. An assortment of pumpkins sat on their front porch and a giant spider web stretched across their window. Halloween was coming up. Of course! "Costume ideas ... for Halloween."

"Oh. Okay." He shook his head, backing up and pivoting to leave. But he stopped midstride, swinging around to me, his eyebrows drawn together.

"Where were you guys today?" he asked.

I scowled, remembering his insulting words from the other day. I started to close the door.

"Wait!" he said, his hand stopping the door. "Okay. You don't have to tell me. But for the record, I was worried." His blue eyes tilted down at the corners.

I folded my arms and stared at the floor, wondering where all this was leading.

He sighed, pulling my eyes to him. "Tru. I'm sorry. About ... what I said at school ... I didn't mean it, I swear."

He'd implied that I had slept with Isaac. It still hurt like an open wound that wouldn't heal.

"I screwed up." He bent down to grab a small bouquet of flowers that I hadn't noticed propped under our doorbell. They were a bit wilted but still pretty. He shoved them toward me and I blinked in surprise. "I was stupid ... jealous." He sighed, his shoulders caving in. "Can you forgive me?" he asked. My eyes traced his face, stopping at the dark circles under his eyes. Something inside me softened.

The thought of Zena crawling all over him made me want to hurt someone. And knowing I was jealous didn't stop it. But I guess I understood why Zander had said such mean things to me. Besides, I knew better than anyone how manipulative Zena could be. She'd wanted me to see them together and I'd played right into her hands. I'd lost my temper and said dumb things, too. I *didn't* know Isaac better than Zander. And despite our short acquaintance, I think I already knew the most important things about Zander—he felt the same tug between us, defied his parents to find me, challenged and lied to his brother for me, and risked his life to save me (more than he realized considering he didn't know his father was the Collector). And even though we'd broken up, he still went out of his way to protect me.

Plus, I didn't think I could live without him.

His jaw clenched as he waited for me to respond. He wasn't faking what I saw in his face right now. I may still have a lot to learn about this boy in front of me, but maybe I knew enough to trust him. And a boy who could apologize—well, that was super cute ... and surprisingly hot. The hollow feeling inside me started to fill up with all kinds of warmth.

I gave him a lopsided smile and accepted the flowers. "There's nothing to be jealous about," I said. "And I'm sorry, too."

His lips tilted up, chasing away some of the shadows in his face. He reached out again, his hands hovering in the air. This time I stepped toward him. He pulled me to his chest, tucking my head under his chin. I relished the signature hum that swept over me and breathed in his scent—redwoods and morning dew. Even though we'd only kissed that one night, something stronger tethered us together. I'd missed him. The anxiety and depression I'd been feeling lately faded away like the darkness at daybreak.

His breath was warm against my ear as he whispered, "May I come in?"

"Yeah." Reluctantly, I pulled away, but I slipped my hand into his before re-entering my house. As we crossed the entry hall, he tugged me to a stop.

"Wait. Is your father home?"

I swiveled around with a frown. "No. He's out with

some friends. Does it matter?"

"Well, would he be upset if I came in while he's gone?"

"Maybe," I said. "I don't usually have boys over." After our last argument, I didn't want him to think this was normal behavior for me.

"That's good." One corner of his mouth crept up.

"Hey!" I smiled, knowing he was teasing.

"Except for now. We need to talk." His mouth flattened into a line.

Even though his voice was as serious as a gravestone, my imagination went wild considering what talking might lead to. "I know." I paused, sucking in my lips. "How great are you at climbing trees?"

"What?" he choked out. "Are you going to smuggle me out your bedroom window?"

"Well, it works in the movies."

"Why don't you just ask your father if I can be here?" he asked.

"Too risky. What if he says no? And we need to talk, right?" I pinched my lips with my teeth, not quite meeting his eyes.

"Fine," he relented with a sigh, but his eyes twinkled, telling me that his reluctance was all pretense. "Lead the way," he commanded and followed me upstairs.

10

THE NASARU

"UM, IGNORE THE MESS," I said, as we reached my room. What was I thinking? Clothes and makeup were scattered across every surface.

He chuckled. "Tru, I've seen your messy bedroom before."

"Yeah, but it was dark then, and now it's way worse." I grabbed a glass from the bathroom and filled it with the flowers Zander gave me before setting it on my dresser next to the doorway.

"I could see with absolute clarity because I was holding you, remember?" A sliver of awe entered his voice. "It was amazing. You were like my own personal flashlight."

When we had been imprisoned together in Dante's cellar, we had discovered that he could piggyback on my ability to see in the dark, as long as he was touching me.

"Oh yeah. Okay, so now you know I'm a slob—"

"And I still like you." He twirled me around. "A lot." His lips were feather soft as he kissed me.

Wow. My heart thumped so fast, I was afraid he'd hear it. I forced myself to step away.

"I, uh, that—" I waved my hand at his face, "should probably be off limits in here."

He raised his hands in capitulation. They hung in the air like a white flag. "I will be the perfect gentleman. I promise."

Was that a dimple I saw? Oh man. It was.

"But," he continued. "You have to stop tempting me."

"What?" I scoffed. "Yeah, right."

This was a course change from the other night when he'd been the one keeping his distance, which at the time, made me doubt he liked me the same way that I liked him—until he explained that he was trying to be respectful and trying to not take advantage of the situation. I liked this playful side of him, but he'd been right before. Whatever this was between us had fire hazard written all over it. It was like I was standing in a dry field holding a lighted match and it kind of scared me. One of us had to be the adult because being alone in my house with him felt dangerous, even reckless. That was Ruthie's Modus Operandi, not mine. The last time Zander was in my bedroom, Dad had been asleep in the next room. Knowing that had kind of been like a raincloud over the flame, keeping my hormones in check.

Not like now. We were completely alone, and part of me wanted to take advantage of that. Was I subconsciously flirting with him? I nodded, agreeing to do my best not to entice him, but I couldn't hold back a small smirk.

"Okay," he said, his voice taking on a mocking business-like tone. "You stay over there." He pointed to the closest side of my bed where my desk sat. "And I'll get reacquainted with this smokin' hot beanbag, if that's all right with you." He plopped down into its squishiness, wiggling until he got comfortable.

I laughed and his fake seriousness disappeared as he joined in.

He finally looked around at the hurricane wreck of my room. "Wow. You and Ruthie sure know how to party. Just tell me there was a pillow fight." He blinked at me hopefully.

"Shut up," I said with a smirk and scooped up one load of clothes from my bed to deposit on my desk. My eyes passed over the photo album on my bookshelf, before jerking back to it. My levity plummeted at the sight of it.

"Zander," I said, pulling down the album. "I've been wanting to show you something."

"Oh, now you want me to sit by you? Yeah, didn't think you would last very long." He leaned back into the beanbag, hands behind his head and wearing a cocky grin.

I rolled my eyes. "Come on. You aren't going to believe it. Look at this picture." I waved him over impatiently.

Zander's normal James Bond grace deserted him as he tried to exit the beanbag. His hands sunk deeply into its sides when he tried to use them as leverage. Beanbags weren't made for speedy or graceful getaways and I snickered at his distinct lack of finesse. When he gave up and rolled out of it, his face was pink and full of laughter. My stomach fluttered. I liked that he could laugh at himself.

I sat on my bed and pointed to the same photo I had shown Ruthie. "This picture was taken a long time ago, before I was born. This is my mom, my dad, my aunt, and my uncle—although he's not my uncle by blood, just a really good family friend."

Zander froze, staring at the picture, all traces of fun vanishing.

"Zander? You recognize her, don't you?"

"Dubois." He sounded surprised and excited.

"Yeah. Isn't that the name of the usemi from my backyard? The one you and Peter were talking about?"

"She ran away. The Nasaru are searching for her." He stared at the picture, but his mind seemed to be far away.

"The Nasaru are like your police?" I asked, urging him back. "Why do they want her?"

"Basically—" he started to say. But he stopped and picked up the album to bring it closer to his face. He bounced his eyes between it and me. "Wait. She's your aunt?" He ran a hand through his hair. "That explains why she was in your backyard. But him?" He said the word *him* with disgust. "The fact that he's in a photo of your family, well, that's ten shades of wrong."

"Who? Uncle Ira? You recognize him?" Now it was my turn to look puzzled. How could he know Uncle Ira and why would he imply that he was a bad person?

"Yes. He's my father's worst enemy, Tru." Zander ran a hand through his hair again, his cheeks coloring. "Uh, my father is kind of a big deal in the Nasaru."

"That's just ridiculous," I blurted. "Uh, the part about my uncle, anyway. Uncle Ira may have his odd moments but he's always been super nice to us."

"I'm not saying that he wasn't nice to you, Tru," he said. "That doesn't mean I'm not right, too." His eyes begged me to believe him.

"Okay. Whatever." I shrugged, not wanting to fight with him again so soon after making up. "Let's forget about Uncle Ira for a minute. She's the one I wanted to talk to you about." I pointed to Aunt Caroline.

Zander opened and closed his mouth like he didn't know where to start. I could see that he didn't want to let the subject of Uncle Ira rest. But after a second he just nodded for me to continue.

"Why do you guys want my aunt? What the heck did she do to you?"

Zander shrugged. "I don't know the specifics. But I do know she's on a reward poster back home. So, whatever she did, it's pretty serious."

I blinked in surprise, imagining her face on a reward poster. But why was I surprised after what she'd done to my mom?

Zander's eyes narrowed. "You know something, don't you?" He swore. "Did Dante say something about it? How did he even know about her?"

I bit my lip. "Maybe the Collector is from the same place you're from?" I suggested, hoping that he might make the leap to his father. If he figured it out himself, I wouldn't have to tell him and risk alienating him. I certainly wouldn't like to hear anything bad about my dad.

"Could be," nodded Zander. "There are a few Nasaru

facilities. He could have worked in one of them and then branched off on his own somewhere ..."

I sighed, not sure if this was the right time to tell him about the true identity of the Collector. "Anyway," I said, moving on even though guilt burned through me like acid. "You're right. Dante mentioned her. Only I didn't know it was my aunt at the time. He called her the *fixer* and said she could heal idimmu when they began to go crazy." I scrunched up my face. "He said I had done the same thing to Bobby." Zander's eyebrows shot up.

"And," I continued, my words coming faster. "I was wondering if she could have the same weakness that other idimmu have." Zander was shaking his head, but I kept talking. "Dante said she was half idimmu and half usemi, so maybe she could be a little crazy herself. He also said she might have overused her healing ability, that it could have caused her to lose her mind even though she could heal herself—I mean, assuming she can do that."

I pressed a hand against the spot where the bullet had entered my stomach. Zander's eyes followed my movement and his eyebrows clenched together. "Maybe I'm like her," I said. "The 'healing other people' part, at least, because I couldn't heal myself without you."

Zander reached for my hands, clasping them in his warm and gentle grip. I swallowed. "I just can't believe what she did," I continued.

"Are you talking about ... your mom's accident?" He had known Dubois killed my mom, but now he knew Dubois was my mom's sister.

"Yeah," I whispered. But there was more to tell him

and it was horrifying. I hesitated.

He squeezed my hands. "What is it, Tru?" he asked, urging me to explain.

I described the dream I'd had about the night my mom died, how I had seen the woman I now recognized as my aunt, in the car that hit her. I thought I would be able to talk about the accident without getting emotional for once, but my voice cracked unexpectedly.

"Sorry. I don't know why it's still so hard." I paused and took a deep breath. "They look so happy in that picture." I nodded toward the photo album resting on the floor. "My parents thought Aunt Caroline was dead. How could she do that to her own sister?" I covered my face with my hands as an unexpected sob welled up in my throat. "Sorry," I croaked.

Zander moved closer until we were hip to hip with his arms around me. He tucked me under his chin.

"Tru, it's okay. You don't need to be embarrassed around me for any reason. Your mother's death must have been unbelievably painful. And now, to learn that it was your aunt who did it ..."

I sniffled, mumbling. "It just sucks, you know?"

"When did you figure this out?" he asked. One of his hands rubbed my shoulder and warmth spread across my back.

"Officially, this week with Ruthie. But I think I've been piecing it together in my head ever since that night at the cabin." The night when I'd been tossed into a dark cellar, broken and hopeless—until Zander showed up.

His arms tightened. That night we'd learned we both had special powers and we'd finally admitted our feelings to each other.

"Do you think my aunt is crazy? She seemed so nice when she was a wolf." A bitter laugh escaped me. "I can't believe I said that, but she is a werewolf, isn't she?"

"Usemi. They aren't werewolves. Werewolves don't exist. Usemi don't forget who they are when they transform, and the moon doesn't control them. Well, at least not much. They change whenever they want to."

I remembered what he'd said about them before, but I still imagined a stereotypical werewolf, like those in werewolf movies. A name didn't change the true nature of a creature.

"And," he continued. "Those *were* usemi in your backyard. I think the female was Dubois, your aunt. I wonder what she wants with you." His hand squeezed my shoulder gently. "I don't know if your aunt is psychotic. And I didn't bother asking why the Nasaru wanted her or what she did before she escaped. I didn't care then. I just needed an excuse to stay here." He kissed the top of my head, and I hugged him.

"I know," I said, my mouth against his chest.

"Even so, Tru, I've never heard of the usemi losing their minds like idimmu do—angry and violent, yes, but not the same insanity of an idimmu. I think I'd have known about that."

He paused, absently rubbing a hand along my shoulder. "I still can't believe she's your aunt." He murmured the words quietly, almost to himself. "But that picture proves she is. She looks almost the same now as she does in your photo album."

I straightened my spine, lifting my head and staring at him in confusion. "How is that possible? My mom was a lot older than her, but she's still got to be way old by now."

"One of the perks of the usemi is longevity and extended youth." He smiled at me, trying to lighten the mood.

"Seriously? How long do they live then?"

"I don't know for sure. Usemi are pretty rare, on the brink of extinction now. But I've heard they can live hundreds of years, so ..."

"No way! If they live that long, why are they almost extinct?"

"Something to do with childbearing. Both usemi and akharu have been dying out because they are having trouble conceiving and even when they do, few carry full-term."

"That's terrible." I could understand their pain to some extent. My parents had been infertile for years before I'd come along. They had called me their little miracle.

"We've been trying to help them," Zander said, interrupting my thoughts. "I mean the Nasaru have."

"I thought the Nasaru was your police force."

"Some of them are. Others are scientists looking for ways to save the usemi and akharu. The Nasaru is basically our government. They have departments for all kinds of things."

That made sense. "And another thing," I said. "Dante said the fixer, aka my aunt, had a child."

"Really?" Zander's eyes widened with wonder. "I didn't know that. That would explain why my father wants to find her so badly. She might be the key to helping others with fertility issues." His eyes glowed with excitement.

Finally, I asked the question I already knew the answer to, wanting to ease him into the same realization that I'd had. "If I can fix people like she can—like what I did for Bobby—will your father be coming after me, too?" Zander's eyes darkened, and he reached for my hands.

"He's not going to take you away from … your home." *From me,* his eyes promised as they stared into mine. "He wouldn't do that." He squeezed my fingers. Was he trying to convince himself?

"Zander, just because he's your father, it doesn't mean he won't, not if it's that important to him."

He pulled away to stand up, running a hand through his hair. I was beginning to recognize this habit.

Was Ruthie right? Was Zander putting me in more danger? The images I remembered of Aunt Caroline when she'd restored Dante's sanity were not those of a happy woman. Her slow, resigned—even robotic—movements had spoken volumes about her state of mind. Hopeless. She had been a prisoner without hope and I wanted nothing to do with those that had hurt her—the Nasaru and Zander's father.

Zander sighed. "He's not the bad guy here, Tru. He's just trying to save entire species from extinction. He has to make a lot of hard choices."

No, Zander, he is the bad guy, I thought. Why was it so hard for me to say it out loud?

"But maybe," Zander said, perking up. "Maybe we can find your aunt before Peter or my father do. We almost caught them last night." Then his face tightened. "They were prowling around your doorstep." He took my hand and squeezed. "You need to be careful."

Bobby had warned me that night. How the heck had he known?

"But if we find her, we can ask her what she knows about the Collector." Zander stepped back with a sigh. "Maybe we can get her to come back with me or Peter, to take the focus off you."

"How will that redirect the Collector?" I asked.

"If we capture her first, then she'll be gone from Scotts Valley—away from you. We can keep him from finding out about you."

"He said they were coming, Zander, as in *on their way right now*. Who knows how long it will take them or if they are already here." Like Zena's family.

"Hey," I changed gears. "Is it possible that the Collector has—" What had Ruthie called them? "Moles living here already."

"Spies? I doubt it. That's what Dante was doing."

"Well, if he does have spies here, then they could be anyone. In fact, I think Zena's family are spies for ..." I broke off, unsure how to unfold my dream about them without connecting the Collector with his father.

"Er, for the Nasaru," I amended hastily.

"Tru," murmured Zander with a look of pity in his eyes. It churned up the anger inside of me. He must have noticed, because his eyebrows shot up in surprise.

"Come on, babe," he coaxed, his hands reaching for mine. "I don't have any feelings for Zena. It's all you."

I blinked several times, stuck on "babe" and the warmth spreading through my chest. It implied so much. Was he telling me he loved me? Then the rest of his words registered and I smiled shyly, squeezing his hands. I looked down for a moment, struggling with the blush rising up my cheeks and the words I needed to tell him.

"It's not because Zena likes you." I bit my lips. How could I explain my dreams to him? "You know how I saw you looking for me the day I was kidnapped?"

He nodded, his eyebrows squishing together.

"I had a dream about the Taylors." I rushed to explain it to him, the words easier now that I'd already described it to Ruthie. But I didn't share the Taylors' comments about being sent away or the child they were looking for. I wasn't sure I should tell him that yet. He listened without interrupting and when I finished, he began to pace back and forth across my carpet.

"Geez, Tru. I believe you saw me that night that Dante kidnapped you—you described my actions too well—but I guess it hasn't sunk in yet. I keep trying to come up with another explanation." He tilted his head and rubbed the back of his neck. "They said Kasadu?"

I nodded, causing him to scowl. "What do you think?" I asked, a sinking feeling in my stomach.

"It sounds pretty fishy. But perhaps they were posted here as regulators, for usemi and akharu. The Nasaru are always looking for unregistered supernaturals. Regulators help count the population and relay information back home." He ran a hand through his chestnut hair. "Anyway, I'll talk to Peter."

Alarms went off in my head.

"Speaking of Peter," I said, my voice trembling. "He's not going to tell your father about me, is he?"

"No!" blurted Zander, his eyes wide. "He promised me that he'd keep it a secret if I helped him find Dubois." He scrunched up his face. "In fact, he didn't want me to talk to anyone at home about her. I'm starting to think he's coloring outside the lines himself."

"What?"

"I'm not positive, but he's been acting strange. Like finding Dubois is a do-or-die thing for him. He's obsessed about her. Anyway, he's being careful about what he's sharing with those back home." Zander shrugged. "I don't care because it works in my favor. It means I get to stay." His eyes heated as he looked at me.

I smiled. "I'm grateful you stayed," I said. "And I'm glad Peter's keeping his gob shut for now." Then my worry resurfaced. "But that's no guarantee he won't tell them about me, eventually."

I pulled up my knees and hugged them. My heart pounded in my ears as my mind screamed for me to just say it. Tell him his father is the Collector! But I still couldn't bring myself to do it. I pressed my cheek against my knees, blinking away the cowardly tears that were beginning to form.

I was so scared I would lose him. And I didn't want to make him choose between his father and me. Besides, Dante had been crazy. He could have been lying or simply living out some psychotic alternate reality. And there was the fact that I had no proof. How could I accuse Zander's father without a shred of evidence? Having just patched things up, my relationship with Zander was fragile. It was based on some shared supernatural experiences and a strange magnetic attraction that bewildered and scared us both. Plus, this wasn't his home. His father could force him to return at any time. My breath caught as panic threatened to overwhelm me.

"Um," I said, scrambling to my feet, desperate to derail my worrisome thoughts. "I'm going to grab a soda.

Want one?"

Zander looked surprised, but nodded. "Sure."

"Be right back," I promised before heading down to the kitchen.

11

SOUL MAGNETS

BUT THE PEP TALK I gave myself as I grabbed some drinks didn't seem to help, and when my chest tightened, I paused and gripped the stair railing, trying to calm down. The odds of our relationship working out weren't good. Maybe I was stupid to keep trying, but I wanted to with every cell in my body. *It's all you,* he'd said. The words triggered an avalanche of emotions and I almost ran up the stairs.

Hurrying into my room, my eyes zoomed in on Zander as he ran a hand over the books on my shelf. I sat at the edge of my bed, dropping the sodas to my side without looking away from him. He wheeled around and caught my fiery glance. The air vibrated with energy as we stared at each other and my hands clenched my comforter, barely restraining myself from leaping at him. His eyes sparked and narrowed, watching and waiting for me to respond to this sudden kinetic attraction. I wanted to trace every curve of his face, run my hands through his hair, and feel the energy our colliding skin created. More than that, I wanted to protect him, even from the hurt that his father could cause. My heart raced and some rational side of my brain scrambled for a reason not to hand over my heart on a platter.

It was a dangerous game, this keeping him close but at arm's length. It reminded of a quote, 'Keep your friends close, but your enemies closer.' If Zander was on his father's side, then he was, technically, my enemy, right? Was it that black and white? I had to think about that before I let myself completely fall for Zander. I held onto that thought as Zander stepped toward me, allowing it to shield me from his devouring, sapphire gaze.

I scrambled for something else to talk about, dropping my gaze and pushing away from the energy pulling me toward him, moving my body backward along the bed and wrapping my arms around my knees. I felt like a stretched rubber band, fighting against its very nature.

Words flew out of my mouth in one long string. "Uh, do you know how Aunt Caroline became usemi? I mean, obviously, she was bitten, but didn't you say usemi have children? That it's *not* some kind of virus?" I sucked in a gulp of air.

Zander froze mid-stride, disappointment and confusion seeping into his face as he came out of his trance. He gave his head a shake and then nodded.

"Right," he said, his voice sounding hoarse. He cleared his throat. "There is no usemi virus, which makes your aunt's story more incredible." He moved over to look out my window, running a hand over his face. "You see, usemi bear children, just like humans, only not as often. It's like comparing rabbits and humans—rabbits having a lot more offspring since they can have multiple pregnancies every year. Normally usemi can only get pregnant every ten years or so, some even longer. But they almost always have twins. Even so, they are heading toward extinction because something's wrong with their fertility cycles. Like I said before, conception is becoming difficult and viable births even more so."

Despite the fascinating information, I kept quiet. Fertility cycles were the last things I wanted to discuss with Zander.

Zander leaned against the window frame, his arms folded. "Your aunt may be the first sign of hope in a long time," he continued. "As far as everyone believes—believed," he corrected, "usemi only mate with usemi."

"But aren't idimmu children of—"

"I didn't say they couldn't 'do it' with other species."

Fascination helped me to ignore the fact that we were discussing sex. "But you said they only mate with their own species."

"Mating isn't the same as having sex. It's different—permanent. With the dwindling numbers, true usemi mates are rare. For a usemi to be mated to a human, well, it's unheard of. And in your aunt's case, we'd have to assume that her mate changed her into a usemi, which is ..." His voice faded in awe.

"Maybe it's an evolution thing, you know, natural selection and diversification. Maybe it's the opposite of diversification. Maybe the usemi species is combining with humans."

Zander's jaw dropped. I rolled my eyes and said, "You

know, that guy named Darwin and all his theories?"

"I know who and what you're talking about. I'm just surprised … I mean you really are as smart as they say, aren't you?" Zander chuckled.

"You know that's offensive, don't you?"

"Sorry. I didn't mean it how it sounded." He grinned. "I just think it's kind of—how would Ruthie say it? Kinda hot. Brains and beauty."

"Nice save." My face warmed all the way to my ears. "Anyway, usemi could be changing to survive, right?"

"It's possible and it would explain why my father is obsessed with your aunt. I bet he wants to locate her mate, too."

"So, what's up with this mate business, anyway? How's it different than a human couple? And why do you assume my aunt mated with someone?"

"Usemi mates are bonded by …" Zander's previous amusement dissolved and he paused to clear his throat. "It's called the *aramusatu*." His eyes shot my way before dropping to the floor. "I, uh, heard Dubois had a true mate. That kind of thing makes news, you see. I figured her mate was in Eden … that's the name of my home. But I suppose she'd never have left if he was."

When he said Eden, I imagined waterfalls and lush forests, lions playing with lambs and a man and woman walking around wearing leaves.

Before I could ask about his home, he continued. "But I didn't know she used to be human. I mean, it's amazing." Zander looked like he was about to drift away on that thought.

"Zander, how could her mate change her?"

He shook off his thoughts. "As far as I know, when

usemi come across their true mate, they are compelled to mark each other with a bite, completing the bond. That's what I've heard happens between two mated usemi. It's probably what sparked the human myth that a werewolf bite will turn you into one."

"But Caroline wasn't usemi," I asserted.

He shrugged. "Yeah. So, my guess is that she didn't bite him. She probably had no idea what was going on."

"But she still changed?" I asked with confusion.

"I suppose the aramusatu bond could have initiated her transformation. The bond is supposed to create a perfect stasis, a perfect balance between two beings, a flawless harmony. So maybe that's what happened."

"Aramusatu." I said it slowly, the word feeling heavy on my tongue. "Where have I heard that before?"

Zander peeked out the window before opening it and removing the screen. He set it down against the wall beneath the window.

"Are you leaving?" I asked, as he continued to fidget with the window.

"Just making sure I can get out of here fast." He cleared his throat. "In case your father comes home." When he turned and moved away from his escape route, his face was closed and shuttered.

"Zander, what's wrong?" He seemed uneasy about something and I ran through the other conversations from the night Dante kidnapped me, wondering what I'd missed.

I jumped up from the bed. "Wait! *Shield of aramusatu*! I have heard it before. In my dream when you were talking to your friend. What was his name? Conrad?"

Zander shoved his hands in his pockets with a sigh. "When I said we needed to talk ... well, there's something you have a right to know."

My eyes widened in surprise and anticipation. He cleared his throat and opened his mouth, but nothing came out. He smashed his eyebrows together and began again. "All of this stuff about your aunt is important, but I need to tell you more about me because it ... affects you, too."

"Okay." The air shifted, feeling heavier. I settled myself on the bed against the headboard, hugging one of my decorative pillows like a lifeline and staring at him with rapt attention. I wanted to learn everything I could about the mysterious Zander Hughes, whose face was flushing an attractive pink before my eyes. I tried to chill out a little, relaxing my strangling hold on the innocent pillow.

He cleared his voice again. "I never explained why I came here in the first place." His brow knitted.

"I thought it was because you were looking for my aunt." I darted a look down at the bed pillow, plucking at a stray string. He'd already told me that I was the one drawing him to this town, but doubt still wove in and out of my feelings for him, and my insecurity begged for him to say it again.

"No, I didn't come here for Dubois. Yeah, my brother and I are still here because of her, but in the beginning I was just using her as an excuse. I never thought we'd actually find her." He leaned back against the wall. "The truth is I ran away from home."

"What?"

"I meant what I said that night. In the cellar," he

said. "You are the reason I came here in the first place. I ran away from home to find you."

"But why? You didn't even know about me. Did you?"

"No. Yes. Maybe." He ran a hand over his face. "It's complicated. You see, I've wanted to come to this area for years. I used to beg my father to take us to Santa Cruz. It was a strange obsession, I admit. But no matter how many camp forms and vacation brochures I showed him, my father always said no."

Zander fiddled with the edge of his shirt. Several expressions flitted across his face—hurt, bitterness, and sadness.

"My father became angry anytime I mentioned anything remotely related to this place. He started punishing me for even bringing up the subject. Needless to say, I stopped talking about it. Then last year, about the same time that your mother died, the urgency to come here became so intense I couldn't stand it. It was more than a 'need,' it was like an involuntary reaction, like something had control of me. I even started dreaming about the ocean, about the redwoods, about this sad girl I wanted to help but could never reach. I woke up every morning completely stressed out. I thought I was going crazy."

I couldn't believe what I was hearing.

"I started thinking that maybe my father was right," he said, "and I should talk to a counselor about my obsession. But something told me I needed to visit this place before I did. And now I'm glad I did." His sudden unguarded expression made me catch my breath. "Tru," he said tenderly. "The girl in my dreams was you. I didn't know for sure until the day Dante kidnapped you." He cocked a lopsided smile and my chest fluttered. "But I suspected it the moment I met you."

He ran a hand through his hair, making it stick up adorably. I felt the corners of my mouth pull up.

"No," he groaned, shaking his head. "Don't get all cute on me. I want to finish what I came here to say— it's been weighing on my mind for days."

I stifled a laugh. I didn't know why I found this so funny. I knew what it was like to think you were going *loco*. But I couldn't help myself. It felt powerful and wonderful to know that I could have this effect on someone. I wanted to hug him, but I could see that he had more to say.

"Ugh!" He swiveled and leaned his forehead against the wall, his hands in his pockets and his shoulders curved in. "I don't think you realize how much trouble I'm in. I joined the military to get my father off my case, yeah, but more to learn how to escape Eden. And when I return home, I'm going to have to deal with the consequences of running away. They will want me to explain it all; on the other hand, I can't tell anyone what really happened because I can't put you in any danger. I'm not sure what I'm going to do."

I swallowed as my earlier doubts regarding his loyalty vanished. But I didn't have a solution, nor did I know how he and I were going to get out of the mess we were in. My best strategy at the moment was to avoid the Collector/Zander's father until a better solution presented itself. Hiding in plain sight was not the best idea, but it was all I had. And until I couldn't hide anymore, I would learn as much as possible, hoping that between now and then I'd find a better resolution.

In the meantime, I still craved details about Zander's life. "Eden?" I asked.

He rotated my way with a timid look. "That's the name of the place I come from, one of the cities of the Nasaru. It's not like it sounds, though. Eden is underground, literally. It's huge, but it's secret. Humans don't even know it exists. Non-humans may know about it, but they don't know how to find it or get into it, unless they are working for the Nasaru. In fact, most non-humans stay as far away as possible because they don't like being told what to do, which the Nasaru does to them a lot. Eden's not our only city, though. There are others. They are all run by the Nasaru and my father manages that organization."

An underground city sounded horrible. I couldn't imagine not seeing the sun, the moon, or the stars. Or feeling a breeze. And to think they had multiple cities. Zander's dad must be very powerful to lead that many people. "Is he your king or president?"

"Something like that. My father is the leader, the *Kasadu*, like his father before him."

I sucked in a breath. "The Taylors!"

He smiled grimly. "Yes. That's why I wondered if they could be regulators."

"So Kasadu is a title?"

"Yeah, like 'president.' As in Kasadu Hughes, but everyone just says Kasadu. He governs all the non-humans."

"And he knows you're here?" My stomach started churning.

"Unfortunately, yes. Peter found me too easily and now he's keeping an eye on me for Father." Zander rolled his eyes. "Basically, *babysitting* me until I get this place out of my blood, or so he says. Um, he did tell Father that he saw Dubois." Guilt had seeped into his face. "But he didn't tell him about you, I promise," he hurried to add.

I couldn't blame Zander for bringing the Collector into my life. That was Dante's fault. And without Zander, the Collector would already have me locked up somewhere.

I smiled, hoping he realized I wasn't upset with him. "So you trust Peter?" I asked.

"In some things."

"Are you guys close?" I asked.

He shrugged. "We used to get along fine. But … he's been different lately. Like I said before, Peter is obsessed with capturing Dubois. I think he wants to accomplish something huge, to impress Father. It made me wonder if Peter needs something from him. I tried to talk to him about it, but he wouldn't tell me anything."

He gave me another sorrowful look. "If I'd known Dubois was your aunt—"

"She's a killer," I said. My voice was quiet but the emotion behind my words made my whole body tremble. Lowering the volume of my voice didn't make them sound less harsh. I thought about her soft fur, her human glances, how she licked my arm, how it healed. I tried to shake off the memory because it weakened my resolve to hate her.

"We don't know her side of the story," Zander cautioned. "She's your aunt, Tru."

He said it as if being my aunt changed things. As if it gave him a reason to doubt her culpability in my

mother's death. But being family didn't make you innocent. His father was the freaking Collector. My aunt had
killed my mom, in cold blood. She'd looked so angry in
my dream. Dante said she wasn't sane. I thought about
Dante and his slow descent into madness. *Had* my aunt
acted in madness?

"Well, the bottom line is that I wouldn't blame you if
you captured my aunt. If she's a danger to others then
she needs to be stopped, crazy or not."

"Thanks."

"However," I added. "I don't think it's right to force
her to heal people or to do it at the cost of her own
health. And I don't think she should be anyone's chim-
panzee in a science experiment just because she's involved with some weird true mate thing."

Zander choked out a laugh. "You're right," he agreed.
"Just so you know," he said, his eyebrows drawing together. "I never intended to hurt her." He leaned against
the wall, closing his eyes. "Tru, I don't want to keep any
secrets from you."

I looked down, hoping the guilt wasn't written on my
face. I was so keeping secrets from Zander.

"And for some reason," he said, almost too low for me
to hear, "I have this involuntary response to—I mean I
know we haven't known each other for long, but it's like
I have no control over it."

"What do you mean?"

He opened his eyes and sighed. "I just need to make
sure you're okay. Like all the time."

My jaw dropped at the rawness in his voice, the intensity of his deep blue eyes. His words seemed to slow
down time, lengthening the moment.

"Anyway," he finally said, looking anywhere but at me and continuing like we were discussing our favorite tv shows or something as lame.

I decided to follow his lead and pretend he hadn't shared something personal, something pivotal, something that I felt was the absolute truth, and that made my heart stutter hearing it. He deserved a better response, but I moved on, scaredy-cat that I was, and pocketed this new information to pull out later and analyze in private.

"Everything's messed up now. Conrad said—"

"The friend who helped to find me that night?" I interrupted, my voice a little breathy. "He's from Eden, too?"

"Yes. He's been looking through our archives trying to figure out why you and I react to each other the way we do." He cleared his throat again. "Why I was drawn here, why I was able to find you, why we are connected."

Here was something to chew on. How had Zander found me? How had he healed me? And why did we feel that hum along our skin when we touched?

"Really?" I said, studying my fingernails, my voice teetering between slightly interested and dying of suspense. "What did he find out?"

"Well, it goes way back. It's a sethian myth or legend—"

"Sethians are your people, right?"

"Yes," he nodded. "Anyway, the legend Conrad found could explain what's happening here, if it's true."

Secret myths and legends again. Was he suggesting that my human aunt changing into a wolf—no, a usemi— could be explained by a legend? Or was it the part about her being someone's true mate? It was bad enough that human myths were turning out to be true. Now the monsters' myths were true?

But I got the impression he was also referring to us. My head spun and I pressed my fingers into my forehead. Our strange and wonderful connection had something to do with an ancient history. That made it sound pretty epic. My heart flipped. I gave myself a mental shake, remembering that I wanted to appear detached and composed.

Zander slid down the wall to settle on the floor. I dropped down to lay flat across the bed, propping up my chin with my hands. Oh, yeah. I could do nonchalant.

"You mean like King Arthur? That kind of legend?" I asked.

"Yeah, only this legend predates that one by a long shot."

It felt like he was dragging this out. "Okay. Spill it already," I urged, impatient to understand.

"Well, reading ancient stuff is kind of a hobby of Conrad's, you see." He chuckled self-consciously. "I mean, I wasn't sure I believed him because sometimes he gets so preoccupied about an old scroll no one will see him for days." He sighed. "Anyway, some of what he's said feels too close to the truth to ignore."

He fell silent, redirecting his attention to the dust bunnies collecting along the baseboards.

"Um. You really haven't told me much yet." I snapped my fingers to get his attention. Realizing that I had dropped my act of indifference, I told myself to chill and tried again.

Zander's mouth pulled up on one side as if he saw

through my charade, but the next second he was clenching his fists. "All right. But it's going to sound crazy and I'm just saying what Conrad thinks. I'm not saying I believe him."

"Go on."

"Well, you know the rare aramusatu bond of the usemi that probably made it possible for your aunt to become usemi in the first place?

"The one that makes them feel drawn to each other?"

"Yeah. It has other, uh, side effects. It's said that the bond connects their souls, that they are drawn to one another before they meet and linked forever afterward."

I froze.

"They are connected psychically and emotionally," he continued. "And they can find each other by sense alone, even over long distances. Essentially, they are like magnets—soul magnets, I guess you could say."

I blinked, my mind gradually processing each word he uttered, my heart feeling the truth in them.

Zander continued, still not meeting my eyes. "The aramusatu bond draws souls together, starting with the male. He's driven to find the other half of his aramusatu, guided by a, for lack of a better word, mystical force. In stories, I've heard it referred to as," his voice broke, "love wandering."

I couldn't help it. I started cracking up with laughter. "Love wandering? Seriously?" It was too corny.

Zander glared at me. "Yeah, sounds stupid in translation, I'm sure. Again, this is all from Conrad. Basically, the male is drawn to the female over any distance and when they see each other, something happens, something unusual, something that connects them and identifies them as each other's mate."

I felt the blood drain from my face. This did sound familiar. When I remained silent, Zander cleared his throat.

"Supposedly," he continued. "The more the two are near each other, the more their connection grows. According to the legend, they become more powerful together, but I'm not sure what that means because we don't have any more details."

I could give him some details. From Zander's awkward glances, he thought the same. No wonder he was so fidgety.

"Um, that sounds cool and cozy for the *usemi*." The only thought keeping me from a full freak-out was the knowledge that I was clearly not usemi. So why was I still worried?

"I guess," he said, not meeting my eyes. "But there's a down side, as well. The aramusatu bond is irresistible to the point of extreme pain and possibly death, *if* ignored."

"What if they decided they didn't like each other anymore?" I asked, passing over the bit about death.

A possessive and dark look crossed Zander's face, but he quickly smoothed it away. "Huh. Good question. With so few usemi, it's rare to find any bonded mates."

"Sounds like it should be called aramu-sucks!" That made Zander smile.

The sound of the garage door opening had us scrambling to our feet.

"Your father's back," Zander said.

"Yes, Sherlock. That he is." I bit my lip, wondering how to smuggle him out of my room. "I thought we'd have more time before he got here."

"What are you doing tomorrow night?" he asked, moving closer.

"Back to School Night with my dad," I said with a cringe.

He swore. "I forgot." He opened and closed his mouth as if he wanted to say more. "Okay," he breathed out. "Guess I'll see you at school tomorrow."

"I'll save you a place at lunch." I tried not to grin. He nodded, looking down at my lips.

"One for the road," he whispered, grasping my face with both hands and pressing his lips against mine. The feather soft strokes melted my mind and I pushed forward for more. Zander groaned, angling his mouth to comply.

Moments later when my dad popped his head in, I was still standing in the middle of the room staring at my open window.

"What are you doing, honey?"

I didn't want to turn away from the last place I'd seen Zander. It was like I was the needle on a compass and he was my true north. I gritted my teeth as I yanked my eyes away.

12

ROCKY MOUNTAIN OYSTERS

WHEN RUTHIE PICKED ME up for school the next morning, dark circles underlined her eyes, despite the layers of makeup she wore. I scooted over to her and leaned my shoulder against her. "Do you want to talk about it?" Yesterday's shark experience must have kept her up all night.

"I don't know," she sighed. "I feel a lot better today. Not scared, just tired." I settled into my seat as she stretched her arms above her head and yawned like a cat. "But I dreamed about that stupid shark." She closed her eyes and rubbed her temples. "And then I dreamed about the dolphin—only there was a mermaid riding the dolphin, and they fought the shark. Cool, I guess. Probably too much Disney as a kid."

I laughed. She must be okay if she was making fun of herself. "I know exactly how you feel, girl," I said.

She smiled at me. "I bet you do. All those dreams you have must really suck."

"You have no idea," I said, nodding.

"Well, then let's talk about something else." She pulled away from my house.

I'd been reliving last night's kiss over and over since I awoke this morning. Happiness tugged up the corners of my lips. I wanted to tell someone and it was the perfect distraction for Ruthie.

"Well," I began. As I told her about Zander's visit, she blinked owlishly at me with surprise and cautious optimism. Then the car started to veer toward the sidewalk.

"The road!" I yelled, reaching for the steering wheel, but she swatted me away and swerved back into a straight line.

"I'm not sure how this thing with you two will end up," she said, ominously. "But I can't argue with the glow around you today." She glanced at me. "Okay, now your secret little smile is getting creepy. Remember, girl. You still have to talk to Isaac today."

A disappointing dose of reality deflated my heart-shaped thoughts. "Thanks for the reminder," I grumbled. But she was right. I had to break up with Isaac, again.

The twins greeted us as we pulled into a parking space. They walked in a circle around Ruthie, peering at her as if they couldn't believe she was standing in front of them. Ruthie beamed and said something about being born again.

Isaac let out a disbelieving grunt, but Phoebe hugged her. "Whatever. I'm just glad you're okay."

Finally, Isaac shrugged, replacing his doubting

expression with his normal flirty one. Whatever suspicions Isaac had about our *miracle* seemed to evaporate as he turned his gaze on me, a flash of possessiveness entering his eyes. I swallowed. Something had to be done about that before lunch and now was just as good a time as any. I squared my shoulders.

"Ruthie, I need to talk to Isaac. I'll see you in class, okay?"

Ruthie wiggled her eyebrows and winked. "Okey, dokey, pokey." She grabbed Phoebe's arm and dragged her away, protesting.

I set my backpack on the pavement and leaned against Ruthie's car. Isaac ambled over to me with a smug smile.

I put one hand up. "Before you come any closer, Romeo, let's get some things straight between us."

He leaned a hip against the car, unperturbed by my tone.

"Sure, Tru."

"Okay. I just want to be very clear this time." I paused. "You know we're not together anymore, right?"

He didn't say anything. I sighed.

"Isaac. We aren't a *thing*. You and me," I punctuated the words by pointing from him to me. "We. Are. Not. Together."

Isaac frowned.

"And," I continued. "We aren't going to Homecoming with each other." I squeezed my eyes shut and cringed. *Geez*, I sounded so rude. I let out the air I was holding and peeked up at Isaac, who scowled now, a red hue darkening his cheeks. I softened my voice. "Look, I'm not trying to be mean about this. I just want to be fair and not lead you on. I don't feel *that* way about you."

"But you did before, right?" His big brown eyes glistened with vulnerability. His puppy dog look.

"Well, I guess so. I mean, look at you! Who wouldn't?"

Isaac smiled and leaned toward me.

"But," I clarified, stopping his forward motion. "It doesn't feel right anymore. Now I just want to be friends. I'm *hoping* we can be friends."

Isaac rotated to angle his chest over the roof of the car, his shoulders drooping. "For *you* it doesn't feel right," he whispered, staring across the parking lot. I finally realized this wasn't just a crush to him.

"Isaac," I agonized, understanding how he might be feeling. Although I'd made up with Zander, the hurt from our breakup was all too easy to recall. "Come on. I hate this. Can't we be friends? Just friends?"

He tilted his head toward me, an almost believable smile playing along his lips. "Sure, Tru. I always wanted to be your friend."

"Good." I smiled tentatively. "Friends it is."

"So what's wrong with going to Homecoming with a friend? People do that all the time." He flipped around, leaning against the car again and slipping his hands into his pockets.

I squeezed my eyes shut, wanting to scream with frustration but praying for patience because I didn't want to hurt him any more than I already had. "Isaac, I don't want there to be any confusion …"

"Are you going with someone else?" he asked, kicking a pebble and watching it skip across the asphalt.

"No," I admitted. "I didn't cancel with you so I could

go with someone else. I wouldn't do that." My stomach clenched a little. I'd like to think I'd never do that, but with Zander I wasn't sure what I was capable of doing. Although I hoped Zander would ask me to Homecoming, for now, it was the truth. I wasn't going with anyone.

Isaac grunted.

"So, we're cool?" I asked.

"Yeah, we're cool, dork face." He snatched up our backpacks and headed out of the parking lot.

"Hey!" I jogged to catch up. "That's not very nice." I wrinkled my nose as I mock-scolded.

"*Friends* get to call each other lame nicknames."

I rolled my eyes. "Whatever, Sasquatch."

He grinned. "That's more like it, short fry."

I scoffed. "Short fry? Sounds like a good one for Ruthie."

He grinned. This felt better. I realized we should have kept it in the friend zone from the beginning. I felt like my relationships were finally settling in as they were meant to.

THE MORNING PASSED QUICKLY and soon it was lunch break. As I reached the path leading to the quad, someone grabbed my arm and pulled me around the corner of the building. I twisted away and swung my backpack at my attacker. Zander blocked me.

"What the heck?" I gasped.

"Sorry," he said, backing away with his hands up. "I just wanted to talk to you alone before you went to lunch."

"All you had to do was ask." I smiled, hoping he

wanted to sneak a kiss between classes.

"I didn't mean to scare you. I just wanted to ask about Isaac." He gave me a guarded look. "Did you work things out with him yet?" He cupped my shoulders, his touch gentle, as he pulled me toward him.

"Why are we hiding?" I whispered, bringing my hands up to his chest. We were tucked between the science building and a hedge that separated the campus from the Redwood forest, and it made me feel sneaky. I giggled.

"Tru, what's going on with you and Isaac? I saw the two of you laughing together this morning."

Had he been spying on me?

"I don't mean to sound jealous," he clarified. "I just need to know that he's clear about us. I don't share," he added, one side of his mouth pulling up.

For the first time I took a second to see this morning from Zander's point of view. Laughing and joking with Isaac probably didn't seem like post-breakup behavior, especially given Isaac's temperament. I sighed, wanting him to trust me.

I inched closer, so close I could see the dark blue flecks in his brilliant eyes that sometimes seemed to glow. "You don't have to worry, Zander. He gets it now. Really. And we're still friends, which is super good. It feels right." I dropped my gaze to my hands, noticing that I'd been unconsciously rubbing my thumbs across the taut muscles of his chest. My teeth bit into my lower lip, and I focused on that pressure as I tried to stop myself from exploring any further.

Zander's palms covered my hands and he pressed his back against the building, pulling me with him. I locked my arms straight, wedging us apart enough so that I could keep looking at his face, loving the way his eyes caressed me.

He smiled boldly, his dimples winking at me. "He knows about us then. That's good."

"Uh ..." I blew out a puff of air. "I didn't say that."

Zander stilled. "Why not?" His voice darkened with mistrust again.

I stepped away with sudden uncertainty, pulling my hands out of his. Lifting one shoulder, I mumbled, "Well, to be honest, I didn't know what to say about us. What exactly are we officially, Zander?"

He squinted at me like he couldn't believe I'd asked him. But I had to know before I let him get any closer.

"Am I your girlfriend?" I said hesitantly, regretting the needy sound of my words.

With blazing blue eyes, he stood to his full height, now towering over me. "Geez, Tru. You're not my girl-friend, you're—"

"There you are!" Bobby skidded around the building and rushed up to me. He came to an abrupt stop when he noticed Zander. "What's going on?" He looked from my red face to the electricity sizzling in Zander's eyes. I could see that he realized he'd interrupted a very private conversation, but instead of leaving, he straightened his shoulders and demanded, "Is everything okay, Tru?"

I squeezed my arms around my waist, as my stomach churned. *No, I was definitely not okay,* I thought. Zander said I wasn't his girlfriend. Bobby couldn't have picked a worse time to interrupt.

"Oh my gosh, I'm fine!" I barked. "Stop worrying about me every second of the stinking day! Geez, don't you have anything better to do?" Although I didn't intend to sound waspish, my frustration with Zander misdirected and landed on Bobby, causing his face to burst into bright red splotches.

Zander edged in front of me, apparently ready to finish off whatever remained of Bobby's self-esteem. "Why would you be worried about Tru?" he interrogated with a scowl. I pushed Zander aside, regretting my harsh words.

"It's nothing," I said, hoping to prevent Zander from accidentally cluing Bobby into any of the strange events currently consuming our lives. "I'll explain later," I whispered to Zander. He nodded, but remained by my side, his body stiff and alert.

Bobby fidgeted, pale and rattled. My heart sunk as I noticed his appearance for the first time. His eyes were bloodshot and his hair stuck up all over the place, as if he hadn't bothered to comb it today. And I would have bet money that his clothes had been pulled from the laundry hamper.

"I don't know why I keep doing this, Tru. I swear. I must be losing my mind." He pressed a hand against his temple.

Was Bobby's recent behavior a side effect of what I'd done? He'd been depressed before. But, while Dante said that I'd fixed him, I wondered if I'd made him more broken instead. Bobby looked up from the ground, his eyes connecting with mine, his face whitening. I reached out a hand to him wanting to comfort him, but he muttered something incoherent and walked off.

I spun around to Zander, wanting to throw myself into his arms and cry, but his comment about me not being his girlfriend hung there like a No Trespassing sign.

He sighed and lifted his arms to pull me close, but I moved away, unable to act as if he hadn't hurt me again.

"I didn't mean you aren't my girlfriend, Tru. I was about to say you are more than a girlfriend before he butted in."

Chiding myself for jumping to the wrong conclusion, I smiled gratefully. But then I choked out a cry and threw myself into his open arms.

"It's all my fault," I sobbed.

LATER, ON MY WAY to my last class for the day, my heart fluttered in anticipation of seeing Zander again. I thought about how patiently he had listened as I confessed that it was my fault Bobby was depressed again. Of course, he'd insisted that it wasn't possible that I'd broken Bobby. I didn't believe him, but I felt better anyway. I looked across the path and the smile I'd been fighting fell away when I noticed Bobby stumbling around like a rudderless boat. I called out.

"Bobby!" He stopped, but frowned when he saw who it was. I rushed up to him before he could take off. "Bobby, I'm sorry I was a jerk. You caught me in a bad moment. I'm really, really sorry."

He continued to scowl at me. I gulped, trying to swallow the sour taste in my mouth.

"You know what?" muttered Bobby. "I thought my troubles started with Dante, but maybe they started with you. Forget I ever said anything. In fact, just stay the hell away from me." He tightened his grip on his backpack and took off, leaving me frozen to the pavement, blinking away tears.

When I made it to English class, I was a little out of breath from running. Zander was saving me a seat and waved me over. Zena sat a couple rows away staring daggers at me, but for once I didn't care. He leaned toward me as I slid into my seat, concern rounding out the corners of his dark blue eyes.

"What happened?"

I smiled weakly, running my hands over my cheeks to brush off any leftover tears.

"I tried to talk to Bobby," I whispered. "And he told me to leave him alone."

Zander lifted an eyebrow. "Really? I could talk to him."

I slumped over my backpack. "Don't bother," I said. "He's so mad at me he probably won't listen. I think he figured out that I did something to him."

Before Zander could respond, the class chatter faded, tipping us off to the woman walking in.

"Good afternoon everyone," she said as we all stared at her curiously. Her smooth ebony skin gave off a youthful appearance, until she smiled, and then wrinkles crowded the sides of her face, explaining some of the gray peeking through the roots of her hair. She looked familiar, like I'd seen her around school somewhere. Her corporate dress style and the confident way she carried herself made me think school administration, which then made me think she was here to tell us bad news. My heart stuttered.

"Good afternoon. I'm Mrs. Jackson." Her brown eyes sparkled as she smiled. "Mr. Mac is working with Mr. Millard on Back-to-School Night plans, so he won't be in class today. However, he gave us an excellent topic to discuss, after which you are to write a short essay regarding your thoughts about it. It's to be turned in on Monday." The class groaned. "But that doesn't mean we can't have fun." She smiled again and I let out a long sigh. No bad news. Just another sub.

She walked to the whiteboard, picked up a marker, and wrote in large capital letters, the word IMMORTALITY.

"I understand that next week you will be moving away from Shakespeare and jumping into Gothic horror literature—just in time for Halloween."

General interest spiked. Halloween was a favorite holiday for most students. Me? My life was already a nightmare. Who needed costumes when real monsters were already roaming our town?

"By any chance, has anyone read *The Picture of Dorian Gray* by Oscar Wilde?" asked Mrs. Jackson.

Students looked around at each other, but no one raised their hand.

"How about Bram Stoker's *Dracula?*"

One hand shot up. Several others said they had seen the movie, but Mrs. Jackson didn't seem impressed. "Unfortunately, the movie won't help you on your AP test."

Then she smiled again. "Let's use our imagination for a moment. What would you say if the mainstream media ran a story about creatures like vampires and werewolves? What if they said they really existed?"

My eyes widened and I shot a glance over to Zander who squinted toward the front of the room with suspicion. Most of the class buzzed with absurd comments, embracing the idea. Mrs. Jackson pumped her hands to bring down the noise level.

"Remember that I said 'what if' before you tell your parents." Everyone chuckled.

She seemed to be looking at me with more attention than the other students, as if she was trying to tell me something. It kind of blew my mind since I already knew these creatures existed, at least similar creatures. But why was she telling the whole class? Or was this discussion generated for me alone? Whoever she was—I was starting to think she wasn't just a school substitute—she probably didn't know about Zander or Zena, at least how they related to the danger this knowledge was sure to engender. Or did she?

"I always thought," she said, "that if I were to write a horror story, I'd write about the hybrid child, perhaps the offspring of a vampire and a human."

"They can have kids?" asked someone on the front row.

Mrs. Jackson shrugged and winked in my direction. "Who knows? It's my story and anything can happen. That's the thrill of being an author."

What was the woman insinuating? I shook my head in bewilderment, knowing in my heart that neither Mom nor Dad was akharu or usemi. I felt someone else's eyes on me and looked up to see Zena staring. For once she wasn't glaring. But I would have preferred it to the speculation I saw in her eyes now. This was a look of new awareness, and it sent a chill up my spine. Zander noticed Zena's interest, as well, and frowned.

The substitute continued. "And in my story, the child would be the hero—or heroine." She winked my way again. "In fact, this character would also have special powers." The class buzzed with ideas. I let out the breath

I'd been holding as she finally looked away from me. I wanted to go hide under a rock.

The rest of class passed in a blur. I didn't even hear the essay question that Mrs. Jackson announced before the bell rang. Zander grabbed my bag and stuffed my notebook and pen inside.

"Come on," he said, leading me by the arm toward the door. I let him direct me, my mind still in chaos. As we passed by the front of the room, Mrs. Jackson gave me an entreating smile, but I ignored her and rushed out of the classroom in a panic, now the one leading Zander. I found the nearest blank wall and pushed Zander up against it.

"What just happened?" I demanded. "Is she ..." I tripped over the words. "Is she one of the Collector's people? Has he figured out who I am?"

Zander dropped our stuff and grabbed my hands. "I don't know, Tru, but I won't let anything happen to you. I promise." He pulled me into his chest, wrapping his arms around me.

"Zena definitely figured something out in there," I wailed. "What am I going to do?"

"Let me handle this," he said his voice brushing against me in soft waves. He lifted up my chin and kissed me, his lips making me forget the dark possibilities raging in my mind.

Loud "oohing" rang out around us and we broke apart to see an audience of students. My face heated up, but Zander chuckled and threw an arm around my shoulders.

"Let's get you home. We'll decide what to do later," he whispered into my ear as we passed through the gauntlet of teasing students.

At my locker, I repacked my bag and headed over to meet Ruthie. While we walked, Zander and I made plans to go jogging together the next morning. We wouldn't get a chance to see each other tonight because Dad wanted me to attend the school meeting with him and then go out to dinner afterward. The hours between now and tomorrow seemed too far away, and after the almost taunting words of the sub in English today, I wanted Zander as close to me as possible. Was the Collector toying with my mind?

"FOR THE LOVE OF puppies!" piped Ruthie as she strolled out to the parking lot with Zander and me. After Mrs. Jackson's very public insinuations, my nerves were already on edge. And, the scene in front of me didn't help ease the spiraling tension in my shoulders. Zander followed my gaze, his face going still. Several cars away stood Phoebe and Peter, talking. No, make that flirting.

I still owed Zander's psychotic brother a black eye or a kick in the kidney. But I couldn't do anything about it. If I did, then he might do something worse than give me the mother of all headaches, which is how it felt when he had tried to erase my memories. If I faced off with him, he would find out that I knew about his mind-wiping ability. Peter was still under the impression that he'd erased my memory and knocked me unconscious for hours. Zander knew the truth but didn't want Peter to know I'd heard the conversation, which had revealed to me the existence of usemi and akharu for the first time, and more importantly, the name of my Mom's killer.

I could almost hear Ruthie's teeth grinding as she

eyed the budding romance in front of us. They weren't the only couple raising eyebrows. Isaac leaned obliviously against another car off to our right with two other seniors. Jenny Bushman had a hand on Isaac's arm and he smiled down at her. If I weren't so disturbed by Phoebe and Peter, I would have made a comment about Isaac moving on. Instead, my eyes switched back and forth between the twins as if mesmerized, aware that this powder keg could explode at any moment. Isaac had always been overly protective of Phoebe, which pissed her off to no end. Sure enough, I saw the exact second that Isaac noticed Phoebe flirting with Peter. But Isaac showed remarkable restraint, remaining in place as he observed them.

With equal fascination, I watched Peter work Phoebe over. Peter had a surprising playboy alter ego and whatever he was saying seemed to be working on Phoebe. I'd never seen her so animated. She twisted a lock of hair with both hands, tilting her head from one side to the other. Three cars away, Jake Tinke glared at the two of them. He was a regular at our lunch table and had an unspoken claim on Phoebe, although she hadn't been eating what he'd been dishing out. Not the case with Peter. No, she was gobbling up his charm like her brother downed pizza.

I tried to look at Peter objectively. Short dark blond hair, brown eyes, and a broad chest. He favored dark clothes, canvas cargo pants and military-style jackets that I knew could hide a gun because I had seen him pull one out and shoot a usemi.

Phoebe ducked her head and sent a frown Isaac's way before bringing her eyes back up to Peter's. It was no surprise when a moment later they pulled out their phones to exchange numbers.

As the entertainment drew to an anti-climactic end, Zander squeezed my hand. "See you tomorrow," he stated, a preoccupied air about him pulling him toward Peter's truck before I could respond. I wanted to ask him what his brother was up to, but he seemed just as startled by his actions as I was.

"OMG," said Ruthie as soon as Zander was out of hearing range. "I so need to set Phoebe straight."

"But you can't tell her the truth," I reminded her, a thread of panic in my voice.

"Nope. But I have to say *something*." We threw our junk in her Mini and headed over to the twins. My eyes darted once more to Zander and Peter as they reached their truck. The stiff set of Zander's shoulders indicated an argument, but Peter didn't engage. Instead, he shrugged his shoulders and climbed into the truck.

When Ruthie and I caught up with the twins, they were already engrossed in one of their staring contests. Ruthie yanked on Phoebe's arm to get her attention.

"What the crap was that about?" blurted Ruthie, waving a hand in the general direction of Phoebe's flirting scene.

She sighed dreamily, misinterpreting Ruthie. "Yummy, isn't he?" She looked at me. "Did you know Zander had a brother?"

I nodded. "Peter," I muttered.

"Yeah … Well, I got his number." She grinned.

"Really?" said Ruthie, still stunned. "I'd delete that, if I were you. And block his calls."

"What the heck, Ruthie!" sputtered Phoebe.

Ruthie wasn't done. "No offense but your jerk meter is malfunctioning. Peter is bad news, like Rocky Mountain Oysters bad news."

"Rocky Mountain Oysters?" Phoebe asked, tilting her head to one side in confusion.

"Bull testicles," answered Ruthie, not dropping a beat. "Peeled, washed, rolled in flour and fried in a pan."

Isaac gagged, his complexion turning green. Phoebe's mouth hung open in shock. I couldn't stop the deep giggle that escaped, so needing a comic moment in my crappy day. Ruthie grinned at me and winked.

"How would you know?" asked Phoebe, her voice peevish. Ruthie smirked.

"I mean about Peter," Phoebe added, a little flustered.

"Trust me, I just do," insisted Ruthie. Isaac crossed his arms and glared at his sister, who lifted one shoulder as if she couldn't care less about what he thought.

"If that's all you have to say, Ruthie, then I'll take my chances." She adjusted the straps on her bag, preparing to leave.

I shook my head when Ruthie made funny eyes at me, trying to get me to spill my guts. There was no way I was going to tell them that there were shape-shifting and blood-sucking supernaturals out there or that Peter was another kind of supernatural that thought he had some kind of authority over them. They'd never believe me. We'd have to find another way to keep Peter away from Phoebe.

13

SET UP

MY ALARM WENT OFF at eight-thirty a.m. I stretched, feeling wonderful and recalling no dreams whatsoever. Sometimes I forgot what normal sleep was like. It felt fabulous. I thought I'd have trouble sleeping after worrying so much about the substitute in English yesterday. Had I done anything different? I retraced my bedtime preparations, hoping that I could recreate my restful night by repeating whatever I'd done. Dinner with Dad, laundry, a half-hearted attempt to clean up my bedroom, and then off to bed. Normal stuff. Except ... when I was lying in bed, I had been thinking about something Zander said, that I was so much more than his girlfriend. And it had conjured up all sorts of warm feelings. Maybe he was my dream catcher. I couldn't wait to see him again. He could be on his way over already.

The thought of seeing Zander this morning sent a

swirl of excitement zipping along my skin. I stood up and frowned at my bedroom, which was still messy from my sleepover with Ruthie. *Oh Ruthie,* I thought with an inward smile. When I told her yesterday about the mysterious Mrs. Jackson, her interest in me, and Zena's reaction, she had shrugged off her shark encounter and worry about me, unloading it like a nuclear bomb. Now my best friend wanted to ship me off to her uncle's ranch in Idaho. I wouldn't have been surprised if she had kidnapped me in my sleep.

The idea of petite Ruthie trying to do that made me giggle to myself as I searched for my running shoes among the clothing piled up on the floor. I almost squealed with delight when I found them. It had been a while since I used them for actual jogging. I used to run all the time. Before Mom died, anyway. Today, it was the perfect excuse to get out of the house alone. I hurried to clean up and pull on my running gear—a pair of black spandex capris and a purple t-shirt that said "Just Do It" on the front and "Doin' It" on the back.

"Watch out for cars!" Dad yelled as I tucked my house key into a pocket and walked out the front door.

Early morning fog hung low above my head, lending a chill to the air, but I knew I'd warm up once I started moving. After a quick stretch, I walked down the street with long strides, continuing to stretch my legs while looking for Zander's blue truck. I spotted it around the corner and picked up my pace.

Zander reached across the cab and pushed open the passenger door. "Hey there! Hop in." I climbed in, meeting his smile with one of my own. He ran his eyes over my face, pursing his lips for a moment before saying,

"Buckle up."

"Where are we going?" I asked as he pulled away from the curb.

"I know a nice trail for jogging, if that's okay with you."

"Sure," I said, rubbing my arms to chase away the goose bumps.

"Here," he said, pulling a gray sweatshirt out from behind his seat and passing it to me.

"Thanks." I wrapped myself in it, warming immediately.

Looking out the window at the foggy neighborhood, I ransacked my brain for something to talk about. I had been so excited to see Zander again I hadn't given any thought to how I was going to greet him. Should I have kissed him? He'd given me a few sidelong glances as we drove, a small smile playing along his lips. But for some reason I couldn't think of a thing to say. Awkward. A few silent minutes later, we pulled over on a damp tree-lined road.

I reached for the door handle but Zander called out "Wait!" making me pause. I watched him saunter around the truck to open my door and my heartbeat picked up. As I stepped down, he tipped up my chin and gave me a soulful look, like he could see inside me.

"I didn't say hello properly," he said. He brushed his lips against mine with feather light touches. The awkwardness melted away and I instinctively leaned into the kiss, letting my hands rest on his chest. Zander wrapped his arms around me and tilted his head to the side, his touch making my brain go numb. It was like nothing existed outside the two square feet of ground we stood on. When we broke apart, my heart was thumping wildly. Zander shook his head with a half smile, as if he didn't know what to do with me. But clearly, he did, because my skin pulsed in a very pleasant way. I trapped my lower lip with my teeth and tried not to grin. Zander's sparkling eyes dipped down to my mouth. I smothered a giggle.

"Yeah, very 'proper,'" I said, tongue in cheek. He chuckled and pulled me away toward the trees. A wide dirt path appeared and we hopped on it.

"So," he said, swinging my hand clasped in his. "How'd you sleep?"

I smiled. "Surprisingly great."

"That's good. I was afraid you would be scared," he said, squeezing my hand.

Yesterday I'd zombie-stared my way through most of English class, feeling like I was being hung out to dry. It was very possible that our substitute had tipped off Zena's family about my less than human qualities.

But right now, my lips were still tingling from Zander's kiss and it distracted me from all the chaos going on around me. He swung his head around to catch my star-struck gaze and I blinked with embarrassment. With a gulp my mind went blank and I couldn't remember what we'd been talking about. I stumbled over a root, pitching face-forward toward the dirt path, but Zander's reflexes were quick and he caught me.

"Are you alright?" he asked, steadying me.

"Yeah," I gasped, cursing my clumsiness. Desperate to redirect the conversation, I blurted, "Dad is making me go to a co-worker's barbecue today. Super boring." My social skills were cringe worthy. Fortunately, they didn't seem to faze Zander.

"Oh man, you're killing me!" he said. "Sure beats the food I've been eating. When is it?"

"Noon or something like that."

He sounded so interested I almost invited him, but Dad was definitely not ready for me to bring home a boyfriend. Lightning raced up my neck. I had a boyfriend! I felt a grin spreading across my face.

"What?" he asked.

"Nothing." I mentally chastised myself once again for getting distracted. I needed to focus on more important matters—such as what had happened yesterday. "Um, what are we going to do about Mrs. Jackson? Do you think she knows about me?"

"Peter checked into it. She's not working for us." His eyebrows squished together. "So, she must be from the Collector."

If the Collector sent her, then Zander's father knew about me. I swallowed through a suddenly dry throat.

"So what do I do about her?" I asked.

"Nothing," he said, squeezing my hand. "I've got this handled."

"What about Zena?" I added. "What if she told her parents about Mrs. Jackson's comments? Won't that put me on your father's radar?"

He tilted his head and smiled. "Come on. Trust me. I'll keep an eye on them, too."

I cast him a doubtful look. He didn't know the Taylors like I did. A burst of frustrated energy swept through me. Time to burn it off.

"Are we going to actually run or talk?" I said, stretching.

Zander grinned and took off, yelling over his shoulder. "Come on, lazy bones!"

THE TRAIL CURVED THROUGH the tall trees for at least a mile. The air smelled alive with the scent of redwoods, eucalyptus, and damp air. Blue jays darted through the trees, chasing smaller birds with loud caws. I soaked in the freshness of the forest, feeling grounded by its simplicity. Exhilarated, I ran faster and Zander and I settled into a comfortable pace that allowed us to still chat. Occasionally, Zander ran backwards. My fast pace was barely a trot for him, but he didn't seem to mind.

As we jogged around a corner, the path straightened and Zander took the opportunity to turn around again, grinning. Before he could say anything, I gasped and pulled to a stop to stare at a tree off to my right. I could have sworn that it had moved, that the bark had bulged like something inside of it was trying to break out. Zander halted in confusion. He looked around to see what had caught my attention just as something flew through the air from the opposite side of the trail. It landed in Zander's leg with a sickening thud and he went down, grunting with pain.

"Zander!" I yelled, rushing to his side. He pulled me down and rolled on top of me.

"A tree moved like a weird alien creature," I whispered. Then I caught a glimpse of it again. "There it is!" I nudged Zander and pointed behind him. He looked over his shoulder to see a figure leap from one tree to another before blending into the bark.

"Akharu," he said. With lightning reflexes, he pulled out a small gun, aimed, and fired. The bullet missed, burrowing into the bark as the figure jumped out of the way and took off into the woods. I tried to squeeze out from under Zander's heavy weight, but he pressed me down.

"Not yet," he gritted out. "The knife came from the other side. There's more than one of them."

"Knife?" That's what that small missile-like object had been. And it had struck Zander. "Oh my gosh, you're hurt! Let me see your leg." I tried pushing him away so I could see the damage, but he continued to pin me down.

He watched the other side of the trail for several long moments. Pine needles and shredded bark covered us. Tiny sticks and rocks poked into my back.

"He's long gone by now," I said. "Let me up!"

"Shhh. Please," he whispered, his voice freezing me in place.

Minutes felt like hours. Zander finally rolled off me and sat up. His jaw clenched in pain, but he remained wary with his gun out and his eyes fixed on the surrounding vegetation.

I looked him over and gasped when I saw a knife embedded into his thigh. If it had been me, I'd be screaming. But except for the pallor in his face, Zander appeared remarkably unfazed. Even so, I doubted he could walk out of here and I couldn't carry him. Our options narrowed down to two: call for help or heal him myself.

This healing thing was becoming a regular occurrence. I didn't struggle with the decision like I did after Ruthie's shark attack, when I had worried what I'd do to her or what I'd reveal about myself. Zander wasn't human and he already knew I was different. Besides, the need to help him was overriding any other concerns.

"Hold still," I ordered. His eyes spun toward me, then back to the steel hilt protruding from his thigh. Seeing the injury seemed to make it more painful. His face paled even more and his hands shook as he set the gun down on the path beside him. He leaned back on his hands and gave me a questioning look that held a hint of dread. "What are you doing?"

"I'm going to fix you. But first, it's going to hurt really bad."

I didn't give him time to think about it before I grabbed the knife and pulled with all my strength. I cringed as it slid across bone and tissue.

"Aaaah!" groaned Zander. He reached out to grab his leg, but I pushed him away and he fell back on his elbows.

"Don't touch it," I ordered, raising his shorts to reveal the gushing blood. I pressed both my hands against the wound. He arched his back, his elbows digging into the dirty trail and his face contorting with pain.

"I'm sorry," I said, my eyes trying to express how awful I felt.

"It's okay," he muttered through clenched teeth. "I trust you."

His words echoed Ruthie's after her shark attack, but Zander's felt different. They evoked feelings I didn't understand. They had their own gravity, linking me tighter to him. And oddly enough, they made me feel older than my seventeen years.

"Tru?" Zander broke into my thoughts.

I sent him a smile, hoping it reassured him, even as I

realized the missing component that I needed. I couldn't see the sun. Not good.

Although much of the fog had dissipated on our run, the tall redwood trees towered above us, blocking out much of the sunlight. I could see fine, but I didn't know if I could lock onto the rays of light like I had done at the beach. I racked my brain for another source of light, believing with all my heart that I had to have it in order to heal Zander. Ironically, we were surrounded by life— lush green ferns, trees, and bushes—but the source of it was above us, out of reach.

Wait! Green. Chlorophyll. Photosynthesis. The plants were filled with trapped energy from the sun. Could I tap into that? I hoped that would be enough.

I called to the plants, begging them to share the energy they held in their tiny molecules. Seconds later, I smiled as rays of green light shined all around us. I directed it into Zander's leg, instructing the light to reconstruct his cells, to nourish and heal his traumatized flesh. As it worked its magic, the searing heat stung my hands, but I didn't yank away as I'd done with Ruthie.

Long moments later the top layers of Zander's skin sealed and smoothed. Overcome with fatigue, I teetered over onto him. He sat up and pulled me into his arms.

"You did it again, Tru," he whispered, brushing his lips across my forehead. "You are a miracle worker."

I thought about the other day on the beach. Maybe it really had been a miracle.

This time, my energy renewed itself in moments. I looked up into Zander's face to see fear and admiration in his glowing blue eyes. I frowned, about to ask what was wrong, but a rustling in the bushes had Zander leaping up, pulling me alongside him. Something dashed through the undergrowth of the forest, already too far away for us to catch up.

"What was that?" I asked.

Zander swore. He looked from me to the rustling in the bushes and then in the direction our assailant had taken, as if he wanted to chase whatever it was. Instead, he shook his head and gently squeezed my arm before moving away to inspect the bushes. Seconds later, he returned with a pair of jeans and a t-shirt. I couldn't make sense of it.

He scowled. "All that's left are usemi tracks and a pile of clothes," he said, his words heavy with dread.

"Usemi?" I said.

"Yeah."

"But earlier I thought you said akharu."

"There was one of them, too. It makes no sense. I've never heard of them working together before." He poked through the pockets of the clothes. When he came up empty-handed, he tossed them back into the bushes with a frustrated snarl.

"I thought they were almost extinct," I said.

"They are," he muttered. "All the more reason to tag them."

"Tag?"

Zander sighed. "It's just a word we use for recording a new usemi or akharu, one that isn't in our records. The Nasaru keep tabs on them.

"Oh," I said. "You could go after him," I suggested. Zander was fast, really fast.

He looked at me as if I were crazy. "I'm not leaving you alone."

The protective look in his eyes sent shivers up my arm. I looked away. "Why would they try to kill you?" I asked.

He shook his head. "The real question is, if they went to the trouble of knifing me, why *didn't* they finish me off or take you?"

Alarm zipped through my veins. "Do you think the usemi stayed to see if I healed you?" I asked.

Zander's already serious expression grew darker, giving me my answer. Someone had set us up, provoking me to use my ability. He ran a hand over his face.

"Tru, I think you should leave Scotts Valley." His eyes were hooded as he gauged my reaction. "With me."

The idea of running away with Zander was tempting for many reasons. First and foremost, we could discover where this delicious physical connection between us would lead. It also felt like a formal declaration, as if it would make our relationship permanent, which appealed to me because I lived with the constant fear he would return home. But I couldn't do it for the same reasons that I'd given Ruthie.

"No. I can't do that to my dad."

Staying meant that I might have to face my foe, that I might even get hurt. But it didn't matter. The one and only time I'd visited Mom's grave, I'd made a promise to my mom that I'd take care of Dad. And I was going to keep it. Plus, I had to look after Ruthie, too.

Heaving a deep sigh, Zander nodded as if he had expected that answer. When I tried to wipe the drying blood off my hands Zander disappeared into the bushes. He returned with a handful of damp moss.

"Here," he said, using the moss as a sponge to clean

my hands. It wasn't perfect, but I felt much better once the red smears were gone.

"Don't worry," he said, tossing the moss into the bushes and tucking me under his arm. "We'll come up with a plan."

14

Liar, Liar, Pants on Fire

WE SLOWLY HEADED BACK along the path to his truck, both of us wanting to prolong our time together. When I asked about the akharu and the bulging tree, he explained that akharu could camouflage their bodies by emitting a type of oil that caused people to hallucinate. Their musk tricked your mind, making you imagine things.

"Like they turn into Brad Pitt or Angelina Jolie on you?" I asked, twisting my face into disgust.

Zander laughed. "Yes, they can make you see them as someone different."

"That's some seriously trippy oil. Sounds like magic."

"What we don't understand, we call magic." He shook his head with a smile. "We've studied it enough to learn how it works. Nature always has a reason for what it does. For akharu, it's a lure to draw people into a trap.

But you have to be close enough to be affected."

"The problem is, you don't know you're too close until it happens." We had walked right into their trap.

"Exactly why they are so dangerous," agreed Zander. "Plus, they have a paralyzing bite. Temporary but effective for their purposes."

I grimaced. "Geez. They're like spiders that poison their prey so it can't defend itself."

"Pretty much," he chuckled. "That way they can suck you dry without a fight."

I shivered. "Do you think they're coming back?"

"No." He took my hand and laced his fingers through mine. "I think they got what they wanted," he said grimly.

"So," I sighed. "You mentioned a plan?"

His hand tightened. "It's time to go on the offensive."

"What do you mean?"

"Well, first we figure out what we have to work with. That means we need to understand our abilities and why you and I are so connected."

My heart skipped a beat. He meant the usemi aramusatu bond. The strange connection we were experiencing sounded similar to it. Could we actually have that? My thoughts backpedaled to when I had tried to convince myself Zander was psychically manipulating me and making me think I liked him. I had avoided him, and the longer I did, the more awful I'd felt. He'd looked miserable, too, like we were both physically sick. Could it have been the mere act of avoiding each other that made us ill? He'd said that a side effect of the usemi aramusatu bond was a couple's inability to withstand long stretches of time away from each other. I frowned. Was that what he meant when he said I was "more than his girlfriend?" I was his mate? Were we nature's science experiment, the first non-usemi to experience it? I frowned.

"I guess I can't avoid it anymore," I said, sneaking a peek at him. Our eyes connected and he half smiled, looking like he understood my reluctance.

I tried to make light of it, thinking some levity might make this conversation easier. "Living as long as a usemi does is a pretty great perk, but if it means you need an aramusatu bond, then..." I paused. "Well, it gives a new meaning to the 'ol ball and chain, right?"

Zander's face fell, making me want to retract my words. But I didn't. Instead, I let go of his hand and locked my hands behind me. "You think we might be bound to each other like that, don't you?"

"Yes," he said, his face softening. "But I don't think it's as horrible as you do."

"I didn't say that," I defended myself. But if I were being honest, I had inferred it. "Besides you said it was something that only happened to usemi, and we aren't usemi, so..."

Zander pulled me over to a log bordering the path and we sat down.

"I've always been told that." He sounded like he didn't believe it, though. The skin along my neck prickled, foreshadowing his next words. "But I think we might be an exception."

"But it's not possible."

"You don't think that the way we feel about each other sounds suspiciously like an aramusatu?" he asked, the corners of his eyes turning down.

I tried again to appear unfazed. "No, not really." I

cleared my throat. "For starters, that *soul magnet* mojo is still ... TBD, to be decided." I waved one hand in the air. "We don't know for sure if that's what's happening to us."

"Tru, I've never heard of anyone being able to do what you can do, what I can do, or what we can do together."

Was he referring to that sizzle along our skin? Or when Dante shot me and I healed myself by drawing on his strength? Maybe he meant the way he could share my ability to see in the dark when we touched. Right now, he looked at me like he could see all of me. My insecurities, my strengths, and my secrets. And I feared he could because I felt my soul shift and move toward him.

"And I have a feeling this is only the beginning," he added, his eyes warm as he stared at me.

My throat closed up and I shut my eyes to block out the intensity of his. Months ago, I would have considered the idea of one person meant to be your other half a romantic idea. But in reality, it carried too many responsibilities, too many expectations. It was choking me. Couldn't we just really like each other? The way kids our age normally crushed on each other?

"Zander, please, can we focus on something else right now?" My voice cracked. "I-I don't want to talk about that." I opened my eyes to see his face brewing with concern.

"Tru, this is what I mean by going on the offensive. If we want to be prepared for whatever is out there trying to hurt us, then we have to face up to the possibility we are true mates."

"Tell me more about where you grew up," I said. "Are there any usemi or akharu there? What about idimmu and humans?"

He tried to stare me down but I hung on and he finally relented. "Okay," he said with a shrug. He leaned back along the rough redwood log. "Eden is pretty much sethian. Other supernaturals prefer living on their own, but some work for the Nasaru as enforcers and whatnot."

"No idimmu?"

"Not really. Since they are genetically inclined to insanity, they aren't very useful. Sethians look upon idimmu as mutants, accidents that should never have been allowed to happen."

Considering I might be an idimmu, I didn't like the sound of that. Zander cast a worried glance at me. I wondered what he thought about being "mated" to an idimmu. I mean, what else could I be? But then maybe he was, too. His abilities were definitely not like most sethians.

"And what about humans?" I asked.

He scrunched up his nose in distaste. "Well, we do have some humans in Eden, but they don't have the same rights as sethians."

"Harsh!" I gasped. "Why the heck don't they?"

"Sethians blame humans for their current weaknesses. Our scientists believe that co-mingling sethian and human gene pools bred out the best sethian traits, such as their long lifespan and their special abilities. And they think it's also the cause for their fertility problems."

I sat up straight, suddenly furious on behalf of humans everywhere. "How do *you* feel about humans?"

"I don't have a problem with them," he said. But his

earlier response made me suspect that he did. It kind of ticked me off that he might be racist when it came to humans or idimmu.

"In fact," continued Zander, "we're trying to protect them from usemi and akharu. We just aren't allowed to have children with them."

I grimaced, disliking the Nasaru even more than I already did. "What about idimmu?" I asked, a hot ball forming in my stomach. "Do you think they're like second class citizens, too?"

Zander's eyebrows shot up, as if he'd finally realized he had stepped into a minefield. "No! Of course, I don't. I think they're … great."

"But you were taught that idimmu are mutants."

He looked down at the ground, kicking a rock across the trail. "My teachers said that sometimes nature screws up and creates things that become detrimental to the rest of us. Sethians—the Nasaru—are just weeding out these mistakes so the rest of us can thrive."

"Weeding out?"

Zander sighed, rubbing his forehead. "Okay. Listen. Crossbreeding across species creates weaknesses. For instance, in the animal world the environment eradicates undesirable mutations, right? That's nature taking its course. But unfortunately, nature isn't doing what it's supposed to and the weak anomalies are propagating, which puts everyone, human and supernatural, in danger. But why let that happen if we can stop it? That's where the Nasaru comes in."

"How?" My stomach felt sick. "How is the Nasaru doing this?"

He hesitated, like he knew I'd hate whatever he was

about to say. "Well, at first, they are observed. If it's decided they're dangerous—let's say they cause an earthquake or they hurt other people because of their idimmu abilities—then they are removed from society. Sometimes they can be rehabilitated."

"Removed?" I asked, knowing there was a darker side to this equation. "Rehabilitated?"

He sighed. "Ultimately, the Nasaru decides whether to remove them from society altogether. In a humane way, of course. Or they just prevent them from, uh, replicating."

In other words, they killed them. And prevent them from replicating? Was that his nice way of saying they were spayed and neutered?

"Wow. Your people sound great." I said in a deadpan voice.

He sighed. "Like I said before, sethians have been protecting humans for centuries. And now they are protecting the original races from extinction. If it means making some tough decisions ..." He frowned.

I tilted my head in confusion. "What do you mean by extinction?" I asked, torn between anger and curiosity.

"The original races—akharu, usemi, and sethians—are on the brink of extinction. Human DNA is the cause. Coupling with humans over time has slowly stripped sethians of their supernatural abilities. And now their birthrate has fallen to an all-time low. Not just theirs, akharu and usemi, too. The big question is how to undo so many years of damage. Our scientists have some ideas and they are beginning to make some progress. In the meantime, the Nasaru is doing its best to keep humans and supernaturals apart."

I couldn't help but think that nature *was* taking its course; it just wasn't the course that the Nasaru liked. I found it odd that human DNA would be dominant and that given free reign nature would weed out all supernaturals. But then look at redheads. They'd existed for thousands of years and I'd read recently that they were definitely going the way of the Dodo bird.

"Okay," I said. "But I don't like it and I'm not sure I agree with your methods."

"I don't love our methods either," said Zander. "But I don't have any better ideas."

"I wonder why akharu and usemi aren't losing their abilities like the sethians. How do you know that the human DNA is affecting them?"

"Well, given what human DNA did to sethians, it didn't take a big leap to figure out that both human and idimmu DNA could be adversely affecting akharu and usemi populations as well. This is another reason we tag akharu and usemi."

"You don't mean tagging like they do to study wild animals, do you?"

"No. It's much more discreet—just a tiny disc under their skin."

"Oh my gosh! That's horrible!" I felt a little sick.

"It's the best way to police them. Cohabitation between supernaturals and humans, or with idimmu, is absolutely prohibited. Breaking these laws incur the severest penalties."

Severest penalty felt too much like a death sentence. I shivered.

"Seems pretty unfair," I said with a frown. "And if you're punishing humans and idimmu, too, then it's a huge conflict of interest. I thought protecting humanity was the Nasaru's primary job? Humanity includes humans and idimmu."

"They are protecting them—at least their future," said Zander. "In a nutshell, supernaturals and humans create idimmu. And unchecked, insane idimmu would destroy the world. The Nasaru also keep the idimmu from exposing the *supernatural* world to humans because they just can't handle the idea of them at all."

I had no defense for his logic, but it didn't feel right.

"Anyway, that's why they track and tag wayward supernaturals," said Zander.

"And then play judge and jury," I said. He looked confused. "You know, decide if they are a threat to anyone."

Zander raised an eyebrow at my slightly mocking tone. I couldn't help it. It all sounded too much like the witch trials, the massive wolf hunts, and vicious exorcisms throughout history. How many innocents had died?

"Tell me more about the abilities that sethians lost," I said.

Zander nodded. "Sethians used to have supernatural talents like idimmu have, but without the bad side effects. They could be anything from enhanced mental powers or extraordinary physical abilities. They made sethians powerful enough to subdue akharu and usemi when necessary. And, like I already said, sethians used to live just as long as akharu and usemi. But not anymore. Now sethians are as weak as humans."

"But I thought they were still in charge," I said.

"Not always. When the sethians first began to weaken there was a period of lawlessness and chaos. It took a while, but eventually, sethians gained the upper hand—mostly through technology that is above and beyond any human tech. Many in leadership positions believe that this advantage over all supernaturals could be temporary if we don't find a way to reinstate our original abilities and longevity. Although akharu and usemi traditionally despise technology, some are changing and evolving with the times. It's a bit of a race to stay ahead."

"You have abilities, though," I said.

His jaw tightened. "Yes. But nobody knows about them."

"But you could be the answer to reviving your people." I was playing the devil's advocate because I definitely didn't want him to go anywhere.

He shook his head. "I've thought about it. But something inside me keeps me from telling anyone." He leaned forward. "It just feels like a bad idea." Then he leaned back, releasing a loud scoffing noise. "Maybe I'm a coward."

I pressed a hand down on his knee, forcing him to look at me. "No, you aren't."

But he dropped his gaze and sighed.

"How do you think they are doing it?" I asked. "Do you really think it's possible to recreate abilities and extend life? I mean, if they can do that, then what can't they do?"

He looked away. "Um, our scientists think so. They have some very promising test subjects."

Zander sounded uncharacteristically vague. Was he lying? Or was he avoiding a direct answer. I wondered why he might do that and then I thought of how excited he'd been when he'd discovered that my aunt had been idimmu before she became usemi. That she could heal idimmu, that she had an aramusatu mate and possibly a child.

"My aunt."

Zander stiffened and looked up at me.

"Was the Nasaru experimenting on her?" I asked.

He had the grace to look ashamed. "I suspect that your aunt was a highly coveted research subject. And I don't think she's on the Most Wanted List because she's a criminal."

"Then the Nasaru made everyone believe she was a criminal so that they could lock her up and do whatever they wanted to her."

"I'm sorry, Tru. It was wrong." His face drooped with regret. At least he knew right from wrong, despite his father and his upbringing.

"You didn't know. But she must have been so miserable," I said. "I'm not surprised she ran away when she got the chance."

Zander seemed lost in thought. Perhaps his imagination was running wild like mine. I thought about how terrifying it must have been for Caroline. In my mind I saw myself being forcibly fastened down on a gurney as heartless doctors drew my blood or worse, screaming as they performed questionable experiments on me. I shivered.

"I hope they never find me," I whispered. For a split second I reconsidered running away with Zander.

"Tru, I won't—no, I *can't* let anything happen to you, to us." His eyes were wide and luminous. Although I knew now that the aramusatu made him feel that way, my stomach reacted with a flutter.

"Besides," he said, excitement entering his voice. "Maybe they don't need to study your aunt anymore."

"What are you talking about?"

"I'm not supposed to tell anyone." He hesitated. "I could be put to death for doing it." Then he shook his head, resolve shining in his eyes. "But it doesn't matter anymore." He smiled. "And maybe this will make you feel safer."

I leaned forward. "So ..."

"Well, our doctors have developed a purifying process that awakens the abilities hidden in our DNA."

I yelped. "They figured it out!"

"They think so. But from what I've heard, the ingredients for the process are limited and take time to produce. Therefore, few have received the gift of purification. Those who get it have contributed in a great way to the Nasaru and they are rewarded with this gift. It's a great motivator to all the sethians."

I deflated with disappointment. Wow. Zander had been living underground way too long. He didn't even realize how awful he sounded. If I heard the word "pure" one more time, I might smack him upside the head. The idea of a reward system sent a new warning tingle up my neck.

"How does it work?" I asked. "Is it some kind of operation or medicine?"

"I don't know a lot about it except that it's a very secret ceremony called the *Blessing*. After the ceremony, they begin to develop special gifts, much like the idimmu, but without the madness. They think that these traits can be passed down to their children."

Blessing. This was what Mrs. Taylor meant in my

dream. And that also explained Peter's mind-erasing ability. "When did this start?"

"Uh, it began about twenty years ago, I think. And sometimes the abilities are kind of lame." Zander made a face. "One person can just change the color of her skin. Not that helpful in a fight."

"Is that why you are so fast and strong? And why Peter can erase memories?" I asked. "Did you get those abilities from your father?"

He shook his head. "No. Father received the Blessing after I was born."

I raised my eyebrows. "How about you and Peter?"

He shook his head. "I haven't," he insisted. I cocked my head to the side and gave him a disbelieving look. "It would explain your special *talents.*"

"I swear I haven't, Tru," he said. "I don't know how I can do what I can do." He scowled at the ground. "But Peter has. He was rewarded this year. And frankly, I'm afraid it screwed up because he's been an ass ever since." He grimaced.

"You think the Blessing turned him into an ass?" I asked with a smile. One side of Zander's mouth inched up. "Probably not."

"So he just grew into one, I guess," I said, raising one eyebrow.

The other side of Zander's mouth curled up. "I guess so."

Pushing that subject aside, I said, "You said 'original' races earlier. Do you mean that sethians, usemi, and akharu were here before humans?" Alarms were going off inside my head even as I uttered the words. This felt wrong.

"Well, I guess not that far back. But almost." Zander stretched and gripped his neck. "I know it sounds weird to you. Our people's origin stories are different from your bible stories. Sethians believe the original races started with three brothers, Cain, Abel, and Seth. Similar to your bible, of course, but the sethian story shifts in a different direction. Like your story, Cain turned against his brother, Abel, and killed him. And like your story, Cain was cursed. *How* he was cursed is where the stories diverge. In our legend, the curse changed Cain into the first akharu. Because Cain spilled his brother's blood, blood became the most important thing in his life, his addiction turning him into a bloodsucker. He and his family were hated and hunted all their lives. Abel's wife didn't think Cain's punishment was harsh enough and sought revenge against him, disobeying her leaders. Consequently, she was cursed sevenfold. She and her six sons changed into animals, wolves to be specific. But they repented and their curse was lightened, giving them the ability to change back into their human bodies. They became the first usemi."

Cold prickles ran up my arm and I blinked at him in confusion. "No way."

"Many humans believe Jonah was swallowed by a whale and lived to tell the tale, so why can't you believe this?"

Because everything in me said it was false, that's why. But I didn't tell Zander that.

"Anyway," Zander continued. "To enforce the peace between the akharu and the usemi, and to protect humans from them, of course, sethians were blessed with their own abilities. Over the millennia, each race has evolved to what we have today. Or I guess you could say de-evolved."

Everything about his story felt like a campfire tale and I struggled to not tell him he was full of hogwash. They all believed this, fashioned their whole society around it, created and enforced laws because of this. I was both awed and appalled.

"Tru? Are you okay?" asked Zander.

I had been scowling in silence for so long, my face hurt. "Sorry." I shook my head and tried to smooth out my features. "That's, uh ..." Crazy? Idiotic? Could I say that?

"That's unbelievable," I finally said.

"I know." He shrugged. "I'd be freaking out, too, if I were you."

"No," I said, placing a hand on his knee. "I mean I don't believe it—I *literally* don't believe it. Sorry, but you're wrong."

A chant from grade school ran through my head. *Liar, liar. Pants on fire.* It ran in loop mode. But deep down I knew Zander wasn't the real liar here. It was his father. He'd created an entire social infrastructure of lies. But how had he done it? And what was the real truth?

Zander's dad was definitely lying to everyone, but Zander was lying, too. To himself. All that talk about *his* people, the *sethians*, how they'd lost their abilities was bullcrap. Zander had abilities that didn't come from their creepy purification process, secret abilities that he'd kept from his family. I knew that he suspected he was different like me, but he couldn't seem to come out and say it. He still lumped himself with his father's people.

I decided there were many kinds of lies. Outright lies,

like the ones his father told, as big as mountains, and so huge they blocked everyone from the truth. There were those you told yourself because you couldn't face the truth, like Zander was telling himself when he called himself a sethian. Or when he said he wouldn't let his father hurt me. When he'd asked me to leave town with him, I knew he'd doubted his ability to protect me. But he still said he would.

And then there were lies of omission, like the one I kept from Zander. His father was more than the Kasadu, the leader of the sethians. His father collected idimmu for some freaky reason I didn't understand, but it had to be really bad. He was the one who'd sent Dante. And he had to be involved with the trap we'd run into along our trail today. The trap had forced me to heal Zander, revealing my ability. But I didn't tell Zander what I really thought. While something inside me told me I was right, I couldn't bring myself to tell him what I believed about his father.

So many ways to lie. How could I be mad at Zander when I kept such a horrible secret to myself?

15

FACT OR FICTION

THE NEXT EVENING, MY dad's strangled voice yelling up the stairs tore through my homework bubble and I bolted out of my chair, almost knocking it over. I hustled downstairs expecting the house to be on fire.

When I skidded around the corner of the family room, Dad was perched on the edge of his leather recliner with the tv remote in his hand. It was almost his football game pose, but the lines on his face were deeper and more solemn grooves than I was used to seeing. He looked like he'd received the worst news ever. I moved closer to the tv screen, to see what had caused this transformation.

"—found behind a dumpster early this morning," reported a newswoman. "Her wounds indicate an animal attack ..."

I tuned out some of the reporter's words as the victim's picture appeared on the screen. It was Mrs.

Jackson, the strange substitute I'd been so afraid of. Pieces of the story infiltrated my paralyzing shock. She was dead, her throat torn out. Family had already been notified. The best guess was that she'd been killed by a mountain lion.

Dad cleared his throat. "They said she worked in your school district as a substitute. Did you ever meet her?"

"Yeah. She subbed for Mr. Mac last Friday." I sunk into the sofa. "I can't believe she's dead."

"I don't want you running by yourself anymore. At least not until they capture whatever attacked that woman."

I wanted to protest. But, how could I? The danger was clearly there.

When I returned to my bedroom, I checked my phone. Ruthie and Zander had texted about the news of Mrs. Jackson's death, both believing a usemi had attacked her. I zipped back replies, telling them I'd already heard the news. They wanted to talk about it, but I wasn't up to rehashing things separately with them. It was time to bring us all together to decide what to do about the Collector.

Ruthie's mom wouldn't let her spend the night as it was Sunday and therefore a school night, so we decided to wait for Dad to go to bed and then get her on the phone after Zander snuck in. His friend, Conrad, would conference in, too.

In the meantime, I brought Ruthie up to speed. She was unusually quiet when I told her about Zander's attack in the woods and how I had healed him. Even though I tried to tone it down, it must have reminded her of her shark attack. I tried reassuring her, telling her that it wasn't just the two of us anymore. We also had Zander and Conrad. She perked up a little, suggesting that we start or own club or gang.

Much later, when I heard the tapping on my window, I hurried over to let Zander in. He climbed through and pulled me close. Without hesitation, I leaned into him. We both sighed. I didn't think I'd ever get used to that thrilling pulse we produced each time we touched.

"Man, you feel so good," breathed out Zander as he curved his mouth into my neck. "And taste so good! Like barbecue!"

I gasped in mock outrage as he nibbled my neck. It tickled, making me giggle and squirm. "Ha ha! That was yesterday." I pulled away to look at his face. "Hey, are you really hungry?" I asked, recalling his food complaints.

His eyes brightened as his eyebrows moved up and down suggestively. I giggled again, surprised by the girly sound I made. "I mean, do you want something to *eat.*"

He pretended to look crestfallen and admitted, "Yeah, I guess I could use some *food.*"

"Okay. Luckily Dad is a deep sleeper. But we'll have to be super quiet."

Zander crossed his heart. "Quiet as a mouse," he vowed.

We crept down the stairs with the stealth of navy seals and pilfered the kitchen for snacks, gathering an odd assortment of candy, popcorn, and apples. Zander carried everything but the chilled water bottles that I grabbed from the fridge.

He paused in my bedroom, perhaps considering where to drop our plunder. A mischievous impulse had me sneaking up to him and pressing a cold water bottle against his neck. He let out a muffled yelp, dropping the goods all over the carpet and twisting around so fast I let go of the bottle in surprise. But Zander's quick reflexes caught it. Then he moved even faster, using his super speed, picking me up and tossing me onto my bed and retaliated with a cold water bottle against my back where my shirt rode up.

"Stop!" I shriek-whispered, laughing at the same time. "You're going to wake up Dad!"

He straddled me, holding me down as the torture continued. "What's the magic word?" he taunted me.

"Please!" I yelped.

He laughed diabolically, the deep sound sending a thrill through me. "Oh, I think you can do better than that," he said. He kept moving the cold bottle to a new patch of warm skin, increasing the agony. I squirmed and thrashed.

"Seriously?" I huffed. He moved the bottle again. "Okay! *Pretty* please."

A second later the instrument of my torture was gone and so was Zander. I flipped over with a scowl only to see him across the room laughing so hard he seemed to be imploding.

"You bully!" I said. Determined to get even, I went into tackle mode. He dodged me, twisting toward the bed, but I captured him by the waist and pushed him down. He landed on the soft bedspread with me plastered across his chest. I lifted my head to see him grinning from ear to ear. I blinked, aware but not caring that I'd been outmaneuvered.

He rose up and pecked me on the lips. When his head

fell back, I followed, concluding that sometimes it was good to be the loser. His soft lips traced mine as if asking for permission before deepening our kiss. And that's when my brain stopped functioning altogether.

Moments later, Zander rolled me over and pulled away, breathing heavily. Tufts of his hair stuck up and his shirt bunched halfway up his torso, giving me a front row seat to his abs. I frowned as he smoothed down his shirt and ran a hand through his hair.

"Damn." One side of his mouth pulled up. "I think I got caught in my own web."

I leaned on my elbows, trying to steady my own breathing, trying to forget the awesomeness of that web.

He groaned and ran a hand down his face. "I promised to be a perfect gentleman in here and … errrrg!"

I felt my face heat up. What were we thinking? As much as I wanted to keep doing what we'd been doing, I was glad he'd stopped us. I wasn't ready for whatever that led to. I looked down at my skin playing peak-a-boo through my clothes. My hair had to be a jumbled mess, too. I left the bed and hurried to straighten myself.

Warm hands twirled me around and embraced me. My stomach did that flip-flop thing again, which was notably different than the "on fire" feeling I'd felt a moment ago.

"Why do you have to be so dang cute?" sighed Zander.

I smiled into his chest deciding right then to do whatever it took to keep his trust. I couldn't imagine my life without him in it.

Once the food was gathered up and pooled in the center of the bed, we surrounded our stash like children with

Halloween candy.

"Ready for Hurricane Ruthie?" I smiled.

"Good name for her," he said. "Should be interesting to see what Conrad thinks. He's a bit unconventional himself."

"Awesome!" I pulled out my phone. "I predict he and Ruthie will hit it off. Based, of course, on the phone call I overheard—you know, in my true dream that night I saw you talking to Conrad."

"*True dream.* Good name for it." Zander dialed his friend first.

"Hey, Zan my man!" A friendly voice spilled out of Zander's phone. "How are those California vibrations?" He started singing *Good Vibrations*. It reminded me of the delicious pulse that Zander and I felt when we touched. Oh my gosh! He must have told his friend. My face heated up.

"Conrad!" Zander hurried to cut off the singing, which only dimmed a little. He held his phone up to his mouth and cleared his throat. "I want to introduce you to some-one," he said.

Conrad stopped singing. He coughed and sputtered. "Am I on *speaker?*" he said in a hushed tone. "What did I tell you about—"

I laughed. "Hi Conrad," I called out. "It's good to meet you."

"Uh, hey Tru," said Conrad, his voice noticeably deeper.

"Yep. The one and only, thank goodness," I said, look-ing up at Zander's twinkling eyes.

"Nice to finally meet you," Conrad said formally.

"You, too." I made a terrified face at Zander and

pointed to my phone, indicating I would call Ruthie. He nodded with a grin.

Ruthie answered in her usual bubbly voice. "Hey girl!" I was glad she was back to normal. I introduced her to Conrad, feeling the need to say a little about her. I told him that if you mixed Sophia Loren with the witty Jack Black and the tai chi butt-kicking Jennifer from our favorite show *Court of Palms*, then you'd get my best friend, Ruthie. Ruthie chuckled in the background.

"Me likey ..." Conrad whispered. "Oops. Did I say that out loud? Rewind and erase."

"O. M. Gravy, Tru. It's like a phone mirror," Ruthie whispered.

I winked at Zander.

"You know what we are?" said Ruthie. She didn't wait for a response. "We're like the Scooby Doo Gang! Zander, you're Fred. I guess that makes Tru, Daphne. And I'm Velma because I'm helping you figure this out. Only I'm the better-dressed Velma. And exchange her glasses for my Prada sunglasses and I'm good." She laughed. "Conny, you get to be Shaggy! Now all we need is Scooby!"

"Hey!" griped Conrad. "I should be the smart one. I work with scrolls, woman! Give me some respect!" Then he added, "Wait. What did you call me?"

"But Shaggy is the center of the mysteries," said Ruthie, ignoring his question. "And he always seems to be the one who finds the real villain. If we had one of your were-wolfies, we would have a perfect Scooby!"

They argued about the characters for a few more minutes before we could lead them back to the real purpose of our meeting.

KAREN LYNN BENNETT

"Oh my gosh," gushed Ruthie in an over dramatized voice. "I can't believe Mrs. Jackson is dead. I mean I didn't know her or anything, but still. She was a teacher—"

"Or not," I inserted. "She may have been posing as a teacher."

"Right," said Zander. "I think it's too much of a co-incidence that she was murdered within a day of her suggesting to the entire class that vampires and werewolves exist, no matter how tongue-in-cheek she said it."

"Are you sure it was murder?" asked Conrad.

Zander felt that we had to assume so, especially after he was attacked by a usemi and an akharu. He certainly didn't believe that the culprit had been a mountain lion. There were supernaturals running around here, and their presence would have scared off other big predators. Someone had followed me and manipulated me into using my abilities. Mrs. Jackson's public comments may have brought her the wrong kind of attention.

"That means she wasn't working for the Collector," said Conrad. "And that means there's more than one person after Tru."

"That's what I think," agreed Zander with a scowl.

"Uhh," started Ruthie. "Maybe ..."

Suddenly I was afraid she'd blurt out what she knew about the Zander's father and I rushed to shut her up.

"Yeah," I interrupted, moving closer to my phone. "That makes sense."

I breathed a sigh of relief when Ruthie dropped it. Zander suggested that Ruthie and I shouldn't be alone anywhere, in case whatever attacked Mrs. Jackson took a swing at us.

"Duh," said Ruthie, sarcastically. "But kind of hard to do."

"Between Peter and me, we'll make sure you are safe," promised Zander.

"I'm not sure that's much better," said Ruthie. "Not after what he did to Tru."

"What did he do?" asked Conrad.

Ruthie happily filled him in, telling him in her colorful way how Peter had tried to erase my memories. Zander frowned throughout her dramatic description.

"And by the way, Z," said Ruthie. "Tru told me about this blessing thing you guys have going on and I have to say your people sound very sketchy. I go to church every Sunday, and believe me, your brother is the opposite of 'blessed.' Nobody can go around parading as 'the blessed' if they've attacked my girl!"

"I have to agree with her," said Conrad. "Peter isn't all right in the head these days."

Zander heaved a big sigh. "I know."

I didn't see any good coming out of rehashing Peter's unsavory qualities. "We don't have all night," I said. "We need to come up with a plan that doesn't involve me running away."

"If the Collector has a bunch of supernaturals working for him, how are you going to protect yourself?" asked Conrad. "Healing power may be amazing, but it's not going to fend off an attack."

We made a list of our assets, and as awesome as Zander's super strength and speed were, it didn't make him infallible. Yesterday's knife attack proved that. Ruthie, on the other hand, seemed awestruck to hear about Zander's superpowers. I could hear the envy in her voice and once again hoped that the "miracle" on the beach hadn't changed her in any way. We all agreed that my abilities were useless in a fight.

When it came to reconnaissance, Ruthie said she could try to come up with information on Zena and her family. Her mom handled their insurance and might know something useful. Conrad claimed the position of chief researcher. Maybe he could dig up more about the Blessing, as well as any sources for the sethian's ancient lore. I agreed that knowledge was ammunition, but frowned thinking that there wasn't enough actual action in our plans. Anxiety started eating away at my earlier happiness. Zander seemed to notice and reached for my hand. Despite our odds in this fight, his touch comforted me.

We racked our brains considering how we could evade the Collector permanently, but nothing seemed plausible. Zander said there had to be a way, that we just needed to think longer. After a long moment of silence, Ruthie gasped.

"Guys," she said. "I don't think we're looking at Tru's powers in the right way. I think she can do more than dream about past events."

"What are you talking about?" I asked.

"Tru," she said. Her voice was tinged with excitement. "You couldn't have aced your tests like you did most of last year in zombie mode—*unless* you have a super sensor. When I asked you how you did it, you said you picked the answers that felt right. I used to think you had some kind of ESP going on but you never seemed to hear me when I tried to speak to you with my mind."

I didn't know what to be more shocked about, the fact

that Ruthie believed I had some psychic power or that she tried to speak telepathically with me.

"So," said Conrad with awe in his voice. "Are you saying Tru is some kind of lie detector?"

I shook my head in denial but Ruthie kept going. "I think so. Maybe we can do a little supernatural true or false."

Zander raised his eyebrows and tilted up one side of his mouth as if to say, *we might as well try.*

"I don't know, guys," I hesitated. "I don't think I can say for sure if something is true just like that."

"Yes, you can, Tru." Ruthie's unwavering confidence in me almost made me a believer.

"Why don't we try it out?" asked Zander, cocking his head to the side and shrugging. "And as you think about the questions and answers, examine how you feel. Maybe you will notice a difference in a true and false answer."

"I've got a question for you, Tru," said Conrad. "Usemi always have multiple births. Are they twins, triplets, quadruplets, or any of those options?"

"What the freak?" yelped Ruthie. "They always have more than one child at a time? Like a litter?"

Zander and I chuckled.

"What's your answer, Tru?" asked Conrad.

"Zander already told me. They have twins."

"Oh yeah!" said Zander. He rubbed his chin and said, "How about this? My birthday is

"A: January twenty-first,

"B: July first, or

"C: September fifth."

I closed my eyes and ran through the possible answers in my mind. My temperature gauge wasn't going hot or cold, but it definitely felt warm when I said September fifth in my mind.

"September fifth?" I suggested, weakly.

"Dang! You got it, Tru," said Conrad.

"Oh no! We didn't do anything for you," whined Ruthie.

"It's okay," said Zander with a chuckle. "It was a long time ago."

"Uh. No, it wasn't," said Ruthie. "It's only been a few weeks."

Zander and I blinked at each other. It felt so long ago that he'd first shown up in our school.

"How did you do it, Tru?" asked Conrad.

I thought about it before answering. "Um. It's a temperature thing? I think I feel warm and kind of cozy when I think something is right. When it's false I feel cold and …" I tried to capture the feeling with a word. "Empty. I feel cool and little empty when it's false."

"Awesome! Here's another one," said Conrad excitedly. "How can you kill a usemi in wolf form?

"A. Shooting it with a silver bullet,

"B. Cutting off its head,

"C. Stabbing it in the heart,

"D. None of the above."

Again, I thought about each answer.

"None of the above?" I said with a surprise. Zander smiled. Conrad hooted in the background.

"But why?" I asked. "Do you mean they can't be killed?"

"Oh, they can be killed," said Zander. "But you answered correctly. Usemi have almost impenetrable skin. It's tough in human form, too, but not as strong. A regular bullet wouldn't work (the silver thing is a myth, by the way), and an ax or knife wouldn't get through either."

"But I thought Peter shot a usemi in Tru's backyard," exclaimed Ruthie.

"That was a special bullet," said Zander. "You could choke one, but they are super strong, so don't count on that. It's better to go for their weaknesses. They have some vulnerable areas, though, like their ears, mouth, eyes, and so on. You could stab them through the eye and penetrate their brain."

I made a face.

"Ew! Gross," said Ruthie.

Zander agreed.

"What's so special about Peter's bullets?" I asked.

"Well, the only things that can pierce usemi skin are the teeth of another usemi or akharu."

"Good gravy!" burst out Ruthie. "Are you saying that Peter's bullets are made from teeth?"

"Yes," said Zander.

I grimaced, but Zander just shrugged. "Okay, guys. So, what if I can spot a lie. It's not going to help against the Collector."

"Don't underestimate yourself," piped in Ruthie.

Zander nodded. "Knowing the truth can be a weapon," he said. "Or it could shield you."

"That reminds me," said Conrad. "Zander told me that you didn't believe the sethian lore he shared with you yesterday. And it's been bothering me all day. Now that we—"

Zander leaned forward, butting in. "Now that we know she's a human lie detector, are you suggesting that we test if our history is wrong?"

I sucked in a sudden breath. Now we were treading on thin ice. I didn't know if I wanted to talk about sethian lore because I was pretty sure Zander's father had made it all up. And the truth about Zander's father, that he was the very Collector we were trying to avoid, was something I didn't want to tell to him yet, fearing that it would change the way he felt about me.

"Exactly," said Conrad.

"I didn't hear about any sethian lore," said Ruthie. Conrad was only too delighted to share it and he wanted to start at the beginning, with Cain and Abel.

"But explain it in pieces," said Zander. "So Tru can tell us if she thinks it's false."

I bit my lip, already knowing I'd be getting a lot of cold and empty vibes. But I nodded anyway.

Conrad's story-telling skills were much better than Zander's. And Ruthie's gasps and sputters lent a somewhat comical background to the scene, forcing me to concentrate harder to discern the telltale signals that Zander was looking for. When he got to Cain being cursed and changing into a blood-sucking akharu an icy chill ran along my skin.

When I shook my head, Zander told Conrad and Ruthie it wasn't true.

"Oh, come on!" complained Conrad loudly. "Some of this has to be true. I mean our whole society is centered around this stuff."

"Wow, Conny!" gushed Ruthie. "The story is riveting. Seriously, this would make a great book!"

Conrad was so disturbed to learn the stories weren't true he didn't even comment on Ruthie's nickname.

"What about the curse stuff? Someone better damn well have been cursed!" he muttered.

I thought about the idea of a cursed akharu and how the curse could be passed on to family members. I felt a warmer tingle.

"Wait!" I said. "I think the curse is real, or kind of. I don't know. It just doesn't feel wrong."

"That's a start," said Zander, clenching his hands together. "Let's keep going. Ruthie and Conrad, make sure you are writing this down."

"You know it!" said Ruthie.

"Let's talk about the curses," started Zander. "Are usemi cursed?"

Coolness. "No, I don't think so."

"Are akharu cursed?"

I paused longer. I strange mixture of cold and warm swirled up my back. I pressed my hands into my eyes. No, I couldn't tell.

"I don't know. Part of me thinks so, and part of me doesn't."

"Maybe some akharu are cursed and some aren't," suggested Ruthie.

The coolness fled and warmth spread through my chest.

"That's it! I think some akharu are cursed."

"What about sethians?" asked Ruthie.

"Why us?" said Conrad. "We don't have any funky shape-shifting, blood-sucking limitations. We're the ones in charge."

But I was already thinking about the sethians. The heat around my heart tingled and spread like a million warm bubbles, warming me everywhere, from the tips of my fingers to my toes. Were the sethians cursed? Yes!

Zander saw my expression of wonder and his eyes widened. "Actually, Ruthie asked a good question," he said. Conrad made a strangled cry.

As much as I hated to say it, that was exactly what my hot and cold sensors were telling me. "I think sethians *are* cursed. Sorry," I said.

After a prolonged silence, a despondent whisper floated out from Zander's phone. "I'm cursed?"

"Wait, guys. What does 'cursed' even mean?" asked Ruthie. "Maybe it isn't so bad."

Zander looked at me. I was starting to feel anxious. My sethian acquaintances included Conrad, Zander and his brother—and the Collector in a roundabout way. I had a pretty good idea who in that group might belong to the cursed category.

"I don't know," I said. "Maybe."

"Well, if we get to vote, I vote that Zander's jerk face brother is cursed," said Ruthie.

Zander scowled but didn't comment.

"I-I think we need more information," I said. "Before we get too upset about this cursed stuff."

The silence coming from Conrad spoke volumes. His head must have been spinning. I wondered if now was the right time to tell Zander about his father, about him being the Collector, Dante's boss.

"You're right," said Zander. "I say we let Conrad try and dig up something to support these ideas before deciding what to do with them." His face was pinched, like he was thinking too hard. I decided I couldn't accuse his father in front of Ruthie and Conrad. It could wait until he trusted me better.

"So, tell me something else about the original races," I said, unwrapping a chocolate and taking a little bite.

Zander stretched out his long legs, rolling onto his back with his arms behind his head. "I've never seen an akharu attack someone for blood, but I know they like human blood most of all, which is how we get the vampire myth."

He glanced at me.

"What does Tru think?" asked Ruthie.

"I'm getting both feelings again, like it's both true and false."

Conrad finally came back to life. "This is so strange, but if you think about it, it's brilliant. If you are going to tell a lie, it goes down better mixed with a little truth, doesn't it? It's an interesting hypothesis anyway. I need to find out how these stories started."

Ruthie cleared her voice, butting into Conrad's verbal musings. I was glad because I didn't think Zander was ready to reach the conclusion that his friend would inevitably make—that Gerard Hughes, Zander's father, was smack dab in the middle of all the lies.

"How about the sunlight? Can akharu be in the sun?" asked Ruthie.

Zander explained that akharu could handle the sun, but that they preferred shadier areas or times of day with muted or no light. Their camouflaging abilities made them almost invisible under those circumstances. Both akharu and usemi could see in the dark, like me. That was no surprise, considering that I must be idimmu, which meant there must be one of them on my family tree somewhere.

"Akharu and usemi also had a heightened sense of

smell and taste," added Zander.

"Are they being straight with us, Tru?" asked Ruthie, her voice shrill through the phone. "Because if they are joking, I'm hunting down Conny in that crypt he lives in and teaching him a lesson."

"Bring it girl!" challenged Conrad with a chuckle. "Besides, Tru just had a close encounter with one."

"As far as I can tell, it's all true, Ruthie," I admitted. "I didn't see it very well—the akharu thing was creepy—but even so, it feels like the truth."

"Wait a meatloaf minute!" said Ruthie. "I just thought of something. Are usemi and akharu born or made by biting humans? Because it just occurred to me that these werewolves and vamps have children like humans. But we know Tru's aunt was turned with a bite. Now I'm confused."

"First of all," said Conrad with a long sigh. "They are not werewolves and vampires. So, stop calling them that."

I rolled my eyes. Ruthie knew they weren't vampires and werewolves. She just liked calling them that. Then Conrad explained that normally sethian, akharu, and usemi procreated and bore children like humans, but not as often. However, in Aunt Caroline's case, the aramusatu bond must have had something to do with her change. That type of bond was not understood very well, but it was the only thing that made sense.

There was an almost reverence in the air whenever he or Zander talked about the bond, like mystical awe. Conrad said that sethians made up all sorts of fairytale-like gibberish about the power of the aramusatu and all that it could do, but few believed it was anything more than fanciful thinking. He theorized that my aunt could be the evidence needed to prove that some of the old legends were true.

"You forgot to tell us how akharu can be killed," said Ruthie. "Do they have tough skin like usemi?"

"No," said Conrad. "But they can regrow their limbs and bones."

"Holy Haggis!"

"I doubt you'll ever be up against one," said Zander. "But if you are, aim for their eyes before they spray you or touch you."

"Oh, that's so gross! They're like skunks!" said Ruthie. "You never said they shoot their trippy oil! Do they kill their victims?"

"Not necessarily," said Conrad. "In fact, you may end up believing you've just had the best kiss of your life!"

Something that Zander had said earlier was nagging me in the back of my mind. "So, are all akharu blood drinkers?" I asked, even though as I said it, something in me denied it. "Do they need blood to survive?"

Zander said, "As far as I know. Why?"

"Because I don't think so. I mean, what about some of them being cursed and some not? Couldn't that mean that there are good ones out there? Maybe some who don't drink blood? Human blood, at least."

"Really, Tru?" scoffed Ruthie. "Are you going all Twilight on us?"

"No," I denied. "I just don't think every akharu is bad. At least that's what I feel."

"At this point," sighed Conrad. "Anything is possible." Disappointment drifted out of Zander's phone in waves.

"Well," I said. "Not all humans are good or bad."

"And therefore, there could be good and bad akharu, too," finished Zander.

"Yeah." I sighed. "Just saying."

"You know, Tru," said Ruthie. "If their brother-killing-brother story isn't true, why does it sound like that dream you had before school started?"

Zander stiffened.

"She's right," I said, remembering. "I dreamed about something similar. It didn't have anything to do with the bible story though."

"What did you dream?" asked Zander.

"Well, in my dream a dark-haired man—"

Ruthie cut me off. "His hair was braided, like in *The Last of the Mohicans.*"

"—Anyway," I continued. "He reeked of evil. I didn't see him kill the other man, who by the way didn't look anything like his brother at all. Anyway, this woman ran up to the dead guy upset and crying while the evil-looking man ran to the edge of this weird-looking forest. The trees had long floppy branches with long drippy leaves and these pretty blue flowers hung from them. Have you ever heard of such a tree?"

I didn't wait for anyone to answer. "The woman was super ticked off when she saw the evil guy running away. She yelled at him saying something I don't remember. He looked at her, kind of smiling like a psychopath, you know? But when he saw her pointing her finger toward him, he ran off through the strange forest."

"That's it?" asked Zander.

"Yes, that's all of it, I think. So, you see, it was similar with two guys and a girl and one guy killing the other, but none of the other stuff Conrad talked about. My dream seems real, but his story doesn't."

"Oh no!" whispered Ruthie through my phone. "Someone's coming down the hall. Mom is probably checking on me. Sorry guys, I need to pretend I'm asleep or I'm in big trouble! Don't talk about any cool stuff without me!! Please!"

Then my phone went silent and she was gone.

"I guess that's a wrap for tonight," said Conrad. "It's late, anyway. And I've got a lot to think about. A lot to research." He muttered something about his stinking curse before hanging up.

Zander stood up, pocketing his phone. "I should get going, too." His brows knitted together with a scowl.

I followed him across the room. Before he stepped through the window, his tense shoulders loosened. When he swiveled around and leaned against the window frame, his expression had smoothed into one of wonder.

"Tru, that dream thing of yours. Well, it's pretty amazing."

"Not if you want to sleep." I gave him a self-deprecating smile.

"Ruthie is right, you know. You don't give yourself enough credit," he said in a low voice. "I think that being a human lie-detector is an amazing ability. It's certainly going to keep me on my toes." He smiled and tipped my chin up with one hand. I sighed as he pulled me closer to rest his cheek against mine.

Tonight's meeting had been illuminating, but I was left with a sense of hopelessness. Despite all the fiction we'd uncovered, one overriding fact remained: we still had no idea how we were going to fend off the Collector.

16

RED-HANDED

MONDAY MORNING, I KNEW something was wrong as soon as I walked into the kitchen. Dad stood in the middle of the room, his hands on his hips and scowling. What now? My stomach clenched. Had he somehow found out about Zander being in my bedroom last night?

"What's wrong?" I asked.

He pressed his lips together, staring at me like he'd never seen me before. Then with a grunt of disappointment, he ran his hands through his hair and pointed to the kitchen table. "Sit."

With robotic movements, I settled into the nearest chair, burying my nervous hands under my bottom.

Dad lowered himself into the chair across from me.

"Tru, I received a surprising phone call this morning. Can you guess who it might have been from?"

With a loud swallow, I said, "No." Who tipped him

off? Did a neighbor see Zander leave?

Dad shook his head. "Tru, I think I've been too lenient with you since your mother ..." He broke off, unable to finish his sentence. "But not anymore," he rallied.

Oh no! Would he keep me from Zander? My stomach started twisting and sweat broke out across my forehead.

"For heaven's sake, Tru, the *police* called this morning!" His hand slammed down on the table and I jumped, not used to him acting like this. He took a deep breath.

"Can you imagine how I might feel knowing that you were in danger? That you didn't bother to mention it to me?"

I looked down, wondering what he knew. Did this have anything to do with Mrs. Jackson's death? Or what about Dante? Wait, it could be Ruthie's shark attack or ... Man! There was too much crap going on. But who would say anything to the police? A name slipped out of my mouth. "Bobby?"

"Yes, Bobby. His grandmother called the police!" Dad looked like he wanted to tear out what little hair he had left.

"But nothing happened!" I insisted, pulling my hands out from under me and spreading them innocently.

"Would you have told me if something had happened?" I saw frustration and worry in his bloodshot eyes.

I didn't know if he would believe me, but I said it anyway. "Nothing happened."

Man, I was getting good at lying, or so I thought.

Dad's eyes narrowed. "Then explain to me what did happen."

"Okay," I said with gulp. "Just to make sure we're on

the same page, you are referring to the day Bobby's friend gave me a ride home from school, right?" I cringed, realizing that I just made it worse.

Dad's face couldn't have looked graver. "Do I need to be concerned about more than one incident?"

"No!" I panicked. "I'm just wondering what you know already."

"Why don't you tell me everything *you* know," Dad said. He folded his arms as if to say I wasn't moving another muscle until I'd explained everything to his satisfaction.

What had I told Bobby? Our stories had to match. I stared at the table, thinking at a frantic pace.

"This guy at school, Dante, he's a friend of Bobby's, or was a friend. Anyway, I know I should have waited for Ruthie after school that day like you told me to, but I just wanted to get home. And they offered me a ride— Shrina, too, although they dropped her off before anything happened."

Dad almost came out of his seat.

"But nothing like you are imagining happened, I promise!" It was the most truthful thing I had said so far. I could guarantee Dad would never imagine what really happened. He gritted his teeth and signaled me to continue.

"So, after they dropped Shrina off, Dante decided to do some Vulcan shoulder pinch on Bobby and it worked. Bobby passed out cold. I was freaked out, yes, and worried. But mostly I was mad because Bobby's been through a lot of crap with his parents dying." I paused, getting ready to tell him the biggest lie. "Yeah, I just, I don't know, I got all mad at Dante and then he did the same thing to me! The next thing I knew, I was waking up at home, on the back porch."

Every line on Dad's weathered face stood out as he scowled. Then he made me go over everything again and describe how Dante had "knocked me out." I tried to keep it vague, because I didn't know anything about how it might work or if it was even possible. Finally, Dad relented. I don't think he bought my entire explanation, but at least he stopped interrogating me.

I looked at the clock. It was way late. Ruthie should have arrived already. I was surprised she hadn't honked. "I have to go to school, Dad. Ruthie is probably waiting for me outside."

"No, she's not." He continued to scowl. "I called her mother and explained that you are not going to school today."

"What? I can't miss school. I have a quiz today." It was a desperate attempt, admittedly, but I was desperate. I hated lying to him.

"You'll live. Today we are going to the police station and you will tell them everything you told me. And then you will describe this Dante person so they can hunt down his ass and find out what kind of psychopath he is. After that, I am installing a security system. And then ... we are going to get a dog."

With each word that came out of his mouth, I deflated like a leaky tire. It had been a long time since I'd seen him so angry, and it scared me. Imaginary bars were going up on all of our windows and shackles on my feet. I would never be allowed out of the house again. Wait a second, did he say ...

"Dog?" I yelped. I had always wanted one. My parents

would never get one before because Mom was allergic. How ironic that her own sister was a wolf! My mind splintered, wondering if she would have been allergic to Aunt Caroline. I shook my head. Yes, I'd always wanted a dog, but Dad sounded like he was going to get a guard dog, one that wouldn't let me leave my new prison.

"Yes, a dog. You should be happy. You are finally getting a dog." He still sounded angry, but he softened his words with the smallest of smiles. "You used to talk my ear off about getting one."

"But when can I go back to school?" I asked, thinking of Zander.

He frowned, and his eyes narrowed suspiciously. "Not today. Maybe tomorrow. Let's see what the police have to say."

Zander was going to be so worried.

"Can I call Ruthie? I bet she's freaking out."

"Yes. Make it fast. Then grab something to eat and let's go," he ordered. His voice was so gruff it sent tremors of unease through my shoulders. The thought of food right now made me queasy. But I just nodded my head and returned to my room to make my calls.

Ruthie had already texted: "What the halibut? Did you ditch me again? Do you need a rescue? Call me!"

I zipped off a quick reply to Ruthie telling her I was okay and I'd fill her in soon. Then I called Zander.

"Running late?" he asked, somehow sounding super sexy with just two words.

"I'm not coming to school today." I tried to keep my voice low so Dad wouldn't overhear.

"Why are you whispering?" Edgy concern had entered his voice. It was still sexy. "Is anything wrong?"

My stomach knotted. "Yes. Bobby told his grandma about Dante and she called the police, who called my dad, and now he's about to turn our house into a prison!"

"That's not good." Although he kept his voice level, it was laced with suspicion.

"No. It's super bad! And I'm whispering because he might be trying to listen in." I talked so fast, my words ran together. "Anyway, he made me tell him every little detail about that day with Dante, which of course I couldn't tell him, so I lied. I hate lying to him! He's taking me to the police station to repeat my story, and now I'm hoping that Vulcan neck pinch thingy is for real. I think I told Bobby that's what happened. I don't know if I can remember it right!" I picked up a pencil from my desk and snapped it in half, imagining it was Bobby.

"Tru, it's going to be okay," he said in a soothing voice. "We'll figure this out. Your dad is worried about you, that's all."

"I know, but how are we going to be a-a Scooby Gang if I-I can't ever leave my house!" I was becoming hysterical.

Zander chuckled. "I think you are channeling Hurricane Ruthie right now."

I cracked the smallest smile, but forced it into a frown, refusing to find the situation funny when my world was spiraling out of control.

"I am seriously upset, Zander." I needed him to commiserate with me, not crack jokes.

"I know you are. It's going to be okay, Tru. And for the record, it is possible to knock someone out if you apply pressure to specific points around the neck. But I doubt Spock did it right."

"I knew it! I should have said something else."

"No, it's okay. Be vague. Besides, you already told Bobby that's what happened and he probably told them." He paused. "When do you think you can come back to school?"

"Dad said maybe tomorrow. It depends on what the police say. He said I have to describe Dante so they can find him. But Bobby can describe him, so why do they need me? You and I both know they are never going to find him." My heart stopped with a new thought. "Wait! Is it possible they'll find him?"

Peter, Zander's brother, was supposed to have taken care of Dante's body. What if he buried him in a shallow grave in the forest? Dumped him into the ocean so that he washed up on shore? Left him behind a dumpster like Mrs. Jackson?

I was stressing about hiding a dead body, the body of someone I killed. Who had I become? I dropped my phone and leaned over, trying to take in deep breaths as black spots started appearing in front of me. Everything that had happened to me was suddenly too much to handle. And now I was having a real panic attack.

"Tru, let's get going," Dad called from the hallway. I couldn't answer. I could barely breathe. Zander's anxious voice called to me from my phone. I wondered if he was feeling what I felt, like he had the night Dante dumped me in the cellar and I busted my ankle. I had to calm down, for Zander.

My eyes bounced around the room landing on the beanbag chair. I thought about how cute and clumsy he'd been when he'd tried to get out of it. I thought about the sweet way Zander had apologized after we argued. I thought about the warm feeling that overcame me every time we touched. The black dots began to recede.

"Tru?" Dad stepped into the room. "Honey? Are you all right?"

I could only nod my head. As I slowed my breathing, I realized that I was curled up on the floor in a fetal position. I didn't recall dropping down. I had just enough mental clarity to reach over and end my call with Zander.

Dad kneeled down and patted my back. When I could finally talk, I said, "I'm okay now. It's just the thought of going to the police ... it made it seem so serious ... I couldn't breathe for a second. Please, don't make me talk to the police!"

Dad stood, pulling me up and wrapping his arms around me. I hugged him, breathing in his Dad smell, which evoked memory after memory of him being there for me. I started to feel a little better.

"It *is* serious, Tru. You could have been in real danger. This boy is bad news. He needs to be stopped before something more serious happens. What if he does something worse and you didn't say anything?"

If he only knew, I thought. He stepped back, looking me directly in the eyes. "Sweetheart," he said gently. "I will be with you every second, I promise."

I didn't fail to notice that he was using my own tactic. Direct eye contact did it every time. How could I refuse when he put it that way or when he looked at me with his soft brown eyes and wrinkled face? Once again, I noticed the folds of loose skin around his neck, the age spots on his hands, and the stress around his eyes.

"Okay. Can I have a few more minutes to finish getting ready?" I asked. He raised an eyebrow. He could tell

I was stalling, but I held his gaze, pleading.

"Okay," he relented. "But make it quick. I've got a lot to do before I'm getting any sleep tonight."

Zander surprised me by picking up on the first ring. He should have been in class, so either he was skipping or his teacher was pretty cool. I didn't even know his first class. Weird. We needed to have normal conversations, about schedules and movies, not about usemi and akharu and all the other unbelievable things that were now my reality.

"What happened? I couldn't breathe!" he said, answering my earlier question.

"I'm okay. I just had a little panic attack. I'm sorry."

"Sorry? It's not your fault. Are you sure everything is okay? Because I can be there in five minutes. I'm halfway there already."

"What? No! I'm fine, really. I'm about to leave to go to the police station with Dad. Everything kind of hit me all at once. And I'm worried Peter didn't take care of Dante well enough. What if the police find him?"

"You don't have to worry about that. He's nothing but a pile of ashes now and they are probably scattered over the ocean."

Poor Dante. Was there no one to mourn him?

"Are you sure I shouldn't come over?" Zander's voice became strained again.

"No. That's a terrible idea. Sorry, but I'll be fine. I'm just not looking forward to being grilled by the cops."

"You can handle it. And I'll stay close by."

"Aren't you going back to school?"

"Tru," he said, his voice deepening. "I only go to school to be near you."

I choked up. It was one of the nicest things anyone had ever said to me. And it made me feel dizzy with happiness in the middle of this nightmare. Did Zander love me? Did I love him? My heartbeat sped up at the thought.

"Okay," I said, my voice a little breathy. I didn't know what to say. I wasn't ready to have this conversation now. Why was he saying this? Maybe he was trying to distract me from what I was about to do. If so, then it had worked.

The floorboards creaked downstairs. Buzzkill. Dad must be pacing. He wouldn't wait forever, and I needed to call Ruthie before Dad hustled me out of here.

"I have to go," I said. "Don't let my dad see you. He may notice you if you're following us. He's extra suspicious right now. And I would like the first time you meet my dad to be a happy moment."

"Why Tru Parker, are you saying you want to introduce me to the family already?" I heard the smile in his voice and imagined how he'd look.

I chuckled. "No, Goober! I just don't want to taint his impression of you with all this Dante stuff going on. He's going to be extra cautious now and I want him to like you so you can come visit me without him pulling a gun on you!"

"Well, hot damn! That's a declaration if I ever heard one." Zander's chuckle vibrated through the line, and a tingle of happiness zipped up my spine. After a slight pause, he added, "Tru Lee Parker, will you … go to Homecoming with me?"

I grinned, biting my lips to try and keep my happy smile from splitting my face in half.

"It's a date!" I agreed.

"Awesome. Now when is this shindig exactly?"

I laughed. "Hope you brought your tux," I said.

"TRU!" Dad bellowed up the stairs.

"I gotta go! Bye!" I ended the call on Zander's laughter and I tried not to smile as I rushed out of my room. Dad would worry I was bipolar if I came down laughing after that panic attack.

17

ACCOMPLICE

THE POLICE STATION WASN'T like anything I would have imagined. Near the entrance, a circular driveway with lush green landscaping separated the building from an ordinary parking lot. A bowl-shaped water fountain with an abstract art design stood in the center of the grassy area. The building wasn't just the police station. It acted as City Hall, too, which might explain the beautiful landscaping.

As we headed to the police department on the first floor, I was surprised by the lack of criminals being manhandled in handcuffs like I expected from my tv experience. Were it not for a couple of uniformed policemen heading out, it could have been mistaken for any other business. In fact, the reception area looked like a hotel lobby.

We approached the sleek-looking front desk where a

woman wearing a brown pantsuit was speaking into a phone. She had a pen sticking out of her gray-brown hair, which was pulled tight into in a bun at the base of her neck.

I thought maybe this wouldn't be so difficult after all, until I spotted Bobby sitting alone in a chair across from a desk, his shoulders hunched. He noticed me and started to get up, but a man with a badge pressed down on his shoulder and my friend slumped back into his seat with a scowl.

I nudged Dad. "That's Bobby over there. Is he in trouble?"

Dad glanced over, pursing his lips. "I don't know, Tru. But if he didn't do anything wrong, he has nothing to worry about. And neither do you."

If. I could almost feel myself shrinking with guilt. Bobby had wanted to go to the police earlier, but I had talked him out of it. I wondered what had changed his mind.

"Can I talk with him?" I asked.

Dad scowled. "Not yet. Officer Winchester is expecting us."

"Is Officer Winchester packing?" I asked in a stage whisper, desperate to lighten his mood.

Dad cracked a smile. "Probably. So, behave." He pulled me up next to him with his arm around my shoulders.

The woman behind the desk finally looked at us. "Can I put you on hold for a moment?" she said to the person on the phone before replacing it in its receiver. "May I help you?" she said, looking at us.

"Yes, we have an appointment with Officer

Winchester," replied Dad.

She looked down at her computer monitor and typed into the keyboard. "Are you Mr. Parker?" she asked briskly in a no-nonsense kind of voice.

"Yes. And this is my daughter, Tru."

She gave me a once over and nodded to herself. "Ah, yes," she said. I imagined that she could see guilt written all over my face and my cheeks warmed with embarrassment. "For a new guy, he sure got busy fast," she mumbled under her breath. Then she picked up the phone and punched a button.

"Mr. Parker and his daughter to see you, sir," she said. She pressed another button and looked at us. "He'll be with you in a moment. Please have a seat."

We headed toward a lobby sofa, but before we could sit down, a short, balding man stepped around the wall, offering his hand to Dad. Although he had little hair on his head, the back of his hand had a black thatch that was unusually long and wiry. I tried not to cringe.

"Mr. Parker. Thank you for coming in." Then he extended his hairy hand to me. "You must be Tru. I'm Detective Winchester." He gave me a toothy smile.

Detective? Yikes. No wonder Bobby was upset. What had he told them? Reluctantly, I shook his hand. It almost crushed mine and I winced. Then he guided us around the wall toward a desk directly across the room from Bobby, who followed our progress with a strained twist of his neck. I wondered if he was still mad at me. A sour-faced, elderly woman that I guessed was his grandmother sat down next to him.

Detective Winchester passed by the desk that I thought we were headed toward, instead leading us down a hallway lit by humming fluorescent lights to another room. A table with chairs took up most of the space. Bolts secured the table to the floor and a metal loop stuck up out of the center. I caught my breath, a sick feeling twisting my insides. Pausing just inside the doorway, I thought about making a run for it.

Dad looked surprised. "Is it necessary to bring us into this room?"

Behind the detective I could see the only window. But it was impossible to see through its dark, reflective surface. I gulped. This looked just like the interrogation rooms on tv. I took a step backward.

"Tru," said the detective, his hands open wide, and his voice cajoling. "Surely you don't mind talking here. It offers more privacy, that's all. It's just you, your dad, and me. No one else is watching or listening to us. I promise."

Dad scowled at the man, but beckoned me in. I shook my head. He came closer and whispered, "Look Tru, I know this is a little intimidating, but he just wants your statement. Then he might bring in someone who will ask you to describe Dante so they can sketch his picture. After that, we'll be done."

"Actually," said the detective, jolting us. We were surprised that he'd heard us. "There's no need for the description," he said. "The other kid had a picture of him on his phone."

That was one less thing I had to do here, but it still didn't chase away the chill I felt. Something was off with this detective, like he didn't fit in here. But the badge attached to his belt qualified him. Maybe it was me. I didn't belong here. Then again, maybe I did. I had killed someone.

"I don't like this room," I said in a hoarse voice. I cleared my throat. "I want to talk out there by Bobby."

"Come on, kiddo," prodded Dad. "Let's just play along and get this over. Please."

Dad rarely said please. I grabbed his hand and walked in with him, hip to hip.

We sat close together on one side of the table while the detective seated himself across from us. He pulled a phone out of his coat pocket, tapped it a few times and set it on the table to record our conversation.

"Just so I don't write your comments down wrong, that's all," he excused himself with a smile.

But his smile did nothing to ease the flutters of panic that threatened to take over.

He announced the date for the recording and turned his full attention on me. "All right Ms. Parker, I need you to tell me what happened after school last Monday."

I tried to stick to the same story I told Dad, shrugging off the Vulcan pinch idea like it was my best guess.

The cold metal chair sucked all the warmth from my body, and I rubbed my arms as I waited for the detective to respond to what I'd said. Silence stretched as his black eyes bore into me like dark lasers. I leaned closer to Dad.

"Vulcan neck pinch, huh?" Detective Winchester finally replied. "That's a new one. Sure you don't want to change your story?" His obvious skepticism made my face redden.

Dad cleared his throat and the detective's eyes shot toward him, narrowing.

"Okay," he gave in, leaning back in his seat. Dad nodded with approval. "What about Dante's car, Ms.

Parker. Can you describe it to me?"

I shrugged. "It was a Blue Suburu WRX, STI, I think. Leather trimmed upholstery."

The detective's eyebrows shot up. "That's very specific." He leaned forward again, giving me another toothy grin. "How did you know it was an STI?"

I looked at Dad and rolled my eyes when he gave me a proud smile. I shrugged. "I could tell by the wheels and the instrument panel."

With the same stupid look plastered on his face, the detective asked me about Dante's behavior before he'd knocked us out. He asked where I had woken up. And then he asked if I had noticed any sign of sexual assault. That was the question I was afraid he would ask, and it was just as awkward as I'd expected.

"No. I don't think he touched me like that."

"How do you know?" asked the detective.

"I think I would be able to tell." I glared at him.

"I'm sorry, but we have to ask. And just to be on the safe side, I recommend that you see a doctor." While Dad looked at me with worry again, I caught the detective's mischievous smile. He was messing with my dad on purpose.

"Dad, I swear, nothing like that happened," I said. He responded with an unsure stare.

Then the detective spoke again, his deep voice patronizing this time. "Now I want to go back to the car, when you saw Dante pinch Bobby's shoulder. Could you demonstrate for me?" He pursed his lips, looking smug.

I blanched. I had to re-enact the Vulcan move on someone? I shook my head. "I don't think I can. I wasn't paying attention that well when he did it. It took me a little while to figure out that Bobby was unconscious."

The detective persisted, his eyes even more beady than before. "Yet you assumed Dante was responsible for Bobby's state of unconsciousness, and you became angry with Dante. Perhaps you two argued?"

"No!" I blinked frantically.

"You said you were angry with Dante on behalf of your friend Bobby. How did you show your anger? How did he respond? Did he pull the car over? Did he apply this 'trick' to you while he was driving, while you were in the back seat?"

The tone of his voice told me he didn't believe a word I'd said. "What really happened, Ms. Parker?" He leaned across the table toward me and I edged closer to Dad again.

"Detective, why don't you ease off for a minute. I don't like what you are insinuating," said Dad as he angled his shoulder in front of me. I was only too happy to move behind him.

Insinuating? Was the detective implying that I had something to do with Bobby finding himself unconscious in the park?

I heard a chair scrape, and peeked around Dad's shoulder. The detective was leaning back in his chair, once again spreading his hands wide, his palms up and out on either side of his body. "Mr. Parker. Frankly, I find it extremely suspicious that your daughter was the last person to see Dante, and yet she has no idea where he is. Also, there was no one to witness that anything happened to her at all."

What? Now I wasn't just frightened, I was angry, too. Angry with Bobby for putting me in this position. Angry with myself for allowing things to get so stupid and complicated. And angry with the detective for going all "bad cop" on me. I knew he was trying to get me to screw up my story and say something self-incriminating. But if the police ever found out how Dante had really disappeared ... well, I didn't think Dad would survive that. And it would put a giant bull's-eye on me, making it that much easier for the Collector to find me.

I stood up almost knocking my chair over. "You're acting like I did something wrong!"

Dad leaped up, pulling me close to him. The detective smiled darkly. "Did you?" he asked, his voice patronizing.

I glared.

"Come now, Ms. Parker," he said. "I just want to find Dante. Tell me where he is and you can leave. I promise."

"I said, I don't know!" I yelled. Dad squeezed my arm.

The detective shook his head with disappointment and looked at Dad. "Mr. Parker, you wouldn't be the first father to be fooled by his teenage daughter. We found Dante's *stolen* car." He leaned heavily on the word "stolen," lifting an eyebrow my way before continuing. "We found it in Salinas, abandoned in a farm field. Your daughter just described it better than most girls know their own vehicles, let alone one they rode in only once." His hands gripped the edge of the table.

Dad glared at the detective. I knew how furious he was by the utter stiffness of his body as he steered me out of the room. My detailed description of Dante's car didn't rouse his suspicion at all. He had starting teaching me about cars when I was in Kindergarten, so I noticed details about most vehicles. I knew he believed me.

Dad left me in the hall for a moment while he returned to the room and spoke in a low, calm voice, perhaps hoping I wouldn't hear, but I did. "I came here hoping to protect my daughter and any other kid out there who might be threatened by this lunatic, and you have the nerve to accuse her of being involved."

"Mr. Parker, you may or may not have heard, but a school employee was killed. This lunatic, as you call him, may have been involved."

"That was an animal attack," Dad retorted.

"Not all the details were made public."

That didn't go over well with Dad. "We're done here," he said in an icy voice.

We headed down the hall to the open room with all the desks. Bobby and his grandmother were gone. Dad marched me out without even saying goodbye to the receptionist. As he opened my car door to help me in, I saw Zander across the street in front of a restaurant. I was too far away to see his expression, but I knew he must be worried. Before Dad got in the car, I typed Zander a quick text.

They acted like I was lying about the whole thing!

Sure, technically I was, but I sure as hell hadn't been Dante's accomplice.

18

WHAT THE SHRINK?

THE DAY WASN'T EVEN half over before a shiny new number pad decorated the wall of our entry hall. Dad had a friend in the home security business who expedited the installation of the new alarm system. Tomorrow the installers would return to take care of the windows.

Dad called in more than one favor. He also had a buddy who worked at the Santa Cruz police department's K-9 unit. They had a retired police dog who needed a home. They said he'd be great for home security.

I texted fast and furiously with my friends. The news of our trip to the police station had already saturated the student body. To make matters worse, the homeroom teachers announced that the police were looking for Dante and asked the students to pass any information about him to the office or the school counselor. Rumors were flying about Dante's possible crimes, including the death of Mrs. Jackson. And since Bobby and "yours truly" were MIA at school, we were also at the heart of the gossip. Even Isaac had been peppering me with questions.

I tried my best to quell Ruthie and Isaac's concerns while Zander told me everything would be all right. He seemed to think everything would die down if we ignored the gossip. His strategy didn't sound promising to me. I'd barely made it through a miserable year of being called "zombie girl" and I knew that the names "accomplice" or "murderer" would be so much worse.

But while the idea of going to school made me sick, the thought of being cooped up at home like a prisoner and not seeing Zander sent me into a full sweat panic. When we planned to meet again tonight with our new gang, I felt a little lighter.

Ruthie texted to say she would drop off homework after school. She'd told her mother a little of what had happened and so, of course, Mrs. Robles called Dad. She'd been keeping tabs on us since Mom died and often dropped off meals and desserts. At some point during the conversations between Ruthie, her mom, and my dad, it was decided that Ruthie could spend the night, even though it was a school night. Pretty rare. Dad must have told Mrs. Robles how pathetic and traumatized I was. It occurred to me that Dad might have allowed the sleepover because of the dinner the Robles were bringing, but as it turned out he was just softening me up for the bomb he delivered later.

"Oh, by the way. I talked to your principal today." Dad concentrated on wiping down the countertops in the kitchen, which should have tipped me off that I wasn't going to like what he had to say. Cleaning the kitchen had become my job lately, so his sudden need to sanitize everything triggered alarm bells in my head.

"What for?"

"Well, he wanted me to know that the school is on alert for any reappearance of that boy, Dante, so there's that for starters." Thanks to Ruthie that wasn't news to me and I gave him my "yeah, so what" look.

But it was lost on him as he continued to avoid my gaze by scrubbing the already immaculate table surface. After a long pause he cleared his throat and said, "Then he set a time for the school counselor to talk to us—"

"What? Why?" Was he freaking kidding me? I'd told him a million times I'd never do that.

"Tru, this wasn't my idea." He threw the washcloth into the sink and braced his hands on his hips.

"I told you I didn't want to see a shrink!" No way was I going to do the couch talk thing.

"I didn't say she was a *shrink*. She's a school counselor, for Pete's sake. That's different. And this is standard protocol for students dealing with violent trauma."

"There wasn't any violent trauma!" I flung my hands out in exasperation.

"The police were involved, honey." He started cleaning the sink. "And she isn't just visiting you. She's going to Bobby's place, too."

"Seriously? Geez!" I clenched my fists. "This is so blown out of proportion." Dad must be thrilled that I was finally going to talk to a psychologist. I bet he was going to ask her to dig into my head about all my mommy issues, too. Then his last words caught up with my brain and my pulse raced in alarm.

"Wait! Did you say she's going to Bobby's *house?*"

"Yes."

"Does that mean she's coming *here?*" It was a clear violation of privacy. I didn't want her in my house, in my space. "But Ruthie's coming over," I whined.

"Don't worry. I talked to Mrs. Robles and she'll keep Ruthie home until we call her."

But in lieu of pulling out my hair, I poured my destructive feelings into my words. "When is the stupid shrink coming?"

"Tru," he admonished in a "you're better than that" kind of tone. "The doctor was kind enough to come here before Bobby's, even though it's a little out of her way. I thought you'd appreciate it because it means you can visit with Ruthie sooner." He acted like the doctor was doing me a favor.

"When?" I said.

"As a matter of fact, she'll be here any minute."

I let out a little scream and headed to my bedroom. He'd waited until the last possible second to tell me. "This totally sucks!" I muttered through clenched teeth.

Before I made a clean getaway, the doorbell rang, but I rushed into my room and shut the door anyway. If Dad knew the real story, my kidnapping, the cellar prison, being shot, the whole *killing* thing, he'd probably check me into a mental hospital. I stopped breathing for a second as the events of the entire day so far mingled with those thoughts and threatened to send me into another panic attack. Even if I did need to talk to a shrink, I couldn't. There was too much at stake.

Dad yelled up the stairs. "If you don't come down here

right now, I'm bringing her to your room."

Alarm kicked up my already fast pulse. I sucked in a deep breath and opened my door. "All right! I'm coming." My brain kept chanting *no way, no way*, as I forced one foot ahead of the other.

I heard him answer the front door. A feminine voice floated into the house. "Hello, Mr. Parker. I'm Dr. Frankler. Principal Millard spoke to you about my visit, I hope."

Her voice was steady and velvety, professional yet personable. She sounded like a shrink already. I took a deep breath, trying to calm down.

"Yes! We were expecting you. Come on in." He ushered her into the living room and my stomach tightened for a new reason. It had been Mom's favorite room. Her knitting basket and magazines still rested next to the sofa. Family photos and small handmade items decorated the various surfaces. It was difficult not to think about her in that room.

I hesitated in the kitchen, wishing I could slip out the back door, but Dad called out, "Tru!" A sliver of impatience colored his tone and urged me forward.

I forced my cement legs toward the living room, my hands fluttering. The woman angled herself toward me as I trudged forward. When her hazel eyes met mine, they seemed to flash yellow-orange for the briefest of moments, so brief, I wondered if I'd imagined it. She smiled warmly and I felt a sense of awareness sweep over me, like something in me recognized part of her. I'd never met the woman before, and the instant comfort I felt had my senses on full alert. There were too many individuals in Scotts Valley lately with unusual abilities to not get suspicious. Although my stomach muscles squeezed in protest, I stepped forward to shake her hand.

"Tru," Dad said with a hint of warning in his voice. "This is Dr. Frankler, the new counselor from school." I limply clasped hands with her, hoping she wouldn't comment on my clamminess.

"It's so nice to meet you, Tru." She smiled and shook my hand like it was a piece of china.

"Thanks," I said. "You too."

"I'm sorry to hear about Mrs. Jackson. Did you know her well?"

I shook my head. "No. I didn't know her at all."

Dr. Frankler squinted at me as if she were trying to peer into my brain, but after a moment she smiled benignly and nodded.

"Please, have a seat Dr. Frankler," said Dad.

Dad and I settled on the couch while the doctor perched on the love seat, crossing her long shapely legs. Her gray pencil skirt showed off her curvy backside. A simple white peter-pan collared blouse made her skin look tan and I was forced to admit she was a beautiful woman, amazing actually, for being … I stared at her, trying to determine her age. She seemed young and old at the same time. She was a doctor, so she had to be at least thirty-something. She wore her brown hair pulled back into a severe bun, and a hint of gray streaked across her temples. I revised my guess, thinking maybe forty-something. But her skin was pearly and smooth with only a few creases around eyes that twinkled under my inspection. She had a kind smile. I looked away, realizing she'd been aware that I'd been studying her.

Dad cleared his throat, pink rising up his neck as he

did his own inventory. I sighed with annoyance. Crossing my arms, I leaned back against the cushions and wished that my ability was teleportation instead of healing.

"What is it you wanted to discuss, doctor?" asked Dad, as if he had no idea what she was here for. I rolled my eyes.

"Mr. Parker. Tru," she said with a momentary smirk that told me she'd seen my reaction to Dad's comment. "I know you are still dealing with a great personal loss, and I don't want to add to your difficulties." She tilted her head to the side giving us both a tender look. "But Principal Millard asked me to talk to Bobby and you, Tru, about your relationship with Dante—"

"Geez," I exhaled loudly. "We had no *relationship*," I said, still stinging from the detective's insinuations.

"I'm sorry," she said with a look of chagrin. "I didn't mean to infer that, Tru. I only meant your connection, association, or involvement."

I wasn't so stupid that I didn't realize that she'd basically recited the dictionary definition of relationship. But those words sounded better to me, so I nodded for her to continue.

"Your comments could help us in the event that Dante is found or if other students come forward with similar encounters." She clasped her hands and leaned forward. "The police didn't give us much information. You are under no obligation to disclose anything to us, of course, but we are hoping you will anyway." She blinked toward Dad, her eyelashes fluttering up and down.

Dad smiled. "Of course, we will help." When he nudged me, I scowled. He could have asked me first. I'd already told everything to the police today, and now he wanted to make me go through everything again. Once more, I feared getting the details mixed up, knowing that Dad might suspect that I was lying if I did. The last thing I needed was my dad thinking I'd lied to the cops.

Plus, he was getting way too friendly with the doctor. She'd been here less than five minutes and he was offering up my cooperation like it was a foregone conclusion. What happened to the ferociously protective dad that he'd been at the police station? Granted, the detective was a total jerk and lacked even an ounce of Dr. Frankler's charm, but still … Then I got an idea.

"I'll talk to her if I can do it alone," I said, biting my lips and trying to appear a little more compliant.

Dad's eyes widened in surprise for a moment before narrowing suspiciously. "Tru, is there more to the story that you haven't told me?"

"No," I denied. "I … uh…just thought it might be nice to talk to her about … uh … other stuff, too."

His jaw about dropped to the floor. I knew I was being temperamental, but he took it in stride. I looked down at my lap in shame. What a lie. However, it was the only thing I could think of to get rid of him. He'd wanted me to see a shrink since Mom died, so I knew he'd agree.

"Oh! Sure!" He stood with a nervous laugh. "Good idea to have a woman-to-woman talk while you can." He nodded to the doctor. "I'll just be in the garage. Take all the time you want. Holler when you're done."

I rolled my eyes as he stepped out of the living room. The doctor was watching me with a keen look in her eyes, and I sat up straighter.

She smoothed her expression before addressing me.

"Tru, I'd be happy to talk to you about anything you need. That is my job, after all."

I swallowed. "Okay."

"But," she said. "Can we discuss Dante first?"

When I nodded, she continued. "How did you meet him?"

"At lunch. He was hanging out with Bobby. I really didn't—I mean, I don't know Dante at all. He was Bobby's friend." I felt more relaxed all of the sudden, that feeling of connecting with the doctor enveloping me again. Before I could become suspicious, words streamed from my mouth like a plane on autopilot.

"He was weird to me. I even thought he called me a dummy once. I mean who says that? But he actually said idimmu—" I slapped a hand on my mouth. What was I saying? I tried to laugh it off. "Um, which is strange, right?"

Dr. Frankler stiffened, but she simply nodded for me to continue.

"Anyway, I got a ride home last Monday with him and Bobby because Dad couldn't pick me up and I didn't want to wait for Ruthie, so even though I didn't get a good vibe, I hopped in the car anyway—"

What was I doing? I couldn't seem to help myself. It was diarrhea of the mouth.

"—I mean, who would have guessed what would happen? And I wasn't the only girl either. Shrina caught a ride, too. She hangs out with Bobby. I think they are crushing on each other. Anyway, after Dante dropped her off, he—" My phone vibrated and rang in my pocket, causing me to pause. What was wrong with me?

"Sorry," I said, grateful for the interruption. I pulled

out my phone and turned off the sound. "It's probably my friend. She's been worried about me." I tried to blink the fog away from my brain. A desire to stay and pour my guts out to this woman warred with a desire to flee.

The doctor's lips pressed together before smiling, as if she understood. "She sounds like a good friend. Do you need to talk to her or can it wait?"

"Oh, it can wait. I'd rather talk to her in private, anyway." Geez! Why did I say that? I stood up, shaking my head to clear it. The doctor's gaze was a little too perceptive. I walked toward the credenza and picked up a picture frame, our last family photo together. We were at the beach at sunset and it was hands-down one of our best family pictures.

"You were saying, after Dante dropped Shrina off at home ..." prodded Dr. Frankler.

And then I was off again, but this time I was able to rein in my words. As much as I wanted to tell her the real truth, I stuck to the same story that I had used at the police station. Focusing on the picture of my family seemed to help me concentrate.

"Unfortunately," I said. "The detective seemed to think I was making it all up, like Dante and I were in on it together. Can I just say, Ick?!"

I had to concentrate hard to stop the words I wanted to say from escaping my lips. I forced out a lie. "The next thing I knew I woke up at home."

I shifted toward her again. She hadn't moved but her eyes still squinted my way. The intensity of her gaze had lessened. I chewed my lips waiting for her to say something.

"It sounds like you are a very lucky girl, Tru. That

could have ended up much worse."

I heaved a sigh. "I guess so." I had almost told her what really happened. It had been like I didn't have a will of my own. But fortunately, I'd been able to push back on that feeling.

"Nothing else happened," I said. I expelled a loud breath, grateful that my head was clearing. What was it about this woman that made me want to tell her—Wait! Was she pulling the truth from me? Did she have super-powers like Zander's brother?

"Is there anything else you want to talk about?" she asked politely, leaning forward with her hands clasped.

"What? No," I said, nervous now that I realized I might be in the room with a supernatural hybrid. Even worse, she might be working for the Collector. "I just wanted to get my dad out of here. He was pretty upset at the police station, so I thought it would be better if he didn't have to hear it again."

"How thoughtful of you," she said without much feeling. It left me wondering if she meant it. "Well, your father isn't going to think we talked about much if we end it here, is he?"

She was right. I should have realized that, but my nerves were rattled. As I set down our family photo, I unsettled Mom's pottery jar next to it. I caught it before it could wobble to the floor but the lid slipped off landing on the top of the credenza with a clang. Paper caught my eye and I realized something was in the jar—quite a few things, actually. I snapped the lid back on, promising myself to investigate it later, and turned to the doctor. I racked my brain for ways to get rid of her without raising her suspicions any higher.

"Good catch," she said.

"Thanks. My mom made it. Dad would have killed me if I busted it."

"It's very nice. It reminds me of a Greek pot that I purchased when I was in Athens." She leaned back and crossed her legs.

"You've been to Greece?" I asked.

"Yes. A long time ago, though. My pot, or jar as they would call it, depicts a scene from an old Greek myth."

"Really?" I pretended interest to prolong our conversation.

"Yes. One of my favorite, too." She clasped her hands in her lap. "Have you ever heard the story of Pandora's Box?"

My fourth-grade teacher had been a fan of Greek mythology and he'd told us many of their stories. "I think so. Something about curiosity, right?"

"You're correct, Tru. It starts out as an origin story, explaining how humans came to this earth."

I picked at my nails absently. "Like Adam and Eve?"

"Yes, but unlike Christians, the Greeks believed in many gods. Pandora's box was originally called Pandora's *jar*, but somewhere down the line of storytellers it changed. It could have been something similar to your mother's jar. I have a jar like it in my office at school. I guess your mother and I had a common interest. You're welcome to stop by if you'd like to see it," she invited, but I refused to take the bait and remained silent.

"Anyway, I'm surprised she never told you the story. Would you like to hear it?" she asked, but she didn't wait for me to answer.

"Let's see," she said, propping one hand under her

chin with a thoughtful look. "There are many different versions of this myth, but the general story is the same. The gist of it—you don't mind putting up with me a little longer do you?"

"No, go ahead." She had to stay longer for Dad to believe that I'd unloaded *all* my emotional crap. Only then would he finally leave me alone. Besides, now I wasn't the one blabbing, she was. And, I had to admit I was a little curious to hear about the myth, especially if my mom knew the story.

"Well, the story of Pandora's Box, or jar, if you will, is a story about the origin of women and also the beginning of evil on Earth."

I rolled my eyes.

The doctor smiled. "Yes, we women do seem to get the blame for everything, don't we? But it was man who first told the story, so ..."

"Figures," I muttered.

"Exactly," she laughed, the sound bringing an unwilling smile to my lips. "Anyway, most of the stories say that two Titan brothers, Prometheus and Epimetheus, created all the creatures of earth, with the help of other gods, of course, who breathed life into them. Prometheus formed them out of clay and his brother gave them their various qualities, such as swiftness, strength, cunning, or physical attributes like fur, feathers, horns and so on. Unfortunately, by the time they came to man, all the best characteristics had been given out. So, Prometheus decided to make man stand upright by stealing Zeus's lightning."

She paused dramatically and then said, "With that lightning, he was able to make fire and give it to man.

Zeus, of course, was furious when he found out because he didn't want man to have anything of his. But it was already done."

Despite my efforts to remain detached, I was fascinated.

"To retaliate against Prometheus and to punish man, Zeus asked Hephaestus to create the first woman, naming her Pandora. He asked the other gods to each give Pandora a gift, which they did. She became beautiful, charming, musical, and *curious*."

"Not much of a revenge gift," I said.

"Not yet." She wiggled her eyebrows meaningfully. "Zeus secretly made sure to add one final ingredient to set the stage for his revenge: a deceptive and lying heart. Since Prometheus' brother, Epimetheus, decided to remain on earth with the humans, Zeus offered Pandora to him as a bride. Epimetheus became besotted by her beauty and charm, forgetting Prometheus' warning about the consequences of accepting gifts from a god."

Dr. Frankler shifted, recrossing her legs. I blinked, realizing I'd moved closer to her. I pressed myself into the couch, grabbing a decorative pillow to squeeze.

"Then," continued the doctor. "For their wedding Zeus gave Pandora a jar, telling her she must never open it. But he knew that her curiosity and deceitful heart would cause her to disobey him, and he was right. Eventually, she opened the jar only to release a swarm of evil upon mankind. Some say they were evil spirits, some say they were all the ills of mankind."

"Sounds a bit like when Eve tempted Adam with the forbidden fruit and they got kicked out of the Garden of Eden," I said, fully engaged in her story.

"Quite right, Tru. Christians have a similar story, for when Adam and Eve left the Garden, they were susceptible to death and all manner of afflictions."

"And in both stories, it's the woman's fault." I smiled wryly.

"Ah yes. That's the eternal plight of women, no? However, Pandora's story doesn't end there. Realizing too late what she had done, Pandora tried to close the lid on the escaping evil, but fortunately she was too late, for the last thing to fly from the jar was Hope."

"Why would Hope be in a jar of evil?" I asked.

"Many have wondered this. Perhaps Zeus took pity on mankind and included it as a balm against the evil she unleashed." Dr. Frankler shrugged, her delicate shoulders lifting up and down. "On the other hand, some believe that hope is false and blinding, and therefore, evil itself."

"That's cheery," I said mockingly.

"Yes," she agreed with a smile. "Personally, I like the idea that hope helps us meet the challenges of life, particularly the ills of this world. Regardless, this is the Greek way of explaining why dreadful things happen."

"Seems pretty misogynistic to me. Why do the women always get the shaft in these myths?"

Dr. Frankler's laughter pealed like bells, making my lips twitch up. "I have to agree with you. Like I said before, women aren't the ones who wrote these stories."

"Yeah. Stupid men did. I'd like to hear some myths or fairy tales that a woman wrote."

"Me too! Perhaps you will write them someday." Her eyes twinkled with amusement. "Well, Greek myths are entertaining, nonetheless. I've always thought that overcoming the tribulations of the world makes us stronger people. I like to think Zeus's plan backfired. Mankind flourished and covered the earth despite all the evil that had been released."

I considered the dark months after Mom's death when I had been drowning in the loss of her. I thought about Uncle Ira and Dad and Ruthie and all the kind things they did for me. The experience had changed me. I became more sympathetic, less selfish, and kinder. My perspective had altered in many good ways. I thought about the children I worked with at the rec center and the joy I felt working with them. I wouldn't have appreciated them before the accident, I realized. Those kids had given me hope and helped me pull away from my depression.

"I think hope is a good quality, not a weakness," I said.

"I think you are absolutely right," she agreed, a knowing smile playing along her lips. "Pandora's curiosity may have released the worst qualities into the world, but she also released one of the best. I can't imagine a world without hope."

I thought about all the questions I still had about my mother and the supernatural events of the past few weeks. Was my curiosity dangerous? I didn't know. And Dante had found me, not the other way around. I had never gone looking for him.

"Tru, how do you like school?" asked the doctor.

"I like it. Well, the school part. Last year I was kind of out of it, but I'm better this year."

"Do you have problems with anyone at school?" Her eyes drilled into me.

"No, I mean, mostly no." Once again, I wanted to sew

my lips closed.

Dr. Frankler smiled. "If you didn't have any problems with other students, Tru, you would be the only one. Trust me."

"Well, I try to avoid the people that bug me." *Namely Zena*, I thought. "So, it's not so bad."

"And your friend, Ruthie Robles, how long have you known her?"

"Since we were little kids," I said, wondering how she knew I was her friend. "We've been best friends forever. She's pretty much my only friend." No, that wasn't true anymore. A warm glow blossomed in my chest. "I guess there's also Zander, Isaac, and Phoebe. Oh, and Bobby."

Why didn't I just shut up? I was starting to like the doctor, but I'd die before I admitted it. Besides, I didn't know her well enough to trust her. I didn't understand the compelling need to confide in her when my mind said not to. It revived my suspicions about her having special abilities. I wished Dad would come back inside now.

"Oh, yes. Zander Hughes. He's new this year, isn't he?" The doctor absently ran her hand along her skirt, pressing out a crease.

"Yeah."

"You two are close?" she said, still looking down at her lap.

"Yeah." At least I was keeping it short.

"Hmmm ... Isaac and Phoebe. The Efoti twins. Tongan twins, quite unusual."

"Their mother is from Taiwan," I blurted.

"Ah, I see. How fascinating," she mused before piercing me with one of her intense looks again. "Tru, have you noticed any odd behavior from your friends, or anyone else? Anything like you may have seen with Dante?"

"What? Why would you ask that?" Of course, I'd seen plenty of oddities about them, but I wasn't going to share them with her. I gripped my hands and tightened my lips.

"All right, Tru. I just thought I'd ask." She uncrossed her legs. "Is there anything else you want to talk about before I leave?"

"No," I said. I felt like I'd given her way more information than I'd wanted to. It was time for her to go.

She got the hint. "I've enjoyed our chat, Tru," she said as she smiled and stood. I jumped up to walk her out. "Thank you for telling me about Dante." She tilted her head to the side. "I know that must have been unpleasant. Please feel free to drop in and see me at school if you think of something that might help us, or if you just want to chat."

I nodded, hoping to propel her out my front door sooner.

"Let me say goodbye to your father and I'll be on my way."

"Sure." I walked ahead of her through the kitchen to the garage door and yanked it open to call Dad in. He had his head under the hood of his old Mustang.

"Done already?" Dad asked a moment later as he stepped into the kitchen wiping his greasy hands on an old rag.

I nodded.

"Yes, Mr. Parker," replied the doctor. "We had a nice conversation, but I'd like to check in with her now and then at school if that's all right with you."

What? I gritted my teeth. So, she hadn't bought my story and now I was stuck doing the couch thing at school. Not good.

"That's a great idea. Thanks for your help, Dr. Frankler." He walked her to the door while I fumed in the kitchen. He returned seconds later.

"So," he said smiling. "That went okay, didn't it?"

I shrugged, not wanting to let on that I was upset. "I don't know why she needs to check on me."

"Ah, don't worry about it. The school wants to keep tabs on the situation until Dante is found. Play along and it will blow over."

Déjà vu. It was the same advice Zander had given me. The thing was, they didn't act like it was nothing. I couldn't go to school, my house was in lockdown mode, and if I ever got out again, I had visits with a shrink to look forward to.

"Can I call Ruthie now?"

"Sure honey." He ruffled my hair like I was six years old and headed out to the garage with a light step.

I scowled as the door clicked closed behind him. I resisted the urge to follow him and tell him I didn't need any more "sessions" with the good doctor, but I really wanted to take another look at Mom's jar, so I turned back to the living room. When I tried to open it, the lid jammed. I shook it and something clinked inside.

I set it down and tipped it to look at the three images painted on its surface. The first was an Aztec depiction of a bird rising from a fire made of thick outlines, simplistic and garish. The second was a dragon breathing fire, its long serpent-like body undulating half submerged in water. Looked Chinese to me. And the third had a

Celtic design made of interlocking weaving patterns that formed a wolf howling at the moon. I thought it odd that there were three vastly different cultures represented on the same piece of artwork, but at the same time it didn't surprise me. Mom could have made it in one of the teacher art classes that she went to.

Maybe I shouldn't open the jar. Maybe I didn't want to know what was in there. What the shrink? Dr. Frankler's story had me believing my mom's stupid jar held secrets that shouldn't be told.

Just like Pandora, I knew I wouldn't leave it alone, though. I needed answers, and I hoped that whatever hid inside it would help me understand the mythical creatures that weren't so mythical after all. The kitchen door squeaked as it swung open, signaling Dad's reappearance. I set aside the jar to call Ruthie.

19

FORT KNOX

IT FELT LIKE AN eternity before Ruthie arrived. Her parents followed her into the house, their arms full of food. I was grateful for the reprieve from Dad's not so subtle questions about Dr. Frankler and what we'd discussed. Our parents visited in the kitchen while Ruthie and I hustled upstairs to my bedroom.

As soon as my door shut, she dropped her bags and pushed me into the Black Hole. The beanbag squished as I settled in.

"Free from my crazy family for another night!" She sighed loudly as she grabbed a few pieces of clothing from the messy floor and shoved them under my door, saying, "Just in case our voices carry ..."

We both jumped as an object slammed into my bedroom window. I crawled my way across the floor after Ruthie, who looked ready to grapple with the devil.

"What was that?" I asked, rising to peek through the side of the window.

"Pfft!" A burst of irritation flew out of Ruthie's mouth as she hauled herself up. "I should have known they wouldn't listen."

She raised the window and yelled, "Mom said to stay in the car!"

Little boy laughter wafted through the window. "Why didn't they come in?" I asked.

Ruthie looked at me like I had a third eye. "Are you crazy? They're human cyclones. Mom would never unleash them on your house." As if to emphasize her point, two more pinecones hit the side of the house, one right after the other.

Ruthie let out a string of threats, some involving tying her brothers to their beds and releasing their ant farms on their feet. I chuckled as she closed the window and yanked the curtains shut.

"I hope you didn't just give them an idea," I said with a chuckle.

Ruthie looked horrified for a second before sinking back into the beanbag with a loud sigh. I dropped down to the floor near her. My window pattered again. "Just ignore them," she said. Then in the same breath she ordered, "All right. Tell me everything! Did they fingerprint you? Did you see the jail?"

"I'm not a suspect, Ruthie." But was I? I certainly felt like I'd been one. "At least I think so," I added. "The detective acted like I was lying." I curled up and leaned my head on my hands.

"What the frickin' chicken?" Ruthie's outrage siphoned away my earlier lightheartedness. "How did he find out? Probably that cop intuition thing ... you know, gut feeling." She tapped her long fingernails against her teeth.

"Yeah, but I was telling the truth when I said I wasn't working with Dante." I lowered my voice, still a little horrified to be saying my next words. "And Zander said Peter got rid of the body, as in his ashes are floating in the ocean."

"Yuck! He burned the body?" She whispered, her face paling. "That's gross. I mean, probably a good idea. But man, sometimes I hear what you're saying and it doesn't compute, you know?"

"Yeah. I know. Like the *X-Files*, right?"

"Totally. There's got to be someone who can help us figure out what's really going on."

"Well, not the police for sure," I said. "I hope I never have to see that detective again. He made me so mad I wanted to punch him in his smug face."

"If your dad has anything to do with it, I doubt you'll see him again. He's going all out with this new security system. How the heck will Z sneak in now?"

I sighed. "I don't know, but it won't be working in my bedroom until tomorrow. Zander is joining us tonight after Dad goes to bed so we can talk about stuff. You know, with you and Conrad, too. That is, if Dad ever goes to sleep."

"Cool! Conny seems pretty awesome, doesn't he? He must be super smart, which is way advanced of me to notice, don't you think?"

"Really? With everything going on you have time to crush on a guy you've never seen before?"

"I would have thought you'd be proud of me! I'm

crushing on a guy I've only talked to—like I was attracted to his brains or something. That's huge! He sounded adorable! How ugly could the guy be anyway? Don't look at me like that. I'm just keeping my options open, that's all."

"What about you and Val? Anything new happen today at school?" I asked.

"If you mean did Val ask me to Homecoming, then no," she said, deflating all of the sudden. "Everyone was talking about you, Bobby, and Dante." She wrinkled her nose with distaste. "Plus, I caught Val laughing and flirting with Zena and her club," she muttered with a frown. "Loser."

"What?" No wonder Ruthie was looking around for a new boyfriend. "Do you think he's into them?"

"I don't know for sure. But he knows I hate her like lice, and I have to draw the line somewhere. The way he was acting around her, well—I wanted to kick his butt!"

I scooted closer. "Ruthie, you deserve better. You don't have to work this hard. There are better guys out there."

"Yeah, that's what I was thinking, too." She smiled sadly. "But I really wanted to go to Homecoming."

"What's stopping you?" A gloomy and disheartened Ruthie didn't seem right. She usually bounced back from disappointment faster than this. "What about Isaac?"

She raised an eyebrow. "I heard he was going to ask Lizbeth. And I approve because she's nice. I don't want to get in the way of that."

I frowned. "Look, if you want, I might be able to hook you up with Maverick from the rec center."

She brightened. "The cowboy computer nerd with all

those muscles?"

I laughed. "There are a lot of guys with muscles there, but yes, he's one of them. I'm sure you'd have fun with him. He's a couple years older, though."

"Even better! Is he in college? College guys are hot!" She leaned forward, eyes sparkling with anticipation.

"I don't know," I said smiling at her sudden mood shift.

"But I'm not sure if I want to go with someone I don't know." She let herself fall into the beanbag. "I wish we could double. Too bad you canceled with Isaac."

I gasped. "Ruthie, with everything going on I forgot to tell you Zander asked me to Homecoming."

She jumped and squealed, rotating on her side and leaning on one hand. "Marinating meatballs! You are holding out on me. When did all this happen? Details. Now!"

I told her how Zander had asked me today, how he said he only went to school to be close to me. She sighed dreamily, swearing that our story was so much better than a sigh-worthy couple's romance on our favorite tv show *Court of Palms.*

A little later, we were both sprawled out on my bedroom floor when someone knocked at the door and called out Ruthie's name. Ruthie's mom opened the door, pushing hard to overcome the clothing and bags in her way. We barely lifted our heads as she wedged her way in, shaking her head at us.

"Well, I can see Ruthie has made herself at home." She gave her daughter a cranky look, saying, "You know I hate it when you block the door."

Ruthie just shrugged. When her gaze landed on me, I

sat up. "Sorry," I said.

Mrs. Robles pursed her lips before giving me a kind smile. "Tru, you seem to be feeling a lot better. And that makes my heart *muy feliz.* But would you do me a huge favor and please help her focus on her homework."

She narrowed her eyes at her daughter again. "Ruthie, if you don't get it done, you will never have a school night sleepover again. I mean it! I really want you to get into a college one day, *mi querida.*"

"Yes, mama," droned Ruthie.

"I'll make sure she gets it done, Mrs. Robles. I've got loads to do myself." I pointed to the pile of papers that Ruthie brought me. "Looks like we'll be up for a while tonight."

"Well, not too late, I hope." She stepped closer and pulled a reluctant Ruthie to her feet, kissing her on her cheek. "See you later, *mija.* And go eat dinner with Mr. Parker before it gets cold. He could use some company, I think. Salad is in the fridge. Oh, and I added some brownies."

"Are they the ones with marshmallows and fudge frosting?" I asked.

"Of course!" she smiled.

"Oh my gosh! I love those brownies!" I exclaimed. The world always seemed brighter when I was eating her special treats. "Thanks so much for helping out. And Ruthie will get her homework done and get enough sleep. I promise." *Even if I have to do her work myself,* I thought.

Mrs. Robles looked like she didn't believe me. "Well, at least try." She gave me a hug and then left.

Ruthie grabbed my hands, giggling. "This is going to be so much fun! Sleepover on a school night—" She lowered her voice to a whisper. "—boys sneaking in, clandestine meetings. It's just like *Court of Palms!*"

"But better!" I said, giving her hands a squeeze. "I'm starving. Your mom brought real food. Dad's going to eat it all if we don't get down there."

"Okay, okay," said Ruthie. "Just let me hang up my shirt for school tomorrow."

I slumped onto my bed, preparing for a long wait. I glanced over some of my homework that Ruthie brought, happy to see the teachers went easy on me. Maybe they heard the gossip and felt sorry. For once I didn't mind their pity.

THE ENCHILADA CASSEROLE RESTED on the counter untouched when we went downstairs, evidence that Dad was out of sorts. He sat at the table reading over the documentation for the new alarm system.

"Hey Dad, want me to get you a plate?" I asked.

"That would be great," he said without looking our way. He walked over to the new panel beside our front door and punched a couple buttons. A British female voice indicated that our doors and windows were secure. I panicked.

"Uh, Dad. I thought they were coming back tomorrow to wire the windows. You know I like to sleep with the window cracked."

He punched in a set of numbers and the woman's voice responded again, stating that the system was disarmed. Dad smiled with satisfaction, glancing my way.

"They're scheduled for tomorrow, but don't worry. The upstairs windows aren't wired. Besides, we won't alarm the windows most of the time."

I sighed with relief and shot Ruthie a meaningful look. She jiggled her eyebrows and started grabbing plates from the cupboard.

"Man, Mr. Parker," said Ruthie as she moved around the kitchen quickly setting the table. "This place is going to be locked up tighter than Alcatraz."

I pulled out the salad from the fridge, thinking she had it about right. This place was starting to feel like a prison.

"Ruthie," said Dad. "I'm not trying to keep Tru here. I want to keep others out. I want to know she's safe when I can't be here."

"Sure, sure! I'd probably do the same thing." She sent me a "your life is going to suck" look.

"How about the dog, Dad?" I asked, rolling my eyes at Ruthie.

"You're going to love him," he said. "Oh yeah! I have a photo." He pulled his phone out of his pocket, brought up the picture, and handed it to me. Ruthie squeezed in close to see.

A gold and brown German shepherd sat frozen like a statue next to a police officer, similar to the picture I saw at the police station today. He looked alert and smart, not playful at all and nothing like the golden retriever I'd always wanted. The whole reason I'd wanted a dog when I was a kid was to play with him. This dog didn't look like he would even catch a Frisbee. There was no way he would be cool about the weirdness of my new world, either. I hoped I could outsmart him, for his own good, of course. There had been two usemi in my back-yard a couple weeks ago, and according to Zander, they'd been on my front porch the other day. Would he run away, tail between his legs or attack? Either option wasn't good. Maybe I needed to learn how to train dogs. Regardless, I couldn't rely on a dog, the police, or my dad for help with the creatures I had only recently discovered. I needed Zander.

Dad had no idea there were supernatural beings out there and a police dog, no matter how trained he was, wouldn't be much help against them. Absently, I wondered how long it would take me to get the dog to like Zander.

"Anyway," Dad said. "He used to work for the Scotts Valley Police Department but when they defunded the project years ago, they transferred him and his handler to Santa Cruz. He helped with all kinds of stuff from drug dealers to tracking criminals all over the county before retiring."

So that might have been his picture I saw today. I hoped there was a little fun still in him.

"Mike says he's amazing," said Dad. "Unfortunately, his handler, his old partner actually, passed away from cancer. Mike was trying to find him a new home, so this is perfect for everyone."

"Poor doggie," said Ruthie. "Bet he misses his partner."

Dad and I exchanged a sad look. Our new pet already had something in common with us. We'd lost someone who meant the world to us, too.

"What's his name?" I asked.

Dad's eyes twinkled. "Knox. As in Fort Knox."

We all laughed. "Great," I said. "Alcatraz, Fort Knox, aka prison! You won't let me out and Knox won't let anyone in. My life just got suckier."

"Hey now," said Dad. "Alcatraz was a prison. This isn't a prison. Fort Knox protects some of the country's greatest treasures. Think of it that way, honey. I'm just trying to protect you, not ruin your life."

"Sure feels like it."

"Come here and let me show you how to set the alarm. If you know how to arm and disarm it, maybe you won't feel so imprisoned."

Dad showed me how to work the new system, and even made me memorize the password. This was going to take some getting used to. I couldn't just walk out the door in the morning anymore because that would set off the alarm. It seemed plain old annoying. By the time Ruthie had tossed the salad, warmed up her personal plate of cheese enchiladas, and filled the glasses with ice water, Dad had finished my instruction.

Before we could sit down to eat, the phone rang. I ignored it, forcing Dad to answer. "Hello? Oh, hello, Mrs. Johnson. Bobby?" Dad sounded surprised. "Just a moment." He paused and looked at me.

"Tru, have you seen or heard from Bobby since we saw him at the police station today?"

"No," I said, wondering where this was leading.

"Hmm ..." said Dad. "His grandmother can't locate him. He's been gone all afternoon. He even missed his appointment with Dr. Frankler."

My throat tightened and I shared a look of fear with Ruthie. Dad told Bobby's grandmother we had no information for her but promised to call her if we found out anything.

When we finally sat down at the table, we ate in

silence. Each of us seemed immersed in our own thoughts. I wondered what could have happened to Bobby. It was too much of a coincidence that he'd gone missing now that he'd told everyone what had happened. Halfway through my meal I noticed the bruises covering Ruthie's wrists.

"Holy crap, Ruthie!" I yelped. "What happened to your wrists? Is that more stage makeup?" The light cotton cardigan she'd been wearing hung from her chair, leaving her wrists bare now.

"What are you talking about?" she asked.

Couldn't she see them? What was going on? Dad frowned. I got out of my chair to hold her arms. Red welts circled her wrists, and they were beginning to darken to purple in places. It looked painful.

Dad came around the table for a better look at her arms. "What is this Ruthie?"

Ruthie stared at the marks, her eyebrows drawn together. "Huh. That's weird. I didn't notice them before. They don't hurt that much."

"You don't remember how you got these bruises?" Dad asked, his face darkening.

"No. But I bet two little monsters at my house had something to do with it," she muttered.

Dad's eyebrows shot up. "I might have a talk with your dad," he said. "For now, why don't you put some ice on them after dinner."

"Okay," she said, her face a mixture of haunted confusion. "Man! It's so weird. I didn't notice them until Tru did." She pulled her cardigan back on, covering up the bruises. Pasting on a smile, she changed the subject. "Well, it's kind of cool that you're getting a guard dog.

And with the new alarm system, this place should be super safe, right?"

Dad agreed, pulling out his picture of the dog again. I picked at my food while casting concerned looks Ruthie's way. I didn't believe her brothers had hurt her. She wouldn't have allowed it. And if Val was getting rough with her, I was going to kick his butt. But if he had, I was sure she would tell me.

At least for tonight I could keep an eye on her. Tomorrow I'd find out what happened, even if I had to talk to Val myself. Perhaps I wasn't the only one who needed a Fort Knox.

20

UNCLE IWA

I MADE SURE THAT I heard Dad snoring before I texted Zander to give him the "all clear." Before that, there had been more than enough time to do our homework, pick out our clothes for school tomorrow, and even tidy up my room.

After homework, we'd moved on to the traditional sleepover activities, painting nails, fixing hair and boy talk. She had described her idea of the perfect school dance with the perfect guy. Her imagination made me laugh. I could have told her to stop dreaming, but I didn't want to squash her dream. So, I'd let her gush while making approving noises. She had gradually transitioned into going to Homecoming with Maverick and how great that was going to be, even though I hadn't asked him yet. When she spent almost an hour on her makeup and hair, I started calling her "Sophia Loren" again because she had that hot Latin look going on with dark, smoky eyes and thick, wavy brown hair. Although her parents were Hispanic and had rich cocoa tans year-round, her skin was much paler. Ruthie joked about a secret *gringo* churning up the family pedigree chart.

Now Ruthie sat cross-legged on my bed, computer in her lap, researching makeup tips. She'd already fixed me up. I slipped into my bathroom one more time to make sure I looked okay. My hair hung in curls down my back and across my shoulders, perhaps a little too fancy for my yoga pants and oversized shirt, which only passed Ruthie's approval because the shirt reminded her of a dancer on the old eighties' movie, *Flashdance*. It was highlighter pink and had a ripped neck. Ruthie said the color made my skin and hair pop. My outfit shouted teen rebellion next to Ruthie's purple sweater and black stretch pants. It seemed that we were swapping personas, but I understood why she chose the sweater. The sleeves were extra long and covered up her bruised wrists. My lips tightened again at the idea of someone hurting Ruthie.

I was just stepping back into my bedroom when I heard a tap on the window. My heartbeat quickened. Zander already had the screen off when I slid open the window. He ducked into the room and scooped me up with a hug. I giggled, wrapping my arms around his warmth. We stood for a second with our foreheads touching. I felt complete, like someone had reattached my arm and I could function normally again.

"You look amazing," he whispered huskily. His nostrils twitched. "And smell good, too."

Ruthie cleared her voice.

"Just in case you forget I'm here ... Hi!" She waved, giving us a wide grin.

Zander smiled, a cocky tilt to his head, and stepped back, clasping my hand. I tried not to smile like a spaz, but failed.

"Ohhh! You two are absolutely cute-ageous! I need to get me a hand-holding hottie!" She sighed like she was watching a good chick flick. Red warmth spread across my face. I tucked in my lips, trying to appear confident and mature rather than the blushing naive girl that I was. It felt like forever since I'd seen Zander. Having him next to me now allowed the heavy thoughts of the day to slide off my shoulders. I wanted to bounce up and down on my toes, but refrained, trying to seem less affected than I was. Zander kissed the back of my hand and let go to reach through the window for his backpack.

"All right, Ruthie, but the best I can do is video chat one in for you." Zander was in a good mood. I wondered if he felt as fabulous as I did when we were near each other. *What if he just felt what I was feeling?* My great mood ebbed a little.

"Not saying he's a 'hottie,'" said Zander. "But remember, the screen adds ten pounds."

We laughed—Ruthie a little too hard. Was she nervous? Had she really started liking someone from one phone call? She rubbed her hands on her jeans and fussed with her hair.

As Zander set up his computer tablet on my desk chair, I caught her eye and raised an eyebrow. She winked back at me. We squatted down next to Zander as he fiddled with the computer settings.

"Yo Z-man!" Conrad announced as his face filled the

monitor. I looked from Conrad to Ruthie, who stared, her jaw hanging just a little.

I could almost read her mind. She had a thing for blond boys, and if she could have picked Conrad's hair color, it couldn't be more perfect. It hung over his forehead, the sides waving back over his ears. His face was long, his nose pronounced. But the eyes—with their cornflower blue color and those curly blond lashes—they were way cute. A light dusting of freckles added to his boy-next-door looks. His scrubby, unshaven jaw and otherwise angular face saved him from looking feminine, though. If the screen added ten pounds, then the guy was reed thin, his shoulders pointing up as he hunched forward toward the camera.

"Hey Conrad!" said Zander. "Nice haircut, by the way."

Conrad ran his hands through his thick mop, letting it flop back into place. "Yeah, I thought I'd try and make a good impression." He grinned, ratcheting up his on-screen charisma a few degrees, which sealed the deal as far as Ruthie was concerned. She was speechless. Normally she would have inserted a saucy comment about him not needing to impress us.

I decided to help her out. "Hi Conrad! I'm Tru." I waved. "It's nice to meet you face to face." I wrapped an arm around Ruthie's shoulders. "That makes this girl Ruthie. She's an angel through and through. Sweet and quiet as a kitten," I added, pinching her arm.

"Hey!" Ruthie finally seemed to snap out of it, which was my intent. "I'm definitely no angel and the only things I have in common with kittens are my claws!" She stretched and curled her fingers, her long nails pointing like claws.

I laughed hard, grabbing my stomach. It was easy to get a rise out of her sometimes. I knew she hated it when her parents called her "angel," short for Angelina, one of her middle names. She despised it as well as any reminders of it. But I knew she'd thank me later when she realized she had been gawking at Conrad.

"Okay, okay!" I gurgled as she punched me in the arm. "Conrad, she may look angelic, but she's really the devil in disguise!" Ruthie punched me again. "Ouch!"

"I see what you mean, Z. She's *zinty* for sure." Conrad and Zander grinned at each other.

"Zinty?" I asked, still bubbling with humor.

"Oh," said Conrad. "That's just means ... uh ... lots of personality."

"In a good way, of course," added Zander.

"Alright, already!" said Ruthie rolling her eyes. "I call this meeting to order. And before I forget, I just want to let you know we've found a Scooby, so the gang is now complete!"

I raised an eyebrow. "Huh? Who are you talking about?"

"Knox, of course," she said, reminding me of the new dog that I hadn't told Zander about yet.

"Oh, yeah," I said with a frown. "My dad is getting a retired police dog to help guard our house—and me, I guess."

"Seriously?" said Conrad, leaning forward so that his face took up the entire screen.

"Great," grumbled Zander. "Your dad is making it hard for us to get together, isn't he?"

"When you said her dad was upset about the Dante

thing, you weren't kidding," added Conrad. "I hate to imagine what he'd do if he knew the real story."

"Well, I think it's going to be fun," said Ruthie. "Tru always wanted a dog. Her parents only let her have a dumb 'ol stuffed dog."

"Hey now!" I said, pretending offense.

"You know what I mean, girl. I know you love your Mummy."

"You named your toy dog *Mummy*?" asked Zander, smiling again. "Do you still have it?"

I tried not to look at my bookshelf, but my knee-jerk glance gave away its location. "No!" I tried to beat him to it, but it was no use. He swiped it from the top shelf before I could stop him.

"Shhhh!" said Ruthie. "Stop horsing around and get your butts back here. We have some serious business to discuss."

Zander held my childhood treasure at a distance, arms extended. "It's kind of cute." That was an outright lie.

"It's a she. I've had her since I was a little kid. She's a little raggedy so I have to be careful with it." The light brown tufts of fur that hadn't been rubbed away by time were matted and, quite frankly, ugly. I didn't care. She was like a security blanket. I'd been forced to stop sleeping with her for fear of destroying her altogether. So, I kept Mummy at the top of my shelf where I could see her from any place in my room.

Zander gently handed her to me. "Sorry. It's kind of sweet that you still have him—I mean her." He smiled.

I sighed, all irritation dispelled by the adorable twinkle in his eyes. "Well, I guess you're forgiven." I carefully placed Mummy back on the shelf.

We bent down in front of the tablet again. Ruthie glanced between a notebook and Conrad as she explained my weird dreams to Conrad.

"Oh, you brought your notes," I said. "Nice."

"Yessiree!" said Ruthie proudly.

"Can I take a look?" asked Zander.

Ruthie handed him the notebook. "So," she said. "What did I miss last night?"

The only thing we had discussed after she hung up was Ruthie, and the fact that Conrad thought this counted as a double date.

"Oh, nothing really," answered Conrad quickly. "Planned this meeting and stuff. Then I started feeling like the third wheel, if you know what I mean, and took off."

"Totally!" she said, letting out a puff of air. "I had to remind them I was here when Zander arrived. Talk about awkward."

I rolled my eyes, knowing she was trying to make me blush. "Speaking of meetings," I said. "How are we going to figure out what's going on around here if Zander can't sneak in anymore?"

"Don't worry," said Zander, his eyes connecting with mine, reassuring and strong. "We'll make it work. We can still talk during school and maybe your dad will let me take you out some time."

Just thinking of going out on a real date with him made my insides twirl with excitement. But I hadn't told Dad about Homecoming yet. I needed to tell him soon so he could warm up to the idea. And then there was the dress ...

Ruthie snickered. "Good luck with that one. He's

seriously gone off the rails this time."

"Come on! I'm sure he'll let you go out with friends, right?" said Conrad.

"Oh yeah, probably," I replied, not selling it very well.

Zander scowled again, but his jaw was set with stubbornness. "What about the big dance coming up?"

Ruthie answered for me. "Homecoming is different. It's a rite of passage. The old man wouldn't dare stand between a girl and Homecoming. Don't worry, I'll make sure she goes."

I shook my head. "Dad's not going to stop everything I do, guys. He just needs to know I'm safe when he's not around. If I lay low for a couple days and nothing weird happens, then I'll talk to him about Homecoming. It will be okay."

"Maybe you could take Knox. You know, blind people get to take dogs everywhere, so why not you, too?" teased Ruthie.

I smirked back at her. "Ha ha."

"No sense in worrying right now," said Zander. "Let's talk about these dreams of yours, Tru."

"What about them?" I asked.

"The first one here," he tapped Ruthie's notebook, "is about a dream of you in a forest fire. Being attacked by a wolf?"

I shook my head. That didn't seem right.

"Yes, it is," insisted Ruthie. "This is the one you told me about the first day of school. It definitely sounded like you were attacked." She snagged the notebook from Zander.

"Don't you remember? You said you were in a smoke-filled forest, you heard a howl, then a wolf came up to

you and tried to chomp on you, and then you woke up."
Ruthie looked up from her notes. "Not a lot, but I can't
remember if you said anything else. I wrote this one down
a while after. Until this week, I thought your dream was
just some kind of premonition because we saw a wolf run
across the road after you dreamed about one. But now
that we know your dreams can be real, like actual things
that happened, maybe this could have happened too?"

I was still shaking my head because it seemed a bit
farfetched.

"Or maybe you got lost in the woods when you were
a kid, Tru," suggested Conrad.

"We don't have wolves here, Conny," scoffed Ruthie.

"Maybe not regular wolves, but—"

"Oh! You mean usemi," Ruthie interrupted.
"Freaky!"

Zander scooted closer to me and clasped my hand.
"It's okay, Tru. Do you remember the dream?"

I did. But it was so surreal, more so than the others.
I squeezed my eyes shut. Zander's hand tightened in mine
as the dream washed over me.

"Alondrea!"

*A ghostly plea, with the intangibility of a dream
within a dream, induced a stabbing panic like I'd never
felt before. It sounded far away, perhaps over that hill—
the one I could barely make out through the smoky haze
filtering through the thick trees. My heart pounded to one
thought—*

Dan-ger-Dan-ger.

"A-lon-dre-a!"

It was a woman's voice, a terrified voice, and it was fading along with the clear blue sky above. I wanted that voice, and the woman it belonged to, but my mind was like the smoke, slipping between the pine needles above me, unable to grasp the moment. I began to cough.

A dog howled, an eerie entreaty echoing through my confusion. Fear stepped back as hope pushed forward. But hitched sobbing pulled me up short. Heavy paws thumped toward a small child. The dog...no...not a dog...a wolf opened up its toothy mouth and reached for the girl's neck, biting into the collar of her shirt and tossing her like a twig over its shoulder. The little girl dug her small hands into the soft brown fur and buried her face in its back trying to block out the smoke. The two raced through green and yellow pines that tried unsuccessfully to dislodge the wolf's rider.

The air cleared long before the wolf stopped running. But finally, it collapsed into a thick and dry patch of grass that marked the edge of the tree line. The girl tumbled off with a yelp, but the wolf mustered up enough energy to grab her shirt in its teeth, preventing the child from knocking against a tree trunk. Then the wolf let go and shuddered as a long wail floated out of its pointy mouth. Its fur convulsed again, the paws stretching and contracting, changing into graceful arms. The rest of the woman reformed in undulating, painful waves, leaving her exhausted and gasping for air. Wavy brown hair covered her like a silk scarf, separating around a jagged tear in her abdomen where blood leaked. Several hundred feet from the edge of trees stood a familiar house. A man ran out the front door and headed toward the forest, toward the woman and child. Evidently, he'd heard the mournful wail of the wolf.

"Jasmine!" he yelled.

The small girl heard him and leaped up. She ran forward on her toddler legs, heedless of the sharp branches of nearby bushes. Smoke and dirt caked her face, her pale skin streaked with wet trails of tears. She cried out.

"Uncle Iwa! H-help!"

"Uncle Ira!" My eyes went wide and I sucked in a long, coughing breath, like I was still breathing the smoky air from my dream. But it wasn't a dream, was it? And Uncle Ira had been there. I squeezed my eyes shut, trying desperately to return to my vision and find out what happened to the wolf that saved me from the forest fire. My head was splitting with pain, but I kept trying. In the background, I could hear Zander and Ruthie calling out to me, their hands shaking me. But as soon as I recognized their voices, they faded, and the light went with them, disappearing like the last rays of a winter sunset.

21

TRUTH BE TOLD

I WOKE UP ON my bed, a wet cloth on my forehead. Ruthie and Zander sat on either side of me, worry pinching their faces.

"What happened?" I asked.

"Hey! Is she okay?" piped in a voice across the room.

"Crap," muttered Ruthie. "We left Conny on the chair." She dashed over to move the tablet to the desk beside my bed. Conrad's eyes blinked owlishly at me.

"How do you feel?" asked Zander, his hands fluttering over me like he didn't know what to do with them.

"Okay, I think." I recalled what I'd seen before I lost consciousness.

"I had the dream again. I don't know how, because obviously I wasn't asleep." I wrinkled my forehead in confusion. "But it couldn't have been a dream because I was awake. It happened before I blacked out."

"Holy Spamburger! Wait just a second." Ruthie moved away again to grab her notebook. I could hear Conrad scrambling for something, too. He mumbled "waking dream" as he scribbled way.

Ruthie rushed back, kneeling at the edge of the bed, pencil poised over her notebook. "Fire away, girl!" she ordered.

"Wait," said Zander. "Only if you want to. How are you really feeling?"

I pulled the washcloth off my head and leaned up on my elbows. "I'm okay now, really. But I felt awful right before I blacked out. Like someone was taking a chainsaw to my head!"

"Too graphic, girl!" said Ruthie, cringing.

"Sorry. It was the same dream I had the night before school started, but it lasted longer. I was trying to see more, like, you know, mentally trying to go back to it, but then I felt an awful pain in my head—like I burst a brain vessel or something—and everything went dark. How long was I out?"

"A couple minutes," said Zander. His face said "two minutes too long." He reached for my hand, squeezing it between both of his. I sighed and entwined my fingers with his. His touch comforted me, making my thoughts more clear.

"This is so freaking weird, Tru. It sounds like you re-dreamed?" Ruthie's eyes were wide, like she was looking at the moon.

"Yes. And I dreamed more than before, too. Dang! I wish I'd finished it."

"Well, no need to keep us waiting. What happened?" demanded Ruthie.

"Okay. But it was strange. You know how sometimes I dream about a younger version of me, but I'm watching it all happen?"

"Yeah," said Ruthie.

"Well, it was just like that. I knew the little girl was me."

"How old do you think you were?" asked Zander.

"I looked like I was just three cr four? I was riding the wolf—I guess it was a usemi."

"What the heck?" Ruthie's voice rose high. "You were riding a wolf? Like a horse?"

"Shhhh! Her dad, remember?" Conrad reminded us.

"Okay, okay, okay," she whispered. "Sorry." We listened silently for any signs that Dad had been disturbed, but heard nothing. I had reinforced the bottom of the door with a blanket before Zander showed up and apparently it had muffled our noise.

"I think Dad is still asleep." I scooted up to lean against the wall. Zander resettled next to me, an arm around my shoulders. I smiled up at him, feeling very cozy. His eyebrows clenched and unclenched, his stoic facade crumbling and rebuilding repeatedly. I ran a hand along his arm, trying to pull him away from his worried thoughts.

"You have to admit that riding a wolf is hecka weird," Ruthie said, rationalizing her outburst.

"Anyway," I continued. Ruthie swiveled Conrad in my direction again, making it an even six eyeballs riveted on me, and I could feel every one of them. I dropped my gaze to the floor.

"What I don't get is that even though I knew the woman was calling for me, she used a different name."

"What was the name?" asked Zander. Ruthie chewed on a thumbnail.

"Um, I think it was *Alondrea?*"

"A-lon-drea." Ruthie practiced it. "Unusual, but pretty."

"I heard another voice calling that name and it felt like she was someone important to me. I was scared and I wanted to run to the voice but I couldn't see a path through the smoke. Then this brown wolf—"

"I thought you said it was like the one we saw, more blond-brown," butted in Ruthie.

"I thought it was, but I was wrong. It wasn't the same wolf. This one was a darker brown, not black, but definitely different. Anyway, it did open its mouth toward me, like I said before, but it wasn't trying to bite me. It grabbed me by the shirt and tossed me onto its back. Then it took off running, like a long time. The wolf was hurt, but I didn't know until later when we were almost out of the woods. She stopped and fell down."

"She?" asked Ruthie.

I nodded, looking up at her. "I could see a house through the trees."

"Yeah, then what?" said Ruthie, pencil scratching away.

"The wolf had some kind of seizure, and then all of the sudden it reformed into a woman with long black hair. She was bleeding from a hole in her stomach and it was bad. I thought you said usemi skin was impenetrable?"

"It is!" insisted Zander, his face darkening. "Except for cutters—bullets made from akharu teeth, remember?"

"Good name for them," said Ruthie with a grimace.

"You know what that means?" said Conrad, ominously.

"It could have been a rogue agent," answered Zander, his eyebrows smashed together.

"Wait," I said. "Are cutters only used by the Nasaru?"

"I always thought so, but I can't believe the Nasaru would shoot at a kid or burn down a forest," said Conrad.

I shook my head, having no problem believing they were behind it. But Zander had closed off his face, and I let it go for now.

"What happened next, Tru?" asked Ruthie gently.

"Well," I said, giving her a disturbed look. "Before the woman changed into a human, she made this wolfie howl and a man came running out of the house."

I reached over to grab Ruthie's hand. "Ruthie, it was Uncle Ira."

"No way!" she half screeched, her eyes going wide.

"Your uncle?" asked Conrad in confusion.

Zander answered. "Not a relative. Close family friend. He's someone familiar to both of us."

"Huh-what?" said Conrad, sounding even more puzzled.

"I haven't seen him since the beginning of summer," I said, blinking furiously as I grappled with what I'd seen in my dream. "He travels a lot and it's not unusual for months to go by between visits. But it has been longer than normal. I've been meaning to ask Dad about him. Uncle Ira got me the job at the rec center this summer and I want to thank him."

"He works there?" asked Zander. "I've been going there and I've never seen him."

"I don't know if he actually does anything around there," I said.

"We think he owns it," replied Ruthie. "But he's never admitted to it. I don't think he wants people to know he's rich. Once I overheard him talking about some investment in Europe. And he speaks a bunch of languages. He's really cool."

"You know how he looks right now?" I said, looking at Ruthie.

"Yeah. Not bad for an old guy," she admitted.

Uncle Ira was tall and lean. I'd describe him as sinewy. And he moved gracefully, like he walked on wind. Unlike my dad, he had all his hair. "In my dream, he looked exactly the same," I said.

"How old is he?" asked Conrad.

"I don't know," I said. "Maybe forty?" I rubbed my eyes, feeling tired.

"On the plus side," said Ruthie. "Alondrea is an awesome name." She smiled.

My lips twitched. "Yeah, better than Tru Lee!"

"Your middle name is Lee?" chuckled Conrad. "Tru Lee? Hilarious!"

Zander remained silent, staring across the room deep in thought. The corners of my mouth lowered as I watched him. He finally noticed me twisted up toward him. By then we were all staring at him.

"I know that look, Z," said Conrad. "Who is this man?"

"Tru, the photo album you showed me before? The one with your aunt in it? Do you still have it here?" asked Zander.

"Yeah, over there on my shelf."

Zander got up to retrieve it. "Where is that picture?" he asked, handing me the album.

I opened it up to the same photo I'd shared with him before. "Here it is," I said, as I propped up the book so Conrad could see it.

"Would you name all the people in the picture for Conrad?" He tipped the photo so Conrad could see.

I moved my finger across the pictures as I said each name. "My mom. Her sister, Caroline. My dad, obviously. And," I started to say who it was, but Conrad gasped, interrupting me.

"It's him!" he said.

"Uncle Ira," I finished, a little miffed by his negative reaction. This picture had upset Zander the other day, too.

"Is this the same man from your dream?" Zander asked, pointing to Uncle Ira.

"Yeah, I already said that," I said impatiently.

"Just making sure," said Zander.

"You've got to be kidding me!" moaned Conrad.

"What?" Ruthie and I said in chorus.

"How do you guys know Uncle Ira?" Ruthie asked.

Zander looked like he was about to deliver bad news. "You know how the FBI has a most wanted list?"

Ruthie and I nodded.

"Your uncle is number one on our most wanted," he said.

I shook my head, refusing to believe it. "Impossible," I whispered.

"Why?" asked Ruthie. "He's super nice."

"All I know," replied Zander. "Is that he's some kind of terrorist, always trying to break into our labs or other

Nasaru facilities and mess up whatever we're trying to do. For instance, I heard he broke in and helped a bunch of criminals escape once."

"I heard he took out twenty soldiers all by himself!" said Conrad. "He's badass!"

"And our greatest enemy," muttered Zander. "My father would probably sacrifice a kidney to get him."

My arms quivered with little quakes that spread all over. First my aunt, now Uncle Ira. It was as if the Collector's lasso around my neck was tightening. Zander's description didn't sound like Uncle Ira at all, but neither had many of his stories. Zander and Conrad had to be wrong. Was now the time to tell Zander about his father being the Collector? I didn't know what to do. Zander pulled me closer, rubbing a hand up and down my arm.

"Uh," hesitated Conrad. "With everything going on I kind of forgot to tell you something, too."

"What?" Zander asked.

"Let's just say your father doesn't have to give up a kidney."

"They captured him?" gasped Zander. "When?"

"Not sure. I think a few weeks ago, but I didn't know how to contact you then because you went off the grid and all..."

"Wait!" I said.

"Does that mean—" Ruthie sputtered.

I scrambled away from Zander. "Are you saying that your father is holding Uncle Ira prisoner?"

"Technically, he's a terrorist," countered Zander. "So—"

"Technically," spat Ruthie. "You guys are a pair of crazy pants if you think Uncle Ira is a criminal of any kind. He's super nice and he's just about the only other family Tru has left besides her dad!"

I was reeling from the notion that Uncle Ira was a prisoner of the Nasaru.

"I'm sorry Tru. If you knew what he's done, you might not feel this way."

"Well, they're all lies." I tried to keep my voice down even though I wanted to scream at him. What would happen to Uncle Ira? Based on my last dream, he had the answers I'd been searching for. He might even know what really happened to my mom. What if he had been trying to avenge her? I could see him doing something like that. He wouldn't sit around and mope about problems like I did.

"Okay, Tru." Zander moved closer, trying to pull me toward him.

"No." I shook him off, ignoring the flash of hurt in his face. I didn't want to be distracted by him right now. While I understood that the real thing making me reject him was the secret I was keeping from him, all I could focus on was the fact that I didn't deserve his comfort. I rubbed my forehead, wondering what to say.

"Great. Now we have another mystery to figure out," sighed Ruthie. "They keep piling up."

"Well, at least that explains why your uncle looks the same today as he did when you were a baby, Tru," said Conrad.

"Huh?" I yanked my head up. "What do you mean?" I stared at the monitor. Conrad leaned forward, his shoulders up to his ears.

"Your 'uncle' is a supernatural. He's been around for a few hundred years."

"No way!" spouted Ruthie. "Awesome! He's like the fountain of youth ..."

My hands shook as I closed the photo album. Zander noticed. "Hey, don't worry. I won't let him hurt you," he said quietly.

"You still don't get it," I said. "He'd never hurt me. He's my family."

Compassion flittered in his eyes, but again, I refused his comfort and I looked away.

"Don't you guys think it's interesting that Tru's uncle is a terrorist—sorry, Tru—suspected terrorist," corrected Conrad. "And her aunt is a super healer usemi/idimmu who murdered her sister? And, that they are both on the run from the Nasaru? Don't you think we should start looking into Tru's parents?"

"Oh, come on, guys," scoffed Ruthie. "I've met her uncle and he's so not a bad guy. Besides, he's not even her real uncle."

"What if you're wrong?" persisted Conrad. "About the bad guy part."

"What if *you're* the one who's wrong?" Ruthie's eyebrows shot up and she tilted her head. "Her mom was a flippin' schoolteacher, an *elementary* schoolteacher. She wasn't a criminal or some freaking supernatural—unless you count how good she was at figuring out kids' lies. I mean geez! She was amazing! She could sniff out a liar like a dog does a bone—"

She stopped suddenly and stared at me. My spine had snapped up straight the second she mentioned Mom's talent for deciphering the truth. No way! It had always been a family joke.

Conrad spoke up first. "So Tru's mom was like a

human lie detector for little kids ... Doesn't that remind us of someone?"

"Barbecued beef kabobs!" Ruthie remembered to lower her voice, but she still wrung her hands and hopped up and down. "Tru, your mom was like you! That means she was idimmu! She must have been if your aunt was. Does that mean your dad is, too? Oh my gosh! This is crazy!"

Was my mom involved in this madness? Could my dad be, too? "No. Not possible," I murmured.

But *im*possible had taken a back seat to *possible* a while ago.

"Tru," Zander said, scooting closer. He rested a hand on my arm tentatively. "Maybe your mom didn't even realize she had a talent like that. It's common for many idimmu to not realize they are different. Just because she could tell when a kid was lying doesn't mean she knew she was idimmu. She may have just chalked it up to great intuition."

"But she wasn't crazy, like idimmu are, I mean." My mom was in her sixties when she died and never once had she seemed insane.

"Hey," said Conrad. "What if living with you, a healer, stopped her from developing those symptoms?"

"Yeah. Maybe," agreed Zander. "It's hard to tell now."

I still wasn't buying it. "But she was pretty old when she had me. How did she manage to last until then?"

"Good question," piped in Ruthie. "She could have had problems before and been on medication, though. Or, her sister may have healed her ..."

Dang it. That made some sense. "I don't think Dad is

idimmu, though." I said, pushing against the possibility that both my parents were non-humans, and that they had lied to me my whole life. "He would tell me if he was something different."

"Are you positive?" asked Zander.

No, I wasn't sure. But I needed a normal dad. I needed one who didn't know all this crazy stuff, because if he did and didn't tell me while I was going through that awful depression last year … Well, I didn't know how I felt about that.

"Has he displayed any unusual gifts?" asked Conrad.

"No. He's just … normal." But he was so much more. He was everything to me right now—my only family. I couldn't count some aunt or cousin I'd never met.

"Tru," said Zander, his eyes connecting with mine. "Use your gift and you'll know."

He was right. I closed my eyes, asking the question in my head. Gratitude filled me as I received an answer. I was getting better at it.

"No. Dad isn't idimmu, but I think Mom was," I said with a frown. Ruthie shared an understanding look with me before brightening.

"Now we know," said Ruthie, pulling out her phone to check the time. "Guys, it's getting late and maybe we should talk about Tru's addition to her dream some more. 'Cause I haven't forgotten that she said she rode a wolf like a horse. What's up with that?" The atmosphere of looming doom lightened as each of us cracked some semblance of a smile.

"Now we know Tru spent time with a usemi when she was a toddler. And we know her uncle was there, so he knows about them." While Conrad and Ruthie moved right into the next big revelation, I was still digesting the idea that my mom had a superpower like mine. Although I was sad that she'd never told me, it made me feel closer to her and miss her more. I blinked away a sudden onset of tears.

"What happened to the usemi in your dream, er, vision or whatever it was?" asked Conrad.

"Vision is a good name for it," said Ruthie.

"I don't know," I said. "That's why I tried to remember more. Uncle Ira seemed frantic. I heard him yell her name and then I called out his name and 'help,' like I knew the woman needed him even though I was just a toddler."

"What did he call her?" asked Zander.

"Jasmine." My chest tightened. "I think I knew her pretty well. I-I need to find out what happened to her."

"If only we could talk to Uncle Ira," said Ruthie.

"No!" Both Zander and Conrad said.

"What the heck?" said Ruthie.

"Seriously, guys!" Anger made my voice sharp. "He would never hurt us! I've known him all my life. He's a good man."

"Look," said Zander, his face chiseled with tension. "It's more like I don't want you anywhere near Eden. If we have to communicate with your uncle, maybe Conrad can get a message to him."

"Fine," I said, a little mollified. "But Zander, we finally have a direction. Someone who can tell us what's going on."

"He's dangerous." He backpedaled when he saw my scowl. "Whether or not he's the terrorist we think he is, he's not the guy you think he is, either." He paused to let that digest. I took a deep breath, realizing he was right.

When I nodded, he continued, "And how do we know he won't lie to us if we are able to talk to him? He might say anything if he thinks it would help him escape."

"He couldn't lie to Tru," suggested Ruthie.

"No. She isn't safe there." Zander glared at her.

"Why?" argued Ruthie. "Because of your father? Dude, you are confused. Get it straight. Either she's safe around your father, the guy you're working for and who seems to have invented a bunch of crap lies about where you guys come from, or she's safe with her uncle, who's done nothing but try to protect her, her entire life," she said, still huffing. "It's a no brainer."

"Ugh!" Zander knocked his head against the wall. "I don't know what's going on. I want to talk to my father, but I don't want to take the risk that he'll come for Tru, for her abilities. Can you imagine how helpful she could be to the Nasaru? A saint would have a hard time not taking advantage of her gifts." Conrad nodded grimly.

"Are you nuts?" I butted in. "You can't tell your dad about me. He'd take me away and make me heal people like my aunt did. She shouldn't be forced to do that, no matter what her talent is or if she is somebody's true mate and can help you guys figure out your problems. Sane people don't hold other people prisoners in the name of science or force them to use their abilities. Your father is the *psycho*." *Like Dante*, I wanted to say. But I'd already said too much. I could tell from Zander's closed-in face as he wheeled around.

"I'm sorry. I didn't mean that like it sounded." Yes, I did. Oh man. I needed to tell Zander about his father. I hoped he would understand and not blame me.

"Tru," he said in a firm voice. "Your uncle is hundreds of years old. You have no idea what he's done. And we don't know the whole story about your mother. Who knows if Dante was telling you the truth?"

My mouth hung open. Of course, I knew that Dante told me the truth. He knew it, too. I could tell by his expression. He was lying to himself again, reaching for straws.

"Dante *was* telling me the truth. Both our families owe us explanations, especially your dad. He's got a lot to account for." My throat hurt as words that I needed to tell him began to strangle me.

"What are you talking about?" A shield seemed to slide down Zander's face, almost as if he had an inkling about what was coming.

The silence dragged as I battled the war inside me.

"Oh, for the love of puppies everywhere!" snapped Ruthie. "Rip off the Band-Aid already."

I stared at her, my mouth forming a silent "No!"

Ruthie shook her head and faced Zander with accusing eyes. "We know that the Collector is your dad, Zander. And we hope your stupid brother hasn't told him about Tru because if he did, then she's toast."

Zander shook his head, his jaw clenched and hard, like petrified wood.

"I'm sorry, Zander," I breathed out. The burden of this secret was finally gone but it left me feeling as lifeless as a deflated balloon.

Zander backed away, looking like I'd slapped him.

"I don't believe it," he said, his face bone-white. "And why would you keep that to yourself this whole time?

Why do you even think it?"

I couldn't bear the pain in his face, and I scrambled to make it better. "Remember when Dante was so excited about handing over both of us to the Collector? That you were a bonus and that the Collector was going to be surprised."

Zander nodded.

"Before you got there Dante tried to make me believe you were using me—"

"I wasn't using you!" he almost yelled.

"I know, I know *now*. But he called you and Peter the silly sons...the *Collector's* silly sons..." I let it sink in. Conrad swore in the background.

"And he kept your father's identity secret from you because he wanted you and your dad to be surprised. He bragged about how funny it would be."

Zander looked so betrayed as he stared at me with disbelief.

"Don't you see? Your father must have *collected* my aunt and found out she could heal people. He's the one who controlled Dante. And now, your father is the one looking for me, only I'm not sure if he knows my real identity. I don't know if Dante told him. Or, if Peter did," I finished lamely.

I could see the devastation in his eyes as he considered all of the awful actions that could be applied to his father, if what I was saying were true—like pulling a thread on your favorite sweater and watching it unravel in horror.

It left me feeling like a traitor, which may have been appropriate because I'd called his father the Collector, enemy number one here in our little sphere of Scotts

Valley. The villain in our world started out as Dante, but he'd only been a tool of the real puppet master. The ramifications of the Collector's identity were too complicated. I wanted to reach out to Zander, tell him I knew what he was feeling, but I was afraid that he'd say something that would hurt more than I already hurt.

I followed him as he walked toward the window. He paused for a breathtaking second before ducking through.

"Where are you going?" I asked, blinking away the moisture in my eyes. I knew his world had just caved in.

He turned and faced me with pain-filled eyes. "I trusted you, Tru," he said, his voice cracking. "You should have told me first."

So that was it. I'd told Ruthie and not him. Guilt poured out of me like blood from an open wound. I opened my mouth to explain, to apologize, but he spoke before I could utter a syllable.

"I need to talk to Peter," he said in a deadpan voice.

"No, Zander!" Fear for his safety overrode my own. "You can't trust him. Don't tell him anything!" I reached for a reason to keep him here. "We have to decide what to do together."

"I just can't right now. I need to think." Then he dropped lithely from the roof to the tree and down to the ground. A second later he disappeared around the street corner.

I rubbed my wet cheeks and turned back to Ruthie. She stared at me, dumbstruck. Regret pinched her face. A sob bubbled up from my chest and Ruthie ran over to hug me.

"I'm sorry," she said.

"He won't tell him." Conrad's voice floated over to us.

I looked over and saw the tablet tipped our way.

"You don't know that," I blubbered.

"He just needs some time. I'm having a hard time with it myself. I mean are you sure? Because this changes everything. My parents work closely with Zander's father, you know. You implicate Gerard Hughes and you implicate my family, too." His voice sounded bitter and betrayed.

Great. Now Conrad was mad, too. And he was in danger. "I swear I'm not making this up. I'm sure Dante said it. You need to be really careful, Conrad."

He held his head in his hands, as if his thoughts were so colossally heavy, he couldn't sit up straight. "We still need proof," he muttered. "Dante was a nut case, remember? What if he was just messing with you?"

"I don't think so. Conrad, I was with him a long time that night. And I've been thinking about it ever since. I-I feel like it's the truth."

"Snap!" wailed Ruthie. "This is messed up. Who do we trust now?"

"If Zander's dad is the Collector," I said, looking at her with the sure knowledge in my eyes despite the hesitation in my words. "And his greatest enemy is my uncle, then it seems like Uncle Ira would be the best person to start trusting. Except we can't because now he's locked up somewhere in Eden."

"Dammit, Tru!" Conrad's boy-next door cuteness was gone, and in its place was an avenging angel. "If our parents are the bad guys, then everything Zander and I believe in is up for grabs! The Nasaru could be...I mean, damn!"

"You know what's worse, Conny?" Conrad didn't

even make a face at Ruthie's nickname for him. "What's worse is that you are smack dab in the middle of enemy territory. You need to watch your back."

"You're more right than you know," he said, sounding so alone. "My mother is part of our triad and my father works in the laboratory with Dr. Hughes. While I hope they don't know what he's up to, it seems—"

"Unlikely," Ruthie finished for him.

Conrad swallowed, and nodded his head. "I need to hide everything. Man! I feel like we stepped into some serious sh—"

"Shish-kebabs," interrupted Ruthie.

"Yeah," sighed Conrad. "The kind you can't shake off."

"Poisonous?"

"Pretty much," I agreed. "I think this is the kind of secret that gets people killed. I think it already has."

No one said a word as we thought that through.

Finally, Ruthie broke the silence with a gasp. "Bobby!" I'd forgotten his grandmother's phone call earlier and blanched. Ruthie filled in Conrad and he grew grimmer with every word.

"What do we do now?" I asked.

Zander was MIA. Conrad had to stop talking to us and cover up his research. And Bobby was missing. My mind sifted through our conversations, going all the way back to the morning after Zander and I had escaped Dante's cellar. I swallowed, feeling a pending bout of panic. The attack in the woods, the Taylors being spies, Mrs. Jackson's death ... It did feel like the Collector was closing in. The note I'd found in my locker sounded eerily like an inescapable fate—

Although his power builds faster and faster,
Your true nature still eludes the master.
But all too soon the blood shall reveal
What you are and break the seal.

"Give it a night," said Conrad, interrupting my brooding thoughts. "Talk to Zander tomorrow. Like I said, I think he's just in shock right now. This is just as earth shattering to us as discovering that usemi and idimmu exist to you."

"All right," I said woodenly, unable to tell them about the note. My throat closed in on itself, preventing any more words. Where was Zander? He had to feel the anxiety already threatening to consume me. Or was I feeling his?

"And Tru," added Conrad. "Don't feel too guilty. Truth be told, you aren't the only one with secrets."

"What the heck do you mean by that?" blurted Ruthie, squinting with suspicion.

Conrad ran a hand through his hair with a sigh. "It's not my place to say. Just give him some space for now. He'll come around." With a sad smile, he said, "I have to go. Keep safe."

Before we could question him further, the screen went blank. Conrad's words hadn't comforted me one bit and now they rang in my head like a warning bell.

You aren't the only one with secrets.

22

LOOSE LIPS LUCY

WHERE ARE YOU?

No response.

I'd been texting Zander since first break. I had hoped to catch him at his locker but he had never showed, which worried me. What if he'd gone home? I imagined the worst if he confronted his father. I wondered if Peter was still around. As much as I didn't want to talk to Peter ever again, I'd do it to find Zander. I didn't know the name of their hotel, but there were only so many in Scotts Valley.

The idea of skipping school didn't even bother me today. I was uncomfortable with everyone asking me about Dante anyway. Now that I wanted a little anonymity, people I didn't even know came up to say how awful it must have been or asked if I knew where Dante was hiding. It was almost as bad as Detective Winchester's inquisition. All I could think of was that I had to get out of here. But I chickened out on my plan to play hooky when I kept running into teachers at the exits. Fuming with frustration, I reversed course and headed to my next class.

The person I really wanted to talk to was nowhere to be found. I had so much to tell him.

Last night I had dreamed erratically about Zander and his father, my mind tumbling from scene to scene like clothes in the dryer. I wasn't sure how much was real and how much was my imagination. For the first time I'd seen his father and it made me doubt Dante's description of him. When I dreamed about Dante, I'd never *actually* seen the Collector, only Dante's reactions to him. And because of that, I'd created a dark and sinister image of Gerard Hughes. Now I could understand Zander and Conrad's surprise, because the guy looked like your average Joe with dark brown hair, hazel eyes, and an easy smile. And he looked younger than I expected, too. I saw him tucking his young sons into bed, kissing them on their heads, and hugging his wife as they left their room. Zander didn't look anything like his father. But the resemblance between Zander and his mother was strong. They shared the same beautiful sapphire blue eyes and auburn hair. She even wore it short, above her ears.

After that I'd dreamed about Uncle Ira and Jasmine, the usemi who rescued me from the forest fire when I was a little kid. I saw Uncle Ira standing over Jasmine's open coffin, grief furrowing his face before he collapsed to his knees. He must have loved her a lot. She died saving me but I'd never felt any resentment from him. In the dream, my tiny body lay curled up in a corner of the room, behind a high-backed chair. I clutched Mummy, my toy dog, the very one currently perched on my shelf, although it wasn't tattered and worn like it was now. Why was I alone? Where were my parents? And why didn't I remember this?

Talking to Uncle Ira had moved up on my priority list. But it seemed impossible now that Conrad was in shutdown mode. Should I ask Dad about my past? What had he and Mom been hiding from me?

All these thoughts had drifted through my mind the previous night as I wrestled with sleep, hoping there were no more dreams. I'd finally fallen to sleep again only to be hit with perhaps the most illuminating one of all.

Uncle Ira and Zander's father were in a lab, arguing.

"You lied to me, Gerard," accused Uncle Ira, waving a sheaf of papers in his face. Despite his beard and lab coat, I recognized him. "You were never planning to release them after the tests. You're keeping them as your own lab rats!"

Gerard's easy smile twisted up to one side and his eyes narrowed. "You can't expect me to let them go, Ira. I've spent too much time and money hunting them down. We need them."

"They answered our questions and gave you blood samples. That was the deal. You can't keep them here."

"There are always great sacrifices in the name of science."

"And they aren't your only prisoners." Uncle Ira waved the papers again. *"You have dozens of idimmu here, too. What are you really after? If you were after an infertility cure, you wouldn't need idimmu. Those poor people are already suffering for our mistakes. Don't compound our crimes."*

Gerard sighed. *"I can see that I can't change your mind, old friend."* He leaned closer, looking into Ira's eyes. *"There are no idimmu here."* He carefully lifted the papers out of Ira's frozen fingers.

Ira blinked his eyes and shook his head, as if he was trying to recall something. Gerard tucked the papers away in a folder on the counter and placed his hand on Uncle Ira's shoulder, drawing his gaze again. Gerard stared into the other man's eyes without blinking.

"You saw the usemi true mates leave this facility. They volunteered to help us and they have completed our tests. We discovered nothing unusual and no longer need their help. They have gone home to their community. You've decided to take that job offer in our east coast lab and you need to make plans to move immediately. Nothing I can say will change your mind. You told me just now of your decision. You are about to return to your office to clean your desk."

When Gerard let go and stepped away, Uncle Ira blinked slowly before reaching for the nearest counter for support with one hand. He pulled out a handkerchief with *his other and wiped his beaded forehead. As he looked up in confusion, Gerard fixed a look of concern on his face.*

"Ira! Are you all right? No wonder you want to transfer. I must be working you too hard. What if we cut back your hours? Would you stay then? Would you stay then?" Gerard grabbed Ira's shoulder to steady him, false concern layering his words.

"Sorry. No, thank you. I-I think moving east is the right move for me." Ira shook his head, his eyes still unfocused. "Sorry! Head rush, I guess. Anyway, I-I just wanted to thank you for the last year here. It was great working with you."

Gerard frowned and held out his hand. "All right. I wish you'd stay here, but I'll start the paperwork. Thank you for all you've done to help the program. If you ever change your mind, though, you have a job here."

Uncle Ira shook his hand. "No, no. I won't change my mind," he repeated like a robot before straightening his shoulders and heading out the door.

When Ruthie had questioned the black circles under my eyes this morning, I'd explained my sleepless night. Fear had seeped into her face as I shared my dreams with her. Gerard Hughes had just become creepier. Afterward, she'd been uncharacteristically sober, but it hadn't distracted her from my face. She'd pulled out her makeup and touched up my eyes so I didn't look like the walking dead.

My thoughts circled back to the present, as I zombie-stepped my way through the school walkways, wondering where Zander could be. I had expected him to meet me in the parking lot this morning. Was he avoiding me? Then again, what if he wasn't and something happened to him?

I wanted to hit something, so I picked up my step, stomping around the closest building, hoping I could find a wall or tree to smack without anyone thinking I was going postal. I skidded to a stop when I saw Ruthie sitting on the ground crying.

"Ruthie! Oh my gosh! What happened?" I knelt down beside her.

She rubbed her cheeks. "I don't know. That's the problem!" She held out her wrists. "I don't know how I got these bruises. And I don't know why my arm is bleeding."

A red line ran down the inside of her arm, oozing blood. It didn't look like a scratch, more like a razor cut. My heart fluttered in alarm.

"My throat hurts, too." She said, swallowing with a grimace. I stared at her red and swollen neck with shock.

"Who did this to you? It was Val, wasn't it," I stated through clenched teeth. Now I knew the person that I wanted to beat up. Maybe I'd stop by the gym to grab a bat.

"No. I don't think so." She wiped her face clean of tears.

"Ruthie. You have to tell me the truth."

She looked up at me with big luminous eyes. "I am! Can't you tell?"

I'd forgotten that I could. I tried to calm down and asked myself if Val had done this. No. Not Val. Then who?

"Okay, so Val didn't do it, but someone did. I should take you to the nurse."

"I don't want to go, Tru. What if this has something to do with all the weird stuff going on? I don't want to make it worse for you."

"Screw me!"

Ruthie laughed, then grimaced and put a hand to her throat. "You just said 'screw you.'"

I smiled. "Geez, Ruthie."

"Sorry. I'm deflecting," she croaked.

"When we find out who did this, we're going to kick the crap out of him."

"Damn straight."

She winced as I pulled her up. The marks on her neck were starting to turn purple. Another burst of murderous rage swept through me. At least she wasn't blubbering anymore. Zena would love to see her this low. Ruthie wiped her cheeks.

"You need something to cover up your neck." I said, determined to help her. "Got makeup in that bag of yours?"

"Of course, I have makeup, but I think I have something faster." She dug down to the bottom of her pack and pulled out a fuchsia scarf, snapping it in the air with flair.

"Perfect. And no smeared mascara. Waterproof, huh? Good call today," I said, making sure she got all the marks on her neck covered as well as her arm and wrists. "I don't think we're going to make it before the bell."

"I know I won't. I still have to cross the campus. You go ahead. You've already got one tardy."

"I'm not leaving your side, Ruthie. Who cares about

tardies?" I cared, but no way was I going to send her off on her own. Why she didn't remember what happened, I didn't know. I linked arms with her and we headed to her next class.

I knew we were going to catch hell from some teacher, but did it have to be Mean Mr. Green, one of the math teachers? He was older than dirt and smelled like it, too.

"You two! Why aren't you in class?"

We froze.

"Oh, barf nuggets!" muttered Ruthie.

"Hello, Mr. Green," said a soft female voice behind us.

It was Dr. Frankler. "You'll have to excuse these young ladies," she said. "They are helping me with a project."

He eyed us up and down before snarling, "Where are their passes?"

"I'm afraid I haven't given them passes yet. I didn't think it would be a problem. But don't worry. When they finish helping me, I'll be sure to have one in each of their hands. Come along ladies," she chirped as she waved us to follow her. Mr. Green glared, but thankfully, he let us go.

Ruthie looked wide-eyed at me, mouthing, "Who is she?" I shushed her and pulled her along.

We followed Dr. Frankler to an office door marked SCHOOL COUNSELOR. The door didn't say "doctor" or "psychologist" like I thought it would. She closed it behind us and gestured toward two cushy chairs in front of her desk. I thought, *huh, no couch* … It looked similar to the principal's office, but she'd softened up the walls with some Monet prints. It was warm and inviting, except for the metal filing cabinet located in the corner.

The only thing on her desk besides her laptop and phone was a pottery jar. I did a double take when I saw it. She'd been telling the truth. It was like Mom's terra cotta pot, except that it had different drawings. Curious images flowed across its surface—a woman lying on the ground, one arm around her own pot and the other thrown into the air. Ferocious creatures were leaping out of the pot. The design looked familiar. I blinked and looked closer. Was that a hand gripping the edges of the pot, like a person was trying to get out? Dr. Frankler caught me looking.

She picked it up, spinning it around it so I could see the backside. "It's a representation of Pandora's jar. Remember our conversation yesterday?"

The scene on it surprised me. A pack of snarling dogs, mermaids with sharp teeth and hollow eyes, and metal-looking birds swarming toward a globe that looked like the planet Earth. The artist incorporated elements from each creature into the rest of the pottery design around the top and bottom of the jar.

"What the heck is that?" I asked, pointing to the horned snake.

"The snake? That represents the evil we spoke about," she replied.

"What about that?" I said, pointing to the hand coming out of the jar.

Dr. Frankler smiled. "I believe that is hope."

"It's a person?"

"Well, why not?"

"Oh, yeah," I said, thinking it made sense given that she was a head shrink. She had helped Bobby be more hopeful. "I guess that works. Anyway, nice jar."

"Thank you, Tru. It's very important to me."

I looked over at Ruthie who was giving me a "what the heck'" look. I lowered myself into my chair.

"Ruthie Robles, isn't it?" asked Dr. Frankler.

"Y-yes," stuttered Ruthie, now that the attention was on her. Thankfully, her voice had recovered a little and now it sounded simply husky.

"I'm Dr. Frankler, the school counselor."

"Nice to meet you?" said Ruthie hesitantly.

"So, what did you need us for?" I asked her, hoping this would be brief.

Dr. Frankler set the jar down and leaned back, her hands clutched lightly in front of her. She eyed both of us, as if wondering what to do.

"Why are you girls out of class?" she asked, one eyebrow raised.

Ruthie pulled her sleeves down over her hands, keeping her wrists out of sight. I bit my lip, wondering what to say and hoping she wouldn't convince me to spill like she had done at my house.

"Just helping my friend with girl stuff. You know." I pressed my knuckles to my mouth and bounced my knee.

"Girl stuff," said the doctor with a smirk. She squinted at Ruthie.

"Uh …" stammered Ruthie, blinking fast. "I really don't know," she said. "Honest."

The doctor looked confused. "You don't know?"

"I don't remember," she admitted, before slapping a hand over her mouth.

I kicked her. She was about to blab everything, and then we'd get hauled off to some hospital for the insane. She looked at me with wide eyes. I understood her desperation. On a normal day and if I were a normal person, I would say I liked the doctor. But I wasn't normal and my life was full of the supernatural right now. Plus, I was beginning to think that there was something not altogether human about her.

"What is the last thing you do remember?" asked Dr. Frankler, her eyebrows clenched in concentration.

Ruthie bounced a little in her chair, pinching her lips with her fingers and looking ridiculous. Any other time, I'd laugh, but my stomach twitched with trepidation. Before I could think of a single thing to prevent her from opening her mouth, she burst out "Leaving Mr. Pham's class, first period."

"But that was well over an hour ago," said the doctor. "What did you do second period?"

Ruthie gasped, the air expelling from her mouth as if compelled. "I said I don't remember!" She bit her lips. Her eyes widened self-consciously.

I had to do something.

"Are you really a doctor?" I asked. Ruthie stiffened, dropping her eyelids with suspicion.

The doctor raised one perfectly manicured eyebrow. "Of course, I am, Tru. Why do you ask?"

"Well, I guess what I mean is ... is that *all* that you are?"

She gave me a look that made me feel like a bug on a petri dish. Then she chuckled, her eyes sparkling.

"My goodness, what are you getting at?" Her words seemed to attach themselves to my brain, digging in and coaxing out an answer.

I pulled my lips in, trying to prevent the words from betraying me, but it was no use. "I-I need to know if you're human. And who you're working for. Other than the school of course."

Ruthie gasped. "Tru!" I looked at her, shaking my head.

"I mean," I kept going. "We just have weird stuff going on right now, and we don't know if it's safe to confide in you."

"Tru. Ruthie." She leaned forward across her desk, her face serious again. "I promise you that you can safely tell me anything. I'm not working for anyone who would hurt you." She paused. "And I suspect that you can determine if I'm telling you the truth, can't you, Tru?"

"How did you know that?" blurted Ruthie. "Oh! You must be one of *them.*"

"Why whatever do you mean?" she laughed, her eyes twinkling with mirth. "I suppose Tru confided in you, didn't she?" Ruthie and I looked at each other in amazement.

The doctor paused thoughtfully, and then slowly tilted her head to the side. "Tru, you said a word yesterday that has me worried you've become involved with some dangerous people."

"You spoke to her yesterday?" asked Ruthie, looking at me.

"Before you came over," I replied. Turning back toward the doctor, I asked, "What are you talking about?"

"You said the word *idimmu.*"

Ruthie gasped. "Good gravy!"

"Wait!" I said. "How do you know it's a word?"

Dr. Frankler relaxed back into her chair. "I want to be honest with you, Tru. Can I trust you?"

"Me?" I asked in surprise, before nodding. "What do

you know?"

"I know quite a lot actually. Sometimes, too much." The corners of her eyes crinkled with humor again, but I sensed a hint of bitterness in her words. "I know that some people have unique talents, unusual talents, talents that are often hidden because most people aren't ready to know about them."

A shiver ran up the side of my neck.

"I think you might be one of these special people, Tru."

Ruthie cast a nervous glance at me.

"And I think your friend, Ruthie, knows this. I think others know about you, too. And that somehow you are involved with some … unsafe people." She raised a concerned eyebrow. "I want to help you. Can you tell me how you are *really* doing so I can help you?"

"Why should we tell you anything?" I asked with a scowl. "How do we know we can trust you?"

"I don't blame you for being suspicious. It's smart to be cautious." She paused, considering me for a moment. "What if I told you I met your mother a long time ago, and that you used to have a different name. Would that help?"

I froze and Ruthie started muttering, "Oh my gravy, oh my gravy, oh my gravy" under her breath.

"I'm right aren't I?" She smiled at our reactions. "I didn't know why I needed to come here until I made that connection." She seemed relieved. "Tru," she said, tilting her head. "It's obvious you don't have anyone looking out for you and I truly want to help you. It's what I do."

"What do you mean, what you do?"

She picked up her pottery jar again. "I help

supernaturals such as yourself find their way in this world." She ran a hand over the jar's painted images.

I was definitely some kind of supernatural in need of help. Perhaps she could protect me from the Collector. I considered telling her everything. If Zander were here, I'd feel better about it. But what if she was playing me? She could be another spy for the Collector. Dante said he was sending people here to get me. They should have been here by now. The possibility gave me very little hope that Zander and I would ever be together. Still, a stubborn spark of positivity flared, hope. The Collector's people couldn't know I was the one they were looking for, could they? I didn't know for sure. I didn't know if I could trust the woman in front of me.

I thought about the way Dr. Frankler made me want to spill my guts and it reminded me of the way Mom could always tell when her students were lying.

"You can do something to people, can't you?" I said. "You can make people talk." She could make people tell them the truth. Yes, that was it. Was it a coincidence that she could do something so similar to me?

"Dang!" said Ruthie, her eyes bugging out as she stared at Dr. Frankler. "You turned me into Loose Lips Lucy!"

The doctor chuckled, her eyes twinkling with genuine amusement. Suddenly, there was a short knock on her door and it swung open.

Mrs. Jones, the school secretary, pulled up short when she saw us. "Oh, sorry, Dr. Frankler. I didn't know you were meeting with anyone."

Dr. Frankler gave us a brief look of frustration. "It's fine, Sharon," she said.

"The meeting about 'you-know-who' starts in five minutes. Mr. Millard asked me to collect everyone. Like I don't have enough to do already," she complained.

"Thanks. I'll be right in."

When the door closed, Dr. Frankler leaned forward across her desk. "Girls, we have a lot to talk about, don't we?" It was a rhetorical question, more like a statement. "I hope you give me a chance to explain. Suffice it to say, I have unique abilities like you, Tru. And I've managed to keep my secret from the same people you are avoiding. You are more rare than you know, Tru, more rare than me. And I've decided that your safety is my number one priority right now. I may be able to make you talk, but I can't make you believe me." She sighed. "However, if you give me a chance to explain, you will be glad you did. There's so much to tell you ... You must be so confused ... This is a difficult stage for you ..." She broke off as we looked on in confusion. Then she sighed. "The most important thing you need to do right now is nothing."

I didn't want to sit around doing nothing. Doing nothing was stressing me out. I stared mutely at her, not ready to confide in her.

"Tru, I have to ask," she said when she realized I wasn't about to promise her anything. "Have you noticed anything peculiar about yourself lately? Things you can't explain?"

Ruthie gasped and my face must have revealed something, for Dr. Frankler's face tightened in worry and she mumbled, "It's too soon."

"What's too soon?" I asked, frightened by her expression.

"I don't have time to explain it to you. But you must

be careful. You may be experiencing the *parinati*. It's the transformation that those with special abilities go through as they ...they ..." She paused, looking like she wasn't sure how to explain it. "Well, during this process your abilities can be volatile, that's all." She bit her lip.

"What do you mean by volatile?" asked Ruthie with an unusual steel to her voice.

Dr. Frankler's eyes slid to Ruthie. "Her abilities may be inconsistent and difficult to control. And dangerous." Lines appeared between her eyes as she scowled at us. "It's very important that Tru not use them right now. The consequences could be ..." She seemed at a loss for words and my heart squeezed in panic as the fear I'd been ignoring each time I healed my friends resurrected itself with alarming fervor. What had I done?

But Dr. Frankler was looking at Ruthie and missed the guilt that must have been written across my face. I closed my eyes and prayed for calm.

"My dear," said the doctor as she leaned closer to Ruthie. "You must watch out for her, for each other." Ruthie gulped and nodded, her eyes wide.

Then Dr. Frankler turned to me. I was sure I still looked guilty, but I must have appeared terrified because the doctor made a soothing noise.

"Tru," she said gently. "The parinati is not to be feared, but celebrated, with those around you who can teach you to control your powers, to help you mold them—for your protection as well as others." A fleeting sadness crossed her face. "I don't know how you came to be alone in this, but you aren't alone anymore," she added tenderly.

Ruthie objected with a "Hey!" but the doctor ignored

her.

She eyed the clock like a child facing a plate of cooked spinach. "I have to go now, but if you would remain home—" She raised a hand as Ruthie and I both opened our mouths to argue. "Never mind. I know you won't do that. And it would be difficult to explain to others. So if you must come to school, could you please let me help you? Can you come to my office after school today?"

"I can't," said Ruthie, her hands squeezing the arms on her chair.

"Me neither," I said. "Dad's picking me up."

"Tomorrow at lunch?" she asked, determination in her face.

Although I wasn't convinced we could completely trust her yet, I hadn't sensed anything false about her. And her dire warnings about this parinati ... it felt like something I shouldn't ignore. Hopefully by tomorrow, I'd have a chance to talk to Zander.

"Okay," I said. Ruthie nodded.

With passes in our hands, we headed off to the rest of our classes. I hated parting with Ruthie, still worried about her missing memory and injuries. If Val wasn't messing with her, who was? The fact that she didn't re-member any of second period was strange.

I checked my messages, hoping Zander had replied. Nothing. It made me so mad. If he meant what he said about us, why wouldn't he call me back? Maybe his brother was messing with him, maybe doing the mind-whammy thing on him. Then it hit me. Peter! Mind-whammy! Zander said he could make people forget things. That could be what happened to Ruthie. But twice now? Why? Then a thought occurred to me and I sucked in a breath as warmth ran up my arm. That was it! I knew it was true because my ability reassured me that I was right as soon as I ran the idea through my mind. Peter was torturing Ruthie for information about *me*. Then he was making her forget it. I clenched my teeth with anger, even as a sliver of apprehension spiraled up my spine. I'd told Ruthie everything, so now the question was, *what had she told Peter?*

23

ETCH-A-SKETCHY

MY PHYSICS TEACHER WAS ancient. He had to be the oldest teacher in the school district, maybe in the whole state. He couldn't hear a thing, so kids got away with murder. The class was a joke. Every time he turned toward the board paper airplane notes flew across the room. I peeked around the edge of the door. It was business as usual. While I debated whether or not to skip it, someone squealed my name and all eyes spun my way. Well, all of the students' anyway. Mr. Gordon continued to talk and scrawl equations across the board.

It was now or never, so I walked over to him, finally getting his attention as I approached from his side. I handed him my pass, to which he gave a cursory glance before tucking it into his shirt pocket and waving me to a seat. I usually grabbed a desk in the front to avoid as many classroom shenanigans as I could, but someone was already sitting in my favorite spot, a new face. She was small, with dark brown hair hanging straight to her shoulders and large cocoa brown eyes. She gave me a smile that didn't reach her eyes, but her dimples winked at me from both sides of her face. She looked familiar, however, I couldn't place her. She was definitely new to this class. I moved past her, resigned to dodging airplanes and spit wads and almost tripped as I passed by another new face sitting in the next desk. His legs stretched out in front of him to wrap around the "new girl's" chair. "New boy" didn't even pretend to be pleasant like "new girl." He pierced me with a pointed glare. I couldn't help taking it personally and wondering what I'd ever done to him. Two new kids in class? "New boy" had wavy blond hair forced into submission by hair gel. His thick eyebrows were drawn together producing a deep V in his forehead. I made my way down the aisle, trying not to dislodge the textbooks and binders hanging over the desks.

"Watch it, freak!" said someone as I passed. It was Summer, one of Zena's minions who had knocked me down weeks ago. I gave her a dark look and moved on. I still owed her for that one, so I backed up a little, colliding with her pile of papers.

"Oops!" I said. A few papers floated across the aisle and Daniel Krueger snagged one. As he read, he started cracking up. I looked at Summer, whose face was beet red. She jumped out of her desk to grab the paper.

Daniel whispered to a boy on the other side of him and they both jeered at Summer. Whatever they were saying made her face crumble. I sat down, reminding myself that she deserved it. But I felt no satisfaction as I watched the boys teasing her from my back row seat.

I pulled out my notebook and tried to make sense of Mr. Gordon's mumbling. When that failed it didn't take long for my mind to return to my best friend. Peter worried me and I had to tell Ruthie what I'd figured out. I pulled out my phone.

Me: I think I know who was messing with you!

Ruthie: Really? Who? How?

Me: Mind-whammy boy.

Ruthie: Mother of meatballs!! I'm going to kick him in the nards.

Me: Maybe you did. Maybe you just can't remember.

Ruthie: Snap! I hope I left bruises! But why me?

Me: Info.

Ruthie: OMG! He gave me the shakedown and then erased me? He's a real life Etch-a-Sketch!

Me: Good one. Etch-a-sketchy is more like it. Seriously, this is dangerous. I need to find Zander. He still isn't responding. What if he's in trouble?

Ruthie: Wanna skip and find him?

The idea was so tempting it took me a minute to reply.

Me: Better not. Besides, teachers are staking out the exits. And Dad barely let me go to school

this morning. He might start homeschooling if I get caught.

Ruthie: What about after school?

Me: Dad's picking me up.

Ruthie: Oh yeah. Dangit! That man is really getting in the way of our sleuthing!

Me: Seriously.

I looked up and saw the new kids staring at me. Weirdos! I blocked out the strange kids by leaning down behind the person in front of me.

Me: 2 new kids in my class. They're staring.

Ruthie: Totally forgot to tell you! Must be Wynona and Luke. They started yesterday. You were in lockdown mode.

Me: Are they related?

They sure didn't look like it, but why else would two kids show up in school at the same time?

Ruthie: No. But he sticks to her like glue. I think they're from some place in the South. They talk like Blake Shelton and Miranda Lambert.

Me: Since when do you listen to country music?

Ruthie: Stuck in Idaho last summer, remember?

Me: Oh yeah. So why are they looking at me?

Ruthie: Dunno. Busted. CU later.

I sighed and spent the rest of class wondering what I was going to do about Ruthie.

"HEY TRU!"

I was almost to the quad when I heard Isaac calling from behind, causing me to pause. *Not now*, I thought, deciding to ignore him. I wanted to make sure Ruthie was safe and sound at our table. I hurried around a corner so I could see the lunch tables. My best friend sat at our usual table with Phoebe. I let out a breath I didn't even realize I was holding. No Val in sight, though. Then I remembered he'd been distancing himself from Ruthie. While I was kind of glad about that, I knew Ruthie's feelings were hurt. I needed to call Maverick and talk him into doubling with me for Homecoming. The dance was coming up fast, so I'd better get on it. And nothing would cheer her up like a date to a dance.

"Tru!" Isaac had caught up to me and he sounded upset.

I whipped around. "What?" I said.

"Are you okay? I heard what Dante did to you and I just wanted to see for myself that you are all right." His eyes raked me from head to toe, his brows knitted. "I was worried," he finished.

"I'm fine." I rolled my eyes. "Really. The whole thing's been blown way out of proportion."

"You know," he said, regret stamped on his face. "I looked all over for you after school that day. I even went to your place."

"Oh, thanks for checking on me," I said, my voice softening. The night Dante kidnapped me, I would have given my right arm for someone to come looking for me. He could be a dork sometimes, but under it all he was a nice guy.

"Well, I'm glad you're okay."

I waved my arms down my body. "Obviously, I'm fine."

When I moved to leave, Isaac blocked me, taking a deep breath. "Tru, one more thing. I also wanted to apologize." His wide shoulders drooped.

"Isaac, we had this talk." I was impatient to get to Ruthie. "We're okay."

"I know. I just wanted to tell you I'm all right with ... Uh, Ruthie talked to Phoebe, who talked to me ... Etc. Etc." He rubbed the back of his neck.

Oh great. What had they told him?

"I mean, I get it now," he said, shoving his hands into his pockets.

"You get what, exactly?" I said, needing him to be absolutely clear.

His little shrug said loads. "You and Zander. It's okay."

This should have made me feel great, but for some reason it didn't. I'd wondered how he'd feel if Zander and I went public. I didn't want to hurt him any more. I still felt a little guilty about leading him on. I had liked him at first, but it had been more of a one-day crush. Who was I kidding? A half-day crush. It was all Zander the second I saw him. I hadn't realized it at the time, though, and I'd let myself be pushed toward Isaac. I could see now that it had been different for Isaac. He'd really liked me. I got that. But he was so not my type. He'd become territorial, following me all the time, getting angry when

Zander came over to study, refusing to take any hints from me. Sure, Zander was a little possessive, too. But for some reason it didn't bother me as much. I thought of my own jealous behavior the other day. Man, who was I to judge?

"I'm sorry, too," I said, meaning it. "I didn't know how to tell you."

"It's okay," he said, his hands digging further into his pockets. He looked dejected and adorable at the same time. I couldn't help but smile.

"Can't we all be friends?" I asked. "You know, water under the bridge, blah, blah, blah?"

"Sure," he agreed. But he hastily added, "You and me at least. I'm not sold on Zander." One side of his mouth pulled up.

"Fair enough." It was a decent deal, considering Isaac wasn't one of Zander's favorite people either. "By the way, have you seen him today?"

"Nope." Suddenly, Isaac frowned, stepping closer to peer at me. I backed up thinking, *what now?*

"What's up with your eyes?" he asked. "Do you have contacts?"

"What?" I laughed. "I don't do contacts." Now that I knew my eyes were drawing such a close inspection, I couldn't seem to stop blinking them. Isaac stepped closer, reaching for my face.

"Whoa, there, buddy," I said, putting up a hand to stop him.

"But they were blue!" he insisted, squinting at me. "Just for a second. I mean I think they were."

Now I knew he was just messing with me. I laughed, "Seriously, Isaac! You're freaking me out." I squeezed my eyes shut one more time before opening them wide for him. He looked confused. "Boring brown." I bent to retrieve my dropped backpack. "I can't believe you didn't know my eye color!" I began walking toward the lunch crowd.

Isaac followed behind me, trying to convince me he wasn't nutters. "Really, Tru! They were blue just a second ago."

I glanced at him with a look of disbelief. He squeezed the back of his neck with a scowl.

"Maybe it was the lighting," he mumbled.

"You mean the bright and sunny sky? Yeah, probably," I said.

He shrugged with a wry smile and we continued over to our table. Val's friend, Jake, was saying something to Phoebe with a grin, but she didn't seem amused. Ruthie looked to her right with a haunted expression on her face. I wondered how one's mind could be erased and if shadows of the memories still remained somewhere. When Peter had tried to erase my mind, it had been excruciatingly painful. Settling in next to her, I put my arm around her and gave her a squeeze.

"How are you doing?" I asked quietly. She rested her head on my shoulder. It was so unlike my strong friend, I wanted to snap Peter's neck.

"Weird," she whispered. "I keep thinking about him and I feel scared. I think you were right. Man! It makes me so mad. I hate this."

Isaac stared at us from across the table, pointedly looking at Ruthie's loosening scarf. I casually reached out and smoothed it over the marks on her neck.

"Do I need to beat up Val?" he asked, his eyes a little

too perceptive, his jaw clenched. Phoebe tilted her head, also staring at Ruthie. Jake was attempting to gain her attention by pulling out his fake ID and spinning a story about his cousin and him getting into a club.

Ruthie and I smiled at Isaac, both amused and moved by his protective attitude. "No," said Ruthie at first. But then she mumbled, "Maybe."

I snorted. "What the heck?"

"Well, he is being a scumbag."

"Yeah, but ... does he deserve to be killed by Isaac just because he hasn't asked you to Homecoming? Come on." I tilted my head toward Isaac's darkening face.

"Uhhhh," she seemed to debate it in her head for a moment. Then she noticed the dangerous glint in Isaac's eyes and sighed. "I guess not."

"What's wrong, then?" asked Isaac, still glowering. Jake finally gave up on Phoebe, who was paying more attention to us than him, and left our table with a "catch ya later."

Ruthie straightened, giving me a sidelong glance. I could tell she wanted to tell them what was going on, but I gave my head a tiny shake. We couldn't bring them into our mess, my mess.

"I think Val and I are over," said Ruthie, looking down at her twisted hands. I sighed in relief.

"But you said you were scared." said Isaac. "I mean, I thought you said something like that." He paused before tacking on, "I have good hearing."

"Who would you be scared of?" asked Phoebe with concern.

"It's nobody," insisted Ruthie, wiggling in her seat.

"Guess what?" I asked, trying to derail the

conversation. When I had their attention, I explained the new prison my dad was creating out of our home. They quickly jumped on board my pity train.

"That sucks big time," said Phoebe, paling a bit. Apparently, the thought of being locked inside my house horrified her.

Isaac's forehead furrowed. "I don't get it. You said it was no big deal, but it sounds like it is if your dad is going to so much effort with security. Does he think Dante is coming back?"

"Nah," I said. "My dad is just way overprotective. He works in San Jose sometimes and this is his way of taking control, that's all. Besides, I know how to switch on and off the alarm."

"What if your dad can control it from anywhere?" asked Phoebe. "I saw a commercial about an alarm system that could do that."

"Well, then yes, that would suck really, really bad." We all laughed.

"And the best part—okay, the only good part—is that she's finally getting a dog!" Ruthie announced.

Isaac perked up. "Hey! That's pretty cool. What kind?"

"He's a German shepherd and a retired police dog."

"Awesome," said Phoebe. "What's his name?"

"Knox."

"Nice name," smiled Isaac. "I'm good with animals. I'd love to come by and meet him. And I can help if you need any training tips."

I frowned.

He raised his hands high. "As a friend!" he insisted with a chuckle. Ruthie and Phoebe snickered.

"Well," I shrugged. "He should be there when I get home. I'll ask Dad about it."

ZANDER WAS A NO-SHOW the entire day. After school, Ruthie said she was driving the twins to their mom's shop and then going straight home. She swore her mom would be there and that she wouldn't leave her house for the rest of the day. With her safety taken care of until tomorrow, I relaxed.

As I headed out to the front of the school to meet Dad, my mind wandered back to Zander. Over the last couple of hours, my irritation had grown into uneasiness. I wished I could do that "finding thing" that Zander did for me.

Mom's white Honda Accord sat at the front of the line of parents picking up their kids. The plan was for me to drive it when I got my license. I had my permit, but I hadn't been able to practice since school started. Dad waved from the driver's seat, catching my attention. I headed over.

"Hey, Honey!" he said. "Wanna drive today?"

I shook my head. My thoughts were too scattered to concentrate on driving, which stressed me out on a good day.

"How's Knox?" I asked, as he pulled away from the curb.

"You're gonna love him! He's a smart dog, Tru. Just amazing."

As Dad went on about the newest member of our family, some of the lines on his face smoothed out. I felt my lips widening into a grateful smile. This dog was already good for Dad, so as much as I worried about Knox putting a damper on my clandestine meetings with Zander, I was grateful that he made my dad happy.

"Isaac and Phoebe are super excited to meet him. Isaac says he's really good with animals."

Dad pursed his lips. "It's too soon to introduce him to others, honey. Mike said that we should wait until he's accustomed to us first. Then visitors. He's not your average dog. He can be lethal when surprised."

"Oh. Okay." Lethal. I sighed. That meant no more Scooby Doo meetings. If we ever had one again, anyway. Oh, Zander. I really needed to talk to him about Dr. Frankler, and Bobby, and … Homecoming? Was that still happening? I frowned at my pessimistic thoughts. Ruthie would be on the warpath if I didn't follow through with our plans. No, I had to be more positive. So, until I heard otherwise, I'd proceed as planned.

"Hey, can we stop by the rec center on the way home?" I asked.

"What for?" Dad raised one eyebrow my way.

"I need to ask Maverick if he'll go to Homecoming with Ruthie." I reached over to turn on the radio, switching it to my favorite station.

"Doesn't she have a boyfriend already?" asked Dad.

"They broke up and Maverick is a nice guy. I think he'll go with Ruthie if I ask. She wants to double." Dang, I hadn't meant to say that.

"Double? With you?" His hands tightened on the steering wheel.

"Uh, yeah. It's okay for me to go to Homecoming, right? I mean, Dad, it's Homecoming."

"Are you going with that Isaac kid?"

"No, another boy asked me. Zander. I'm going with him."

"Zander who?"

"Zander Hughes. He's new this year. I think you'll like him."

Dad's hands loosened as he veered around a corner. "Well, I do like that Maverick kid at the gym. Very polite and seems mature. As long as he's coming with you guys, I guess it will be okay. When did you say this was?"

"It's in a few weeks. Um," I bit my lip, expecting a battle. "And I need to get a dress, too." He had to know Homecoming dresses weren't cheap. "Ruthie and I found some great ones online," I added.

"Sure," he said, surprising me. Maybe he didn't know how much formals cost. No sense in telling him until I had a dress in hand.

Dad waited in the car outside the entrance to the rec center while I dashed inside. Kids streamed into the building, goggles and swim caps in hand, their mothers toting large bags. The automatic doors slid open and the smell of chlorine washed over me like a friendly hello. I smiled in relief to see the very person I was looking for behind the front desk and called out a greeting. He looked up from the computer.

"Well, if it isn't Tru Parker," he smiled as I walked up to the counter. "How's school?" Maverick was a cute mix of Irish and Filipino, with brown hair and gray eyes. A smattering of freckles dusted his cheeks and his eyes tilted just enough to make him look like he was smiling even when he wasn't. He was a little taller than me with wide, muscled shoulders.

"Homework sucks."

He laughed, a quiet throaty chuckle that showed off his even white teeth. I leaned an elbow onto the counter. "I thought it would be more quiet around here once school started." Over the summer, the place had been filled with children and families going to swim lessons, basketball games, and camps. Although it was autumn the building seemed almost as busy.

"It's peaceful here before the kids get out of school." He grimaced. "Then the ducks start invading." By *ducks*, he meant all the tweens. The small children were *chicks*, the older kids were *ducks*, and the teenagers were *swans*. Maverick had little patience for middle schoolers. "And now we have a year-round swim team starting up." He shook his head wearily. "Really could use you here. Interested in working after school?"

That's the last thing I had time for, although I did miss everyone. I hadn't realized that my co-workers had become so important to me until I quit. It was nice to know they missed me, too.

I grinned. "Wish I could."

He sighed. "Oh well. Think about it. Even if it's just weekends."

A young mother and her two children came in, already dressed in their swimsuits. Maverick paused to check them in, barking out "Walk!" to the kids as they tried to sprint toward the indoor pool. Their mother grabbed their arms, curbing some of their enthusiasm.

When he pivoted back to me, I leaned on the counter, ready to drop my plan on him. "The reason I came in today—"

"What?" gaped Maverick in mock surprise. "You didn't come in to chat with your 'ol pal and catch up?"

"Yeah, yeah. My dad's waiting for me in the car."

"Oh, that's right. You're still a non-driving individual. Geez, get your license already."

I rolled my eyes. "I will. Anyway, I have a favor to ask you."

"Really?" He seemed genuinely surprised. "Okay, what's up?"

"Well ... My friend, Ruthie ... Remember her?" She had been gone all summer, but before she left, she visited me at the rec center a few times, mostly to ogle the fitness instructors.

"Dark hair? About this tall?" He held his hand about shoulder height. "The one who ditched you for Idaho?"

"Yep. But Idaho wasn't her fault. Anyway, she wants to double with me to Homecoming—"

Maverick's eyes rounded and his lips twisted in distaste. I hurried my explanation.

"You see, she just broke up with her boyfriend and we want to double, so I was hoping you'd come with Zander and me as her date." I sucked in air and waited.

"You can't be serious?" He stretched to his full height, which wasn't quite six feet, and puffed out his chest. "I'm too old for you kids.

"No, you're not," I pressed. "What are you? Eighteen? Nineteen?"

"Almost twenty," he declared, placing his hands on his hips. "High school dances sucked enough when I was in high school. It would be punishment now."

"Come on!" I begged. "You went to school in Santa Cruz. Scotts Valley is better."

He raised his eyebrows, giving me a look of disbelief.

"Also, Maverick, my dad won't let me go unless I

double with you." I gave him my best puppy dog look, but he seemed immune.

"Oh? You have a boyfriend now?" He leaned forward. "Do tell!" he whispered dramatically.

I blushed, but plowed forward. "His name is Zander Hughes and he's new this year."

Maverick straightened, rubbing his chin. "Hughes? That sounds familiar. As in Alexander Hughes?"

"He goes by Zander." My eyes narrowed. "Why? Do you know him?"

Maverick leaned toward his monitor and ran his hands across the computer keyboard. "I think so. At least I think he's the same guy that comes to the gym." He turned the monitor toward me so I could see a membership photo. It was Zander, but like all membership photos, it was blurry and unflattering.

"That's him!" Belatedly, I remembered that he had told me about coming to this gym, when I'd told him Uncle Ira owned it. Maverick looked serious now, with deep lines between his eyes.

"So, you're going to Homecoming with this *Zander* guy?" he asked, squinting at me.

Great. First Dad, now Maverick. "Yeah. So?" Why was I getting the first degree every time I mentioned going to Homecoming with Zander?

"Uh, I don't know. There's just something about him." He paused. "When's this dance?"

"In a few weeks." I gave him the date.

He tapped his fingers on the counter, thinking for a moment. Then he leaned forward, the earlier tension gone. "So, how bad do you want me to go?"

I had a feeling Maverick was messing with me now—

or he was moving on to extortion.

"Maverick!" I whined, worried he'd screw up my Homecoming plans.

"Okay," he laughed. "I'll go with your friend. On one condition."

I sighed. "What?"

"You fill in for me here when I need you, no questions asked."

"What? I don't have time—"

"Nah-uh. Deal or no deal."

I sighed again. "Fine. Just once."

"It's a *high school dance.*" He punctuated the words like they were individual beatings. "Three times."

"Two! And that's final!"

He held out his hand with an evil smile. "Deal." I shook his hand, thinking I wouldn't mind the mundaneness of this center after the last few crazy weeks.

"It's casual dress, right?" he asked.

"Maverick—" I started, afraid I'd have to strike another deal to get him dressed up. But then I realized that he was joking again. I reached over the desk to smack his arm. He pretended it hurt.

"You're such a baby," I teased. "Wear a tux or Ruthie will be crushed."

"Yeah, yeah. Got it covered."

"You do?"

"I don't always wear gym clothes you know." He laughed. "I don't own one, but I know a guy who knows a guy ..." He waved his hand.

For some reason I had a hard time picturing Maverick in anything but gym clothes and swim trunks. I giggled, looking forward to seeing another side of him. "This is going to be fun!"

"Hey, I don't have to pay for anything, do I? You know, tickets and dinner?" he asked.

I smiled ruefully. *Classy*, I thought. "No. Ruthie has it covered."

"Really? I was kidding, but hey, that's great." He leaned closer, lowering his voice. "She knows this is just a favor, right? You aren't trying to set me up?" He glared at me with potential retribution.

"No!" I raised my hands in surrender before hiding one hand behind my back with my fingers crossed. "Total favor. I mean she thinks you're cool, but she just wants to have fun." I laughed hysterically inside my head. *Oh Maverick*, I thought. *You have no idea what you are getting yourself into.*

"Thank you!" I gushed. "It's going to be awesome. You'll love it." I spun around to head out before he tried to weasel anything else out of me.

"Hey!" he yelled.

I twirled around.

"What's your friend's name again? Her whole name?"

"Oh," I smacked my forehead and returned to the desk. I grabbed a piece of paper and wrote down her name and number. "It's Ruthie Robles. You'll recognize her."

"Do I have to call her?" He scrunched up his face.

"No, I'll tell her." I beamed. "We can meet at my house and head to the dance from there. Thanks, Maverick! It's going to be super fun! Really! I'll call you with the details."

He nodded. "Remember, you owe me."

"Okay, okay." I hurried out to Dad before he changed

his mind.

24

Rules, Shmules

Knox was inside his crate in the spare bedroom when we got home. Dad told me to stay in the living room until he brought him down. He said it could take a month to get Knox to bond with us, and we couldn't leave him out of his crate while we were away from the house until then. That surprised me. It was going to be a while before he was a full-fledged guard dog for us.

I heard a bark, the foreign sound echoing in our house. I wasn't sure if it was a happy bark. Dad had said that everything had gone well between him and Knox today. His friend, Mike, had let Knox stay rather than try to integrate him into our home over several days. It proved what an exceptional dog he was. Dad boasted about how surprised Mike had been when Knox quickly accepted his commands. I had to admit I was impressed with Dad's dog know-how. He'd never told me before today that he'd had dogs growing up. Probably because Mom hadn't wanted to get a dog.

I heard the clipping of dog paws against the wood. Excitement trickled through my veins and I knelt on the floor like Dad had instructed me. I wasn't supposed to approach Knox; instead, I needed to let him come to me.

Dad paused at the door, Knox's leash in his hand, and squatted down to scratch him under the chin. Knox leaned into him, his long tongue lolling out of his mouth. "That's a good boy," Dad said. He held out a dog snack and a wet tongue licked it up. "This is Tru," Dad whispered into one furry ear. It twitched upward, as if he understood.

Knox stepped closer, obediently sticking to Dad's side. "Tru, meet your new brother, Knox." Too impatient to wait, I leapt up and reached forward.

Knox froze, his tail rising. He sniffed, bared his teeth, and let loose a low growl. *What the heck?* I thought, as I scooted away. Knox followed me.

"Stop!" ordered Dad. At first, I didn't know if he was talking to Knox or me, but both of us stopped in our tracks.

"Knox. Come," Dad commanded. Knox returned to Dad's side. He was on a leash, but Dad hadn't needed to yank him back.

"Sit," said Dad. Then he passed him another treat. I thought it was wholly undeserved since he'd growled at me. This wasn't what I had expected from our new pet.

Dad laid a hand on Knox's fur and said, "Stay." Then he stepped over to me. He pulled me up and put his arm around me, grinning at Knox. "He's doing well, don't you think?"

"Are you kidding me? He almost attacked me."

Dad laughed. "No, he didn't. You were supposed to remain still until he came to you. He was just trying to protect me. It's amazing! I didn't think he'd bond so fast, but he's already showing the signs."

"Well, I don't think he likes me much," I pouted.

"First rule to remember is to be calm and positive. Dogs pick up on our feelings innately." He grinned, giving me a quick squeeze.

I looked over at Knox. He sat in a relaxed pose, tail thumping and tongue dangling again. He didn't look aggressive any more.

"See," remarked Dad. "He just needed to know you weren't a threat. He sees my arm around you and that I'm happy." Dad laughed as if to punctuate his words. Knox started huffing faster, and his tail swished side to side across the floor. He gave a little whine.

Dad kneeled down, pulling me with him. "Come, Knox," he said. Knox was in front of us in two seconds, licking Dad's hand. Dad laughed again. "All right, boy. I've got another treat for you." His hand paused before withdrawing a plastic bag from his pocket.

"Tru," he whispered. "Why don't you feed him?"

"Me?" I screeched. "He might bite me."

"No, he won't. Look how happy he is. He's saying hello when he licks me like that."

"Or he was just looking for more food," I said dryly.

"Tip number two, honey. Always reward good behavior and ignore bad. Also, love is the best reward, food is a close second."

"Sounds like you," I teased, calming down as Knox began sniffing me. His cold nose tickled as it tentatively moved up my arm. "Okay, give me some of those dog prizes."

Dad dropped a few brown balls into my hand. They looked like leathery Cocoa Puffs. I took one and held it in front of me. Knox gobbled it up. I laughed when his wet tongue tickled my palm. He nuzzled my other hand, already sniffing out the goods.

"Don't give in yet," said Dad. "Give him a command and make him earn it."

I reached out my snack-free hand and carefully scratched under his jaw. Knox whined a little, his eyes half closing.

"Oooh," crooned Dad. "Looks like you have the right touch."

I smiled. "Good boy!" Then I let him gobble up the snacks in my other hand.

"Hold on there, honey! That's like me handing you hot cocoa and then giving you a ten-dollar bill for saying thank you! You're going to spoil him."

"I can't help it," I said, smiling from ear to ear. I leaned in and hugged Knox. A wet tongue licked the side of my face.

"Ew! Dog breath." But I smiled anyway.

"I guess I need to lay down the rules," mused Dad as he stood. "First, no dog on the couches or beds. He sleeps in his crate."

"No problem," I agreed, before scratching Knox's throat. I cooed to my new buddy in a silly voice. "Who wants to sleep with doggie breath in their face?" He widened his mouth and huffed as if smiling.

"Also," Dad continued. "He eats in the kitchen only. Always in the same place."

"Okay," I said absently.

"And we have to take him outside to do his business a lot, until we get to know his pattern. You'll have to help clean up his messes."

"What?" My head jerked up in disgust. "Isn't he trained?"

"Yes, but for some reason he's not using the toilet yet," replied Dad. "Until that happens, you have to pick it up with your dainty little hands. The doo-doo bags are in the closet."

"Great." I rolled my eyes and frowned in distaste. "You know, he was your idea, not mine."

"He's *our* dog. *Our* responsibility," Dad said firmly.

"Fine," I relented. Knox sat politely as I petted him from head to back. "Not your fault, I suppose," I told Knox.

"We also need to walk him twice a day," added Dad.

"Twice? I don't have time for that," I said, starting to worry about all of these new chores.

"Why don't I do it in the morning and you in the afternoon or evening? It's important for his health, but also for his training."

Maybe Knox could get used to Zander faster if he joined us on our walks. "Okay. Sounds fair."

"What would be even better is if you took him jogging," suggested Dad. "He's a big dog and needs to run. And he'll protect you out there."

I couldn't see Dad ever jogging. He might not be fully retired from work, but he had been retired from exercise for years. Mom had tried to get him to go to the gym ages ago, but then she gave up on it, too. Man, my dad was old, and he seemed to be getting older faster these days. At least Knox brought out a younger side to him. I guess I could take Knox on a run once in a while.

"Okay. When can I introduce him to my friends?"

"I thought we'd have to wait a few weeks until he was bonded to us, but since it seems he's about there already, you might be able to do it sooner. Let's see how he progresses over the next few days. He may seem like a harmless pet at the moment, but make no mistake, he's been trained to protect and kill, if necessary. Never forget that," he warned.

"You already told me. I got it." I smiled when Knox pressed his nose against my arm, as if to encourage me to keep petting him. I ran a hand down his brown and yellow mane. "How long ago did his owner die?" I asked.

"It's only been about a month. Knox was having a hard time adjusting to his death, but it's hard to believe it looking at him now. Dogs are smart creatures, though, and very intuitive. I wouldn't be surprised if he didn't recognize similar mourning signs in us. Perhaps he's found kindred souls."

I hugged the little guy. He'd lost the one person that meant everything to him. At least I'd had my dad and my best friend. I vowed to myself that I'd become his new best buddy. Well, other than Dad, who was already feeling connected with him. Perhaps having Knox here was a great idea after all. He'd get used to my friends eventually. Then he really would be the new Scooby in our gang.

ALTHOUGH I STILL HADN'T heard from Zander, I knew he'd been in my room some time today because his bag and laptop were gone. I'd left my window unlocked, hoping he'd come get his stuff after school. I didn't think he'd miss school. But the fact that he had snuck in to get his stuff made me believe that he was okay. I'd worried that he'd gone off half-cocked and done something stupid, like accuse Peter or his father of all the awful things we'd figured out about them.

But my anxiety level rose again when he continued to ignore my text messages. Had I blown it by not telling Zander about his father earlier? Was he somewhere hurt, needing help? At some point, I realized it was the aramusatu doing its thing with me. He had to be feeling it, too. So what would keep him away? I decided to give him another day before tracking him down.

I knew one thing that would cheer me up. I hadn't told Ruthie about Maverick yet. As expected, she was thrilled. Ruthie and I spent at least an hour fantasizing about Homecoming and making plans, carefully sidestepping the fact that Zander was ignoring me at the moment. We both agreed that he needed more time to digest the big bomb we'd dropped on him about his father. We did spare a thought for Conrad, hoping that he was okay.

Much later, after Dad went to bed, I was still awake. Despite Dad's rules, I was dying to get Knox out of his crate. I felt sorry for him. If I got claustrophobic in my own home, I could only imagine how horrible Knox must feel in that box. Knox was beginning to fill an emptiness I didn't know I'd had. I pulled Mummy down from my shelf, smiling at its threadbare appearance. It wouldn't last much longer if I cuddled with it. I knew what I needed to do, but I had to wait until Dad was asleep.

Thirty minutes later, I opened my door and peeked

into the hallway. Dad's door was ajar, and I could hear the low sound of grinding gravel drifting out of his room. I tiptoed to shut his door before returning to switch on my light. Its brightness shined across the hall, into the spare room and into Knox's crate. As I got closer, I could see him standing, one paw sticking out through the metal grid. I smiled, realizing that he'd known exactly who it was before the light came on. Dad said dogs could smell something like a hundred times better than humans.

"You poor baby," I crooned, as I hurried over to unlock his crate. He didn't come out. What was the word that Dad had said? Oh yeah, duh. "Come," I commanded. Knox hustled out, his tail wagging. "Good boy! You are so polite, Knox." I gave him a hug and scratched his neck. I didn't have any treats for him, but I had endless hugs.

"Wanna hang out with me in my room?"

Knox dipped his head and licked me. That was answer enough for me.

For the next hour he helped me tidy my room, which was the last thing I wanted to do. But he kept picking up things from my floor and bringing them to me. If I tossed them down again, he retrieved them as if it were a game. The only way I could stop it was to put each item back where it belonged. Before long, my floor was clean. Freaking miracle. Dad was going to keel over in shock. Blasted dog. I punished his sneakiness with a good wrestle, which ended with us both huffing and sprawled out on the floor. Feeling a little sticky, I hopped up to open the window. A cool breeze flowed in. Knox jumped up to place his paws on the windowsill beside me.

"Ahhhh," I sighed. "Doesn't that feel awesome,

Knox?" I yawned loudly and Knox glanced over.

"Just sleepy," I said. I walked to my bed and fell into it. A second later I heard Knox panting near my legs. I sat up to see him sitting patiently. waiting for me to do something. "You don't wanna go back to that crate, do you?" I asked with a wince.

He glanced at the window and then leaned his head against my knee. "Okay, boy. Just for a bit. Dad will freak out if he wakes up and you're not where you should be." I patted the spot next to me and said, "Come." Knox hopped up and settled next to me. I curled around his warm body. There was something about him. I wondered if a cat would be as comforting. I doubted it. I swear Knox grinned at me, which earned him another good ear scratching. No, I couldn't imagine a cat wrestling on the floor with me.

"You're the best," I whispered before dozing off.

Zander jogged down a dark road wearing the same clothes from our last meeting with Ruthie and Conrad. He stopped, sliding his hands through his hair and looking from right to left. The street sign under the lamplight read Larkspur Ct, which was my court. He took off through an open lot and exited it to enter the forest. He moved too fast for a normal person, but no one was around to see. In seconds, he was well within the tree line, free from potential onlookers.

"Aaagh!" Zander yelled, his face livid. A second later his fist slammed into a nearby tree. It toppled over in a cloud of dust and flying pine needles. His knuckles came

away bloody.

He moved to another tree and leaned against it, breathing heavily. He brought his hands up and squeezed the sides of the trunk, gouging the bark. He grunted and stepped back, surveying the damage. Again, he seemed to swell with aggression. He dropped his backpack and took off running, pounding the forest floor, leaping over tree trunks, bushes, small streams, and dodging jagged branches. He was miles and miles into the woods before his blind and thrashing sprint turned into an easy gait. His scowl vanished as the bliss of the run took over. His feet seemed to know the shape of the land, and he leaped gracefully over ditches and logs, easily avoiding wayward branches. Then he sped up again, pushing himself harder. He melted into the scenery as if he belonged there. He moved so fast, he sped past a small herd of deer before they even noticed.

After a while he slowed to a jog and stopped, a look of surprise rendering him immobile. He waved one hand in front of himself, his face full of amazement. He looked to the right, then the left, and smiled, pleased about something.

Then he turned directions and slowly headed back, taking note of the plants and animals he passed, and the paths that wove through the brush. Suddenly, he stopped and crouched down, staring at a set of footprints. Not human, but dog-like, only larger than the everyday dog.

He followed them and found another set. Human this time. He started poking around the nearby bushes. Under one, he found a woman's blouse and jeans. He dropped them as if they burned him. Then, a look of determination crossed his face. He turned back to the set of animal prints. Carefully, he followed them, wandering about a few times when he lost the trail. But it didn't take him long to find it again. Soon, he came upon a modern-looking cabin, a large two-story building with a two-car garage.

He crept around the edge of the house and paused every few seconds to listen. When he saw a silhouette in the window he jerked back, dropping his body low to the ground. When no one came running out of the house, he quickly retraced his steps, moving like the wind through the forest.

The dream blended into another.

Zander and Peter yelled at each other in front of a small kitchenette. One bar stool lay knocked over on the floor.

"You lied to me!" bellowed Zander.

"Would you stop already?" Peter hollered back. His eyes were white with surprise. "Nobody lied to you."

"You said you didn't know anything about Dante or this Collector!"

"I don't," Peter said.

"You knew Dante worked for Father!"

"I didn't know—until I did a little research on the kid." He had the decency to look a little sheepish.

Zander swung at him. Peter ducked just in time and grabbed Zander's arm, twisting it and pinning him against a wall. Zander barked out a dark laugh and pulled away from his brother's stronghold, knocking him to the ground.

"What the hell, Zander?!" Peter leaped up, looking at him in amazement. *"Did you receive the Blessing?"* Peter asked in surprise. *"Why didn't Father tell me?"*

Zander ignored him, his face thunderous. *"You should have told me about Father,"* he said. He took a step toward Peter, who backed away through the bathroom door, stopping only when he bumped into the glass shower stall.

"Zander," he said, spreading his hands wide, as if to placate his brother. *"That was need-to-know information and I didn't have the authorization to share it with you. But I swear I didn't know Dante was here. I would have told you if I'd known you or Tru were in danger."*

Zander clenched his teeth before charging, but Peter rushed forward and closed the door. Zander slammed into it with his shoulder. The door crushed in, leaving a dent the size of a basketball. He stepped back with a curse.

"Hey!" yelled Peter. *"What's wrong with you? Are you on drugs? I don't make the decisions. We do what*

we're told and we're told as little as possible. You know that."

Zander blinked at the mangled door before running a hand over his face. He took a deep breath, then another. When he'd calmed down, he walked across the room and leaned against the wall.

"You can come out now," Zander said. "I'm not going to hurt you." Under his breath, he added, "I think."

The bathroom door cracked open, still functioning despite the damage. Peter swung it in all the way and stepped into the room, his eyes bulging at the sight of the ravaged door.

He tracked Zander across the room. "I didn't lie to you," he insisted, his voice low and calm.

"But you knew Father was kidnapping idimmu, even if they weren't doing anything wrong." His jaw clenched. "Dante told Tru that the Collector had tons of idimmu. What kind of monster takes people away from their families for no reason other than to 'collect' them?"

Peter narrowed his eyes. "You still haven't told me what's so special about Tru Parker. What's her story, anyway?"

Zander glared, but kept his mouth shut.

"Okay, okay," said Peter, his hands rising up, as if surrendering. "But you know I'll find out eventually."

Zander whirled around to face his brother. "You said you'd leave her alone if we found Dubois."

"Yeah, yeah," grumbled Peter. "But we haven't found her yet, have we?"

Zander looked like he was about to have another go at his brother, but before he could, Peter spoke up. "You know what happens to them, Zander. So what if Father is being proactive. His end goal is still the same. He's trying to help them."

Zander shook his head, clearly disliking what he was hearing.

Peter huffed and continued. "He's working on a cure, and until then, he needs the Fixer. That's Dubois. She's the key to helping these poor, sick people. And us, too, Zander. She may also be the key to the survival of all supernaturals." Peter watched Zander for a moment, and seeing that he was in no immediate danger, he stepped over to the small refrigerator and pulled out a soda. He cracked it open and took a long swig.

"You get it, don't you?" Peter said, leaning against the kitchen counter.

"But what about what's best for Dubois?" said Zander. "What if she doesn't want anything to do with our people or the idimmu?"

"If she was a nice person, she'd choose to help us. She wouldn't have left them. It's for the greater good."

Zander looked up, his eyes haunted. "What if Father isn't who we thought?" he asked.

Peter's eyes narrowed to dark slits. "Zander, if Dante

was bringing Tru in, then she's idimmu." He paused when Zander began to puff up with anger again. Peter raised his hands. "I'm right, aren't I?" he insisted. Zander fumed in silence. "Look, one of these days Tru is going to need the Fixer. It's in her best interest, too."

Zander shook his head. "You expect me to believe that crap? Tru is not insane. She won't—" He cut himself off and then restarted. "That's not how it's supposed to work. I went through the training, too. The Nasaru aren't supposed to interfere unless they have a reason. If Father really was trying to do the 'right' thing, he wouldn't abduct a girl from her family, and especially before she showed any signs of mental problems."

"I read the school's files on her, you know. She was definitely having mental problems."

"Her mother died!" yelled Zander. "And she's much better now."

Peter shrugged. "Why wait for idimmu to go insane? You can't blame Father for looking ahead. It's a lot easier to explain what's going on to a rational idimmu than one who's already lost her marbles."

"Then why is he called 'the Collector'? And why wouldn't he talk to Tru's father instead of kidnapping her?"

"You know the rule about involving humans." Peter swept his arms wide. "Here's a thought. Why don't we ask Father first before deciding he's the boogie man?"

"It's too risky. Wait! You promised you wouldn't tell Father about Tru—"

"Relax. I haven't," promised Peter.

Zander ran his hands through his hair. "What if he— I mean, how do we know he's telling the truth?" Zander let his body sink down into a small sofa, his action kicking up a breeze and unsettling a pile of papers on the side table. A paper wafted to the floor. The logo "Redwood Regency" was stamped across the top of it.

"We need to trust him, Zander," Peter insisted.

"I-I don't think I can," admitted Zander, leaning over his knees, his head in his hands.

"I get it." Peter moved closer. "I would be confused, too. But we need to hear Father's side of this before we make any judgments. We don't have all the facts. What if you're wrong?"

Zander stared up at his brother like he wanted to believe him.

"Why do you care so much about this girl?" asked Peter. "It's intense, almost like—" He cut himself off. A speculative glint had entered his eyes. He looked from Zander to the broken bathroom door.

Zander stilled, his face going blank. "I just think she's a nice girl, Peter. I lost my temper, that's all. Her family has been through a lot since her mother died. Separating Tru from her dad right now, the way Dante treated her … It's just not right."

"*Come on,*" *said Peter, smiling.* "*Let's talk to Father together. In person. We can head home tomorrow.*"

Zander shot up to his full height, several inches above Peter. "*No. He might not let me—us come back here.*" *He ran a hand through his hair.* "*Besides, I, uh, found something new.*"

"*What do you mean?*"

Zander squeezed his eyes shut, as if his thoughts were painful. Then he opened them and took a deep breath before saying, "*I think I know where to find Dubois.*"

Peter looked almost gleeful. "*Great!*" *He grabbed his jacket and keys.*

Zander put up a hand to stop him. "*Wait! I mean, I think it's her. Let's do some groundwork first, to be sure. We don't want to scare her off by running in, guns blazing. And we have no idea how many others are with her. There's at least one, remember?*"

"*We can handle them,*" *Peter said as he opened a drawer next to one of the beds and pulled out a gun.*

Zander moved to block the door. "*What if I'm wrong and it isn't Dubois?*"

"*If it isn't them, then they're probably unregistered usemi. We tag them. It's our job,*" *Peter emphasized.*

Zander's eye twitched. "*Okay. But I swear I'm not taking you there unless we do this my way,*" *insisted Zander.* "*First, we wait until it's light outside.*"

Peter replaced his jacket. "*Fine,*" *he drawled, resting his hands on his hips.*

The dream fizzled away and I groaned, desperate to see what they found. As if on cue, another dream drifted toward me.

Zander and Peter walked through the redwoods dressed like forest rangers, complete with nametags. Suddenly, a tall figure loomed in front of them.

"Are ye lost, mates?" a deep voice boomed, the Australian accent clear. It was Isaac and Phoebe's dad. His creased forehead and scowl contradicted the friendly question.

"Good afternoon!" smiled Peter, his manner easy. Zander wore a bland expression, but it seemed forced. He stood tensely next to Peter, letting him lead the conversation.

"We're following up on a report of a bear. Just checking out some of the nearby regions." Peter chuckled, like it was an absurd idea. "Have to follow up on all complaints, you know." He looked self-consciously at the man in front of him. "Do you live all the way out here by yourself?"

Mr. Efoti's face lightened at the mention of a bear and he chuckled, his laugh booming.

"No," he said stepping closer to shake Peter's hand. "I live up there with my family." He pointed up a nearby hill. "But I can't say we've seen any bears around here

... ever."

Zander reached out a hand. "I'm Jack, kinda new to this area. What's your name?" Zander asked before wincing as his hand was enveloped and squeezed.

"We're the Efotis," he said letting go of Zander's hand.

A dog whined and a wet nose pressed against my arm, pulling me from the dream. I sat up, disoriented to see the walls of my room instead of rough tree bark. What a life-like dream. No, a vision. In fact, multiple visions. I'd never had so many in a row. And I'd answered my own questions about Zander, like I'd had some control over what I'd seen for once.

First, and foremost, he was safe. The next pressing concern was the fact that Knox had stayed the whole night with me on my bed. I was already breaking Dad's rules. But it was still early. Maybe I could get him back into his crate before Dad found out. Knox trotted stealthily to his crate without balking, making me wonder what kind of work he'd done with his police partner. If only he could tell me. I returned to my room, the fear of waking Dad fading away, along with my anxious pulse.

I replayed my visions, trying to understand them. The sun was beginning to rise and I still had an hour or more of sleep before I had to get up. But I couldn't sleep. No way. I wanted, *needed*, to ask Zander about what he'd found in the forest and if they had discovered Aunt Caroline. Trying to sleep while I stewed about it wasn't helping either. I hopped out of bed.

Moments later, dressed in shorts, a t-shirt, and

running shoes, I stuck my head into Dad's room.

"Dad!" I whispered loudly, afraid to frighten him out of a sleep.

It had been years since I'd been up before him, years since I'd awoken him. No, not true, I thought, as I stared at his rumpled gray head. He looked so fragile curled up on his blankets. With regret, I remembered that I'd awoken him plenty of times over the last year with my screams and crazy dreams. Now I realized they were visions. I'd been changing into something else while I slept. A shiver went up my spine. At least I wasn't screaming in my sleep anymore.

"Dad!" I said a little louder.

"Tru?" He sat up abruptly, looking dazed. "What are you doing up? Are you all right?" He started getting out of bed.

"Don't get up," I said. "I just wanted to tell you I was going running, with Knox."

"What?" He looked shocked. I couldn't blame him. I couldn't remember seeing a sunrise since grade school.

I laughed. "I know. But I couldn't sleep and Knox was whining a bit," I added, although it was untrue. "He must need to pee or something. I'll take a key."

Dad still looked like the world was tilting. He pursed his lips, obviously fighting with the idea of me going out by myself this early and getting out of bed to take care of Knox himself. He looked toward his window. The dim morning light was beginning to peek through the edges of his blinds.

"Okay," he mumbled. "But stay close. Keep him on his leash. It's hanging by the door. And don't forget the alarm."

25

YOU-KNOW-WHAT

WHEN KNOX AND I returned from our run, the wonderful smell of waffles hit us as we opened the front door. Knox's feet made clipping noises as he hunted down Dad. I hung up the leash and stretched before following him into the kitchen.

"Hey!" I said, catching Dad pinching off the corner of a waffle for Knox. "I thought we had to feed him dog food."

Dad popped the waffle piece into his mouth like that was his plan all along.

"That's right," he said. "Sorry, buddy," he told Knox who huffed at his heel. "I've got yours right here." He pulled out a bag and poured the dried dog food into the bowl on the floor. Knox hesitated before padding over to eat his breakfast. "That's a good boy," said Dad.

I snatched up a fresh waffle and smothered it in butter

and syrup. Dad grabbed a whip cream can out of the fridge and waved it in my direction. I took it gleefully and sprayed an artistic pile of white fluff on top of my not so healthy breakfast. "So how was the run?" asked Dad.

"Fun," I said between mouthfuls. "Much better with Knox. We stayed in our neighborhood though. Maybe I'll take him out further tomorrow."

Dad nodded his head as he dug into his own breakfast. "By the way," he said. "I can drop you at school today. I have to leave about the same time as you normally do. Let Ruthie know?"

I started to pout, but in another effort to abolish my snotty attitude from last year, I said, "Okay," instead. Dad raised his eyebrows, opened his mouth as if to argue, but realizing that I had agreed with him, he just nodded. "Alrighty then," he said.

There was plenty of time before we had to leave, so I added another fifteen minutes to my shower, enjoying the warmth on my sore muscles. I should run more often. Reluctantly, I turned off the faucet before Dad banged on the door to remind me not to waste water. I sighed heavily and started getting ready for the day. Despite the run and the long shower, I still felt out of sorts and stressed. All through my run, I'd debated whether or not to tell Ruthie what I'd dreamed last night. Peter was already on the top of her "people-who-needed-to-die" list, not to mention her "people-who-creep-me-out" list. I didn't want to make it worse.

Several things bothered me. First of all, I knew Peter was lying to Zander. About what, I wasn't sure. Secondly, it bothered me that Zander believed his brother when he said that their father was the good guy. He clearly was not the good guy, nor was Peter. Why couldn't Zander see through them? I felt sorry that Zander's family was turning out to be rotten. I knew he was hurting. But he'd come around, right?

Another thing that annoyed me was that Zander had taken Peter to find Dubois. Zander knew she was my aunt. I may not like her. I may want revenge for what she did to my mom, but she was family. And I felt a bit betrayed by him.

Then there was Mr. Efoti. The usemi trail that Zander found had led them to Isaac and Phoebe's dad. What was that all about? Were they in danger?

RUTHIE CLUTCHED THE STRAPS of her backpack while she waited for me along the school walkway. She waved when I hauled my stuff out of Dad's car.

"Oh my gosh!" she gushed, grabbing my arm and pulling me off to the side.

"Hey!" I said, waving goodbye to Dad. As he drove away, I took a good look at Ruthie, checking her over. She wore a purple scarf around her neck and long sleeves again. I frowned, knowing she was covering up her bruises.

"How does your neck look today?" I asked. She blinked and pushed her scarf around on her shoulders a bit.

"Oh, not too bad. At least it doesn't hurt. But I seriously had to go rocker chick to cover these." She lifted her wrists to reveal thick leather bracelets covering each one under the sleeves of her leather jacket.

I wrinkled up my nose. With her black-heeled boots and dark lipstick, she did, indeed, seem a little hard rock. "Yeah," I said. "Not your normal vibe."

She shrugged. "Whatever. I didn't have a choice today. If Peter even shows his face, I'm going to shoot him," she whispered, patting her pocket.

My eyes widened in alarm. "You have a *gun*?" I knew her dad had a handgun because sometimes he went shooting with Dad. But this was just wrong.

She laughed. "No, of course not. It's just pepper spray," she whispered wickedly.

Relief warred with apprehension. "But that could get you expelled," I whispered.

"Na," she waved off my concern.

I trailed behind her as we headed to our first class, moping and feeling guilty that she was breaking the rules because of me. It was only because I'd involved her in my crazy problems. But she turned back to grab me, pulling me along with an arm through mine.

"Seriously, Tru. After all we've been through and with the Collector coming for you, it's not that big of a deal. I'd rather be expelled than killed." When I tried to stop, she continued to drag me, her tiny body stronger than it looked. "Remember that Dr. Frankler said I had to look out for you."

She'd also wanted me to stay home because I was going through some change. *Into what?* I wondered. Was I that dangerous to everyone around me?

"All right," I said, giving in. Part of me was impressed that she had the nerve to bring a weapon onto campus. But was it courage or something else? Could I have messed with her head accidentally when I'd healed her?

"Ruthie, if I did anything bad to you, I'll never forgive myself," I blurted. "Oh my gosh! What if I'm becoming some kind of monster?"

"Are you talking about when you healed me?" she asked, pausing to look me in the eye.

I nodded.

"Are you serious? You saved me, Tru! Sometimes when I close my eyes, I can feel the pain and the terror from that day." She shuddered. "I'm so glad you were with me and that you were able to make me better." She clutched me to her in a quick hug.

She pulled away saying, "And you aren't turning into a monster. If anything, you're turning into a superhero!" My eyes shot to hers in surprise. I hadn't voiced that fear before, although it had been on my mind for a while.

She rolled her eyes. "I swear, Tru. You are always thinking the worst about yourself." Her grip softened. "But you'd never hurt anyone. All you do is help."

I blinked away the moisture building in my eyes as Ruthie pulled me alongside her, marching me to class. As we rounded a corner, she whispered, "Besides, I'd rather talk about something else." The excitement in her voice was almost tangible. "You will never guess what I heard!"

I rolled my eyes, now feeling like the one leading her to class. "Ruthie, I think we have more important—"

She stopped again and yanked me toward her. "Ouch!" I said.

"Tru, it's about Zander!"

My feet suddenly grew roots and I stared at her. "What do you mean? Have you seen him?"

"No, but apparently he's been talking to Zena."

As my jawed dropped, she continued. "Yeah, Zena's throwing a party tomorrow night and he's going to be there!"

"Why would he do that?" I tried to suppress a feeling of betrayal. The very thought of Zander going to Zena's party after what he knew about her was like a knife in the back. A surge of anger washed over me.

Ruthie rubbed my shoulder. "I don't know, sweetie. It doesn't make sense. I mean, he's totally into you. Like he's *all* about you, you know? What if he's ..." She leaned closer. "What if he's *spying?*"

"You mean ... because I told him her parents were from 'you-know-where'?"

She nodded vigorously and my anger subsided. I chewed my lips, still not liking the idea of him in the Taylor's house one bit.

"But," continued Ruthie. "I totally got your back! Val's going and he invited me!"

"What? No! Val's treating you like crap. How could you agree to go to with him?"

"I know," she said rolling her eyes. "I'm not going with him like that. I'm meeting him there. Anyway, don't worry. He's history," she promised. "I just thought I'd use him to get us into the party, you know? A little pay-back." Her heavily outlined eyes narrowed with venge-ance.

I wasn't sure if I believed her because I knew she was still nursing a little heartache over him. "I don't know, Ruthie. I don't want him to hurt you any more than he already has."

"It's okay. I can handle it. Plus, I can't wait to see his face when I walk into Homecoming with hunky

Maverick." She grinned so maniacally I laughed.

"Still," I hedged. "I mean, come on! We'll be hating it there. It's going to be her crowd and they *loathe* us."

"No," said Ruthie. "Lots of other people are going, like we'd be the only ones not there if we don't go." The warning bell rang, and we started walking again, hustling this time.

"My dad will never let me go. Remember? Fort Knox?" I insisted.

"I've got you covered." Her eyes twinkled. "Mom said you can spend the night Friday!"

"Okay," I nodded, finally getting on board with her wicked plan. "That might work." I smiled. I didn't know what I'd do without her. I wished I could do more for her. Then I realized there was something I could do after all.

"Hey!" I pulled Ruthie over to the side of a building.

"What the—"

"Your neck," I said. "I healed you once already. I might as well get rid of the bruises now." Dr. Frankler's warning sounded in my ear. "Wait," I said. "Maybe I shouldn't ..."

She smacked her head. "Why didn't I think of that? I had to be really sneaky to hide them from Mom. She thinks I have a hickey." When she saw me shaking my head, she placed her hands on her hips, her elbows out. "Stop thinking about what that *crazy* doctor said," she ordered. "Besides, what's done is done. Erasing a few bruises is nothing compared to a freaking shark bite." She grimaced at the memory.

I swallowed hard. *What's done is done,* I thought. It sounded so final, like there was no returning. Perhaps she was right.

We slid around the building so there'd be no witnesses. It was easier now, and within seconds the bruises were gone. She hugged me, and for the first time I felt proud of my ability.

FOR THE REST OF THE morning, I constantly checked in with Ruthie. I wasn't going to risk Peter hurting her again. I even arranged to cross paths with her between classes. I had to run to make it to mine in time, but it was worth it to know she was okay.

When I rushed into Physics, I was glad to see I'd arrived before the new kids. I slid into my normal seat just as they walked through the classroom door. Their eyes zoomed in on me darkly. As they trudged to the last row, their heavy gaze made me feel like I'd done something wrong. What did I ever do to them? All throughout class I felt their eyes burning a hole into my back. I didn't understand their interest in me. When Physics ended, I hurried out, relieved to get away.

Shrina greeted me at my locker before lunch. "Hey Tru."

"Oh. Hi Shrina. Any news about Bobby?" My stomach twisted.

"Nope." She pulled on her bag nervously.

"What's wrong?" I asked.

She seemed to be wrestling with something. "Were you and Bobby ..." She hesitated. "I mean, did you and Bobby ever ..."

I blanched. "What? Bobby and me?" She thought he and I had something going on. "Are you kidding? He likes you! Besides, I'm with someone else."

Her face reddened. "Isaac."

"No," I hurried to correct her. "We broke up. It's ... Zander."

"Oh." She said, surprised. "I knew you and Bobby weren't ... I mean, well. He talked about you so much. It made me wonder."

I felt horrible. "I swear we were—are just friends." Geez, was I already writing Bobby off? No, he had to be alive!

Her expression clouded over, but she nodded. "The day before he disappeared, he had a fight with you," she said.

"What?"

"Don't deny it. He told me."

I blinked at her in dismay. What in the world had Bobby told her?

"Uh ... yeah," I stammered. "I may have yelled at him. But, honestly, he just caught me at a bad moment. I apologized already."

She heaved a big sigh. "Did he tell you about his new gypsy skills?"

Oh great. He had told her. I shook my head.

Her eyes drooped. "Yeah. He started getting psychic vibes about weird stuff like picking up the phone before it rang, saying your name before you walked into a room. Stuff like that. Do you have any idea what might have caused it?"

Of course, I did, but I couldn't tell her I'd done something to Bobby, like turned him into an idimmu. Or that the Collector might have him now, if he was still alive.

"He was so worried," Shrina said when I didn't reply.

"He felt he had to talk to the police, even though I told him not to be so stupid." Her forehead wrinkled. "Looks like I was the stupid one. I should have believed him."

I closed my eyes, regret eating me alive. If only I'd left Bobby alone from the beginning. Everything happening to my friends, Bobby's disappearance, Ruthie's bruises, not to mention Mrs. Jackson's death—none of it would have happened if I'd left him alone.

"TRU PARKER AND RUTH ROBLES, REPORT TO THE OFFICE. TRU PARKER AND RUTH ROBLES, REPORT TO THE OFFICE."

An intercom speaker blared the announcement over our heads. Shrina raised an eyebrow and I shrugged.

"I wish I knew more," I told her. "Really. I want Bobby to come home, too." I poured as much sincerity into my words as possible. They were the truth.

She smiled sadly. "Thanks, Tru. I'm glad I talked to you."

"Me, too," I said, frowning as I watched her walk away.

"TRU PARKER AND RUTH ROBLES, REPORT TO THE OFFICE. TRU PARKER AND RUTH ROBLES, REPORT TO THE OFFICE."

"Agh! I'm coming!" I grumbled.

RUTHIE LOOKED FRIGHTENED WHEN she met me at the office. "What's happening, Tru? Why are we in trouble?" I shrugged as we stepped through the doorway. She grabbed my arm. "Do they know about you-know-what?" she whispered, panic seeping into her words. She had to be referring to her pepper spray. I made a face.

"Man, I hope not. Is it still on you?"

She shook her head.

Mrs. Jones waved us over. "You two. I have a note for you from Dr. Frankler." She handed us an envelope, then dismissed us to answer the phone.

Ruthie and I huddled together just inside the office as I tore open the letter. "What does it say?" she asked.

I scanned the hastily scrawled words. "Dr. Frankler has been called away by an emergency. She can't meet with us today."

"I totally forgot," exclaimed Ruthie.

"Me, too. Good thing she can't meet, then, right?"

"Yeah."

"But she still wants to talk, like this weekend," I said, scanning through the rest of the note.

"What? Over the weekend? That's weird, right?"

"It is," I agreed. "I guess it's important. You know it's about you-know-what, right?"

"Which you-know-what?" she asked.

"Not today's you-know-what," I said with exasperation, knowing she meant the pepper spray again.

"Oh," Ruthie breathed out loudly. "Of course. That you-know-what. When?"

Mrs. Jones suddenly announced, "Just a few more minutes, young man."

I hushed Ruthie, realizing we had an eavesdropper. The new boy from my Physics class sat in a row of chairs opposite the office counter, obviously waiting for someone. His blond head bounced between Ruthie and me with fascination, his sky blue eyes twinkling.

"New kid," I said with a glare. "It's rude to stare."

He smiled a toothy smile. "You-know-what?" He

replied mockingly in his southern drawl. "I don't give a damn." Ruthie laughed and then slammed a hand over her mouth. He gave her a half-lidded look.

I pulled Ruthie out of the office so we couldn't be overheard.

"Dr. Frankler wants us to call her this weekend," I said. "She left her number."

"Okay," said Ruthie. "We have Zena's party on Friday, which means we're totally sleeping in Saturday. Mom has me doing stupid chores most of the day after that. Think we can talk with her on Sunday after church?"

I nodded.

As we headed to lunch, Ruthie talked about what we should wear to the party. Most of the conversation was one-sided. I made a few comments, but I wasn't really listening. My heart had started beating faster, hoping that Zander would be waiting for me at our table. My stomach caved in when I didn't see him anywhere on the quad. Several kids jeered at us as we passed their table.

"What did you do this time?" yelled one girl as her friends broke out into hushed titters. Any time you heard your name over the school loudspeaker … it was pretty much not good. We ignored them. Well, at least I did. Ruthie stuck out her tongue.

Isaac and Phoebe were sitting alone, and as we settled in next to them, they peppered us with questions.

"We aren't in trouble," wailed Ruthie for the third time.

"It was just the school counselor," I admitted.

"What did she want with Ruthie?" asked Phoebe.

"Excuse me?" I said. "You think I'm the only one who

needs to see a school counselor?" I was slightly offended by her question. Isaac spoke up to defend me, causing Phoebe to roll her eyes. She gave up getting a real answer. Ruthie took the opportunity to tell them about our Homecoming plans. I groaned inwardly. Isaac gazed around the lunch tables, but I could see that he was uncomfortable with the topic.

"You guys are going, right?" asked Ruthie.

Phoebe shrugged. "Jake asked me, but I told him no."

"What???" Ruthie practically screamed. "Don't you want to go?"

"I don't really care about the stupid dance," Phoebe replied. I caught her quick glance at Isaac. Could she have declined Jake's invitation because of Isaac? There was no way I was entering this conversation to find out, though.

"Oh, come on," whined Ruthie. "You seriously need a life. You guys are so boring sometimes. I mean, why wouldn't you want to go to Homecoming? It's epic! A milestone!" She moved on to Isaac.

"Isaac," she begged. "You have to convince her. She'll always regret it if she doesn't go."

Isaac scrunched up his forehead and Phoebe shook her head.

"Come on, guys," Ruthie continued. "We can all meet at the dance and hang out. It will be great!" When they didn't reply, she frowned. "Isaac," she snapped. "Just because Tru bailed on you—no offense, Tru." She rolled her eyes at me before leaning toward Isaac. "It doesn't mean you can't go. There are tons of girls who would cut off their pinky toes to go with you."

"Ew!" I made a sour face. But I felt obligated to back

her up. "But it's true," I admitted to Isaac. "Half the female population here is in love with you."

Isaac sported a cocky grin now. "I know," he admitted. I rolled my eyes this time.

"Oh my gosh! You are so full of yourself," I said. We all laughed when Isaac pretended to look offended.

"Anyway," Ruthie said. "You guys really should go. Besides, I know someone who's going to ask Isaac."

Isaac jerked toward Ruthie and opened his mouth, but she cut him off. "Oh no. I'm not telling you who it is. Spoilers."

"You know what?" Phoebe finally said. "Maybe I will go. If only to keep an eye on him." She jerked a thumb toward Isaac.

"I don't need a babysitter!" blustered Isaac. Phoebe raised an eyebrow and smirked. Ruthie and I burst into giggles.

26

HEARTSICK

FRIDAY FINALLY ARRIVED, and our plans weren't going as expected. Ruthie's parents were going to *Phantom of the Opera* in San Francisco, keeping them out late. We planned to sneak out after her brothers went to bed and corner Zander at the party. We'd still have plenty of time to get back before her parents. Anyway, that was the plan until Dad said I couldn't sleep over.

I pouted, I whined, I pleaded. And I didn't care that I was being a snot this time. But nothing worked. He took one look at the circles under my eyes and my pale skin and said I needed more rest. It was true that I looked like crap. I even felt achy. But I wasn't sick in the conventional way. I was Zander-deprived. As ridiculous as it sounded, I needed him like I needed air to breathe. It was the aramusatu—aka aramu-*sick*. But Dad had no idea about that and eventually lost his patience with me. He yelled that the discussion was over, scaring me because it was so out of character for him. At that point I knew all was lost and stomped off to my room to make the dreaded call.

"Well," said Ruthie, without missing a beat. "You're just going to have to wait for him to fall asleep and then sneak out."

My chest tightened at the idea. The last time I'd done something like that was the night Mom had died. And if Dad caught me, it would be the final nail in my coffin. I'd never get out of the house again. I'd never see Zander again.

Zander. Why wasn't he calling me back? He'd missed school again today and people were starting to talk. They wondered if he had gone missing like Bobby, or if he had something to do with it. They speculated that he might be with Bobby. I tried to say as little as possible. And I could honestly answer that I didn't know where he was. Then Zena had to open her mouth and say that she'd seen him and that he was fine. She even said she was hanging out with him this weekend. I'd wanted to scratch her eyes out.

Ruthie's voice coming from my phone pulled me out of my vengeful thoughts. "Tru? Are you still there? I didn't send you into shock, did I? I know this is a big deal for you—"

"I'm okay," I said. Thinking about Zena had steam coming out of my ears. If sneaking out was the only way to get to Zander, then I had to do it. And if I could piss off Zena in the process, even better. "I'll try it," I promised, biting my lips, foreboding twisting my insides.

"Wow," she gushed. "I didn't think you'd really do

it."

"I don't think I have a choice," I sighed. "I feel so crappy."

"You poor thing," she crooned.

"I look like a dead girl walking."

Ruthie sighed. "Okay. I'll bring makeup. We'll be in and out. Can you get through your alarm?"

"Of course," I replied.

"All right then. We're really doing this?" she asked.

Desperation made me braver than I'd normally be. "Yeah. We are."

"Okey dokey," she said enthusiastically. "Next question. What are you wearing?"

DAD DIDN'T STICK HIS head in my room to say goodnight until ten-thirty, but I pretended to be asleep. When I heard him close his bedroom door, I texted Ruthie and told her to come over. I'd meet her outside as soon as I heard his snoring.

Knox whined softly as I slipped out of my room and down the stairs, but fortunately Dad slept through it. I covered the little speaker on the alarm and hit the Silent button before switching it off. Ruthie's car idled alongside the curb outside.

"Finally!" she yelled, as I quietly opened the car door and got in.

"Shhh!" I whispered.

"Why?"

"Knox can hear everything! He's a super smart dog," I replied.

"Oh," she whispered and pulled out onto the street.

"If he can hear us, then wow. Imagine what the usemi can hear."

Now that was a scary thought. Ruthie looked at me as I twisted my hands nervously.

"Don't worry. You'll be back before anyone's the wiser," she reassured me. "Zander's going to be ticked when he sees you. He won't be able to concentrate on whatever secret mission he's on once he sees you." She laughed.

My mouth dropped open. I hadn't considered that he wouldn't want me there or that I might get in the way of whatever he was doing. I tightened my lips. No, he deserved whatever happened because he should have called me long ago. He had to know how this was affecting me because it would be affecting him the same way.

"I'm sure he'll be able to finish whatever he starts there regardless of me," I said stubbornly.

Ruthie made a disagreeing noise. "Well, anyway, here's the necklace I was talking about," she said, handing me a gold statement necklace with red glass accents. "That will look good with your top."

She'd talked me into wearing black jeans, a ruffled black tank top, and my strappy red sandals. The necklace dressed up the outfit.

"When we stop, let me cover up those circles under your eyes," she added.

"Thanks," I said, clasping the necklace around my neck. My hair hung in curly waves, and it looked more blond than usual against the black shirt. Ruthie wore a sparkly plum colored top with navy leggings. Gold zippers went up the sides of her legs. Glittery bangles dangled from her ears and spiky heels made her legs look longer.

"You look sexy," I smirked.

"I feel sexy!" she laughed. "I decided that if it was going to be a quick stop then I needed to make an impact. You know, throw it in Val's face." Her brown eyes glittered with purpose.

"Yeah, but don't you dare take him back. Nice makeup, by the way." She looked like a magazine cover.

"Gracias," she said, smacking her glossy lips together. "Don't worry. I'm done with him." She glanced at me with concern. "Are you okay? You look really pale."

I frowned. "I think it's ..."

"The aramusatu thing?" she finished.

I nodded. "Aramu-sick!" I blurted, warming up to the nickname.

"Aramu-sucks!" Ruthie giggled. "The aramu-sex better be worth it."

I gasped, my face heating up, but cracked a smile. "Geez, Ruthie."

"Just saying ..."

WHEN WE PULLED ONTO Zena's street, cars lined both sides and we could hear the music blaring. There were only a few houses, which meant it was less likely that neighbors would complain. Plus, I wouldn't have been surprised if the neighbors were afraid of Mrs. Taylor like everyone else I knew. The huge houses sat on equally large lot sizes. Several kids lounged around the sculpted front lawn, drinking out of plastic cups and laughing. I didn't see Zander's truck, which made me worried.

"Stop scowling, girl," said Ruthie as she touched up

my makeup. When she was done, I heaved one final nervous sigh and stepped out of the car. Ruthie pulled me along with her, vibrating with energy.

The front door stood open, allowing the music to flow outside. Ruthie had been right. Every upperclassman seemed to be here and they filled the mansion with vibrating energy as they danced and swayed to the music, many with cups in their hands.

"So how should we do this?" asked Ruthie. "Stick together or split up? There are a lot of rooms here."

"Maybe split up? We'll cover more space that way." Now that I was here, I really *didn't* want to be here. An icky sensation swirled in my stomach. "Call me as soon as you see Zander. And I'll call you. Keep your phone on Vibrate. We won't hear anything over the music."

"Okay," agreed Ruthie. With a quick squeeze, she took off toward the left side of the mansion. I headed to the right.

"Well, if it isn't Tru Parker!" said a familiar voice from the bottom of the stairs.

I almost groaned out loud. You'd think I'd get five feet in this crowd without running into Zena. This had been a bad idea from the beginning. She was going to throw me out and my face warmed as I anticipated the humiliation.

"No," she said, reading my face. She looked at me like an aristocrat peering at a commoner. "You may stay." Her groupies hung around her elbows, imitating her like monkeys. "Your life must be so sad these days. People like us have to do what we can for people like you." Her entourage nodded their heads with disingenuous sympathy. I suddenly wanted to reverse directions and walk out, but I reminded myself that I was here for a reason.

Zena pressed one hand to her heart. "Consider it an early Christmas gift." She showered another benevolent smile on me before laughing. It was a plastic kind of sound that made me think of her mother. Zena started to walk away, but turned back. "Oh, and if you're looking for Zander, I left him upstairs in one of the bedrooms." She smacked her lips. "He was amazing."

"Burn!" said someone in her group. Then they slipped away through the mass of bodies.

I stood there, my heart in my stomach. He would never do that to me. I knew it. But it hurt anyway. I wanted to run after Zena and rip out her hair, but I clenched my jaw, resolving again to track Zander down. I headed toward the second floor. Did I believe Zander would go up there with Zena to fool around? No way. But some needy part of me had to know. I started up the stairs.

I dodged an unstable guy holding a frothy cup. Between bouts of laughter, he talked ten decibels louder than necessary. Halfway up the stairs, I stepped over a couple going to second base. Ew. I quickly looked the other way. At the top of the stairs was a large landing area where a group of people, mostly guys, were playing Foosball while onlookers yelled, their shouts like sonic booms every time someone scored. I passed by them and headed down a darkened hallway. The first door I came to was locked, but the next one swung open into a dark room. The light from the game area fell across the face of someone who yelled "Hey! *Ocupado*, moron!" I slammed the door shut.

I leaned my back against the wall, wondering what

the heck I was doing. But it didn't take much imagination to think of Zander and Zena in one of these upstairs rooms and despite believing he wasn't up here, I couldn't stop myself from continuing. As I carefully opened the next door, a shadow suddenly came up behind me and pushed me inside.

Even as I yelped in surprise, a cloth covered my mouth and nose, a hand pressing it against me and another arm pulling me tightly against a warm body. I struggled, kicking and scratching with my hands, but the person holding me was stronger. Moments later, my strength waned and my body became heavier, making my efforts to overcome my assailant even less effective than they had been. But the cloth remained against my face, and after a few more moments I started to lose consciousness. I still tried to fight it, but soon felt my body slump, my eyes shutting. Someone lifted and carried me to a soft surface.

Voices floated around me. "Are you sure you know how to do this?"

"Yes. I've got it. We just need a little blood."

Brightness filtered through my eyelids, but I couldn't open them, couldn't even drum up the appropriate hysteria that should accompany being jumped and laid out on a bed. I felt a sharp prick against the inside of my elbow. That's when everything began to fade. I knew there were people in the room, talking, but nothing they said made sense. The sounds whirled together in my mind until there was nothing.

"Tru!"

Someone shook me hard, rattling my teeth. I dragged my eyelids open, but it was too bright. I put a hand over my eyes.

"Too much light!" I moaned.

"Geez, girl! You scared me to death!"

I squinted at a strange object. It was Ruthie with two heads. As I blinked, one of the heads turned into Phoebe.

"Phoebe?" I murmured.

"Yeah, it's me. I took Ruthie's advice to live it up a little and look what happened. We find you passed out in a bedroom. How much did you drink?" she said, her lips pinched with disappointment.

I stretched my mouth, feeling parched. Ruthie helped me to sit up. "Seriously, Tru," she wailed. "What happened? Did you ever find Zander?"

Ding! I suddenly remembered everything and squeezed my head with both hands. "No!" I muttered between clenched teeth. "Someone pushed me. Knocked me out. I think he stuck a needle in me." I ran a hand along a tender spot in the crease of my elbow.

"They knocked you out and brought you up here?" asked Ruthie.

I shook my head, feeling stupid. "No, I came up here to look for Zander."

"Upstairs?" asked Phoebe.

"Zena." I squeezed my eyes shut in shame. "She said that he was up here. That they ... I knew it wasn't true, but I had to check."

Ruthie frowned. "Tru, opening all the shut doors at a house party is way uncool, you know." She grabbed my arm to check for a needle mark. Sure enough, a small red puncture dotted the skin.

"Yeah, lesson learned," I sighed.

"Why would someone stick you with a needle?" asked Phoebe.

"More importantly, what did they do to you," whispered Ruthie.

I felt the color leach out of my face as I scrambled to my feet unsteadily. I checked my clothes. Everything seemed to be in place and I felt okay, except for the light-headedness.

"I-I think I'm all right."

Ruthie pulled me into a tight hug. Then she ripped herself away. Holding my shoulders, she yelled, "Don't you ever do that to me again!"

"I'm sorry," I said, feeling like an idiot.

"It's not your fault," said Ruthie weakly.

"But you said—"

"I know what I said," she huffed. "You scared me, that's all. This has to be the worst thing Zena has ever done to us. If we went to the police with this—"

"No," I said, gritting my teeth.

"Are you sure?" asked Phoebe, frowning. "This isn't anything to take lightly. They could have done any number of things to you."

"I'm fine," I insisted. "What time is it?"

"Midnight," said Ruthie ruefully.

"What?" I yelped with dismay. "Your parents may be home already!"

"I know. But I couldn't find you and I couldn't leave without you. Luckily, I ran into Phoebe and she helped me locate you. It took her like two seconds. Do not play Sardines with her!"

"Thanks," I said, directing it at both of them. "Now

let's get out of here."

"Isaac is waiting outside," said Phoebe.

Great. One more witness to my utter stupidity. We hurried downstairs, stepping over bodies and around couples only to come to an abrupt stop. Zena and her groupies formed a wall at the bottom of the stairs.

"Oooh, are you finally coming downstairs, Tru? Man, she was up there a long time, wasn't she, Chrissy?"

"All night," said the brunette to her left. "No wonder half the football team stayed up there."

Oh no she *didn't*. I froze, trying to reign in the desire to strangle someone. The tips of my fingers felt like they were burning.

Everyone gawked at me, some with disgust, others with eagerness, hoping I'd take the bait. It was vastly different than the way they had stared at me when they thought I was crazy. Now I was the football team's slut.

"Nice party you have here," said Phoebe icily, stepping up next to me. She pulled both Ruthie and me down the rest of the stairs, forcing Zena and her friends to back up. "I didn't know you were into having your guests roofied," said Phoebe in a dark voice.

All eyes shot to Zena. Ruthie moved forward, facing her.

"If *anything* nasty happened to her," she roared. "I'm coming for *you!*" She stabbed her forefinger at Zena, who jumped backward with a yelp. Ruthie whirled around to me, grabbed my arm and started walking us out.

A low chant of "Fight, Fight, Fight" started up, growing louder and louder.

Ruthie stopped. "No," she said, as if speaking to herself. Then she spun around to Zena again. "You are the nastiest piece of crap I know. You deserve everything you get." And then she crossed the distance between herself and Zena, quickly swinging one leg out and around, catching Zena in the chin and knocking her to the ground. The crowd "ooohed."

But Ruthie wasn't finished. She grabbed Zena by the hair and said, "You'll never be like us, no matter how much money you throw around or how many people you blackmail into being your friends. You're *nothing*." She dropped her to the ground with a loud thud. Zena scrambled away, whimpering.

Isaac met us at the front door, where everyone continued to stream in, hoping to catch the fight. He looked past us to see Zena cowering on the floor and raised an eyebrow. Phoebe grabbed his arm before he could say anything and pulled him along with us.

When we reached the car, Ruthie let out a frustrated scream. "I hate her! I hate her!" she yelled, her fists clenched and tears streaming down her cheeks.

I pulled her into a hug. "Ruthie," I gasped. "What were you thinking? She's going to tell her parents and they'll come after you with the police!"

"What the hell happened in there?" bellowed Isaac.

"No, she won't, Tru," said Phoebe, shaking her head. "What Ruthie did to Zena is nothing compared to what she did to you. You got roofied at her house, and now everyone knows it. You can tell the police and they'll file charges against her entire family. And you know how important their reputation is to them."

"Roofied!?" yelled Isaac. I quickly shook my head.

"I didn't get roofied … I got knocked out with chloroform."

"But what about the needle? What do you think hap-pened?" asked Ruthie, wiping her smeared mascara.

"This sounds weird," I said. "But I think they took some of my blood." Then I remembered that it wouldn't make any sense to Isaac and Phoebe, so I laughed it off. "Just kidding. It just feels like that, you know?"

Ruthie stared at me in shock. Isaac and Phoebe were doing their intense staring at each other thing again.

"Guys," I said. "Ruthie and I need to get home. If there is a God, then maybe we will still be able to sneak back into our houses without getting caught. But we have to leave now."

"Okay," they agreed, but their expressions promised that we'd be explaining later. We said our goodbyes and took off.

On the way home, Ruthie went into full freak-out mode. "What the hell do you mean they took your blood, Tru? Why would someone do that? No," she said, not letting me get a word in. "Let me tell you. We got conned into going to a party at Zena's house. Zander was never there! Zena and her family are working for Zander's dad, who is looking for someone who can magically heal peo-ple. Crapity crap! This is so bad."

"I know," I said, breathing shallowly as shock began to settle in. "Believe me, I'm freaking out, too."

She shot me a glare. "Well, you're way too calm."

My stomach was in knots and I felt like throwing up. "Believe me. I'm freaking out inside."

She let out a frustrated breath. "Tru, once they look at your blood, they may know everything!"

"And Zander was never there."

"Damn," muttered Ruthie. "She made it all up. I

walked right into her trap."

"Me, too. I knew he was never upstairs with her, but I couldn't stop myself." A sickly stiffness tightened the muscles along my neck and shoulders. I hurt all over. "I feel so awful."

"You look awful," Ruthie frowned. "What are we going to do?"

"Nothing," I said. "At least not yet. First you need to get home before your parents discover you're gone." By this time, we were pulling up my street. "Text me when you get in."

"Yeah. Score one for team Zena. I'm going home to lick my wounds."

I paused outside the car to lean in. "Ruthie, everyone at school is going to be talking about how you kicked Zena's butt. You were amazing. I think she may have peed her pants."

Ruthie laughed and I quietly shut the door. She zoomed away as I hurried up to my front door. I tiptoed in and reset the alarm. Upstairs, I splashed cold water on my face in the bathroom, hurrying to wash off my makeup. As I dried my face with a hand towel, I stepped into my bedroom and almost face planted on my floor as I tripped over my backpack. Angrily, I kicked it out of the way. Unfortunately, it was unzipped and as it rolled over, all the contents tumbled out.

"Ugh!" I groaned in frustration before kneeling down and shoving things back in, not caring if I bent the papers. As I did, a tiny slip of lined notepaper slid out. I grabbed it, and thinking it was trash, I turned to toss it into the garbage can. But something stopped me. I unfolded the paper with a frown, trying to remember what it might be. There was writing on it and the words hit me like a slap in the face.

Although his power builds faster and faster,

Your true nature still eludes the master.

But all too soon the blood shall reveal

What you are and break the seal.

I started shaking, the words "the blood shall reveal" blaring at me like a Las Vegas billboard. This was the note I'd found in my locker. The one I assumed was one of Zena's sick jokes. But now it seemed more like a premonition.

My hands trembled and the note fluttered to the ground. I stood up and almost fell over with dizziness. My heart beat so fast I thought I might be having a heart attack. Perhaps I was going into real shock now. There was only one thing to do.

When I unlocked Knox's crate, he fussed around me as if he knew something was wrong.

"Yeah. I screwed up big time, buddy," I mumbled, climbing into bed and turning toward him. A tear slipped down my cheek and onto my pillow. Knox stared up at me, his mouth open and huffing. His ears twitched. I reached out and ran a hand over his soft fur, letting his warmth calm me.

"Come on," I said, patting the covers next to me. He leaped up and licked the salty tears on my face. I had no doubt that the Collector would soon have my blood, and subsequently know exactly who Dante had found so long ago.

The hole in my chest that ached for Zander widened.

I was heartsick for him, for my family, for my future. Sleep was a long time coming, but when it did, I slept like the dead.

27

DONAVITCH

AN OBNOXIOUS WASHCLOTH sweeping across my face woke me way too early Saturday morning. I pushed it away and snuggled into my pillow, but it returned, swiping me from chin to forehead with one sloppy lick. My eyes popped open and I jerked up as soon I registered that the odd sensation wasn't a washcloth at all. Instead, it was a warm, wet dog tongue.

"Gross, Knox!" I said, glaring at him. Upon making eye contact, he whined, jumped off the bed, and looked toward the bedroom door.

I sighed. "You gotta pee, buddy?" I asked. He whined again. Light was starting to creep around the edges of my curtains, but dark shadows still stretched across my bedroom, indicating that it was the crack of dawn. At least I thought so. I rarely ever saw it. Ugh. Why was Knox in my bed? I ran a hand through my hair, trying to wake up.

Then I remembered, and an angry flash of heat ran up my throat. I wanted to rewind last night and help Ruthie beat the crap out of Zena. But if I could change something about last night, I'd never have snuck out of my house. Perhaps a run would put things in their proper perspective. I had to take Knox outside anyway. I cleaned up, scrambled into my running gear, and left a note on Dad's door.

Knox did, indeed, have to take care of business, so I left him to it while I stretched my stiff muscles. A few minutes later, we moved on to the business of exercise. The last time we'd run together, we'd stayed close to the house, and I'd let Knox lead the way most of the time. This time I wanted to venture further. I tested a few commands on him as I walked to the end of my court. He passed with flying colors, even staying at my side when an orange tabby cat streaked across the street.

"Good boy," I crooned, passing him a treat from the plastic bag I had stuffed in my sweatshirt pocket.

I glanced around, hoping to see Zander's truck. There was no sign of it. The last time I'd seen him was in my dreams. Pieces of my recent visions flashed through my mind, like the sign I saw when Zander ran down the street. I looked up at it now: Larkspur Ct. In my dream he'd been running down my street wearing the same clothes he'd worn on the night he'd made a hasty exit out my window.

The dream had also shown me his hotel, the name of it stamped on a paper in his room: Redwood Regency. It was one of the nicer inns in Scotts Valley, tucked away from the main section of town. Fortunately, it was within running distance of my house. I estimated that Knox and I could run there in thirty minutes, if we ran fast. I didn't feel like running, but the possibility of seeing Zander motivated me like nothing else, even sending a surge of adrenaline up my legs.

After a mile or so, I found my groove and picked up speed, letting my hair fly behind me like a sunny banner waving in the breeze. It felt automatic, like breathing. I was going to Zander and that thought erased some of the pain of our separation. It was as if I had wings—my feet didn't seem to touch the ground.

Knox was suddenly a dead weight pulling against his leash and I jerked to a stop. With horror I realized he hadn't been yanking on the leash at all. Instead, I'd been running so fast, I'd been *dragging* him. *What the hay?* He lay on his side, huffing with his tongue lolling out of his mouth.

"Sorry, sorry, sorry, Knox," I said, offering him a handful of treats to assuage my guilt. He was so out of breath he didn't even want them. I knelt on the sidewalk, not caring that stone and dirt pressed into my knees. I hovered over Knox, afraid I'd damaged him beyond repair. Almost reflexively, I called to the light above us and linked its healing powers into Knox who sat up and sniffed at me as if nothing were wrong.

Biting my lip, I checked out our surroundings and realized with surprise that we were halfway to the hotel. How was that possible? I'd been running faster than a German shepherd dog, fast like Zander, and pulling the weight of Knox behind me without realizing it. *Speed and strength, like Zander,* I thought with awe. Had I tapped into his abilities?

During our mutual captivity, we'd hypothesized that he might be idimmu, too, although he'd continually referred to himself as sethian. But I didn't think he was sethian at all. We hadn't really discussed it, perhaps because he didn't want to face the idea that his parents weren't who he thought they were. Neither were mine, I admitted, but my father wasn't a lying supernatural leader who committed unspeakable crimes against, against … well, it didn't seem like his father drew the line with anyone.

Another thing we'd discovered in that dark cellar was that Zander could see in the dark when he touched me. Seeing in the dark was my thing, not Zander's. Yet somehow, he had tapped into my ability. In the other night's vision, Zander had been able to see in the dark again. It was such a normal thing for me that I hadn't realized what he had been doing until now. But this time he'd had night vision without touching me.

I thought about Knox and how he was bonding to Dad and me, how his behavior changed to be more protective. Is that how the bond between Zander and me worked? Had it changed our behaviors, our gifts? Zander could see in the dark without touching me and apparently, I could run fast like Zander, even when he was nowhere nearby.

Knox wagged his tail and pressed his nose against my neck. His breathing sounded normal now.

"I'm so sorry, buddy," I said, rubbing his neck. "I didn't know I could do that. I'm not sure you're ready to run yet, so let's walk for a bit." I started off, keeping an eye on him, but letting my mind wander to my new borrowed talent. It was amazing and I couldn't wait to tell

Zander.

As we rounded the final bend to the hotel, a black sedan slowly passed by on my left, so silently that I jumped in surprise. A Tesla emblem decorated the trunk. Stupid, creepy electric cars. This one even had tinted windows, making it impossible to see who was in the car. Unfortunately, I didn't have X-ray vision. My gift didn't allow me to see through the darkened glass, just like I couldn't see through the spooky fog that often settled down in our little town. The morning sun had brightened in the sky, lighting up our surroundings, but it was still early enough that the nearby homes were quiet and dark. I scoped out my exit options. A fence blocked my left, and off to my right ran a gully, dropping at least ten feet from the side of the road. Apprehension tingled up my arm, and I wondered if we needed to make a run for it. Something felt off with the car, and despite Knox's police training, I didn't feel safe anymore.

My anxiety heightened when the Tesla pulled over ahead of us. The driver's door opened. I slowed down, debating on running in the opposite direction. But it was possible that someone needed directions. It wouldn't be the first time I'd given them. The driver was tall and broad shouldered. He wore sunglasses, which was disconcerting because it still wasn't that bright outside. Then the passenger door opened and a shorter, bald man stepped out.

It was Detective Winchester. Now I really couldn't turn around. Besides, he knew where I lived.

"Ms. Parker. I thought that was you," the detective called out, his voice jarring in the silence of the morning. He stepped into my path on the sidewalk, forcing us to stop. Knox growled. The detective gave him an annoyed look.

"Heel," I commanded. Knox quieted.

"What are you doing out so early?" the detective asked, his voice cordial, as if meeting like this was normal. My eyes narrowed. He was acting too nice.

I held up the leash, as if it was obvious. "Taking him on a run."

Although Knox stood stiffly by my side, he was poised to leap forward and I worried that he'd attack them and get me into more trouble than I was already in, maybe even get him taken away from me.

"It's okay," I said, petting Knox.

The detective inched closer. "Well, a fortuitous meeting then. It saves me a call. I wanted to see if you remembered anything new about our discussion the other day."

Discussion. Yeah, right. Alarms were going off in my head, despite his friendly demeanor. Why was the detective in my neighborhood at this time of day? I glanced at the driver. The dark-haired man had long sideburns and wore a dated black leather jacket that screamed of the seventies. He leaned over the hood of the Tesla, watching us like he had all the time in the world.

"No, I told you everything," I said, hoping he'd go away.

Knox growled again. Even he felt something wasn't right. I reached down to scratch him under his neck, taking my eyes off the two men for a second.

Suddenly a hand ran down my arm. I jumped, turning around swinging. It was the driver. I looked at the car in confusion. He'd been all the way over there a second ago.

He grabbed my wrist with a low laugh, yanked me toward him and pressed his face against my ear before taking a long sniff. I yelped and tried to pull away, but he held me in place with one hand.

Where was Zander's super strength when I needed it?

Knox abruptly tore into the man's leg with a snarl. He howled in pain, attempting to wrench himself free by shaking his leg and boxing at Knox. My stalwart protector let go only for a second before diving for the man's free hand, putting himself between me and my attacker. Knox shook the man, causing him to flop back and forth like a wet mop.

The man's sunglasses fell to the ground with a clatter, revealing his eyes. I stared in horror. He had red eyes! And I'd seen them before on Dante's secret web site. They glowed like evil rubies as he glared at me. A string of curses fell from his lips as he kicked Knox in the side. When Knox didn't let go, he smacked him in the ear. This time Knox yelped and fell away into a patch of weeds next to the sidewalk. He didn't move. I started toward him, but the red-eyed man grabbed me, pulling me back against his chest.

"I was simply getting your scent," he snapped. "But now you owe me." He bit down into my neck. Unbelievable pain seared through me, spreading from vein to vein. My mouth opened in a silent scream, but I couldn't make a sound, couldn't move. I saw the detective pull out a gun and aim it at me.

"Stop, Donavitch. I'll shoot if I have to," he growled, his eyes glowing an orange yellow this time and I realized he wasn't human either.

The vampire at my throat didn't budge as he gulped

away, moaning with pleasure. The detective growled out another threat, and I thought I saw his face shift. My eyes began to droop, my vision getting foggy and dreamy, making me question what I saw next.

Out of nowhere, something slammed into the detective, knocking his gun into the road where it clattered. It was Isaac, and he followed up his attack with an explosive upper cut to the temple. The detective went down and didn't move. Then Isaac leaped over to me, grabbed the man at my throat by the hair and punched him in the kidneys, but the leech remained suctioned stubbornly to my neck, as if sucking my blood was more important than saving himself. He reached out with clawed hands to swipe at Isaac, but he ducked out of reach.

"Move," someone yelled, and Isaac jumped away.

A second later, my attacker howled in pain and fell away from me. I looked back to see a knife sticking out of his back. Before he could flip around to see who had stabbed him, Zander wrenched his head to the side, breaking his neck. He fell to the ground in a heap.

"Unfortunately, it won't keep him out for long," said Zander, catching me as I slumped forward into his arms, too numb to stand on my own. My mind screamed *Zander* as my skin warmed at his touch.

"I've got her now," he said. "You need to get out of here." He was talking to Isaac as though they were working together. Impossible. Or was it? Zander laid me carefully on the ground, ripped off his t-shirt, and held it against my neck. I stared at him, my eyes running from his tight abs up across his muscly shoulders and to his bright blue eyes staring down at me with concern. He was so beautiful. I really hoped I wasn't drooling. Despite his impressive physique, dark smudges outlined his eyes and extra creases lined his forehead. Yes, he'd been suffering from our separation, too, but now that he was near, my heart sighed with relief and the desire to wrap my arms around him almost choked me.

His face softened for a second before he clenched his eyebrows, turning them into angry ridges. He peeked at my neck and cursed. "Damn it, Tru! What were you thinking?" he said, ruining the reunion I'd envisioned.

The warm feelings I'd been swimming in dried up. This attack wasn't my fault and if my limbs weren't frozen, I'd have shoved him away and told him to go to hell.

"I'm not going anywhere until I know she's safe," Isaac said, reminding me that Zander and I weren't alone. He stood over the detective's body. "Besides we can't leave these guys here."

"Then throw them in the trunk for now," said Zander impatiently.

While Isaac took care of the bodies, Zander checked me over for other injuries, running his free hand over my skin. I tried to talk, but my mouth wouldn't work.

"You're going to be okay," Zander promised gruffly, tracing the top of my head with a gentle hand. "I just need to get this to stop bleeding." He pressed a hand against the bite on my neck. "Akharu usually seal their bites," he muttered. I couldn't tell if he was talking to Isaac or me, or to himself. "But I guess I didn't give him the chance."

"The bastard didn't look like he was stopping any time soon," said Isaac.

I could hear Zander's teeth grinding. "I should kill him."

The car trunk slammed shut. "Do it," Isaac said. "He was going to suck her dry."

"Lock the car and hand me the keys," demanded Zander.

Isaac scowled. "Let's chuck the keys," he said, preparing to heave them into the gully.

"No!" said Zander sharply. "I'll need them to get rid of these guys."

Isaac paused, before nodding in agreement. He moved closer to hover over us as Zander checked my neck again. Suddenly I remembered Knox, and tried to speak through my frozen lips.

"What?" said both Zander and Isaac.

"Dog," I mumbled incoherently.

"Doug?" asked Zander.

"Dog," I tried again, rolling my eyes toward the last place I'd seen Knox.

They looked down the sidewalk, noticing for the first time Knox's body in the bushes. Isaac stepped over to examine him.

"Oh, she said *dog*," said Isaac. "It must be Knox, Tru's new dog."

Zander let out an exasperated breath. I knew he wasn't excited about me having a guard dog, but Knox had already found a spot in my heart and I didn't want him left behind, even if he was dead.

"P-lease," I said, hoping he was still alive. I wanted to try and heal him, but my paralyzed body refused to move.

Zander looked over at the Tesla. Was he worried they were going to wake up? Impossible. Isaac had knocked the detective out cold, and Zander had stabbed

Donavitch. Plus, I could have sworn Zander had broken his neck. I reminded myself that they weren't normal. They weren't human. Their eyes had been like the creatures on Dante's computer.

But I couldn't think about that now. Knox needed help and I prayed that he wasn't dead. What would Dad do if he died? No, he had to be okay. Dad needed him, even more than I did. But I couldn't heal him, paralyzed as I was. Wait.

"Z," I said. My voice sounded gummy. The words felt fat, like I'd been mega overdosed at the dentist's office. I was starting to feel a million tiny pinpricks all over my body, which had to be a good sign. "Heal me."

He shook his head, glancing at Isaac. Maybe he didn't want me to reveal my ability to Isaac. But I cared more about saving Knox than revealing what I could do.

Isaac ran his hands down my dog's legs and ribs, checking for injuries. "He's hurt pretty bad, Tru," he said uncertainly.

"Please," I whispered to Zander.

Zander bent down. "You first," he said, one hand still pressing down on my neck. He laid his other hand over my heart and closed his eyes. I said a little prayer. It seemed to have helped the other times I'd healed people.

Nothing.

"It's not working," Zander said. "Must be the akharu venom. It takes a while to wear off, but the fact that you're able to talk a little means that it's wearing off faster than normal."

"Knox," I repeated, a tear running down my cheek. Then I had an idea. "We ... fix."

Zander blew air through his lips like I was wasting his

time, but then scooped me up and carried me over to Knox.

"Dude," said Isaac, "you might need to take her to a hospital. She lost a lot of blood. And Knox needs a vet. I don't think there's anything we can do for him."

"Maybe," said Zander with a sigh. "First she wants to hold her dog."

Isaac frowned in disapproval, but he moved out of the way. Last week, I wouldn't heal Ruthie until Isaac left. Now I didn't have the same privacy. If Knox was going to make it, I had to risk Isaac finding out about me. Based on this morning's events, I didn't think he would freak out. Obviously, he was good with weird already.

Zander settled me next to Knox's still form, placing my hand on his neck. His fur was wet and sticky with blood. More blood dripped from his ear. I realized that I wasn't numb everywhere. I could feel tears dripping from my eyes. If I could cry, then we might be able to save Knox. Zander kneeled over me, blocking Isaac's view. I think we both knew that we could share our abilities, especially when we were touching each other. This had to work. He laid one hand on my shoulder and one on Knox.

"Okay, Tru," he whispered, so softly I almost didn't hear.

I debated how to go about this. Clouds had floated in and they covered the sun, blocking out the best light. I called out to the sun with my mind and tried to draw whatever energy I could from its weak morning light. Then I combined it with the life in the green plants all around me, and pushed that energy into Zander. He gasped.

"Together," I whispered.

As we both squeezed our eyes shut, I tried to conjure up the fiery heat like I'd done before. I chanted, "Be well" over and over in my mind. Then I heard Zander's voice echoing my own. Suddenly, a burst of heat jolted through me, spreading down my arm to the hand resting on Knox's side. Zander stared in wonder. He'd repeated the words I'd spoken in my mind, which suggested that he'd heard my thoughts. All of a sudden Knox twitched, then lifted his head my way, whimpering and licking me. I smiled, or at least tried to. I probably looked like a sad clown. Although I couldn't move, I could feel the ground, Zander, and Knox. That was an improvement.

"How did you do that?" Isaac crouched down beside us, petting Knox. Surprisingly, Knox allowed it. He pressed his nose to Isaac, then to me, then Isaac again, whining.

Isaac ran his hands down the sides of Knox's face, staring into his eyes. Knox reached out with his tongue and licked him. Smiling, Isaac checked out the bloody ear and assured us that the bleeding had stopped. He crooned, "She's going to be okay, Knox. Don't worry."

He looked at Zander. "She is, right?"

"Yeah," said Zander, scowling at him. "She's just temporarily paralyzed. And I don't think she needs a blood transfusion. She just needs time to recuperate." He didn't look at Isaac when he said this. I was thinking that Isaac was way too calm. I mean, he saw a freaking akharu drinking my blood and Zander and me healing Knox. He must be putting it all together.

"What next?" asked Isaac. "How are you going to explain this to her dad?"

Oh no! I didn't want to involve Dad.

"Tru," said Zander. "Is your dad awake yet?"

"No," I mumbled.

Zander pursed his lips. "Maybe we can sneak her back in."

"Dude!" Isaac shot up to his full height. "She can barely talk! Her dad is going to flip out."

Zander settled me next to Knox before rising to face Isaac. "I think it's starting to wear off faster than normal. She'll be fine by the time we get her home," Zander said.

"Okay," shrugged Isaac. "Even if we get her to her room before her dad finds out what happened, what are we going to do about them?" He pointed to the trunk of the car.

Zander's jaw tightened. "I'll take care of them," he said firmly.

Isaac scoffed. "What are you going to do? You can't call the police."

My pulse jumped. They didn't know that one of them was the same detective who had interrogated me at the police station.

"No," said Zander. "No police."

Isaac's jaw clenched. "Who are they, anyway?"

Zander looked away, not answering.

Isaac sighed. "If you aren't going to tell me, just say so," said Isaac.

"D-detective," I mumbled.

"Detective?" asked Isaac, staring down at me. "From the police station?"

I blinked, trying to relay the affirmative.

"Great," muttered Isaac. "Talk about dirty cops."

Zander's lips thinned. "I said I'd take care of it," he

repeated, his voice hardening.

"Fine," said Isaac. "But you can't get her home *and* take care of them."

Zander ran his hand through his hair. "Can you get her home, then?" he asked, teeth grinding again, as if it killed him to admit he needed help.

Isaac smiled. "Easy as pie, dude." He hauled me up in his arms, smiling down at me.

"Careful," warned Zander, his face darkening.

Isaac rolled his eyes. "That train left the station. We're just friends now. Aren't we, lazy butt?" He smiled. "Let's get her home, Knox."

Zander looked unsure.

Stop it. I'll be fine! I thought. Zander's head whipped around to me so fast that I wondered if he'd heard my thoughts. Isaac was too busy with Knox to see our exchange. When Isaac looked back, Zander was shaking his head like a Magic 8-Ball.

"Dude, you have problems," Isaac said. "Dangerous problems. If you really care about Tru, you should go back where you came from."

Zander's head shot up. "Dangerous?" he said. "I'm dangerous?" He walked up to us, almost in Isaac's face. "Your family is more dangerous than I will ever be. I'm trying to protect her, while you're trying to brainwash her with your music."

A tick started in Isaac's jaw, but he didn't defend himself. Zander looked down at me, grabbing a dangling hand. "Don't go anywhere today," he said softly, making it sound like a request. But it wasn't, and I didn't like to be ordered around.

I tried to shake my head. It wiggled slightly. His eyes

drilled into me. "Please," he begged, his face sagging.

Oh man! The sad, little boy face. It made me want to forget how he'd abandoned me these last few days. It made me want to hug him. My arm twitched, letting me know that the venom was starting to wear off. Maybe I should listen to him.

"I promise to call you," Zander said. "After I take care of—" he waved behind him. "Really. I'm sorry I didn't call you. But I'll explain everything, okay?"

My visions had revealed some of the things he'd been doing, but not everything. I had so much to ask him, to tell him. But I had to get home before Dad woke, and Zander had to get rid of that car and the bodies in the trunk.

Okay, I thought. Again, Zander seemed to hear me. His eyebrows shot up, before drawing together with confusion.

"Take care of her," Zander told Isaac, who grunted in response and began walking away down the sidewalk. I wanted to look back but I couldn't. Knox padded along next to us, his feet making soft thudding noises, his leash dragging along the ground.

Isaac kept up a one-sided conversation all the way home, and even though I felt that I could have contributed at some point along the way, I kept my mouth shut. If he thought I couldn't talk, then he wouldn't demand any answers.

Besides, I'd remembered why the name "Donavitch" had sounded so familiar. My gut twisted. I could still feel the teeth in my neck, blood being sucked out, and hands gripping me, clenching and unclenching. Dante had told me about a "Donavitch." He'd said he was a mean blankety-blank who worked for the Collector.

And that meant Zander's father knew who I was and where I was. My time really was up.

28

TURNED

As Isaac stepped toward the front porch he asked, "Think you can stand?"

"Yeah," I said, stretching my mouth from side to side. My whole body tingled, sensation returning like shifting sand.

He carefully stood me up, bracing my shoulders in his large hands while I found my balance. I slowly straightened my spine, and he let go one finger at a time, his hands hovering as if he expected me to collapse. When I remained upright, he cocked an eyebrow and grumbled low in his throat, reminding me of the way Knox sounded when I played tag with him. Did Isaac find this funny? I shot a glare at him. With a resigned smile, he backed away. Knox moved with him, pressing his nose into his hand. I moved up the steps, toward the front door with little robotic jerks and unzipped my pocket to pull out the house key. Because I still lacked full sensation in my hands, I had to concentrate on holding the key. It felt like an extra thick layer of leather covered my skin, and without the sensation of direct contact, I just poked at the edges of the lock awkwardly.

"Let me," offered Isaac, taking the key. With a quick twist it unlocked and he inched open the front door, tilting his head to hear if Dad was moving about. "Seems pretty quiet," he said. "Your old man's probably still asleep." He listened again. "Yep. Snoring."

"You can hear that?" I asked as I stretched my hands, generating painful tingles.

"Sure, can't you?" he said. He bent over to scratch Knox under the chin.

I narrowed my eyes at him. Hottie Efoti had a serious mystery vibe going on. He knew about vampires—no, *akharu*, I corrected myself, even though vampire described my attacker perfectly. I thought about the other night, when I told "the gang" that only some of them were cursed. If they were all like Donavitch, then I understood Zander and Conrad's reluctance to believe me. Donavitch had the creep factor dialed up to a ten. And Isaac's surprisingly calm reaction to him this morning left me wondering how the Efotis fit into things. He sure wasn't confessing anything now, but neither was I.

I looked down to see Knox rubbing his nose against Isaac's hand, like they were best buds already. Knox's reaction to Isaac made me feel stupid for questioning his motives.

"I can't believe he's already so comfortable with you," I said with a pout.

"Told you I was good with animals," Isaac smirked.

Knox let out a wail of satisfaction as Isaac reached down to scratch under his ear. The corner of Isaac's mouth tilted up in amusement.

"Shhhh ..." I said, grabbing for Knox's leash, my clumsy fingers missing it. "He's going to wake up Dad."

Isaac whispered into Knox's ear and he straightened to attention. I gave them both an irritated look before stretching my back and shoulders, relieved that the painful prickles and stiffness were wearing off.

"Want me to help you up to your room?" Isaac asked.

I raised an eyebrow. "No, thanks. I think I can handle it." As I stepped into the foyer a series of unanswered questions piled up in my mind. I turned back to Isaac, opening and closing my mouth, but didn't know how to satisfy my curiosity without saying too much.

"Yeah. I know we need to talk, but not now." He moved forward, his large frame crowding the doorway. "Regarding what just happened with Knox ... and the other day with Ruthie," he whispered cryptically.

My surprised gaze locked with his. "Uh, I guess that's fair," I admitted. "Hey, how did you know I was in trouble this morning?"

"I didn't," he said with a shrug. "I was out for my morning jog and happened to run across you. Zander showed up at the same time."

"What you saw ..." I said.

"Crazy, right?" he said, not looking at me. "I've never seen one of those before."

I squinted at him. "You knew about them?"

He took his time answering, but eventually, he looked up with a grin. "Sure. I watch movies." There was a sad tilt to his lips that told me his knowledge didn't come from movies.

I shook my head. He knows. He really, really knows. It would be nice to have another person on the inside of this asylum I called my life these days. What happened this morning could definitely send a person over the edge. I wondered what Zander would do with Donavitch and the detective. What *could* he do? I didn't think I wanted him to kill them, but I didn't want them to come back for me, either.

"Hey. Are you sure you're okay?" He reached out, brushing a hand over my shoulder. It reminded me of Donavitch sneaking up on me, how he had stood by his car in one moment and then suddenly appeared on the sidewalk in the next caressing my arm. I flinched and jerked away, wrapping my hands around myself. I immediately regretted it when Isaac's face flushed and his jaw tightened. He had misunderstood my reaction.

"Sorry," we both said at the same time.

He raised his arms. "Sorry," he repeated. "I just—" He started, and then sighed, looking at me with concern. "You're still really pale. Promise me you will drink lots of liquids and get some rest." His eyebrows smashed together. "You shouldn't be alone," he added, a question weaving through his words.

"I'm not alone. Dad's here." I pressed a hand against my neck, where Donavitch had bitten me. The skin was smooth now. Perhaps the act of healing Knox had healed me, too. I pulled my long hair over my neck just the same, knowing I'd feel the wound there for a long time. "I'm fine," I insisted.

Isaac's eyes narrowed as he watched my movements. "Are you going to tell your dad what happened?"

"No! Of course not." The idea horrified me. I'd do whatever I could to protect Dad from learning about that monster. It would give him a heart attack.

"But you need someone to talk to," he persisted.

"Knox is here, and I'll call Ruthie."

"Tru," Isaac said, his voice low and entreating.

"I'm fine," I promised. "Besides, Zander's coming by later."

I tried not to think of Donavitch's cold lips on my throat, the stabbing pain of his teeth, or my blood pumping out of my neck. Did I look as haunted as Ruthie had after the shark attack or after Peter's attack? My old regret about involving Ruthie revived itself. She would be better off without me.

Wait. Just because Zander was taking care of my attackers today, it didn't mean there weren't others. The Collector's people could be running loose in Scott Valley. *Of course, they were.* They'd already taken Bobby. I was all but sure of it. I needed to call Ruthie.

"I've gotta go," I said, starting to close the door.

"Okay." His shoulders drooped, making my heart squeeze with shame. I seemed to hurt my friends no matter what I did.

"Pffffttt!" I sputtered, regretting my rudeness. I swung open the door. "Wait, Isaac. You saved my life today—and Knox's. Thank you."

He smiled, turning to lean one hand next to the door. "Anytime." Something sparked in his eyes and for a few seconds my brain fogged over with confusion as conflicting feelings for Isaac and Zander warred for control in my mind. Then a chill went up my neck. I wanted to look around me to see who was staring, because I definitely felt someone there. The phrase "someone walked over my grave" came to mind, adding to the spooky moment.

"I'll talk to you later," I said quickly, and shut the door in his surprised face. I leaned against the smooth wood.

"Drea."

I shot up straight. What the heck? Someone *was* here with me!

"Who said that?" I yelped.

"You can hear me," replied a faint and surprised voice, a feminine voice.

I walked through the downstairs rooms, peering into each corner with Knox padding alongside me. But each room remained quiet and empty.

"Who are you?" I asked, passing the mirror in the foyer. With shock, I backtracked to it to see my face reflected there, but not *my* eyes. At least not the brown eyes I should have. They were blue!

Happy laughter spilled through my mind. "I never thought I'd—" The voice and the blue eyes faded away until all that remained were my own brown ones, and the silence of the house. For some reason, I felt unquestionably lonely.

"Hello?" I said, feeling foolish talking to my reflection.

"Is that you, Tru?" Dad hollered, causing me to almost jump out of my skin. As he climbed down the stairs in his old flannel pajamas, Knox barked out a greeting and padded over to him.

"Have a nice run?" asked Dad, plopping down on the bottom step to give him a good rub. Knox wailed the same happy sound he'd made when Isaac had found his sweet spot.

Then Dad noticed the dried blood in his ear. "Hey, what's this?" he asked. "Is this his blood?" He started running his hands along Knox's fur, checking for possible injuries.

"Huh?" I pretended ignorance. "Wow. I can't believe I didn't see that. I let him play in the bushes down the road because I had a cramp. Maybe he found a dead animal."

"Hmmm ..." murmured Dad. "Perhaps I'll take him in for a checkup, just to be sure." I sighed with relief.

My mind drifted back to the voice I'd heard. Great. I was hearing voices now. As I rubbed my arms, I realized that Donavitch's numbing venom had worn off. But now a fine sheet of sweat covered my skin and the room was starting to spin.

I blinked, raising a hand to my forehead. "Actually, Dad, I'm suddenly not feeling well." And this time it was true. "I think I caught a bug or something."

Dad stared at me. "You are pretty pale. Stomach thing?"

"Yeah, and chills," I added, wondering if it was a reaction to the venom.

"I guess you're going back to bed then," Dad observed. "Think you'll be okay if I go to Hayward today? I need to get some parts for the car, and they have this shop—anyway, you know the drill. Good thing we have Mr. Knox here to protect you." He smiled, scratching Knox under his chin. He straightened, as if acknowledging Dad's statement.

"Sure, I'll be fine," I said, making my way to the stairs. "I think I'll take a shower before going to bed, though."

"Okay, honey," he said. Then I remembered Isaac's counsel to drink fluids and retraced my steps toward the kitchen.

After I had settled down on my bed, I texted Ruthie a short, but dire warning to not leave her house today. My phone rang a few seconds later.

"What the hairy hog butt happened now?" she blurted.

I told her. Everything.

"Whoa! Do you think the Collector is in town, too?" she asked in a quiet and solemn voice.

"Probably not. Why come when you have a dirty cop and a vampire to take care of things for you."

"Not to mention Zena and her family."

"You can't go out today, Ruthie. I'm worried about Peter and any other monsters like the ones I saw today."

Ruthie sighed. "I'll try to avoid it. Mom's already up making breakfast. I'll tell her I'm sick. All I have to do is think about that creep, Peter, ransacking my brain and I feel like throwing up. He gives me serious heebie jee-bies."

"I know what you mean," I said, rubbing the side of my neck.

"Hey," chirped Ruthie. "Don't forget about Dr. Frankler. Or did you already call her?"

"Crap! I forgot. I'll do that now."

"Okay. Keep me posted," said Ruthie. "Bye."

I rang Dr. Frankler, hoping I hadn't waited too long to call her.

"Tru," she answered, relief in her voice.

"How did you know it was me?" I asked with surprise.

"You didn't call me, so I contacted your father last night. You were already asleep, but he gave me your number. Is everything all right?"

"No," I said glumly. "Nothing is right." I sounded like I was whining to my mom. A sudden yearning for her pierced my heart. I could use an adult perspective right now. And Dr. Frankler knew about idimmu, akharu, usemi, sethians, and all the crazy stuff I'd been learning lately. She knew what I was and what was happening to me. And I felt that I could trust her. A sense of relief and hope brightened my gloomy mood.

I launched into my experience at Zena's party. When I finished, Dr. Frankler remained silent for so long that I had to ask if she was still there.

"Yes," she replied. "I'm still here, Tru. But I sense you have something else to say."

"Yeah," I said with a sigh. Then I told her about my encounter this morning with Donavitch and the detective. Another long silence followed my revelations, but I waited patiently. Finally, she suggested I pack a bag and come to her. Disappointed, I let myself fall onto my bed. I'd been hoping she'd tell me everything was all right, the way Mom used to do.

"I'm not running away," I said, grabbing a pillow and throwing it across the room. I was getting tired of everyone saying that. It seemed so cowardly. Dr. Frankler argued that it wouldn't be forever, but I remained firm. No way was I abandoning my dad or the friends I'd already involved in this mess.

She changed the subject. "You said Zander and Isaac rescued you?"

I had mentioned that, but she didn't know who

Zander was, what he could do.

"Yeah ... about that ..." I paused, unsure of what to say.

"How much does Isaac know about you?" she asked.

"Nothing," I said, although I knew he suspected I did something to heal both Ruthie and Knox.

"What does he think happened this morning?" Her voice rose with disbelief.

"I'm not sure. I didn't have time to talk to him about it," I hedged.

"Well, I guess we'll have to cross that bridge when we come to it," she said, her voice business-like again. "Zander is another thing, though. I'd like to talk to you both today. Can you meet me at my place?"

I had a feeling Zander wouldn't be available any time soon. "I don't know if Zander can come. He's been pretty busy."

"How about Ruthie?" she asked.

"She can't get away today, either." Going out was a bad idea, especially today. But Dr. Frankler was my best source for supernatural information right now. Maybe we should make time to talk with her as soon as possible. I rolled my achy shoulders. Just not today. "Maybe tomorrow?" I suggested.

"Hmm. All right." She seemed disappointed. "Meet me tomorrow morning, as early as you can make it."

"Okay," I agreed, hoping Zander would check in by then.

"Tru." There was a sense of urgency in her voice. "You must know that you are in terrible danger. You shouldn't even be going to school. That's where they will look for you first." She sighed. "At least tell me that your father will be home with you today."

"Uh, Dad's going to Hayward. But don't worry. I've got an alarm system and a guard dog."

She grunted, unimpressed. "That's better than nothing, I suppose. Here's my address." I raided my desk for a pen, grabbed a loose paper, and wrote down the address. With a last warning to stay inside, she hung up. I stared at the address on the paper, blinking as I realized it was in San Jose. Dang it! She lived almost an hour away. I chewed my lip as I debated calling her and bailing on our scheduled visit. But I reminded myself that she'd said it was really important. Plus, if she thought I was in danger here, then going to San Jose might be a good idea after all.

I thought longingly of diving under my covers and sleeping for the rest of the day, but the grime and sweat on my skin was starting to make me feel itchy and agitated, and I didn't want to desecrate the sanctuary of my bed with my nastiness. My irritated feelings went deeper, though. The out-of-control events in my life were tormenting me on every side. The tension in Dr. Frankler's voice had only added to that anxiety. What kind of shrink made a person feel more stressed?

I called Ruthie again, to arrange Sunday's meeting. When I told her where the doctor lived, she didn't utter one complaint. She even agreed to sneak out of church to pick me up. Then I texted Zander about our appointment, offering him a ride and telling him I'd explain as soon as we talked. I hoped it would motivate him to finally come over.

I chugged down some more juice before hitting the shower. The warm shower revived me and kept me going until Dad checked on me before leaving, bringing up a sandwich. "Knox is eating his lunch downstairs," he said, setting the food on my desk.

"Thanks, Dad," I said. He smiled and squeezed my shoulder. "Rest up, honey."

I managed to finish my homework and clean the bathroom before dragging myself to bed and giving in to my exhaustion. But worry spiraled out of control in my mind, keeping me from sleep. I rose and wandered uselessly around the house. Knox trailed after me. I considered vacuuming or doing the laundry, but dismissed the notion the next instant. As I passed through the living room, my gaze fell upon Mom's jar on the credenza. It was time to give the lid another try.

It opened easily, and I yelped in triumph. I dropped to the floor and dumped out my newfound treasure, which turned out to be pictures and letters. I spread out the photographs. Several were of babies, all about the same age. Some were of Mom and her sister Caroline as young adults. The others were of the two of them as children, as well as some additional pictures of my grandparents. I wondered why these weren't in a photo album. Setting them aside, my attention shifted to two small stacks of envelopes bound together with rubber bands. One stack contained dated envelopes. On top of the other stack was an envelope addressed to my mom from Caroline Dubois. Another had the seal intact. It was addressed simply "To Caroline, From Lydia." It had never been mailed. My fingers prepared to rip open the envelope, anxious to hear my mother's voice again, even if it was just in my head and she was talking to someone else. Then I stopped, my conscience battling with my curiosity. I sighed and gathered up the pictures, placing them back in the jar. But I kept the letters, taking them upstairs and tucking them under my pillow. When I was ready, I'd read them. I looked out my window, hoping to see Zander sneaking up. But the street was quiet and empty.

I decided to push through my fatigue and clean up the rest of the house before Dad came home. Perhaps I was feeling guilty about all the secrets I'd been keeping from him. Whatever the reason, Knox settled down near the top of the stairs to watch me work. By the time I had finished, it was past dinnertime and Dad still wasn't home. So much for impressing him with all of my work. I decided to crash on my bed with an unfinished book. I patted the blanket beside me and Knox hopped up on my bed.

"But you have to get down when Dad gets here," I instructed him.

I ran my hand down Knox's side, comforted by his warmth. He and Isaac had sure become friends fast. I thought about Isaac's mysterious behavior this morning. He had a temper, that much I knew, but he'd handled a psychotic vampire with the aplomb of James Bond. There was definitely something going on with him. I tried to concentrate on my book, but the words started to blur and I closed my eyes, finally able to sleep.

The Efotis were seated around their kitchen table, eating dinner. Isaac's plate looked like a mountain. Unlike her brother, Phoebe approached her meal with little enthusiasm, trailing her fork through her food. A stranger sat with them, but he looked so much like Mr. Efoti that I assumed he was a relative.

Mr. Efoti was talking. "Of course, you may stay longer, Iosefa, as long as you and your mate need."

Mrs. Efoti pushed back her chair and stood, her small body stiff. "Toluta'a," she almost barked. Her small body strained with anger and her dark eyes darted between her husband and the man called Iosefa. Then she marched across the room and out of the kitchen door, which led to the back porch.

Everyone at the table looked at Mr. Efoti, no one daring to breathe as they waited to see what he would do. Clearly, his wife wanted him to follow, but would he? After a moment, the large man heaved a sigh and stood up to follow her out of the room.

As the door closed behind him, the scene shifted and I was outside on the deck watching the Efotis argue. Mrs. Efoti had her hands on her slim hips, her long dark hair trailing down over her shoulders to her waist. Mr. Efoti's face was shuttered, as if he were bracing himself for something unpleasant.

"How dare you let them stay in our home, my home!" screeched Mrs. Efoti, her delicate features warping with anger. "You might as well put a bulls-eye on our house, on our children!"

"Ruby," said the large man, his voice cajoling. "He's family. They're family. They've been through so much.

You of all people should understand that."

"Yes!" she snarled. "I do. I remember all too well, mate." She drew out the word "mate" with scorn. "And that's why they need to leave. My first allegiance is to our children, as yours should be. Imagine what would happen if he ever got ahold of them." Her face pinched, as if the thought brought her physical pain.

Mr. Efoti tensed. "As your mate, your first allegiance should be to me."

She looked away. "That's just it, isn't it? We aren't true mates. We're half-mates. We were experiments, and now our children are, too."

The emotions pouring from the Efotis were almost tangible and I backed away, feeling like an intruder. I expected to bump into the door, but I fell through it instead, my body moving like a feather in a breeze. I floated toward the dining table where the man called Iosefa sat in awkward silence with Isaac and Phoebe. They looked uncomfortable and sad as they pushed their food around on their plates. The sound of their parents' raised voices could be heard through the door.

Phoebe didn't look like the self-assured goddess that I saw every day at school. She lifted a graceful hand to her face and wiped away the moisture leaking out of her eyes. Isaac appeared shaken, too. He reached out a hand to his sister, but she shoved it away and rose quickly from the table to stalk out of the room. Isaac looked at the man across from him with anger and hatred.

The man looked away, hanging his head. "I am sorry, nephew. A great evil is at our door." His voice was deep like Mr. Efoti's, and now I could see the resemblance. They had to be brothers.

"Because you brought it here," bit out Isaac.

The man pulled back the collar of his shirt to reveal a bandage covering his collarbone. It was stained and seeping blood.

"No," he shook his head sadly. "Evil was here before I arrived. And I'm afraid you were already involved. Your mother may think she can control everything, but she can't. And now you've gone and made the wrong kinds of friends."

Isaac wrinkled his forehead in confusion. "What the hell do you mean?"

The large man sighed. "It's not your fault. It's just the way of things. The way of our kind. The road is never easy and we cannot remain hidden in the shadows for-ever. Alone, we are weak. Together, we are strong." His accent was like his brother's, Australian. "And I hope your parents will see that someday. Before it's too late for you and your sister."

"You're talking crazy," Isaac growled. "Just like your mate," he sneered.

The man growled, a low and menacing sound. "I could snap your neck with the flick of my wrist, bitzer, so show some respect." Isaac looked afraid for a second before bowing his head.

"Uncle," interrupted Phoebe from the doorway, her voice conciliatory and drawing Iosefa's ire away from her brother. "Why did you come here? And who are the Nasaru?"

He blinked in surprise before shoving his eyebrows together. "Your parents have been keeping too much from you. If you don't know your enemies, you can't avoid them." He rubbed his face with one hand. "Ahh, I didn't mean to cause a blue between your parents. And I don't want to bring more danger to your family, either." Somehow, his Aussie accent made his angry words less heavy. "But it's here now. It may not be my place to say, but you need to know, for your own safety going forward. I'll be having that conversation with my brother before I leave ya."

"What happened to your shoulder, uncle?" asked Phoebe.

Iosefa leaned back in his chair, stretching out his legs and pressing his hand against the bandaged area of his shoulder. He glanced toward the sounds of his brother and sister-in-law with worry wrinkling his forehead, before looking at Phoebe.

"A scuffle with our enemy. But it's just about healed now, thanks to my mate's healing gift."

"She can heal people?" asked Phoebe, leaning

forward. "I've never heard of that before. How does she do it?"

Iosefa smiled at her. "I'll let her tell you, if she wants to. She is a jewel among jewels. A diamond still being polished. And a fighter." His eyes darkened. "She has been through more anguish than anyone should have to suffer." He looked toward the back porch again. "Even more than your folks." Then he smiled hopefully. "With time and with me, she will shine bright again. It is a gift of true mates."

Isaac butted in, confusion tinting his words. "What did you mean about our enemies, Uncle? Is our family really in danger now?"

Shadows moved across Iosefa's face. "The Nasaru are a danger to everyone, even to their own people. Gerard Hughes must be stopped if the usemi are ever to be free, to feel true peace."

Isaac and Phoebe stiffened as Iosefa spoke the name of Zander's father, and I wondered if they had made the connection to Zander, or if they'd even known him at this point in time. Their uncle seemed lost in his own thoughts.

"He and his kind are evil beyond any I've ever encountered in my many years," Iosefa said bitterly. "My poor wee Caro. The things they did to her." He shoved back his chair to stand and stalk over to the fireplace. In a husky whisper so soft that I could barely hear, he said,

"You know about the aramusatu, I assume, since your parents have it."

The twins nodded.

"Yes, well, it is supposed to be a beautiful thing—the binding of two souls. It is not common anymore, almost a fairy tale, thanks to that butcher." He was silent for almost a full minute, causing the twins to fidget uneasily. Finally, he picked up the conversation again. "I believed my whole life that if I were so fortunate as to meet my shi mate, I would be the luckiest usemi ever, and the happiest. But perhaps for us, it would have been better if we'd never met."

"Why, uncle?" Phoebe asked.

He looked up then, his eyes hot coals of anguish. "When I found my shi mate she was human, an idimmu." He bowed his head. "And she was already mated to another."

The twins gasped.

"It's not supposed to happen, I know."

"What?" snarled Isaac. "I thought that was impossible!"

"They weren't true mates. But they loved each other deeply. I never dreamed I'd find her at all, let alone like that, in the arms of another. The shock made me rabid for a bit, I admit."

Isaac swore and Phoebe braced herself against the wall, her mouth hanging open.

Their uncle pressed his lips together grimly before continuing. "I attacked her mate. I'm ashamed of it, yes, but it was pure instinct. Honestly, I don't know if I could have stopped it. And worse still, after I thought he was dead, I committed the forbidden—I bit her right then and there."

The twins stared at their uncle in shock. "Then it's true?" gasped Phoebe. "You can turn a human?"

He nodded his head. "Yes, but only a shi mate. I didn't know that at the time. My behavior was instinctual."

Isaac looked fascinated.

"Our wolf instincts protect us," said Iosefa, raising his eyes to the twins. "But sometimes they need to be checked." He stared at Isaac.

"But it worked!" said Isaac with amazement.

Iosefa's eyes narrowed on his nephew's overenthusiastic response. "Don't get any ideas, boy. Learn from an old man." Iosefa's eyebrows collapsed with shame. "Force is no way to win the love of a mate. My crime was twofold, for I didn't know she was pregnant. To think I almost killed—"

"I've often wondered how events would have changed if you had succeeded in killing him, Io-Ara." All eyes shot to the stairs leading to the second floor.

"Aunt Caroline!" said Phoebe with surprise.

Iosefa straightened from his slumped position and

rushed over to the woman. "Caro!"

She looked to be in her forties or fifties. Her long blonde hair was streaked white, giving it a striped appearance, her eyes as blue as the ocean when the sun was out. Lines punctuated her eyes and mouth. She looked tired and ill-used.

Iosefa's face mirrored her weariness as he folded her into an embrace, blocking her from view. "I didn't realize you were awake, Caro-Ara."

Her voice whispered just loud enough for me to hear. "Io, my human love paled in comparison to ours. You know that don't you?" Her voice was soft, but resolute. "I loved him as a human, but you as usemi, my ara-musatu. You understand, don't you?"

"Hush, Caro-Ara. You are my every reason for living." He kissed her gently, like she was as fragile as fine glass. "Hush, now," he repeated. "We need not discuss the past. It's too painful. Come and eat. You must be hungry."

A bark woke me. Knox. But it came from downstairs. I sat up, rubbing my eyes and cracking them open to see light filtering through my window.

Someone was pounding on the front door and my phone vibrated on my desktop. Dang! I must have switched off the ringer. I zeroed in on my clock. 9:00 a.m.? How was that possible? I'd slept through the night and it was already Sunday morning.

I scrambled out of bed and picked up my phone.

Ruthie had left me several text and voice messages. A quick scan of them told me that my best friend was standing impatiently at my front door. I leaped out of bed and rushed out of my room almost missing the note stuck to my bedroom door. I squinted with bleary eyes at my dad's messy scrolls.

You were asleep when I got home last night. Hope you're feeling better this morning. Already took Knox on a walk. Visiting Sean and Sandy today. Stay home and take care of Knox.
Love, Dad

Crap! I'd slept through the night and late Sunday morning. Ruthie and I had an appointment with Dr. Frankler and we were late. The doorbell rang again. I trudged down the stairs, still disoriented. Knox stood at the front door growling.

I pulled open the door. "Ruthie, I'm sorry!"

"Girl, I've been here for half an hour! Well, at least fifteen minutes." She frowned and stomped in.

Knox let loose a particularly blood-curdling growl before lunging forward. I grabbed his collar before he could reach Ruthie, who screamed and backed up, almost toppling down the porch steps.

"What is that!?" She pointed at Knox.

"My new dog, remember?"

"I know, but he's huge! And he has so many sharp teeth. *And* he tried to bite me!" Ruthie wailed.

"Quiet, Knox." He shut up. "Ruthie, you just startled him. I should have put him in his crate. I forgot he didn't know you."

"Yeah, you go put him away, please. I don't think he likes me." She stared at him, her eyes round and fearful. "Great. Scooby hates Velma," she muttered.

I hustled Knox toward his crate, apologizing over and over for doing so. But I didn't want him scaring Ruthie again. I dropped a pile of snacks in front of him to make up for locking him in.

I hurried back downstairs, but Ruthie met me halfway, grabbing my face and looking me over. "You look especially horrible, no offense. Is it the aramu-sick thing?"

I rolled my eyes. "Maybe," I sighed. Sleep had helped but my entire body ached and I was breathing hard just walking up the stairs.

She pushed me toward my room. "Sucks big time. But seriously, Tru! Did you just wake up?"

I scratched my head. "Yeah. It's so bizarre. I was reading a book last night and must have fallen asleep. I didn't wake until I heard the doorbell and my phone going crazy."

Ruthie hustled me into my bathroom. "Well, you're going to need my makeup skills again. Get showered. I'll throw you some clothes."

As the hot water swept away the sleepy cobwebs clinging to my thoughts, scenes from my dream became clearer. The mystery surrounding the Efotis, particularly Isaac and Phoebe, had just turned a corner. With a new sense of excitement, I rushed through the rest of my shower, eager to tell Ruthie what I'd discovered.

29

KISSING COUSINS

BY THE TIME I was ready to leave Ruthie was beyond rattled by Knox's barking. As she started her car, she wailed, "He hates me!" over the sounds of an alternative band singing about a ghost. The haunting notes fit my mood with eerie accuracy.

Although Dad had asked me to stay home and look after Knox, it had sounded more like a request than a command, so I didn't feel too bad for leaving. Besides, Dad's friends lived in Salinas, and whenever he visited them, he was gone all day. I'd probably get home before him. Going to see Dr. Frankler was important.

"You need to get ahold of yourself," I told Ruthie with a frown. "Because I have a lot of crap to tell you and it's not for the faint of heart."

Ruthie made a pouty face by sticking out her bottom lip. "By the way," she said. "You've been holding out on me!" She drew something out of her side door panel. I recognized the letters that I'd tucked under my pillow. "What are these?" she said, one eyebrow raised.

I grabbed them from her purple-painted fingers. "Hey! You were snooping!"

"Well yeah! What else was I supposed to do while I waited? Besides, Knox was driving me crazy." She pulled away from the curb, working her way through the streets with slumped shoulders.

I sighed, not surprised by her pilfering.

"And I wasn't *snooping*," she said, crinkling up her nose. "They were hanging out from underneath your pillow, just begging me to take a look."

"You read them?" I asked, biting my lip.

"Well, not all of them. I only made it through some of them."

"Dangit, Ruthie! I haven't even read them yet. I only found them yesterday."

"Well, then. I won't spoil it for you." She made a zipping motion across her lips.

"Gee, thanks." I tucked them into my back pocket.

"The ones without dates on them looked pretty interesting," Ruthie said in her best salesperson voice. I knew she wanted me to read them to her, but I didn't have time for them yet.

"Actually," I said, worried she might drive into another car when I told her about my dreams. "You should pull over while I tell you what I learned last night."

"I thought we had to go to Dr. Frankler's house asap, which is a weird thing to do on the weekend. Takes the 'no-school' out of the weekend, you know? It's like we're having detention."

"Too bad," I said. "We have to go. But she can wait while I catch you up."

We were still in my neighborhood so Ruthie pulled over to the curb, letting the car idle. She switched off her stereo and turned her full attention on me.

"Spill," she blurted, curiosity gleaming in her eyes.

I told her about the dream, every bit that I remembered. My heart raced with every word, especially when I explained that Phoebe had addressed the woman as "Aunt Caroline." It was a relief to unload the scenes that had been playing on a repeat cycle in my mind.

"OMG," sputtered Ruthie as I finished. "You kissed your cousin."

I blinked in confusion. "What?" I asked.

"You and Isaac," she gushed. "You're freaking cousins!"

She explained while I stared at her in bewilderment. "It sounds like your aunt married—mated, or whatever—Isaac's uncle. So you're like, cousins or something. That's so stupid-weird. You're like 'kissing cousins' now." She snorted with a grin.

I grimaced in horror. "Nooo!" I wailed. Leave it to Ruthie to make things even weirder. "Besides, we aren't really cousins. And for the record, I didn't kiss him. He kissed me."

"Oh, now it's all about who kissed who, is it?" Her eyes twinkled with merriment.

"Who kissed whom," I corrected absently. "But Ruthie, that's not the point. The point is that Mr. Efoti's brother is usemi, which may mean ..." *Wait for it, wait for it,* I thought.

I saw the light go on in Ruthie's eyes. "You mean the

twins' dad is usemi?"

"Yeah ... so it seems ..."

"But wouldn't that mean Isaac and Phoebe are usemi, too?" she sputtered.

"Maybe. Or they're idimmu. It would explain why Isaac was so 'yeah, whatever' about Donavitch."

Ruthie's eyes widened. "Oh crap! I forgot to check your neck."

I pulled my hair away, baring my neck for her. "It's healed already."

She stared in wonder. "Wow. That's amazing." Then she made a disgusted face. "What did it feel like?"

I shivered, remembering the blood being sucked out of me. "Not good." I didn't want to talk about it, so I asked, "What are we going to do about the Efotis?"

She eyed me shrewdly. "You want to find out what kind of supernaturals Isaac and Phoebe are, don't you?"

"Duh!"

One side of Ruthie's mouth pulled up. "We could ask them."

"Really?" I scoffed. "Like you'd go up to Phoebe and say 'Yo! Are you a werewolf?'"

She let loose a mischievous grin. "Something like that. She's been texting me about what went down at the Zena's party. She's trying to get me to admit that there's more to the story. But look who's keeping secrets, now."

"After yesterday, Isaac has no doubt that we *are* keeping secrets. You know, like where that son of a bitch, Donavitch, came from."

Ruthie cackled. "Nice one."

I shrugged. "Actually, Dante came up with it."

"Even better when a crazy guy says it," she said.

I nodded, thinking of Donavitch's bright red eyes and the way he moaned as he gulped against my throat. I closed my eyes and tried to shake off the memory. Ruthie squeezed my hand and I looked up to see her eyes swimming with understanding. Ruthie's shark attack was only days ago, and I couldn't help but be impressed by how recovered she seemed.

"Zander probably staked him out in the desert," she said. I squeezed her hand, grateful once again for her compassion.

"I don't think that would kill him."

Ruthie shrugged. "What a bummer. I like that vampire myth."

"Anyway," I said, moving on. "Whether or not the twins are usemi, they are involved now. We should warn them about Peter. Especially since he put the moves on Phoebe the other day."

Ruthie scrunched up her nose at the memory. "Yeah. Right." She took out her phone.

"Who are you calling?" I asked.

"Isaac," she replied, meeting my gaze.

I bit my lips as we stared at each other. Seconds stretched as we waited for him to answer. Then we heard Isaac's voice asking us to leave a message.

"Fish balls!" snapped Ruthie. "Well, that's just not going to work for us." She pulled abruptly away from the curb.

"What are you doing?"

"What are *we* doing, you mean," she said, before continuing in a singsong voice. "And the answer is, we are going to find our friends because they have some explaining to do. And after that we are going to tell Phoebe what a psychopath Peter is so she'll never talk to him again."

"Are you crazy?" I yelped. "We don't know their parents at all. Do you even know where they live?" Mr. and Mrs. Efoti were extremely intimidating, and I didn't feel like facing them.

"Don't worry," said Ruthie. "We won't even see their parents. They're working at this time of day. And, as a matter of fact, I do know where they live. I drove to their place a few times last year, to drop off schoolwork, because you know they miss so much school."

"What about Dr. Frankler?" I reminded her with a frown.

She shrugged. "Tell her you'll be late. We have all day."

"Fine," I conceded. "But if we get hurt, I'm totally going to kill you."

THIRTY MINUTES LATER, WE were driving down a dark road into the forest of trees that were so tall, they blocked out most of the sun. The further we drove into the woods, the more I doubted our decision to track down the twins.

"You realize this is exactly what the stupid kids in all the movies do right before they get killed, right?" I said, chewing on a fingernail.

Ruthie hunched over the steering wheel, driving a little slower.

"We need to know what's going on, right?" she said, her voice a little breathy. "Besides, Isaac and Phoebe wouldn't hurt us. And they won't let anyone else hurt us, either. Phoebe can't possibly be usemi. Can you imagine her turning all furry and toothy?" She shook her head and continued without waiting for a response. "Isaac is a different matter altogether. I mean, this might explain a lot about him."

I debated texting my location to Dad so he would know where to look for our bodies when we didn't return. "What if they are running around in these very woods that we are driving into, like right now," I said. "And what if there are others like them that aren't friendly?"

We both stared out the windows. The forest was getting darker with every mile. I wondered how far out they lived. We hadn't passed another car for at least ten minutes.

Ruthie's hands clenched and unclenched around the steering wheel. "Crap on a stick," she muttered. "I didn't think of that."

"Maybe we should call someone, just to let them know where we are," I suggested.

"Like who?" scoffed Ruthie. "My parents, who would ground me for a month if they knew I skipped Sunday school? Or your dad, who would ground you for ... *forever*. Wait, you're already grounded. What about Zander?"

I pinched my lower lip with my teeth. "I sent him a text about Dr. Frankler, but he never responded." Again, I wondered what he had done with the detective and Donavitch. The fact that he'd never come to my house like he'd promised hadn't escaped me, despite our current situation. I was both worried and pissed off at him.

"Great," sighed Ruthie. "He can be pretty lame, if you don't mind me saying so."

"I think we need some more friends," I tried to joke.

"I could call Val, I suppose," Ruthie threw out. "But he's on my crap list right now."

"Did you ever see him at the party?"

"Yes," she replied with a frown. "But he pretty much ignored me. I was so going to brush him off. It was a total letdown. He was probably a key player in the whole trap to get you there."

That made sense. I felt a fresh wave of humiliation over the slut calling I got from Zena and her entourage. Monday at school was going to suck.

"Well, after you went all martial arts on Zena, your reputation should be stellar. Bet Val's finally going to give you some respect."

"Yeah, maybe," she said morosely. "If I even care."

"Hey! I could call Maverick," I said.

Ruthie clapped her hands and squealed. "I can't believe he's going to Homecoming with me!"

"Hands on the wheel, Ruthie! Geez. If the usemi don't kill us, your driving will."

"We get to double! I'm so excited," she continued, ignoring my concern.

"Anyway," I said, secretly wondering if we'd ever make it to the dance with everything that was going on. "I could call him, just to be safe. I could say that I'm calling about our plans for Homecoming."

"Good idea," she agreed. "I think the Efotis are only about ten minutes away."

"I had no idea they lived so far out here."

"Now you know why we never hang out at their place," Ruthie arched an eyebrow.

I dialed the rec center's main number, hoping to catch

Maverick at the front desk.

"Valley Recreation Center," his deep voice answered.

"Hey Maverick. It's me, Tru."

"What up, stranger?" I could hear the smile in his voice.

"Uh, just getting our Homecoming plans figured out."

"Oh yeah," he said. "What's the drill?"

"How do you feel about Mexican food?"

"Love it."

"Good, uh ..."

"Tell him where we are!" Ruthie whispered loudly. "We're almost there and I thought I saw something over there." She pointed out her window with a trembling finger.

I began to get that "watched" feeling again. Could wolves be following us? My pulse picked up. I held my phone to my shirt for second. "We *are* those stupid girls, aren't we?" I said.

Ruthie accelerated and screeched, "Tell him before the wolves eat us, already!"

"Tru, are you still there?" said Maverick, his voice muffled by my shirt.

"Uh, sorry about that, Maverick," I said, pressing the phone against my ear and trying to sound normal.

"Hey," he said, a seriousness entering his voice. "Is everything all right? You sound funny, Tru. Where are you calling from?"

"No, I'm fine, I promise. Well, actually Ruthie and I—uh, are driving deep into the woods." I laughed hollowly. "And you know how silly I can get. Um, it is kind of freaky and dark out here and we might have seen a big furry animal, and well—"

"Tru, what the hell are you talking about. Where *exactly* are you?"

"I don't know for sure," I said. "I think we're still on—" I looked at Ruthie. "Are we still on Olive Springs Road?"

"Yeah, as far as I know," she replied.

"We're way down Olive Springs Road," I told him. "You know where that is?"

"Turn around now," he ordered flatly. He sounded different, more adult than I was used to and it sent a sliver of alarm up my arm. I gripped the car door.

I gave Ruthie a worried glance. "Wh-what? Why?" I asked.

"Just do it." I heard him sigh. He began speaking to someone else, but I couldn't make out what he said.

"Look, Tru!" Ruthie pointed through the windshield. "I can see their road right there. They still have that stupid orange mailbox. I can't believe the mailman comes all the way out here. But their place is just down that road."

Then Maverick returned. "Did you turn around yet?"

"No need, Maverick. We are almost there. Ruthie found the right road. So, no worries after all." I laughed with relief. "Sorry about that."

"Tru! Y-do-eed-dange—cchsshhhh..." His voice started breaking up and was quickly cut off.

"Guess my phone doesn't get reception this far out," I said, scrunching up my nose.

"Perfect," muttered Ruthie.

A few seconds later, Ruthie turned down a dirt road full of rocks and dips. Her Mini Cooper bucked and wobbled as we drove slowly forward.

Fifteen minutes later a two-story house appeared around a crop of giant redwoods. It was modern looking with large windows. A two-car garage connected to one side of the cabin. It looked like the cabin Zander found in my vision. I gulped.

"Oh, wow. It seems so normal," I said, glad to see an end to our bumpy ride, but nervous about what the twins might tell us.

"What did you expect? Something from the movie *Cabin in the Woods?*" She giggled.

"Actually, yes," I admitted, grinning.

"Thank goodness it isn't," sighed Ruthie.

We pulled into a gravel driveway, next to a black Range Rover. Ruthie switched off the engine and we stared out the window. The Efoti's home was a multi-leveled house with treated wood on all sides. A pot containing pink flowers sat next to the front door, brightening the covered porch. Tall trees and lush green foliage surrounded the little driveway. A large black raven squawked and swooped down from a tall redwood, chasing away a blue jay.

"So," I said, "How should we do this?"

"Easy," Ruthie said, suddenly all business. "Just let me handle it. We're here to talk to the twins about schoolwork. That's our story in case their folks are home." When I darted an accusing glare her way, she added, "But they shouldn't be."

"Then whose Range Rover is that?" I asked.

Ruthie shrugged as if she wasn't concerned at all by the strange vehicle or how far away from help we were. But I noticed a slight trembling in her hands and realized she wasn't as confident as she pretended. I hesitated before opening the car door. Right now, her car was the only thing protecting us from these sinister-looking woods and whoever might be in that house.

Ruthie stepped out first. I took a deep breath and with one final thought of Zander, I followed her. We practically ran to the front door. When nothing jumped out and attacked us, we giggled nervously before ringing the doorbell.

A moment later the door swung open. My jaw dropped. I didn't have to ask Isaac if he had an uncle named Iosefa, because the man from my dream stood before me, and behind him was none other than the elusive Aunt Caroline. The woman who killed my mother. My hands clenched.

Surprisingly, Ruthie hadn't figured out who they were yet, so while I glared at them, she launched right into the reason for our visit. "Hi, we're friends of Isaac and Phoebe and we need to talk to them about a school project, which is really important and they didn't answer their cell phones." She stopped abruptly because she ran out of breath from speaking so fast.

The two adults were staring at me, Caroline kneading Iosefa's arm with both hands, her eyes wide with recognition. When Ruthie stopped talking, Iosefa shifted his attention to her.

"The twins and their parents aren't here now," he said, his accent softening his tone.

"Oh," said Ruthie with drooping shoulders. Then she brightened and said, "Hey, are you from Down Under?" She chuckled and then looked at me. I signaled to her with my eyes, and finally, she caught on.

"Oh my gosh! Are you—" she blurted before slapping

a hand over her mouth. I grabbed her by the arm and started backing away, aware that the people standing in front of us were lethal supernaturals.

The woman pleaded with the man. "Please, Io-ama." He started to shake his head, but when he saw her face, he sighed with resignation and stepped forward. Ruthie and I took another step backward.

"Girls, we would very much like to invite you in," he said with a smile. "Perhaps for a bite?"

Ruthie yelped and turned to run. I was reversing direction right along with her when I felt a firm grip on my arm. It was the woman and she was laughing, a surprisingly beautiful sound.

"Oh, my goodness! I think you girls have a wild imagination," she said, trying to herd us to the house. "Don't worry. Phoebe and Isaac will return soon. Until then, you can wait with us. We have some chocolate chip cookies and milk."

The lines on her face had smoothed out and she appeared much younger than before. But as our blank faces stared at her, she frowned indecisively. "Or are you too old for that? What about some chips and soda?"

The man rolled his eyes, but he smiled with good humor. Although he tried to hide it, I could see that her laughter had delighted him. He opened the door wide and waved us in. Ruthie was still trying to edge us toward her car, shaking her head. But I pulled against her, spellbound by the woman's gaze. I needed to confront the woman who'd destroyed my world and I didn't think they would hurt us here in the Efoti's home. This was my chance to fulfill the promise I'd made to myself. To make her pay.

"Come on, Ruthie," I said, yanking her hard.

"Ow," she gasped. Then she glued herself to my side. With trembling legs, we followed them into the house.

.

30

FAMILY REUNION

RUTHIE AND I SAT like conjoined twins, connected at the hip. I looked around the room. For some reason its well-kept state surprised me. Late afternoon sunlight shone through the windows and reflected off the white walls, brightening the room. More light filtered through the sun lights in the vaulted ceiling, casting a warm glow wherever it landed. The decor was rustic and worn with a mix of furniture styles with accents of denim blue and deep red. A black pot-bellied stove sat in the corner near a large fireplace. The home was cleaner than I'd imagined. The phrase "a den of wolves" had conjured up rough furniture and sloppiness. *Userni*, I corrected myself.

I absently rubbed a hand along the couch, its fabric worn down like my favorite jeans. In the corners, bright red pillows popped with color, as did the matching valances that trimmed the large windows overlooking the forest valley. From the driveway, I hadn't noticed that the landscape dropped off behind the house, so the beautiful view out the windows caught me off-guard. They could probably see the ocean on a clear day. Currently, the fog was beginning to recede as it often did in the later morning.

The couple, *my aunt and uncle*, I reminded myself, had disappeared into the kitchen to fetch some snacks. They were polite, and as un-intimidating as my neighbor's Yorkshire terrier, although I certainly wasn't feeling like giving either of them a belly rub. Ruthie's grip on my arm had downgraded from "I'm so scared, I'm going to puke" to "calm but ready to bolt at any moment." Wincing, I tried to peel her fingers off me while mouthing the words "chill out." I didn't want to speak out loud because I suspected that our hosts could hear every word we said. When she squeezed tighter, I realized she hadn't understood me. So much for taking control of the situation like Ruthie meant to do.

Now that I saw the woman from my visions up close, I marveled at how much older she seemed compared to our pictures of her. She did, indeed, look like she'd been to hell and back, making me wonder what the Collector had put her through. She didn't seem crazy now. I supposed that it worked in our favor, but if she was sane, what excuse did she have for killing my mother?

By the time the two usemi returned from the kitchen an unhealthy rage was boiling in my chest. They placed a plate of cookies on the coffee table and sat down across from us. I tried to even out my emotions.

"I apologize for not introducing myself earlier," said

Caroline, rubbing her knees. When we didn't respond, she leaned forward with a tremulous smile. "My name is Caroline." She blinked owlishly at me, pausing as if waiting for me to say something. But I kept silent. She sighed and continued. "And this is Iosefa, Isaac and Phoebe's uncle."

Of course, Ruthie couldn't possibly not react to the news, which I might add, she had already deduced, but once again—drama girl. I rolled my eyes as she gasped out an "OMG" and let go of my arm to cover her mouth with both her hands. She behaved like someone had died. Seriously, I was beginning to doubt her acting skills.

Unfortunately, the two adults went into combat mode. Iosefa jumped up and swiveled around as if he expected an attack. Caroline bent over near the edge of her seat looking around. Talk about gun-shy. They looked hilarious.

I bit back a smile and elbowed Ruthie. "Nice. So subtle," I whispered. To the couple across from us, I said, "Don't mind her. She's a little melodramatic."

"Oh, I'm so sorry!" Ruthie slapped her head with a shrilly laugh. "I just remembered that I'm supposed to be home soon because I need to babysit my brothers, and my mom gets really crazy about schedules and all that ..." Her voice faded as she recognized their irritation.

Iosefa settled into the couch again and shook his head. "Sounds like someone's telling porkies," he said to Caroline.

"Huh?" said Ruthie in confusion. I pinched her leg and she yelped. This time our hosts didn't react.

"You drove all this way," said Iosefa. "The twins should be home soon and it would be a shame to miss them." He crossed his rather large arms, and his biceps bulged out from his hard chest. I heard Ruthie gulp next to me.

While Iosefa's words invited us to stay, I couldn't help but think he'd be happy to see the backside of us. Caroline, however, stared our way as if she wanted to devour us. The way she looked at me—I felt like she could see into my soul. I shifted in my seat and reached for a cookie.

"Thanks for the snacks," I said, politely.

"Oh, you're very welcome. Can I get you girls anything else?" she asked eagerly.

"I'm good." Ruthie followed my lead and grabbed a cookie. She munched away, her gaze darting all over the room.

Caroline didn't seem to care that she'd lost Ruthie's attention. Her cerulean blue eyes sparkled as they remained fixed on me, concern spilling through them.

"Tru," she said, hesitating. "Are you alright, my dear? You look a little ill."

"I'm fine," I lied. "Just getting over a cold."

A familiar expression crossed her face, so much like my mom's when she knew I was lying that I bit my lip nervously. But a moment later her mouth formed a trembling smile.

"You seem familiar to me," she said, letting the words dangle in the air like a carrot on a string. But I didn't take the bait. She ran a hand along her jaw and tried again. "Do … do I look familiar to you?"

Was it possible that she knew who I was? And if she did, why would she want to talk with me after what she did to my mom? The room spun for a moment as I considered the fact that my aunt and I were seated across from each other talking like strangers. I thought about the dream I had of her the night of my mother's death. And now I was eating cookies with my mom's murderer? Uncertainty crept into my thoughts as I watched her. *Could* I have been wrong? Ever since Zander and Peter had mentioned my mom's murderer, I'd been working toward finding her and confronting her. I gulped, but pressed forward intending to take advantage of this opportunity to finally get some answers.

"Um, yes actually. You look like an aunt I had. But she died before I was born. Weird, huh?" I paused when I saw a tear slip down her cheek. I steeled my nerves and plowed ahead.

"And strangely, enough, my aunt was named Caroline, too," I added in a mocking tone.

A harsh laugh fell from her lips as she wiped her face with her fingers. Iosefa tried to pull her to him, but she gently shook him off.

"I know what you're thinking. But that would be impossible because while I am Lydia's sister ..." She paused, biting her lip. With a deep breath, she continued. "I am not your aunt."

"Caro," said Iosefa. "Do you think now is the right time?"

"It's never going to be the right time." She stood and walked rigidly to a bookcase, sagging against it. Despite her distressed and somewhat worn-out appearance, I recalled my dream about the man and the woman in the forest, and the wolf that attacked them. Sympathy bubbled up inside of me, but I pushed it down as I tried to process what she had said and why Iosefa looked so worried.

How could she be my mother's sister and not my aunt? It sounded like a stupid riddle.

The two adults looked at each other, communicating in a way I didn't understand. I noticed again that she seemed a bit older than Iosefa, and it suddenly registered that she was a lot older. My mother had been in her sixties when she'd died, but Caroline seemed decades younger than her actual age. Perhaps it was the unusual white streaks in her hair that aged her. If I ignored the lines of strain on her face, she'd appear quite young. Zander said usemi aged slowly, living for hundreds of years. Seeing the evidence of that in person was astonishing. That also meant that Iosefa could be much older than he appeared, as well.

Caroline met my gaze, the sorrow in her eyes like a cyclone absorbing everything in its path. "I know this is confusing," she began. "And I don't want to cause you any more pain than you've already been through." The more she talked, the more she rushed her words, until they began to jumble together.

"Tru, a mother would never hurt her child on purpose." Her eyes pleaded with me to understand. But I didn't.

"You may not believe me when I tell you. But it's the truth. And I need to tell you. I've wanted to tell you since I saw you with Lydia the night she—" Her voice cracked. "Died." She drooped, hanging limply like a vine torn from its wall. I was afraid she was going to fall. Iosefa jumped up to ease her back down to the couch.

I pushed aside the compassion that welled up again. She had been there that night. And she'd practically confessed. She really did it! The urge to hurt someone forced me up, my fingers curling at my sides. I ignored everything but the woman in front of me.

"It was you! I saw you!" I was about to leap across the coffee table when the back door burst open, and the rest of the Efotis dashed in.

Isaac and his father charged ahead into the room, but pulled up short when they saw me. Isaac looked dumbstruck. "What are you guys doing here?"

I barely registered their interruption as I threw myself at Caroline. But I didn't get very far because Ruthie pulled me back with a whimper.

"Let go, Ruthie!" I snarled, almost not recognizing my voice.

"No, Tru!" she yelled. "Don't you get it?"

I tried to shake her off, but she held me tightly, her long nails digging into my skin. "Oh, I get it, alright," I snarled. "She murdered my mother and I'm going to kill her!"

Ruthie's grip loosened briefly as she cringed and gaped at me, but she didn't let go. "You're being stupid, Tru. I don't think we know everything. Phoebe, Isaac! A little help here?" The twins rushed over.

Feelings of anger and revenge lent me extra strength and I fought wildly against them, my hair whipping around my face, my legs kicking out, but they were too strong and held me in place. Out of breath and unable to move, I suddenly became aware of their voices, some telling me to calm down and some arguing a few feet away. My chest heaved as my wild breathing began to slow down. Hatred still simmered near the surface, but it wasn't spewing all over the place anymore. Blinking, I realized that I was on Isaac's lap, and he had me wrapped up in his arms and legs. I couldn't budge an inch. I noticed Phoebe on the floor rubbing her jaw and looking a little put out. My eyes went to Ruthie, who stood apart from us with shock and dismay on her face. I knew that look. It reminded me of the day I had that panic attack at school. Shame engulfed me, dousing the anger. Isaac must have felt me relax because he slowly let go of me. I scrambled away, putting distance between me and everyone else.

Silence.

My eyes swept the room, taking in Isaac's wariness and the stiff posture of Phoebe sprawled out on the floor. Caroline gasped. Iosefa stopped arguing with Mr. and Mrs. Efoti and looked at Caroline. Her eyes were wide, an awed expression on her face as she stared at me. Iosefa stepped forward and Caroline moved up beside him.

"Io, did you see her eyes?" she whispered.

"Yes."

"They glowed just like her father's." Her eyes teared up.

I blinked, remembering something Ruthie had said moments ago when I'd been too angry to listen, something about not knowing everything. But I knew enough to know that she killed my mother, didn't I? I shook my head.

Staring at my mother's murderer, I said, "Ruthie, what more do I need to know? She as good as admitted she killed my mom. And she doesn't seem too broken up about it."

Ruthie squeaked, "Ask her why she isn't your aunt."

I looked toward my friend with confusion. "Of course,

she is. She's just trying to confuse us," I said.

"No, Caroline is not your aunt," said a deep, accented voice. All eyes pivoted to Iosefa. Even the Efotis looked baffled.

I decided I was done with this crowd. Perhaps the police could figure this out.

"Whatever you say, Mr. Not-my-uncle." I was mocking him now, but I was so over this little charade, and it was better than attacking them physically. I pulled out my phone. "This is me not-calling-the-police."

Before I punched in a single number, I was pressed against the wall, my phone knocked from my hands, and a strong hand around my throat. Iosefa growled into my face. He had moved so fast, I hadn't even seen him until it was too late.

"Get away from her!" Isaac growled, bent as if to pounce.

I could hear Ruthie swearing up a storm in the background, albeit, her own brand of swearing. Suddenly, a growl that was both feminine and deadly-sounding made Iosefa and Isaac swivel their heads in surprise. Caroline crouched near the side of the sofa, her head up and lips pulled back to show her elongated teeth. Her hands stretched out from her sides and her fingernails grew into long and pointy claws. My eyes widened and my chest clenched with fear.

In a deep, guttural voice, Caroline demanded, "Get your hands off my daughter."

31

RABBIT HOLE

CAROLINE'S WORDS TRIGGERED A shift in me. I felt something changing and I feared it was me, or at least my life, as I knew it.

Everyone moved in slow motion. Iosefa pulled away like I was burning him and Isaac moved toward me. I started falling ever so slowly toward a spinning void of darkness, like the space of time between wakefulness and sleep. And then with a sudden swcosh I plummeted like Alice down the rabbit hole, spinning and weightless, my chest seizing up with fear.

But after the longest time, my downward descent slowed. I opened my eyes to reassess my situation and gasped with astonishment. Different scenes floated around me, a different home with Caroline and another man, the Euro-looking man from one of my visions, happy, both of them holding blond-haired babies, teasing them while another baby crawled around on the floor.

Swoosh. I accelerated downward again before slowing once more. Another scene displayed before me. Three small children, two girls and a boy playing with toys.

Swoosh. The same children eating dinner with Caroline and that man.

Swoosh. The children running through the woods with a large wolf, one riding the wolf, the man jogging alongside.

I continued to fall from one vignette to another. I saw Uncle Ira holding a familiar dark-haired woman, Jasmine, and my heart tightened at the sight of her, the memory of her death still fresh. A playground in the woods. Caroline singing at bedtime. The man reading to the children, older now, the girls curled up on either side of him and the boy swinging a toy sword at the foot of a bed. The more I saw the man, the more I wanted to call him "daddy," but Dad's wrinkled image was stronger, inserting a sense of betrayal into my thoughts. In another scene, one of the girls clutched a stuffed toy dog as she waddled around the house. The toy resembled my own, the one I'd named Mummy.

Then gravity pulled harder and I swirled downward so fast that I screamed in fear as my body twisted around and around without anything to grab onto. Gradually, I stopped twirling until I hung suspended in the air, my hair floating around me, as if the forces of nature themselves held their breath. A new dreamscape formed before me.

Caroline and Jasmine each held the two little girls, hugging and kissing them fondly. Uncle Ira had an arm curled around Jasmine. They were a striking couple. Both tall. His blond hair a sharp contrast against her rich, dark brown. Uncle Ira seemed so happy. There were fewer lines on his face. Jasmine's hair curled and hung past her shoulders and Uncle Ira stroked it absently. As Jasmine smiled, her green eyes twinkled with merriment. They reminded me of grass in springtime. Freckles sprinkled her face. There was something poignant and familiar about this scene. I recognized the girl in Jasmine's arms. Me. A three-year-old me. The other little girl looked to be the same age and we resembled each other so much, we had to be sisters—same blond hair, same face shape, but different eyes, mine amber brown and hers marine blue. Pouting, we reached for each other, but the women kept us apart.

"Now Alondrea," said Jasmine, "we're only going to be gone a little while and then you can have your sister and mommy back. Don't you want to play with Auntie Jasmine?" She hugged the little girl, who sniffled and buried her face into Jasmine's neck.

"That's right, Alondrea," said Caroline, her voice

cajoling. "You and Shannandoah will be back together in no time." The little girl in Caroline's arms frowned, her eyes wide and sad. But she nodded, rubbing her eyes and looking toward her sister. "It's okay Dwea," she said. "I had my pwaydate wiff Auntie Jazwin yesterday and she was a wot of fun. She wet me wide on her back and then we had ice cweam." Her eyes lit with excitement as she whispered. "And I saw your favwut in her fweezer."

Alondrea perked up at the news, her head lifting with eagerness. She placed both hands on Jasmine's cheeks to bring her face around to her and demanded, "Weally? Do you have Wainbow Shoobit, Auntie Jazwin?" she asked, butchering her words like her sister had.

Jasmine and Uncle Ira laughed. "Yes, my little angel," cooed Jasmine. "Chocolate Chip Cookie Dough for Shannandoah and Rainbow Sherbet for you. I wouldn't forget your favorites!"

Alondrea bounced in Jasmine's arms, tears already dried up. She clapped her hands in anticipation. Uncle Ira's deep chuckle blended into the feminine giggles. Over the girls' heads, Caroline mouthed "Thank you" to Jasmine, who smiled.

The scene skipped to Alondrea and Jasmine in the forest, walking along a trail, looking for treasures among the beautiful leaves, funny-shaped rocks, and bugs. All of it seemed to enchant the little girl as she repeatedly brought Jasmine her findings. Jasmine oohed and aahed over the items the girl dropped into her backpack.

Despite the joy on both their faces, my heart tightened with fear, as if I knew what was coming.

Suddenly, sounds of gunfire sounded in the background, and Jasmine snatched up the girl and started running back toward the small compound of buildings. She zipped through the trees like a gazelle before stopping near a large trunk to lower the little girl.

"Alondrea, darling, we must be very quiet. Can you promise me not to say a word?" She looked down at the anxious girl. Her eyes were wild with fright, demonstrating her grasp of their situation. Jasmine's mouth tightened, but smiled with pride as the girl nodded.

Jasmine peeked around the tree. Armed soldiers ran from house to house, where screams and staccato gunshots sounded. The inhabitants of each residence fought with inhuman strength, but they lacked the skills and weapons to outmaneuver the armed soldiers. Large wolves, usemi, launched into the scene, but fell as bullets slammed into their fur. Jasmine's arms tightened around Alondrea, who yelped softly. But the woman seemed unaware of hurting the girl, as if she were frozen in shock.

When the soldiers began lighting the houses on fire, Jasmine whipped around and covered her own mouth. She closed her eyes and squeezed Alondrea even tighter. The little girl squawked her discomfort into the woman's shoulder. Jasmine relaxed her grip.

"I'm so sorry, sweetling." Clutching the child to her, she dashed back into the forest, but a shout behind them told them that they had been spotted. Ducking through a thicket, Jasmine placed the girl on the ground and made sure Alondrea's small backpack was secure on her shoulders.

"Didn't I promise you a ride?" Jasmine said, forcing a smile that didn't reach her eyes.

"But w-what are they doing to our houses, Auntie? W-where's my family?" She was crying, but there was no time for comforting.

"I'm sure they're fine. Don't worry about that now. We will have to meet them somewhere else." She ran her hands down the girl's golden curls one last time.

"I'm going to change and I want you to get on my back. Don't let go no matter what happens, okay?" The girl nodded and Jasmine moved. As more shots rang out, the little girl whimpered with fear and backed into the underbrush, watching her aunt with panic-streaked eyes. In the distance, a woman's voice called out Alondrea's name.

Jasmine cursed, seeing that the girl was bracing to take off, but remained in place. Her clothing ripped as she changed, human hands transforming into paws and her face morphing into a wolf's snout that stretched to display a mouth full of sharp teeth. The little girl screamed in surprise. Soon the transformation was *complete and the wolf shook out its fur. This broke the spell that pinned the little girl in place and she ran. A mournful cry broke through the clearing, causing her to increase her pace. An instant later, a wolf's soft muzzle tickled the girl's neck before biting down on the collar of her shirt and swinging her up onto her back. Alondrea wrapped her little arms around the wolf's neck as best she could as it took off, away from the screams and gunfire.*

Swoosh. Again, I spun and fell through the tunnel. Only this time I didn't fight it. Instead, I surrendered to that sinking feeling, as the images replayed in my mind. Despondent emotions threatened to tear me apart. But a sense of self-preservation kicked in and I was able to switch off my feelings, embracing the numbing cold that followed.

And yet, a prevailing sense of dread still haunted me, like smoke that wouldn't dissipate. As much as I tried to, I was unable to escape its clinging tendrils, nor the truth that the little girl was me and the life I had been living was all a lie.

My eyes popped open and I gasped in confusion. Isaac held me while everyone else kneeled around us, their hands pressed against my bare skin. They released me slowly as varying shades of horror, sympathy, and pity marked their faces. I cringed with embarrassment.

I'd had a series of waking dreams, but they had been

different this time, in more ways than one. They felt like my own memories. What had triggered them? The moment before I fell down the metaphorical rabbit hole, I'd threatened to call the police. Iosefa had been choking me! My head jerked up to glare at the large man standing above me. Then I remembered Isaac leaping toward us. He stared down at me, too, scowling with concern. On the other side of us knelt Caroline, her face wet with tears. I twitched, remembering that she'd done something to make everyone stop. She had looked scary, all toothy and long nailed. And she'd said something...

Daughter. She had called me *daughter.*

Caroline clutched me, weeping. Iosefa knelt down, wrapping an arm around her. He looked very pale.

"Oh, Tru," cried out Ruthie. She sat at my feet, her eyes and nose red. "That was another vision. It was like the one you had before school started, wasn't it?"

"How did you know?" I asked.

Ruthie placed her hand on my leg. "When we touched you, we could see what you were seeing. It was almost like we were there. It was so sad." Her eyes tilted down at the corners.

"How?" I gasped.

Ruthie shook her head. "I don't know. You're changing I guess."

"You saw it? Everything?" I couldn't believe it.

"It was hard to keep up with you," said Isaac's dad. "You ran through images so fast, I had a hard time deciphering them. Like it was in fast motion."

"They were memories," said Caroline, looking at me with liquid eyes. "They happened to you ... to us. The last time I saw you ... before ..." She grasped my face between her hands. A few moments ago, I would have slapped them away, but now ... now she was my *mother.* My chest tightened at that treacherous thought. How was this possible? It was like my math teacher insisting a circle was actually a square. It didn't compute.

Caroline rubbed her thumbs over my cheeks, forcing me to look at her—not unlike little Alondrea when she wanted her auntie's attention. *That was me,* I reminded myself.

"You used to do this to make sure we were paying attention to you because I always seemed split between the three of you." She smiled, her lips trembling. "I thought you were dead, you know, or I would have tried to find you."

I was beyond uncomfortable, being smashed between Isaac, Caroline, and Ruthie. And it didn't help that everyone stared at me as if I were as disturbing as a Greek tragedy. But that's what I was, I realized. I couldn't take it a second longer. Their pity resurrected too many insecure memories. I wiggled loose and stood up, but the awkward factor only increased the longer no one spoke.

I expelled the breath I had been holding and pushed the hair away from my face. I wanted my safe place, which used to be Dad, home, and my wonderful queen size bed, but over the last few weeks it had changed. Now it was Zander that I longed for, his arms wrapped around me, promising to keep protecting me.

Straightening, I looked at Caroline. "I guess we have to talk." *Mother.* I couldn't say it out loud. The memories might have returned, but they didn't feel real yet.

She nodded somberly and walked through the kitchen and out the back door. A quick glance to my friends let me know they felt some of the devastation assaulting me at the moment, but I attempted a tremulous smile, knowing that as I walked out that door my life was changing again, and I couldn't help but think this was so much worse than learning I had indeed been the freak of nature I'd always feared.

32

GREEK TRAGEDY

I FOLLOWED CAROLINE THROUGH the door and onto a covered wooden deck. The backyard was basically a mountainside that provided a natural amphitheater-like setting to the tragedy playing out before us. Beyond Caroline's slumped form I could see the retreating fog unveiling miles and miles of pines and redwoods. She crossed the deck and climbed down the steep steps to a well-worn path that led to the side of the house. An outdoor seating area appeared with wooden lounge chairs surrounding a fire pit. She led me to the chairs, sinking down with a deep sigh.

I nibbled my lip, trying to contain my internal tremors. My life just took another spin on the crazy ride and I was experiencing motion sickness. Would my life ever settle? Did my dad, the man who raised me, know who I really was? Did he know about this strange supernatural world? I mean, what the heck? I was adopted? It wasn't even that simple. *I* wasn't that simple. I was freakishly complicated, like the woman who gave birth to me.

Caroline pulled up a knee, leaning her chin on it. Through an opening in the green canopy above us the sun shined down, creating a spotlight effect around her. I started to sit across from her, but when her face began to fall, I moved to the chair next to her. She smiled gratefully.

"You really forgot everything, didn't you?" she said.

I looked down at my lap, feeling sorry for something I'd had no control over.

"Oh darling," she said reaching out to pat my arm. "It was a blessing, really. I love that you've had a normal life. I'm grateful that you did."

That word again. Normal. Pieces of my latest vision swam in my head, images of a family. "I remember ... a sister? A brother?"

Caroline's face tensed, her eyes darkening. "Oh, Tru. I just can't ... not yet."

That meant that they were dead. That's why she couldn't talk about them. Tears leaked from her eyes and guilt stabbed me. If I'd had siblings and they were dead, I should be feeling the same pain, shouldn't I?

But my memories of life with her weren't filled out like hers. There were only slivers of feelings that I couldn't interpret, so I changed the subject, going back to my mental list of questions.

"I bet Mom ... uh, your sister ... was surprised by how young you look."

My mom had been seventy years old. And according to the family records, only a few years older than

Caroline. The woman before me couldn't be more than forty. She could have passed for someone even younger than that.

Caroline sniffed and wiped her face. "It's true. I am much older than I look. I've always looked good for my age, though," she said, one side of her mouth pulling up. "It's a side-effect of my ability."

"I know usemi don't age."

"I didn't age like everyone even before I became usemi. My gift is healing." She paused to watch my reaction.

"I still don't get it," I admitted, perplexed. "How can healing make you not age?"

"Aging is simply a process of the body breaking down and my body heals by itself, constantly. I can't intentionally heal myself, but for some reason my body automatically heals from the damaging effects of growing older. It made my life easier with Uriel, that's for sure." Her smile was fragile, but at least she wasn't crying.

"I don't think I totally stopped aging," she continued. "But I age very, very slowly. However, I've learned that extreme stress increases the rate of aging." She ran a shaky hand over the streaks in her hair subconsciously.

I looked at the bands of white, evidence that she'd gone through something horrible. I thought about Zander and me, how awful it felt when we were out of sync and I cringed inwardly thinking of how she must have suffered during her separation from Iosefa. Her frailness worried me and I searched my mind for a lighter topic.

"Your ability is pretty amazing. I bet you could have made billions in the face cream market." I laughed at my joke, knowing we could never submit ourselves to that kind of scrutiny no matter what kind of money was offered to us.

Caroline paled. I wondered what the Collector had done to her. She forced out smile, but I could see the torment in her eyes. I wished I could take back my words.

"That day in your backyard—" Caroline started.

"It *was* you," I said, cutting her off.

"Yes." She smiled with chagrin. "I'm sorry I scared you. I was so curious about you—I told myself I'd leave you alone, after what I did—" She frowned. "But I couldn't seem to stay away, at least not completely." She bit her lip again, shame drawing her eyes down. Then her face brightened. "I believed you were dead for so many years … I had to see you. I wanted to learn as much as I could about you. You've grown into a beautiful young woman."

"You healed my arm, didn't you?" I held it out to show that there was no scar. She gazed proudly at it.

"Yes. You should definitely not run with knives, you know." The censure in her words was softened by a mocking smile.

My lips curved upward. "Yeah, I've heard that before, somewhere." She laughed quietly. It was a pretty laugh, and familiar, I realized with a tiny burst of shock.

"You can do more than heal an injury, though, right? Someone once told me you could help idimmu with mental problems."

"Someone told you, huh?" she said with a sigh. "Well, I won't lie. I can help with mental disorders, but I'm not very good at it. It's never permanent." She scowled. "My enemies want me because of that ability, but …" She sighed. "It exacts a heavy toll on me." She ran a hand over her hair along a wide streak of white.

"Is it possible for someone to inherit a gift?" I asked, knowing the answer already.

Her eyes widened, her breathing hitching up. "Can-can you heal, Alondrea?" she stuttered, leaning toward me, capturing my hands and squeezing them urgently.

"Uh," I stalled at the intensity of her gaze, her touch uncomfortable. I had a feeling she would be very upset if I admitted the truth and blinked furiously.

"You can!" she said. Her face tightened. "Oh, Alondrea, you aren't safe here."

"I go by Tru now," I reminded her. I tugged against the grip of her hands, but she held on, not letting go of me. "It doesn't matter," I said. "The Collector already knows about me."

"No," she gasped.

"Dante kidnapped me but I escaped. I'm not completely helpless," I added.

Her face began to ripple as if the wolf wanted free. Sharp points pressed into my hands and I looked down to see that her fingers had become claws.

"Ow!" I jerked against her with renewed effort, afraid she would transform into the creature that killed my mother.

Just as swiftly, her skin shifted back to her human self and she jumped up, moving away from me. "I'm sorry. I'm sorry." She said quickly and then took a deep breath before letting it out. "Strong emotion makes me lose control." Her eyes drooped in regret.

Note to self: Don't poke the wolf. I thought she could use a dose of "the fixer" herself. I stood, moving forward to lay my hand on her arm. "Could I heal you?"

"No!" She pulled away, speaking so harshly, it startled me. Then she drooped, sinking down into the nearest chair. "I'm sorry again. I didn't mean to scare you. I-I am not myself yet," she said. Her hands trembled as she rubbed her arms.

I sat next to her. "Why can't I help you?" My natural inclination was to do something and her refusal hurt for some reason.

"Oh, you have, dear," she said with a sad smile. "Being near you is help enough. I'm much too damaged for you to attempt healing me. It would take too much from you. There's a side effect to my healing. I assume for you, too?" She didn't wait for me to answer, but sped on. "It weakens me for a time and-and you cannot afford to be weak with the Collector after you. No, I will be fine, don't worry."

I did feel weak after healing others. But I recovered fast. I was willing to bet I recovered much faster than Caroline. However, I could see that she wouldn't give in. And since she was scary when she got angry, I let it go.

I thought of Isaac, how his temper was always close to the surface. Earlier this morning, Zander said Isaac's family was dangerous. I could see how a house full of quick-tempered usemi could become perilous at the turn of a hat. An insane usemi would be way worse.

I swallowed as I asked the most important question. "What really happened the night of the car accident? How-how could you do ... what you did?"

She released another heavy sigh, her eyes drifting away to stare into the woods again. "Oh Alon—Tru. It was a horrible mistake. I promise you I didn't mean it to happen. I wish every second of every day I could take it back. I wish my last words to Lydia were kinder." She bent her head and her shoulders trembled.

"I had a dream about that night," I said, driven by our moment of honesty to confess it. "You were in my high school parking lot, in a car. You looked at Mom like you hated her."

"You dreamed that?" She stared at me, confused. "But that wasn't a memory. At least not one of your memories." She waited for me to explain, but I shook my head.

"All right, we can return to it later," she said, her eyes promising me she wouldn't forget. "That night, at that moment, I honestly did hate her. It didn't help that I wasn't in a very good place mentally. I'd only recently escaped. My emotions were raw, my sanity questionable. And I was very easily angered. And physically, well, I was in the process of coming off some medication—kind of like a detox. I should never have approached Lydia in such a state."

"You were on drugs?"

"No," she burst out defensively. "I mean, yes, but not anything I gave myself, trust me."

I raised my eyebrows.

"You can't think ..." she sputtered. "Did Lydia tell you I was on drugs?" Her face grew shuttered as if she didn't want to hear what I might say.

"Well, I guess I better fill in our thirteen-year gap a little. You see, the day Jasmine ran off with you—" She trailed off as a shadow crossed her face. "Jasmine was ... " she began. I thought of an earlier vision. The one that showed me how Jasmine died.

"I know who Jasmine was. And I know that she's dead

now."

Caroline pressed a hand to her mouth. "I'm so sorry. That day, she must have thought we had all been killed. But some of us weren't. We were captured and held prisoner by evil people. I was given drugs to keep me under control. And because of my particular gift, medicine doesn't work as well on me, so they experimented with new drugs." She paused, squeezing her eyes shut. "To make a long story short," she said as she lifted a slim hand and waved it inconsequentially in the air. "After many years, I escaped."

I squinted at her with a frown. She was leaving out a whole lot. But I wasn't going to push her.

"As you can imagine," she went on. "Going off the drugs so fast wasn't easy on my body or my mind. I was more animal than human. The day I found out you were alive the wolf took over. My instinct was to get my child back any way I could." She stood up and took a few steps away before stopping and wrapping her arms around herself.

"Before that, though," she said. "When I first arrived here, I didn't know you were alive. I was told everyone at the compound except a couple of us had died." Her mouth wobbled, but she stiffened her lips and continued. "I contacted Lydia, needing family. She didn't believe it was I at first. There were a lot of reasons for that, I suppose." She laughed hollowly. "Anyway, I wanted to come to her house but she wouldn't let me. I didn't understand why and her refusal hurt me. I thought she didn't want me in her life."

My hands trembled as I came to the unsatisfying conclusion that the senselessness of my mom's death would not be solved, but remain even more tragic than it already was.

Caroline sniffled and her voice floated over to me in a whisper. "I've had some time to think about it, of course, and I've come to the understanding that she was just trying to protect you."

"From you?"

"Yes," she said a little louder. "I stupidly thought we could pick up where we left off, and, well ... it had been so long since I saw her last. You see, I lost touch with her when I started seeing Uriel, your father."

"Why would that matter?"

"It was just easier, I guess. When I chose him, I also chose his life of secrecy—at least from the human world. If we had remained involved in Lydia and James' lives, they would have begun to notice we were different. Human knowledge of supernaturals isn't allowed and it would have been unsafe for them to know of it."

"You must have really loved him to do that." I couldn't imagine giving up my family for anyone. But then I thought of Zander and I wasn't so sure anymore.

"Oh, I tried to make it work for a little while. I wanted both lives. But I found myself lying all the time." She sighed. "I think Lydia knew I was lying about something; she was always good at recognizing lies."

I nodded with a smile. Caroline chuckled darkly. Thinking about Mom's annoying intuition sent a wave of loss through me and I blinked away tears. A flash of jealousy passed over Caroline's face for a moment before fading to resignation.

With visible effort, Caroline continued. "Anyway, at some point, I realized I had to let her go in order to keep

Uriel. And I loved him more than anything at the time, you see."

To leave someone you had loved forever to be with someone you loved more—well, I had to admit it was pretty epic.

"When I returned here last year, I didn't tell Iosefa about my sister. Not at first. He's fiercely protective of me and he wouldn't want me to risk discovery by reaching out to anyone who knew me in the past. I knew he would try and stop me from seeing her. I snuck away, though."

She sighed heavily. "I expected Lydia to be surprised but her reaction was ... let's just say, disappointing. She was reserved and suspicious. I thought she'd open her arms and love me like she always had before. Her behavior triggered a wolf-response and I began to stalk her."

Caroline sat down across from me, staring my way without seeing me. Flashes of guilt and remorse reflected on her face. "I followed her to work, to home, watching her every move but hiding."

I held my breath, not that surprised by her words, but they still cut me to the quick.

Her face crumbled for a moment and she paused before continuing. "Can you understand how upset I would be to see a daughter I thought long lost to me? And a grown daughter, too, making me realize all the years I'd missed?" Her voice cracked. "My sister never mentioned you. And then one night I saw you get into her car. I heard you call her *Mom.* You were mine, *mine.*" She held a fist to her heart.

I gulped.

"Usemi can be very protective, very possessive of

those we love, so much more than humans." Her eyes
stared past me as she continued in a haunted voice. "A
wild instinct took over, and I could feel the change begin.
I knew I should have gone home, but I was already out
of control. I followed you. When I heard you call her
Mom ... It was the final trigger."

Stillness settled over me as my perception of that
night changed.

"I'm so sorry," said Caroline, her words heavy with
sorrow and self-loathing. "I don't remember what happened after that, but I can guess. I think my rational
mind deserted me. I let my animal instincts take over,
simplifying my choices at that moment. All I thought
was that I had to remove the obstacle between you and
me."

We both knew who the obstacle had been.

"I have to live with what I did," she said. "And I could
have harmed you, too." Her voice hitched. "I don't remember all of it ... I only know that I ran back to Iosefa
and confessed everything, vowing to stay as far from you
as possible." Her head drooped. "But even knowing what
I did, I didn't keep that promise."

Tears dripped down my cheeks. It was the saddest
story I'd ever heard. Guilt laced my sorrow. Perhaps if I
hadn't been acting like a spoiled brat, Mom would have
seen the car coming and been able to get out of the way.

I rubbed my face with my hands, wiping away the
moisture I wasn't aware had been there. I was finished
with this topic. I had my answers and they gave me no
peace, no real closure. But if I could do something to help
Caroline feel better, then maybe I'd feel a little better,
too.

I drew Mom's letters out of my pocket. Caroline jerked out of her dark thoughts.

"I think you should read these," I said, holding out the two letters between my mom and her. "I found them in Mom's pottery jar. It looks like she never gave you one."

For a second I worried that whatever was in there would be unkind, but I quickly banished the thought. I knew my mother. Plus, it was with all of her family memorabilia. It had to be good.

Caroline stared with fascination. "Did the jar have interesting pictures on it? Of wolves and …"

"A bird and a dragon?" I finished.

"Yes!" She smiled thoughtfully. "I gave it to Lydia the last time Uriel and I saw her. It's an ancient artifact of Uriel's and it's worth quite a bit of money. I'm pleased to hear that it's still around."

"Really?" My heart stuttered as I recalled how I'd almost dropped it.

"Yes, and I put a couple of pictures in it. Pictures of Lydia and me as children."

"I saw those," I said. "Mom must have added more because it's almost full of stuff. These were in it." I held out the letters to her.

Caroline took them, pausing as she saw the unopened envelope from my mom. Her chest swelled and she sucked in her lips. I could see that she wanted to read it.

"Go ahead," I said.

She nodded and carefully tore open the envelope, pulling out the colorful stationary my mom was known to use. As she read the letter, she wiped away the moisture that had built up in her eyes and slipped down her face.

She laughed as she finished, looking at me with brilliance shining from her face.

"Oh, thank you, sweetheart." She clutched the letter to her chest. "She wanted me to know how much she cared for you, as if you were truly her own daughter. And she wanted me to know how much she missed me and wished she could ask me about you. And ..." Caroline stopped and smiled. "Oh, she did love me." She moved closer, clasping my hands. "I'm grateful you had her as a mother, Tru. At least one of my children grew up with a normal life. I wish things had been different. I owe her everything, and the only way to pay her back is to take care of you. She would want us to be happy, don't you think?"

I frowned. Was she saying what I thought she was saying? I didn't think I could embrace a different woman as my mother. No way.

33

WORLDS COLLIDING

THE WOODEN STAIRCASE ABOVE us creaked as someone came down the deck. A moment later Isaac's dad walked toward us along the path.

"We have company," he said in a deep voice that made him seem even larger than he already was.

Caroline bristled with concern. "Who?"

"One of Ira's guys."

My ears perked up. "Uncle Ira?" I asked.

They ignored me. "What does he want?" asked Caroline.

"He wants to know if Tru is safe. He wants to see for himself."

Caroline sighed and tucked away the letters. She ushered me into the house with a quick comment about continuing our talk later.

When we passed through the kitchen, I was shocked

to see Maverick standing by the front door talking to Ruthie. He looked relieved to see me and stepped my way. Isaac and Iosefa blocked his approach.

"Get out of my way," I said, pushing Isaac to the side.

"Tru, are you all right?" asked Maverick. He searched my face with concern. I knew I looked like hell warmed over, but it didn't have anything to do with the Efotis and I needed him to chill out.

"I'm fine," I said, trying to sound convincing.

"Are you sure?" he asked, doubt on his face.

I sighed. "I look horrible. I know. I haven't been sleeping lately and I was sick yesterday. But I'm fine, I promise." But it was a hollow promise. I was beginning to wonder if Zander's absence would be the death of me. I didn't think I'd last much longer without connecting with him in some way. But my explanation seemed to mollify Maverick.

"What are you doing here?" I asked.

"I couldn't get you back on the phone," he said. "I thought you might be in trouble."

I should have known he would worry. "Sorry to drag you here," I said with regret. Then I remembered that Isaac's dad had said one of *Ira's* guys was here. "What does Maverick have to do with Uncle Ira?" I asked Mr. Efoti.

He glowered at me. Isaac matched his father's scowl. No help there.

I looked at Phoebe who lounged on the couch, but she shrugged.

It was Caroline who finally answered my question. "Tru, Ira Sans Sebastian is a friend of mine—of ours. He helps us keep our secrets."

My jaw dropped. "Of course," I said with a dry laugh. It shouldn't have been a surprise after what I'd learned about him through my dreams.

"That makes sense, Tru," said Ruthie. "Remember the dream you had about yourself as a little kid? When Uncle Ira introduced you to your mom?" She paused with a confused look. "Wow, that sounds so weird."

I agreed with her. We were way beyond weird though.

"I guess the cat's out of the bag now," Maverick muttered. "Or should I say, wolf?" Ruthie giggled, but she snuffed it out when no one else laughed.

Eyeing the Efoti family with trepidation, Maverick adjusted his stance, placing his hands on his hips. "Tru, you might as well know that I do more for Ira than help at the rec center. That's just a cover. It's really an organization called *Polaris*. Ira started it and we protect and aid supernaturals, like the Efotis."

Isaac's dad growled.

Maverick stepped back. "Well, we do. Ira set up your family here, didn't he?"

"Maybe him, but not you," he said.

Once again, my world adjusted to make room for another reality. "You knew about ..." I gestured to everyone. "... all of this?" I said, directing my question to Maverick. "The entire time I was working with you?"

He gave me a wry smile. "Tru, I couldn't tell you anything then." Everyone seemed to be looking at me like I was some sad little reject again. No. I didn't need this. It was time to go. I threw up my hands. "You know what, Maverick? You and Uncle Ira can just—"

"Ira is missing."

"I al—" I started to say. In my anger, I almost told

him I already knew that. But I stopped myself because I couldn't admit that I already knew about Uncle Ira or I'd have to tell them how I'd come by that information. Now was definitely not the time to tell everyone about Zander and Conrad.

"I'm telling the truth," Maverick said. "Ira has been missing for months. We think the Nasaru captured him. You were always really important to him, Tru. The last thing he told me was to look after you, and that you were to be protected at all costs. That you were the key to changing things for all nons."

"Nons?" said Ruthie.

"Non-humans," said Maverick. "Idimmu, usemi, akharu ..."

I was the key? What did that mean?

"Cool," piped in Ruthie.

"So," said Maverick, "when your phone cut out on your way here, I had to make sure you were all right."

"Because he told you to," I said.

He tilted his head to one side. "Yes, but also because you're my friend, Tru. I would have come even if he hadn't told me to watch over you."

Out of the corner of my eye, I saw Iosefa put an arm around Caroline. She lifted her face to his.

"We need to tell them, Caro," said Iosefa before turning to us. He looked guilty. "Last year, Ira helped Caroline to escape, but it wasn't easy. The Nasaru threw everything they had at us when they discovered her missing. We didn't think we'd make it, especially since Caroline was unwell. Ira suggested that we split up. For weeks, he led them away from us. My brother took us in. Eventually, Ira came home, too. Coming here was a mistake, though. We'd led them right to Polaris. When some Nasaru scouts showed up in Scotts Valley, Ira left abruptly, once again drawing them away from us. And from Polaris, too. This time he stayed away for months."

"Why didn't he let us help?" asked Maverick, his face full of confusion.

"If you didn't know about it, then he must have been trying to protect you. The Nasaru have some very dangerous idimmu in their arsenal. I don't think he could risk having Polaris discovered. Anyway, the last time we heard from him he told us he was trapped. He believed he was about to die and he wanted us to know what happened to him and to tell you." Regret and sadness pulled Iosefa's face down. "I'm sorry, son, but he's gone or worse—captured."

"No," denied Maverick, shaking his head. "Why didn't you tell us?"

"He was protecting me." Caroline's voice was a soft whisper and we all leaned toward her. "Iosefa didn't want anyone, even Polaris, knowing about me. He knew you'd want to interrogate me and my mind wouldn't have been able to handle that."

"Why would Ira help you when it was such a suicide mission?" asked Maverick. His face had turned pasty white.

"We had help on the inside," said Iosefa. "The odds were good enough to chance it. Once Ira saw Caroline's condition, I think he realized she would have died if we hadn't been reunited soon. No true mates have survived what we have. He knew we wouldn't last long if either of us was captured again. Ultimately, Ira sacrificed himself for us."

A tear slid down Caroline's face. "He was my friend and I can never repay him," she murmured. Iosefa raised their clasped hands and gently kissed the back of hers. She looked into his eyes and suddenly I felt like we were intruding. There was so much pain and love there.

Maverick cleared his throat. "What do you mean?" he asked.

Iosefa wrapped one large arm around Caroline pulling her closer to his side. "Our mate bond requires close proximity. It was a miracle we survived all those years during her captivity," he said.

I could easily believe that. My separation from Zander was definitely weakening me. He had to feel it, too. If he could get to me, wouldn't he? Had something happened to him? I pressed a hand against my heart as it thudded loudly.

"How did you leave her in the first place?" asked Isaac, his words like a challenge to his uncle. "How could you walk away after marking her?" Isaac's father sent him a warning growl.

But Iosefa put up a hand. "It's okay, brother." Mr. Efoti nodded. "It was the hardest thing I've ever done," he admitted to Isaac. "When Caroline told me she was pregnant and wanted to raise her baby with its father, I had to honor her wish and hope that I could last until we could be together. I put as much distance between us as possible. I went home to Australia."

Caroline pressed her face into his chest, as he continued. "For some reason our bond allowed it. It was very difficult, but bearable. I'd already hurt her and her family enough. Many years later I traveled to the States on business, and the closer I got the stronger I felt that something was wrong with my mate. I tracked her to the Nasaru but I couldn't find a way in. I became a madman trying to get to her. I turned to my family for help and my brother connected me with Ira. He wasn't easy to convince. He'd believed that Caroline perished with the rest of her family. But when he discovered that I was telling the truth, he agreed to help, for they were old friends."

Maverick appeared to be in shock. I wanted to tell him Ira was alive, but I couldn't until we were far away from the Efoti's house and their usemi hearing.

Caroline looked up at her mate. "Our enemies are coming for Alondrea, Amo. For Tru. She has my gift."

Iosefa's head snapped up to stare at me. "No!" he breathed out in horror. He gripped Caroline's shoulders. "I thought Gerard's sons were here for you. What if ..."

"What if they are here for all of us," she said weakly.

"Sons?" asked Maverick.

"The sons of Gerard Hughes are here. Peter and Alexander Hughes. We've seen them."

Isaac's father and Iosefa growled menacingly, causing the hair along my arms to rise. The twins looked guilty. I met Ruthie's horrified eyes. She and I both knew more than we wanted to say right now. I wanted to defend Zander, but they'd never believe me. A great urgency to hightail it out of this house sent my heart fluttering.

I noticed Maverick watching me and I didn't like the glitter in his eyes. If he hadn't known who Zander was before, he suspected now. And he knew I had plans to go to Homecoming with him. Fortunately, he didn't say anything and I sent him a grateful look.

"We have to leave tonight," Iosefa told Caroline.

Caroline pulled away from him. "I won't leave her," she cried. My heart twisted at her words. That she would risk her life for me. I just couldn't deal with it now.

"I need to go," I said, hoping to leave before any more was said. "I was supposed to meet with my school counselor. Dad will get upset if I don't keep my appointment." Lies, lies. They came so easily to me these days.

Caroline stepped toward me. "Alondrea! ... *Tru,* I just got you back. There's more you need to know, more about your real family." She lifted her arms as if to embrace me, but I just stared at her empty hands. I thought about Mom. I considered how hurt Dad would be if I left him, if I embraced this insane woman begging me to stay.

"I already have a family," I said, moving toward the front door while ignoring the disappointment hitting me like sonic waves. Only Ruthie understood. I could see it in the sad lines of her face.

My worlds were colliding and I couldn't deal with it.

We walked out the front door toward our car. Maverick spoke privately with Iosefa before shadowing us. The Efotis, all of them, crowded the front porch like unwanted orphans. Isaac and his dad scowled at each other as they spoke in low grumbling voices that I couldn't understand. When I heard Mr. Efoti raise his voice, I looked back to see Isaac bowing his head submissively. Phoebe leaned against the side of the house, quiet and thoughtful, as if used to their behavior.

"We need to talk," said Maverick as we headed to our vehicles.

"No kidding," I said. "But not here." I looked at the Efotis, knowing they could hear every word we said. The strange behavior between Isaac and Phoebe all this time made more sense now. Ruthie exchanged hurtful looks with the twins. She must be feeling more betrayed by their secret than me.

"I'll follow you then," said Maverick, walking to his truck.

I dragged my feet through the gravel, wondering if things would have been better if I'd kept my vengeful thoughts and unquenchable curiosity to myself. My need to know the truth about everything had uncovered more demons and mysteries than the ones I'd started with.

My family wasn't who I thought they were. Not just my family—the Efotis, too. And Zander's. A tidal wave of need rushed over me. I pressed a hand to my aching heart, praying with every fiber of my soul that he was alright.

What were we going to do now?

Zander's father had rewritten the entire supernatural history, coloring it with false myths and lore in order to control the different races. Somehow, he had covered up the truth. The truth that he was conducting horrific experiments, for reasons that were still unclear to me. The truth that sethians had usurped their authority with racism and lies. The truth that he was the very Collector hunting us down. I still didn't understand everything, but what I did know had changed me forever.

And it wasn't over yet. I couldn't run away. I couldn't hide forever. There was no way to rewind. I could only move forward, wherever that led.

I climbed into Ruthie's car and pulled the door shut clicking my seatbelt into place. Looking through the windshield at the darkening forest ahead I mentally braced myself for whatever came next.

If you enjoyed *Secrets of the Lore*, look for *Secrets of the Prophecy*, book three in the *True Nature Series*, coming out at the end of this year. In no time at all you will be able to dive back into Tru and Ruthie's adventures! Find it on Amazon.com.

Visit karenlynnbennett.com for deleted scenes, sneak peaks, news, lexicon and more.

ACKNOWLEDGEMENTS

I cannot publish this book without expressing my sincerest gratitude to all of those who helped me out with editing and beta reading. Your feedback meant the world to me—and the story.

Ludwiga, you are a true friend, and so incredibly multi-talented. There's a book editor inside of you that I never knew about, but somehow it didn't surprise me. Thank you for your many hours of reading, analyzing, editing, and then rereading the rewrites. I feel so grateful for your help.

Thank you Jalaire and Amy for your comments and time, too. Your positivity cheered me on when life became overwhelming.

About the Author

Karen Lynn Bennett grew up with seven other siblings in a small farming town in central Washington. She now lives in northern California with her husband and two daughters. She finally went public with her secret writing life and now spends endless happy hours conjuring characters and plot lines. When she's not at her keyboard, she's brainstorming story ideas as she entertains her other hobbies—exercise, cooking, and traveling. Keep up to date with her books at karenlynnbennett.com.